WHISPER OF THE LOTUS

GABRIELLE YETTER

MEANDERTHALS PUBLISHING

ISBN-978-0-9962370-2-4

Dedicated to two of the most significant people in my life: My mother, Colette Said, who encouraged me every step of the way, and my husband, Skip, who inspired me, edited me, brainstormed with me, and supported me from the first word to the last.

And to the wonderful people of Cambodia for giving my soul a home and for stimulating me to write about this magical country.

PROLOGUE

Charlotte stared along the corridor. Fluorescent hospital lights cast a yellow tinge on the walls and the gentle throb from the air-conditioner vibrated in her ears. Ahead, four doors were numbered: 23, 24, 25, 26. The last door—number 26—was the door to his room.

She took a deep breath, remembering what she'd learned from her time in this part of the world: *Relax. Be here now. Trust all will be well.*

Her mind flashed back to a day seven years ago; the last time she'd seen him. The tone of his voice when he'd spoken to her mother was cemented in her mind; the sadness in his eyes painted in her memory. And she'd always be haunted by the image of him walking down the path, getting into his car, and driving away. Now he was steps away, and she was scared.

Her thin, cotton blouse stuck to her clammy back and her hand trembled as she tucked a lock of hair behind her ear. It was too late to turn around. She'd set the wheels in motion and couldn't back down now.

Clutching her handbag under her arm, she pulled back her shoulders and slowly walked down the corridor, the leather soles of her shoes clicking on the tile floor, her eyes focused on the shiny, white door in the distance.

She stopped in front of Room 26, her heart pounding in her chest. Then, she took another breath and pushed open the door.

1

57 DAYS EARLIER

'Ladies and gentlemen, the Captain has turned on the fasten seatbelt sign. We are now crossing a zone of turbulence. Please return to your seats and keep your seat belts securely fastened.'

Charlotte tugged her seatbelt tighter and glanced through the window, willing the dark clouds to disappear. She drained the wine from her plastic cup and shoved the half empty miniature bottle into the seat back. Then she held her breath and waited.

Suddenly, her tray table started to rattle, and a baby screamed in the seat behind. She gripped the arm rest and a violent jolt tossed her sideways. Her bag flew off her lap. Flashes of lightning lit up the cabin and she clenched her fists to control the trembling. *Make it stop!*

The rumble of thunder sounded as though it was inside the plane. A knot tightened in her stomach, and for a moment she felt physically sick. Then a moment of calm, followed by another powerful bump that tilted the plane sideways. A tear rolled down her cheek as her grip tightened. She should never have come.

Don't worry, you'll be fine. Roxy's voice chattered in her head. Then the louder voice of her mother: *You're such a fraidy cat. You can't do anything well.* She battled to block them out. *Just get through the next hour. You're almost there.*

Beads of sweat gathered on her upper lip and with a quivering arm, she reached up and turned the air nozzle to full blast, squeezing her eyes shut.

Then a gentle voice in her ear. 'A million people travel safely by plane every day. According to statistics, you'd have to fly every day for two hundred years before you were in an accident.'

Opening her eyes, she glanced at the man in the seat next to her, wondering why he'd addressed her this way. Bony knees poked the thin fabric of his grey trousers and his slender frame appeared to fill only half of his neatly pressed suit. Huge, hairy eyebrows hung low on a wrinkled forehead, and tufts of grey hair sprouted from his ears. His complexion was dark and leathery, his cheeks etched with signs of age. A yellow handkerchief peeked from his breast pocket and he looked at her, eyes twinkling, as she scrutinised him.

'I'm fine. It's all fine,' she replied breathlessly, wishing he hadn't noticed her nervousness. The plane lurched again, and she flinched.

The man patted her arm, a gold chain bracelet clinking on the metal piece of the armrest. 'I like to think of turbulence as bumps on a road,' he said. 'Does it bother you when you go over potholes in a car?'

She shook her head, reluctant to engage further. She wasn't

one for the easy banter with strangers and was in no mood for conversation, but the importance of good manners had been pounded into her set of values. Perhaps he'd get the message and leave her alone.

'Imagine the sky's a road and the plane's a car.' He waved toward the window. 'A few bumps don't make the journey dangerous, do they? Besides, there's less traffic up here.' He took the handkerchief from his pocket and dabbed his eyes. As he did, a crumpled paper fell to the floor and he gasped. 'Oops, there goes my customs form. I haven't filled it out yet. Would you mind helping me, please? My sight's not so good.'

Charlotte sighed. He wasn't going to stop. But he needed her assistance and she didn't want to let him down. The form lay under the seat, so she'd have to undo her seat belt to reach it, and she was afraid to move. She twisted toward the window, slipping a miniature wine bottle out of the seat pocket and unscrewing the top. She quickly poured it into a crumpled plastic cup and guzzled it.

Before she had the chance to answer the man, he thrust a silver fountain pen into her hand. 'Use my lucky pen,' he said. 'It might make the journey smoother.'

She ran her thumb over the *RCF* initials engraved into the cap and silently scolded herself. He was a well-meaning old man who needed help. 'It's beautiful,' she said. 'They don't make pens like this anymore.'

'Old things aren't cherished the way they used to be, are they, Charlotte?'

She widened her eyes. 'How do you know my name?'

He nodded toward the seat pocket. 'It's on your crossword book. I can see large print. And I pay attention.' He grimaced and pointed to a small Band-Aid taped to his chin. 'Except when I'm shaving.'

She smiled. The turbulence was easing so she undid her seat belt and bent over, scooping up the paper and quickly buckling herself back in. 'Okay, then. What's your name?'

'Doctor Rashid Farouk. Please call me Rashid.' He shook her hand. 'Now, we've been formally introduced.'

'I'm Charlotte, as you know. Charlotte Fontaine.'

'French?'

'Belgian. My father's from Brussels. Mum's Scottish, so I'm a mixed breed.'

'Ah, another multicultural partnership. My wife's English, so people are always confused when someone named Mrs. Farouk has blonde hair and blue eyes. Do you live in Scotland now?'

'I never did. My mother met my father at a golf club in Inverness. He was on a business retreat. She was the beautiful girl in the pro shop.' She lowered her gaze. 'She didn't work in the shop much longer.'

'Forgive me for being bold, but you must take after her. And your eyes—they remind me of someone I used to know.' He lingered on the last phrase, as if remembering something from his past, then took a deep breath. 'What do you do for work?' he asked.

'Public relations.' She made a face. 'More like holding clients' hands and putting out fires most of the time, though.'

'You like it?'

She shrugged. 'It's okay.'

'And your father? What does he do?'

'He ran a finance company in Belgium. When he moved to England, he started a consulting firm.'

'And now?'

Her face warmed. She didn't want to divulge her family history and wished she hadn't drawn attention to herself by letting him see she was scared. If she started talking about her life, she might never stop. There were too many words she'd never said, too much desire for someone to take an interest. This wasn't the time or the place.

She pointed to the form. 'Let's get this completed, shall we? What shall I put for nationality?'

'Bangladeshi.'

She breathed a sigh. The moment had passed. 'Place of residence?'

'London.'

'Date of birth?'

'October 26, 1943.'

She did a quick calculation. Seventy-seven. Travelling alone with poor eyesight. 'Where were you on the first leg of this trip?' she wondered as she filled in the last line.

'I've been with you all the way from London. People don't always notice me.'

She didn't realise she'd spoken out loud. And he was right, she hadn't seen him. But the initial twelve-hour journey from London to Bangkok had been such a blur she hadn't paid attention to anything. Her mind had been focused on one thing: she'd taken the biggest step of her life. And until the plane had left the ground, she'd been terrified something might still prevent her from going.

It had been more than a month since she'd bought the ticket and she'd been jumpy every day since then. Each time her phone rang, she'd imagined it to be Roxy telling her not to come, or her boss saying he'd changed his mind about time off. And every night after she came home from work, she'd held her breath waiting for her mother to find a way to prevent her from going. She was old enough to make decisions without her anyone's approval, but there'd been too many years of emotional programming that made her anticipate disaster whenever her mother was involved.

On the day of departure, she'd turned off her phone as soon as she'd left home, still terrified her mother might find a way to summon her back. And while the idea of sitting on a plane for endless hours sounded like torture, it was better than what she was leaving behind.

The first leg of the flight had been smooth—what she could recall of it, since she'd had a couple of Bloody Marys and a large glass of Chardonnay to calm her nerves. But this final stretch from Bangkok to Phnom Penh reminded her why she hated flying. From the moment she'd heard the announcement, 'Ladies and gentlemen, we are expected to encounter turbulence,' she'd ordered a second mini bottle of wine before she'd even finished the first, then stared through the window, waiting for the storm to hit.

Another bump jolted her seat and she yanked her seat belt tighter and squinted through the window. The outline of land was visible. They'd almost made it. She glanced at her watch. Only twenty minutes to go.

Rashid leaned toward her, a slight smile on his lips. 'Our adventure is about to begin,' he said. 'Thank you for making this flight more enjoyable for me. It makes me wish I'd travelled more when I was younger. And I'm sure I would have impressed my wife with my wonderful story about potholes.'

Charlotte laughed, relieved at the distraction. And for the next fifteen minutes, Rashid regaled her with stories from his life: how he'd broken away from family tradition and married an English woman, why he'd decided to study medicine (he'd watched his mother die of pneumonia), and how he'd managed to win a scholarship to a prestigious medical school in London. He also poked fun at his obsession with perfect punctuation and told her he could identify every flag from every country in the world (except the new ones, he was quick to add).

Charlotte was entranced by this intriguing stranger. He made her laugh out loud at the same time as evoking compassion for the tremble in his hands and the lengthy pauses in his speech. She'd never met anyone like him and couldn't remember the last time she'd enjoyed a conversation more.

He finally stopped talking and pointed through the window. 'Almost there,' he said.

'Thank goodness,' she said. 'Do you have a visa yet?'

He shook his head. 'I'll get one when I arrive. This trip was a last-minute decision and my wife planned most of it. I shouldn't really travel this far, but it's for a special purpose.' He chuckled. 'I'll never outgrow being a stubborn old goat when there's something I want to do.' He shifted in his seat, the bony fingers of his left hand working the creases of his trousers, then took a small jar of Tiger Balm from his pocket and massaged a thin film into his temples.

'You're a bit like me, aren't you?' he said. 'Not a stubborn old goat, just someone who's determined to get things done. You're scared of flying but you're off to Cambodia. That takes courage.'

Charlotte shook her head, resisting the impulse to hug him. Nobody had ever described her as courageous.

'Do you believe in a higher power?' Rashid asked. 'One that inspires you to do something you never imagined?'

'I'm not sure what you mean. I've experienced some odd things recently, and I...' She looked down at her lap, wondering why he'd raised the subject and if he'd think she was weird if she told him about her experience. 'I had a strange feeling before I left Heathrow. As though something bad had happened.' She glanced at him, predicting a reaction, but he was paying careful attention. 'I put it down to being too sensitive.' She paused. *Stop talking, Charlotte. You've had too much wine.* She rubbed her eyes. 'Sorry. I'm rambling. Must be nerves.'

'No need for apology. You're an interesting young lady. Is this your first time flying?'

'No.' She paused. 'Not really.'

Painful memories of her first flight came tumbling back. She'd been twelve, travelling with her parents to Spain. Her mother had taken advantage of the free alcohol and was drunk thirty minutes after take-off, flirting with the male attendants and falling onto a passenger on her way to the toilet. Her dad had been so embarrassed he hadn't spoken to her for two days, so Charlotte had spent most of her holiday at the hotel swim-up bar with her mother who whined nonstop. On the way home, they'd flown into a thunderstorm and the flight had been rough—physically and emotionally.

She was hoping this trip to Cambodia would be more pleasurable. She'd just turned twenty-four and it was the first thing she'd done for herself since enrolling in a yoga course last year. Her mother hadn't approved of that, either. It had kept her out of the house for too many hours; time that should have been spent cooking, doing housework, and taking care of her incessant needs. But this journey to visit Roxy was so much more than a holiday. It was emancipation.

She turned back to Rashid, suddenly giddy with excitement at what might lie ahead. 'Are you going to Cambodia for work?' she asked.

'My days of practicing are over,' he said. 'This journey's a little more personal. I haven't travelled much since I moved to London. That was...' He raised his eyes. 'Goodness, that was fifty years ago.' He exhaled. 'Always too busy. First study, then work. Constantly occupied. Don't misunderstand me, there were many good times. I married a beautiful English rose, lived in the biggest house in the neighbourhood, and bought a new Jaguar every year.' He toyed with the Band-Aid on his chin. 'I'm not telling you this to brag. Just to remind myself what I thought was important.'

'What line of work were you in?'

'Neurology.' He picked a thread from his sleeve. 'I was what you might call a success, but I lost many things along the way. I hope it's not too late to get them back.'

He looked down at his hands and Charlotte resisted the impulse to ask more. Something in his eyes belied a sadness she couldn't put her finger on, despite his light-hearted banter. His words also struck a chord with her: *Too late*. Her father said the same words when he'd exited her life seven years ago.

Her parents' final argument still played over and over in her mind, the ebb and flow of shouting as their quarrel escalated into something deeper, harsher, more threatening. The slam of the front door and the ensuing silence. Then, her mother's voice outside Charlotte's bedroom, imploring her to let her in. When the door had finally swung open, she'd run to slam it shut. But it hadn't been her mother who'd stepped inside. It had been Roxy. Somehow, she'd always known when Charlotte needed her.

'He'll come back,' Roxy had told her. 'He always does.'

But the following morning, her father's coat hadn't been on the hook in the hall, and there was an empty space in the cupboard where his slippers used to be. Days stretched into weeks and months, and the sound of his voice became a distant memory. No matter how hard Charlotte pictured him home, he never returned.

A voice on the PA system jolted her back. 'Ladies and

gentlemen, we're about to land in Phnom Penh. Please fasten your seat belts in preparation for arrival.'

She gripped the armrest, bracing herself for a bumpy landing.

'Remember that road, young lady,' Rashid said. 'Bumps are just little adventures along the way.' He slipped his customs form inside a book and Charlotte glanced at the cover: *Twisted Roots Under Solitary Trees.* It reminded her of her father's favourite Churchill quote: 'Solitary trees, if they grow at all, grow strong.'

'That's my Charlie-horse,' he used to tell her. 'Stronger than anyone I know.' If that's how her father perceived her, why didn't she?

She looked out as the plane slowly descended. Phnom Penh's landscape was dotted with red tile roofs and the graceful curves of pagodas. The sky was now almost cloudless and tinged with a mid-morning haze that hovered above a patchwork of brown and green squares of earth. Tiny houseboats crowded the edge of the river. Colours were muted from dust in the air, and flat stretches of land disappeared into the dusky horizon.

They touched down and Charlotte exhaled with relief as they taxied along the runway. She smoothed her hair and applied a slick of lip gloss. Roxy would probably tease her if she looked less than perfect. She grinned, anticipating their long overdue reunion. It would be wonderful to see her again and slip back into the comfortable company of the girl who was like a sister to her. Life hadn't been the same since Roxy left.

She turned toward Rashid sitting stiffly next to her, his briefcase balanced on his lap. 'Have you been here before?' she asked.

'I haven't. And it will probably be the last new place I go.

There's no point going somewhere if you can't see well, is there? How about you? Is this a holiday?'

'My friend Roxy moved here five years ago, and she's been begging me to visit. I didn't get a chance to come sooner.' She paused. 'And I didn't want to sit on a plane this long.'

'So why now?'

'I had a feeling this might be the right time.'

'Trust those instincts,' he said, nodding. 'It's something I'm starting to learn. There's more to life than reason and fact. I waited much too long. I married late, had a child late. Too late to…' His voice drifted away.

Charlotte touched his arm. 'Are you okay?'

'Yes. Yes.' He took a comb from his pocket and pulled it through the last wisps of grey hair on his head. 'Just reflecting. You're a good listener. That's hard to find.' He smoothed his trousers and drew a silver-topped walking stick from between the seats. 'Thank you for helping an old man,' he said. 'I believe this trip will bring more than you anticipated and less than you feared. There's a Bengali saying that goes *Pagole kina bole, chagole kina khay.* He chuckled as her eyebrows shot up. 'It means one cannot predict what a mad man will say or what a goat will eat. Things aren't always foreseeable, you know.' He looked directly into her eyes. 'Olivier is lucky to have a daughter like you,' he said softly.

Charlotte froze. How did Rashid know her father's name? She didn't think she'd mentioned it. She recreated what she could recall of their conversation, then shook her head. It must have been the wine.

The lights went on in the cabin and she unbuckled her seatbelt, noticing a magazine half hidden beneath the seat in front of her. She leaned down to pick it up and turned toward Rashid. 'Is this your—?' she asked. The words caught in her throat as she found herself looking at an empty seat. She leaned into the aisle, craning her neck to look down the passageway, but there was no one there. Surely, he wouldn't have risked getting up while the plane was still taxiing to the gate.

She looked at the magazine in her hand: a recent copy of *National Geographic* with a cover story about Angkor Wat, the ancient temple complex of Cambodia. As she flipped through it, a white envelope fell from the pages. It was imprinted with the logo of St. Bartholomew's Hospital in London and contained a single word, written in a distinctive, awkward scrawl: *Chris*. She stuffed it into her bag along with the magazine. Rashid must have gone ahead to the arrival hall; she could give it to him there.

A ping went off in the cabin, followed by the crew announcement that they could disembark. Passengers sprung from their seats and hauled bags from the overhead compartments, so Charlotte draped her linen jacket over her arm and followed the line of passengers from the plane. As she entered the terminal, a blast of icy air hit her. She inhaled sharply. Roxy had warned her about the heat. But this? She glanced outside and saw perspiring baggage handlers hauling suitcases from the plane in sleeveless shirts, then chuckled to herself. *Come on, Charlotte, you're not that daft. Remember air-conditioning?*

She passed through the terminal, then found the immigration line where a uniformed customs official with a broad smile took her passport. '*Sua s'day,*' she said, using one of the Khmer greetings she'd memorised.

'*Sua s'day.*' The officer nodded at her. 'You speak Cambodian so well.'

She flinched, embarrassed. 'Oh no. It's the only thing I know.'

He returned her passport and she looked around. Ornate murals adorned the walls and orange and gold lanterns hung from the doorways of shops. Her vision blurred as tears welled in her eyes. There had been so many times she'd imagined herself here, but she'd never been able to get a clear image of how it would feel. She wanted to soak up every sight and sound so the moment would be indelibly imprinted into her memory.

A group of people brushed past and she took a deep breath. She had to find Rashid. On the other side of the hall, a man with a stick shuffled toward the exit door dragging a suitcase. Charlotte ran toward him. 'Dr. Farouk!' He didn't respond. 'Rashid!' she shouted louder, thrusting herself between a group of passengers and grabbing the man's arm. He turned, dropping his stick with a clatter, and she found herself looking into the eyes of a man with a Fu Manchu moustache. 'Sorry,' she mumbled, picking up his stick and handing it back. Her face warmed in embarrassment. 'My mistake.'

She looked toward the *Visa On Arrival* counter. Most of the people in the queue were loaded down with enormous backpacks and there was not a single elderly man among them. Perhaps he'd be at baggage claim.

A buzz sounded from inside her handbag, so she stopped and fumbled for the mobile phone she'd switched on after landing. Surely nobody would be contacting her here. Her fingers curled around it and she flipped open the case and checked the message.

Welcome to Cambodia, Charlotte. You have 57 days.

2

Charlotte stared at the text. It came from a number she didn't recognise, just like some of the messages she'd received before leaving England. She shrugged and put the phone back in her bag. *Technology*. She'd try to figure it out later, but there were more important things to think about now, like where to retrieve her suitcase and how to find Roxy. She tried to swallow but her throat felt like sandpaper. Hopefully, Roxy would bring something to drink since tap water was almost certainly not drinkable in this part of the world.

'Cambodia's a third-world country,' Roxy had written in her last email. 'Leave your stilettos behind and bring lots of bug spray.' Charlotte didn't remind her she'd never owned stilettos—that was Roxy's style, not hers. She also didn't tell her how much she detested the heat and was petrified of bugs. Roxy had been so excited she was coming that Charlotte was determined to keep an open mind, follow her friend's lead, and try to ignore her own anxieties.

It had been three years since their emotional parting, and Charlotte now realised she'd made a mistake. She should have gone too, instead of being wed to that pathetic obsession with 'duty'. She'd never been the adventurous type, but she longed for something more exciting than sitting in a cubicle nine hours a day waiting to return to a house that no longer felt like home. As to be expected, Roxy had finally run out of patience and had gone alone. Then, every time Charlotte received an email gushing about India and Vietnam and Laos; every time she'd seen a photo of the temples in Siem Reap or the beach in Nha Trang or the bars in Vientiane, her day had felt a little gloomier.

As she walked through the airport looking for Rashid, she was struck by its simplicity in comparison to Bangkok's terminal. While the Thai airport was filled with stylish designer boutiques and chic cafés, Phnom Penh's Pochentong was a cavernous space with luggage conveyor belts and LED video billboards. Droves of people scurried around, pushing trolleys piled with suitcases and cardboard boxes. Women in shiny high-heels and Chanel handbags checked iPhones, while two young Cambodian girls wearing pyjama-like garments giggled and hovered near the baggage carousel. At the edge of the hall, a man in a suit mopped his brow with a handkerchief and, next to him, a pair of orange-clad monks fingered wooden prayer beads. It was all colourful and exotic and strange.

She followed a line of people from her flight and caught a glimpse of her reflection in a plate-glass window. Her ponytail had come loose, and her face was glowing, no doubt from heat and nerves. She retied her hair, pulling strands free from her tiny, silver hoop earrings, and glanced down at her clothes. After travelling almost sixteen hours, she didn't look too bad. Her linen slacks were wrinkled, but the rest of the outfit looked almost as fresh as when she'd put it on. She tucked her blouse into her waistband and straightened her collar. The neat freak in her wanted to look perfect for her arrival. She wasn't sure why, since Roxy always told her she was obsessive, but it made her feel calm. It was one thing she could control.

A man bumped into her with a luggage trolley and she jumped aside, realising she'd been standing in the same place for several minutes, staring. People milled around, collecting bags and chattering with friends; some fanned themselves with slips of paper and others hefted overstuffed luggage, enormous plastic bags, and odd-shaped boxes onto trolleys. A few westerners stood at the edge of the baggage carousel, claimed suitcases from the conveyor belt, and swiftly exited. Charlotte watched them disappear through the large glass door and hoped Roxy was on the other side of it.

Twenty minutes later her suitcase appeared on the conveyor belt wedged between two cardboard boxes. She pulled it free and followed a group of passengers toward the exit. Automatic doors parted, and she stepped onto a stone pathway lined with lush, tropical plants and mobile phone booths selling SIM cards. A gust of hot air blew in her face, smelling of frangipani flowers mingled with fuel exhaust, and dust. Dozens of eyes stared in her direction and people jostled for space on the pavement, some clutching bouquets of flowers, some holding greeting signs, some jabbering on phones in a language jarring to her ear. Behind the crowd a disorderly mishmash of two and four-wheeled vehicles was crammed into a narrow corner of a dusty road. This wasn't what she'd expected. Where were the porters? Airport buses? High-rise buildings?

She wiped a film of sweat from her upper lip and looked for Roxy. It wouldn't be surprising if she'd forgotten to come to the airport. Her gaze fell on a Cambodian family standing near the entrance. Two tiny children ran in circles around a handsome young man who was checking a phone, and an old woman with a shaved head clung to his arm, her long skirt skimming a pair of flip-flops. The glass doors swung open and a slender young woman walked toward them with a huge smile. Charlotte expected them to rush into one another's arms, but the man merely nodded, took the woman's suitcase, and ushered them all from the airport.

Then, from the back of the crowd, a voice rang out and Roxy burst through. 'Charlo! Charlo!' she shouted, shocks of spiky, peroxide hair bobbing as she tossed handfuls of silver and gold confetti into the air. She grabbed Charlotte by both hands and whirled her around. 'Charlo, you're here! You're in Cambodia!' she shrieked, using the nickname she'd given Charlotte in kindergarten, then she wrapped Charlotte in a hug, filling her nostrils with intoxicating aromas of musk and patchouli. 'You're really here!' she repeated. 'I'm so bloody excited you finally made it!'

Charlotte hugged her back, laughing. 'Yes, I finally made it!' she said, then held her at arm's length. 'Just look at you. Cambodia agrees with you.'

Roxy was a sight to behold. She'd always been among the first to embrace every new trend back home, and Charlotte had watched her change from punk to Goth to ripped overalls faster than she'd changed her boyfriends. Today, she looked as though she'd fallen from a box of Crayola. Tight pink leggings ended above silver plastic flowery flip-flops, her bouncy bosom stuffed into a purple strapless top, and a calf-length chartreuse silk chemise swirling below her knees. Streaks of brilliant pink flashed in a mop of bleached platinum hair, and silver bell earrings tinkled as she leapt around like a baby bear.

'A bit different from the Brighton Goth, hey?' Roxy

dramatically placed one hand on her forehead and waved the other in the air, attracting the attention of a taxi driver who thought she was hailing him. She shooed him away and grabbed Charlotte's suitcase. 'This way. Let's get away from this crazy mess,' she said, dragging the case to the edge of the kerb. 'In the meantime, look at you. How on earth d'you manage it? You just travelled for ninety-seven hundred hours, and you look like Nicole Kidman. Don't you ever eat?'

A man approached and reached for Charlotte's bag. 'You want taxi, lady?' Roxy grabbed it back. '*Ot-tay, akun, bong. Yeung meen tuk-tuk, howee.*'

Charlotte's eyes widened. 'What on earth was that?'

'I told him we already have transportation. At least, I think I did.' She reached out and picked specks of confetti from Charlotte's hair. 'Hey, what d'you think of my new creation? I make it with the girls at my shop. We spray mountains of rice with silver and gold. I'm trying to think of a name for it. What d'ya think of *rice-fetti*? Thought it would be great for weddings and parties. M*ega* perfect for Gay Pride too, don't you think?' She yanked Charlotte's arm and steered her toward the parking area. 'But now I'm gonna show you my Cambodia.'

A round-faced Cambodian man drew up beside them, an enormous smile on his face. He sat astride a motorbike that pulled a two-wheeled orange wagon fitted with a canopy and wooden bench seats. Emblazoned across the rear were two words scrawled in black paint: *Super Tuk-tuk*.

'My man, SomOn!' Roxy slapped him on the shoulder, dripping silver and gold confetti down the back of his shirt. 'Charlo, meet SomOn, the best tuk-tuk driver in Cambodia. Maybe the world.' She turned to Charlotte. 'Say *Khnom chmoa Charlotte*. That means, my name is Charlotte.'

'Ker-nom jermo Charlotte.'

SomOn chuckled. 'Oh, you speak such good Cambodian, Jallod.' He lifted her suitcase onto the vehicle and donned a helmet.

'Well done,' Roxy said. 'That's your first Khmer lesson. You'll also need to know *akun* which means *thank you*. And *ot tay*, which means *no*. You'll be using that a lot with all the tuk-tuk drivers competing for your business.' She cupped a hand over her mouth and whispered to Charlotte, 'Everyone here will say you speak good Cambodian, or Khmer, which is what the language is really called. People are so lovely, and they all want to do is be helpful and encouraging. You'll see.'

Charlotte grabbed Roxy's arm as she started to climb onto the tuk-tuk 'Just a moment, Rox. There's someone I need to find first. There was a man sitting next to me. He—'

'Must've been a good flight.'

'Don't be daft. This fellow's seventy-seven and looks like Ravi Shankar. I've got something that belongs to him.'

'Almost everyone from your flight has left.' Roxy shook her head. 'If it's really important you can leave it at Lost and Found.' She pulled a face. 'Maybe not. Someone's likely to pocket it.'

Charlotte hesitated. 'But he might need it.'

'What is it? Something valuable?'

'A letter.'

'A letter? What does it say?'

Charlotte shook her head. 'I didn't read it. But it might be something he needs.'

'Tell you what. Let's read it later and see. In the meantime, we're blocking the road. Gotta move on.'

They climbed aboard the tuk-tuk and the vehicle pulled into the line of cars, causing the women to tumble into one another. Charlotte's bag fell open and the contents spilled out onto the floor: a pair of earplugs, bug spray with 70 percent

DEET, SFP 50-plus sunscreen, a box of aspirins, and a plastic bag filled with plasters, antacids, and antiseptic cream.

Roxy burst out laughing. 'Oh honey! D'you think you need to protect yourself from everything?'

Charlotte stuffed them back into her bag. 'Just being well prepared. You know me.' She silently squirmed. Did she look like an idiot? She'd never been anywhere like Cambodia and wanted to be organised. The guidebooks had warned about mosquito-borne diseases, sunstroke, and stomach ailments in this part of the world and her mother had told her she'd definitely get sick. With a slight shrug, she closed her bag and thrust her phone toward Roxy, eager to change the subject. 'Look at this. Is it from you?'

Roxy took the phone and looked at the message. 'Fifty-seven days?' She raised her eyebrows. 'Are you daft? I'm not paying international rates to send you a text that says fifty-seven days. What does it mean anyway?'

'No idea. It's the latest weird message.'

'Latest?'

Charlotte sighed. Did Roxy ever read her emails? 'These texts. I've been getting them for a while.'

'What's a while?'

'Since December.'

'December? It wasn't me. I was on Rabbit Island. No Wi-Fi. No phone. *Nada*.'

Charlotte smiled to herself. It had been so long since she'd last seen Roxy that she'd almost forgotten their sisterly wrangling. Many people who spent time with them thought they quarrelled all the time, and few understood the familiarity the two girls shared, having grown up together and knowing every detail of one another's lives. It hadn't taken long for them to fall back into the same pattern.

'I didn't say it *was* you,' she replied.

'So, what did it say?'

'*You will receive a gift of time.*'

Roxy snorted. 'Probably an ad from a phone provider, or a watch company.'

'I thought so, too. But two days later, my boss told us about reorganising the agency. Guess what *that* meant: A gift of time.'

'I think you're being a bit *woo-woo*. It must've been a Christmas promo.'

Charlotte sighed. Was Roxy paying attention? She'd imagined she might be concerned, or at the very least intrigued by these strange messages; possibly even offer a suggestion about how to figure them out. But Roxy was off on her own agenda and Charlotte regretted bringing up the subject. 'Never mind,' she said. 'You're probably right.'

'Don't stop now,' Roxy nudged. 'Are there more? If you don't tell me, I'll push you off the tuk-tuk.' She prodded Charlotte in the ribs. 'Didn't you miss me?' she said, giggling.

'Like a bad rash.' Charlotte replied.

'So? Tell me. Was that the last message?'

'No. I got another the following week.'

'Did it say, *Happy New Year, go visit your friend in Cambodia*?'

'I'm serious, Rox. It said, *Someone from your past will come to rescue you*. That was right before Uncle Alistair called to say he was coming to live near us. It kinda freaked me out.'

A motorbike roared past, drowning out Charlotte's voice. 'Hey? What d'you say?' Roxy shouted.

'I said the message told me someone was coming to rescue me. Don't you think that's weird?'

Roxy wrinkled her brow. 'I guess. What did you do?'

'Called the number back and sent text message replies, but nobody answered. I figured it must be someone playing around or a wrong number. But then I got another after I booked my flight. There was some…' She stared at Roxy, her eyes widening.

'What's the matter?' asked Roxy. 'Looks like you just saw a zombie.'

'The message I got. After I made my reservation. It said *March 3.*'

'So?'

'Today's January fifth, right?'

'Sure is. Why?'

'March third is fifty-seven days from today.'

3

Clouds of acrid dust flew from the street as SomOn swerved to avoid gaping potholes in the tarmac. Charlotte put her phone away and stared at Roxy. 'What do you think that means?' she asked.

Roxy sighed. 'You've just arrived, hon,' she said. 'Just be here now, as Ram Dass used to say. And get a new phone number. I think he said that too.'

A dog darted across their path and Charlotte grabbed Roxy's arm and shrieked. The highway pulsated with motorbikes, cars, trucks, bicycles, and buses, and the gusts of hot wind in her face made it hard to breathe. She poked Roxy in the ribs. 'Tell him to slow down,' she yelled over the noise of the traffic. 'We're going to turn over!'

'Don't worry,' Roxy shouted back. 'This is normal.'

Charlotte gripped the metal bar on the tuk-tuk and squeezed her eyes shut as motorbikes sped across the pavements, often in the opposite direction to traffic. This was almost as bad as the flight.

Roxy pointed to a group of street vendors scooping noodles into Styrofoam containers. 'The best street food in town,' she yelled. 'Gonna take you there.'

Charlotte opened her eyes to see two men with bare chests stirring a large metal pot. Noodles from a street stand? It sounded horribly germ-infested. They weren't even wearing shirts. Strands of hair blew from her ponytail, so she brushed them away then peeled off her light jacket. Her blouse was glued to her back with perspiration and it was only mid-morning. Couldn't they have taken an air-conditioned taxi?

The tuk-tuk drew up alongside a minivan and Charlotte glanced inside. Passengers were packed like rag dolls in a toy box; a helter-skelter of arms, faces, and shoulders behind glass. She caught the eye of a woman who had one arm twisted behind her head, the other pushing against the ceiling of the van for balance. Charlotte quickly looked away, afraid to be caught staring. But the woman's face broke into a smile and she nudged the woman next to her who did the same.

Roxy shouted in Charlotte's ear. 'It's a shared taxi.'

'A what?'

'An insane way to travel! People pay a pittance and drivers pack them in like bloody sardines. Sometimes they even sell the seat *under* the driver or let someone sit on the roof. Everyone seems in good spirits, though, don't you think? Imagine people crammed like that on a bus in Brighton. Not so sure they'd be waving and smiling.' Roxy gave a thumbs up to the woman in the minivan who returned the gesture. Some of the passengers waved.

'It's a crazy place, hon,' Roxy said. 'Hectic, nutso, and overwhelming. But I love it all. It isn't pretty and clean like your holiday lodge in the Highlands, but there's much more personality.' She wrinkled her nose as they passed a rubbish pile. 'If you don't mind the smells.' She leaned forward and patted SomOn on the shoulder. 'This man will take care of you when I'm at work. He picked me up when I first arrived and saved me from getting lost almost every day. He became my regular guy till I realised I was spending too much on tuk-tuks and bought a motorbike.'

Charlotte spluttered as dust blew into her face. 'A motorbike? In *this?*'

Roxy nodded, then lowered her voice. 'I'd like to give SomOn the business, but it's cheaper to have a moto. I usually drop Peter at work in the morning, then Tnout and I usually spend time together till I open the shop.'

'Tnout?'

'My pup. Well, not really mine. He belongs to our Cambodian landlords, but they're not very good with dogs.' She pulled out a bag of M&Ms, stuffed a handful in her mouth, and offered them to Charlotte, who declined. 'Tnout means *palm tree* in Khmer,' she continued, her mouth full of chocolate. 'Don't blame me, I didn't name him. Daro—one of the landlords—is happy to let him hang out with me, so I buy him treats and he rides with me on my moto. Tnout, that is, not Daro.'

She shovelled the rest of the M&Ms into her mouth, crumpled the empty bag, and stuffed it beneath the seat. 'I've got to take you to *Edgar Allen Paw*. Lots of pooches. And sometimes cute owners too. Get my drift?' She nudged Charlotte. 'But first, the Roxy-Peter pad. It's near *Psar Toul Tumpoung*. Not much, but it's our home.' She took a can of Coke from her bag, had a sip then offered it to Charlotte. 'Am I talking too much? It's just so darned good to see you. Can you believe it's been almost three years?'

Charlotte caught the M&M wrapper mid-flight as it blew

from beneath the seat. 'Edgar Allen Paw? Sar tooltam pong? I haven't a clue what you're going on about.' She folded the chocolate wrapper and put it in her pocket, then took the can from Roxy, wiped the rim with a tissue and drank from it. She didn't like fizzy drinks but right now she'd drink almost anything.

Roxy threw back her head and laughed. 'Edgar Allen Paw's a doggy café. Great coffee for humans and the best dog biscuits. I know, I've tried them. And Psar Toul Tumpoung's the Russian market. It's called that because of the Russians who shopped there in the eighties.' She jangled an armful of silver and turquoise bracelets. 'I bought these there. It's the best place to buy trinkets and stuff your face with cheap spicy food. Gets a bit hot and stuffy but...' She shrugged.

Charlotte's heart sank. This wasn't what she'd pictured. She'd known it would be different—probably exotic and unpredictable like Roxy—but she'd been hoping for something more comfortable. It was her own fault. She usually dissected every smidgeon of information about everything, but this time she'd been so excited about getting away from home and seeing her dearest friend she'd assumed everything would be fine. Roxy had told her Cambodia was special—that had been enough for her. But she hadn't said she'd be working every day and she hadn't told her it would feel like *this*. In the past, they'd always done everything together. Roxy had done the scheduling and Charlotte had been happy to go along with her plans. She'd expected it to be the same here. She suddenly realised her vision of exploring a romantic faraway land with her friend had been a fantasy. Roxy had been gone for years. Their communication had been patchy. Of course, things had changed.

Roxy put her arm around her shoulders, as though sensing her discomfort. 'Why so quiet?' she asked. 'Jetlag?'

Charlotte shrugged her arm off. She didn't want Roxy to feel badly for her. Faking a smile, she said, 'Probably,' and took another sip of Coke. 'Tell me about Peter. I know nothing about this man you married, and I can't wait to meet him.'

'Ah, the wonderful Peter,' Roxy replies, her eyes twinkling. 'He's the Punch to my Judy, the Clyde to my Bonnie, the Rhett to...'

'Roxy, be serious.'

'I am. He completes me, Charlo.' Roxy grinned. 'I've no idea what a smart, gorgeous man like him saw in a chunky Englishwoman like *moi* but,' she shrugged, 'I won the jackpot when I found him.' She leaned forward, twisting the wedding ring on her finger. 'You'll see when you meet him. Right now, I want you to check out the neighbourhoods.' She pointed down a side street where two women sat on the pavement next to a basket filled with fruit, an infant rolling an apple on the ground beside them.

Charlotte followed her gaze along the road and was struck by the miniscule size of the houses. Many had long lines of laundry dangling from the windows and some had awnings above entrances that were grey with age and dirt.

'Wait till you see our home,' Roxy said. 'It's a weeny little place near the market.' She slipped off her flip-flops and dangled her bare feet over the side of the tuk-tuk. 'It's one hundred and seventy-two steps from a great internet café with air-conditioning. You'll be needing that. We only have aircon in the bedrooms and don't use it much as it's mega-expensive. Then if you walk four hundred and eleven steps you'll get to the Russian market.'

As Roxy talked, Charlotte started to unwind. She had

forgotten how her friend measured distance in steps. Back home, her texts always said something like, *Meet me at the King's Head. 349 steps from the number nine bus stop*, or, *Leave your house, turn left and walk 653 steps to the Goldfish Café*. It was a relief to see some things had stayed the same.

She flinched as a motorbike pulled alongside. The driver was a young man in faded jeans and a black sleeveless T-shirt, a blue and white checkered scarf knotted around his neck. A small boy balanced on the seat between his legs, and a young woman sat behind him feeding a baby from a milk bottle. On the rear, an old woman sat side-saddle, her legs dangling, both arms wrapped around the woman with the baby.

Charlotte looked at Roxy and widened her eyes. Four people on one seat? Five, if you counted the baby. The boy caught her eye, raised his chubby hand, and blew a kiss. The mother and father looked at Charlotte and Roxy, smiled and waved and sped away in a cloud of dust.

'That's Cambodia for you,' Roxy said. 'Everyone smiles back.'

Charlotte relaxed her grip on the metal bar as they turned onto a main road. Perhaps she'd been too quick to judge. She'd slipped into her typical response: run away from anything uncomfortable. But there were plenty of fascinating things to see, even in the sixty-minute drive from the airport, and Roxy was doing her best to entertain her.

Roxy's voice cut into her thoughts. 'Look at that,' she said, pointing to a western woman standing at the edge of the road. '*Tourist* written all over her.' The woman hovered on the pavement, apparently paralysed with fear at the prospect of crossing the steady tide of humans and steel. The traffic light changed to red and cars filtered through. The woman ran across the street, zigzagging between motorbikes, stopped at a concrete barrier in the middle of the road and froze. *That'll be me,* Charlotte thought. *I'm not going anywhere without Roxy.*

The tuk-tuk swerved onto a bumpy back street and Charlotte grabbed Roxy's knee as they veered around the corner. A couple of children ran alongside, kicking a ball across the road, and three men stood in the middle of the street, waving their arms in animated conversation. Upon seeing the tuk-tuk, one of them walked toward them brandishing a machete.

SomOn slowed down as the man approached. Charlotte gasped and dug her fingernails into her palms. 'What the...?'

'Coconut, laydee?' the man asked, gesturing to a pile of enormous fruit with the machete.

'*Ot tay*. No thank you,' Roxy replied.

SomOn accelerated and continued along the road. Charlotte took a deep breath then groaned and clamped a hand over her mouth and nose. 'Oh yuck! What's that awful smell?'

Roxy slipped her feet into her flip-flops. '*Loo teuk saoy*,' she said. 'Stinky canal.'

'Stinky canal?'

'Phnom Penh's least attractive site— the open sewer.' She pulled a face. 'Sorry. Didn't realise we'd be coming this way. Don't worry, we're almost there.'

A few minutes later, they pulled up in front of a three-story yellow building embellished with tiny wrought iron balconies. The street was barely wide enough for the delivery lorry that lumbered past them, and the building was sandwiched between a high-rise block of flats and a large open-fronted restaurant. A blend of aromas that smelled like fried chicken, garlic, and a sour fishy odour made Charlotte gag a second time.

Roxy leapt from the tuk-tuk and waved her arm toward the

building '*Ptea yeung*! Our home.' She hoisted Charlotte's duffel bag onto her shoulder as SomOn unloaded the suitcase. Suddenly Roxy let out a high-pitched squeal. 'Tnout!' she cried. 'Darling doggy.' A stumpy dog raced toward them, yapping, and wagging its stubby tail. Roxy crouched down and swept the mucky animal into her arms, her silk chemise dangling in the dust. 'Look who I've brought to see you,' she said to the dog, then dropped him back onto the ground where he ran to Charlotte, sniffed her leather sandals, and retreated into the building.

'He's shy with strangers,' Roxy said. 'Rather like Peter. But they're both extremely loveable when you get to know them.' She handed some dollar bills to SomOn and pushed open the front door to the building 'Grab the other handle, hon. We're going up.'

They hauled Charlotte's suitcase up a narrow concrete stairway, stopping every four steps to take a breath. When they reached the third floor they were sweating and panting. Charlotte leaned against the wooden door and inhaled deeply. 'Jeez, Roxy, don't they have lifts?'

'Not when you're paying three hundred dollars a month, darlin'.' She wiped a sweaty arm across her forehead. 'You know me and exercise. I bloody hate it. Told Peter I'd never live in a place with more than thirty-five steps. Then he found this place. Guess how many steps it has? Thirty-seven.' She fumbled for the key. 'I told him he'd have to carry me up the last two if he wanted to live here. Know what? He did. For the first week. Then he started to complain about back problems and ankle sprains, and some disease he didn't have. Told me we'd have to move if I couldn't manage all thirty-seven steps. Of course, I'd fallen in love with the place by then. So, I'm stuck with forced exercise.' She grimaced and pointed to herself. 'But look at me, still no Victoria's Secret model.' She unlocked the door and waved her arm in a flourish. 'Ta-dah! Welcome to Wicker World!'

The door swung open, and Charlotte gazed into a small living and dining area with a shiny wood floor and more wicker than she had ever seen in one place. In the middle of the living area, a white wicker couch was covered with red cushions that had been hand-embroidered with yellow sunflowers. Near the window was a circular papasan chair painted a shade of silver, its black cushion embellished with tiny sequin stars. And in the middle of the room sat a yellow wicker coffee table and a dresser covered with brightly coloured bottles and jars, some with fabric flowers poking from the top. A ceiling fan spun in wobbly circles above them.

Charlotte laughed with delight. 'It's so *you*! I love it.'

Roxy's smile stretched from ear to ear. 'I painted most of the furniture myself. Wicker's mega cheap. Peter thinks I'm mad, but he doesn't care what I do as long as there's space for his work. Come see your room—sixteen steps from the front door.'

She led Charlotte down a narrow dimly lit corridor, past a kitchen barely large enough to contain a four-burner stovetop and small fridge. The sink was piled high with dirty dishes and some of the cabinet doors were wide open with most of the shelves empty. At the end of the passageway, she pushed a door open with her shoulder and ushered Charlotte inside. 'Here you go,' she said. 'My artist cavern.'

Charlotte dropped her bag on the single bed which was draped with a purple tapestry decorated with miniature mirrors and gold thread. Above the bed, a mobile of coloured glass and painted feathers hung from the ceiling, and boxes of beads, buttons, glass pebbles, and coloured string were piled high on a wicker dressing table. On the floor was a stack of cardboard boxes with paper hand-written labels: *Scarves. Fabric. Animals. Paper. Fish.* She kicked off her shoes and saw a frame on the bedside table containing a photo of two teenage girls standing in the middle of a field. The tall one was dressed in a velvet medieval gown, auburn ringlets falling around her shoulders. The other had a pierced nose and a gaudy jester's costume. She picked it up and held it out to Roxy. 'The Herstmonceux Medieval Festival! What are you doing with this?'

'You'd be surprised at the things I've carried around the world,' Roxy said. 'Remember that day? We entered an archery competition and I almost shot a friggin' sheep. Your dad dropped us off, and we spent the taxi fare on that dreadful fermented mead.'

Charlotte laughed. 'Then you persuaded a couple of policemen to take us home, and my mum thought we'd been arrested.'

Chuckling, Roxy pulled the cord to open the window shade and knocked a plastic vase onto the floor. 'Peter thinks that's the perfect portrayal of us, by the way. You're elegant and gorgeous, and I'm the clown. And he hasn't even met you yet!'

Charlotte picked up the vase and put it back on the table. 'We had so much fun, didn't we? I'm so grateful.'

'For what?'

'There aren't many Roxys in my life. I could count them on...on one finger!' She sighed.

'You only just arrived and you're giving me the finger?'

'I'm serious, Rox. If it weren't for you, I'd probably be a solitary bookworm with no friends. And look at me now. I'm in Cambodia.' She spun in a circle, then planted a kiss on Roxy's cheek.

'Enough of that, Charlotte O'Hara. You're getting sappy. Get yourself settled. Unpack, take a shower, eat a KitKat, whatever you want, then come chat. We've lots of catching up to do.'

She left the room and Charlotte flopped onto the bed. She pulled the band from her hair and shook her head, then connected to Wi-Fi. She should let her mother know she had arrived safely. She leaned through the window, snapped a photo of a rats' nest of telephone and electrical wires tangled around a telephone pole and forwarded it along with a brief note. Perhaps if she kept in touch, her mother wouldn't stay angry.

Rummaging in her bag for a hairbrush, her hand landed on the rolled up *National Geographic* and the envelope she had found on the plane. She didn't want to read the letter as Roxy had suggested, but she wondered if it might contain Rashid's schedule or an address where she might be able to find him.

There was a slight tear at the top of the envelope, so she eased it back and peered inside, then caught herself. She hadn't intended to read it. But she realised it may be her only way to find him, so she slit it open and pulled out two sheets of paper, both covered with neat cursive handwriting written in the curly script of a fountain pen.

Dear Chris. I have started so many letters in the past year, but I've torn them up as I didn't know what to say or how to reach you. This time I plan on finding you so I can give this to you in person.

She stopped. This was private and she was intruding. But the temptation to know more was too great, so she continued.

When you left, I was angry and disgusted. I wanted to eliminate every memory of you. I felt you had ruined our lives as well as yours by the way you lived your life. I wanted you to stay away forever.

For three months I didn't care to think about you. You were no longer my child. You weren't like me—that's all I knew. Your mother cried every day and begged me to talk to you, but I refused to listen to her. After Christmas, I went into your room to clear it out and found a notebook. I read your words about forgiveness and life purpose and began to understand you a little better.

Later that week, I saw your friend Jose at the coffee shop. He told me about the work you had done for his shelter and how you were their shining star. He said he missed you and cried a little when he talked about you. He told me you'd gone to Cambodia but didn't know how to find you (if he did, I'm sure he wouldn't have told me).

I see things differently now. I realise I never took the time to know you or understand your lifestyle. I'm sorry I hurt you and dismissed you from my life. I'm sorry I caused pain for your mother. Most of all, I'm sorry for all I *have lost. I never realised what a special child you were until it was too late.*

I am writing this letter in case you refuse to see me. I understand you may not want me in your life, but I want you back in mine.

I love you.

Baba

Charlotte swallowed a lump in her throat. She had sensed something had been troubling Rashid, but she'd put it down to anxiety about his sight. She slid the pages back into the envelope and felt something hard in the bottom. She turned it upside down and tapped it, and a tiny felt bag embroidered with silver thread fell to the floor with a muffled clink. Inside was a gold ring and a note. *It's time for you to have my grandfather's ring. I understand why you didn't want it but I'm bringing it to you with no expectation.*

The heavy band was studded with three small sapphires and etched with an ornamental design. It was clearly expensive and must have sentimental value. As Charlotte stared at the envelope, she realised that somewhere in Cambodia an old man would be worrying about the loss of two things: his ring, and his son.

4

Blaring car alarms and yelping dogs snapped Charlotte out of a deep sleep. She looked at her watch through blurry eyes. It was 3 p.m.

The door creaked open and a shock of platinum hair appeared through the crack. 'Hey,' Roxy said, with a twisted smile. 'You can sleep when you're dead. Come talk to me before Peter gets home.' She disappeared, leaving the door open behind her.

Charlotte stuffed Rashid's letter into a trouser pocket, brushed her hair, and splashed water on her face. She felt groggy from hours of travel, so she picked up her overnight bag and went into the living room, before succumbing to the temptation to go back to sleep.

Roxy was curled up on a beanbag reading a yellowed copy of *Artists Weekly*. She patted the seat next to her. 'Come sit. I'm so friggin' excited you're here I could bust out of my bustier. Which isn't a good idea!' She tugged her strapless top up toward her shoulders.

Charlotte flopped down and wrapped her arms around her. 'Amazing, isn't it? I'm in Cambodia. And you're married. Who woulda guessed? Rambling Roxy has settled down.'

'Hey! I'm an independent woman. I don't need anyone to make me happy.' Roxy blushed. 'Except maybe this one. He's rather special.'

'You're the special one. He's just lucky.'

'Yeah, you're right.' Roxy grinned. 'I'm amazing. Hey, I can't wait for...'

Charlotte interrupted. 'You know you never told me the story. How you met this magical man.'

'Course I did. I emailed you from Yangon, or was it Chiang Mai? No, I wrote to you from a guesthouse in Krabi. I remember telling you I found him at a night market.'

Charlotte rolled her eyes. 'Whatever. I never got it. So, you met him in Thailand?'

'No, Phnom Penh. Before going to Thailand. He was at the night market and I fell over him since the daft fellow was sitting on the ground. Then, we met again on a bus to Thailand and ended up in the same guesthouse in Krabi. I walked into his room one night by accident.' She chuckled. 'They all looked the same. No alcohol involved, of course.'

'And that was your first date?'

'Not really. He wasn't too happy to see me as he was sleeping and I was—well, drunk. So, I made it up to him by taking him breakfast and showing him I was actually a caring, sober-minded, totally fascinating individual. Turned out he was planning on coming to Cambodia to do some kind of benevolent work and it also turned out this incredibly fascinating woman serving him muesli would be a perfect business partner. And that, of course, turned into...' She shrugged and grinned.

'You're amazing. How do you do these things?'

'I have my ways.'

Charlotte took a deep sigh.

'You okay?' Roxy asked.

'Sorry. My head feels like it's stuffed with cotton wool.' She rubbed her eyes. There wasn't much air circulating in the small flat, but she didn't want to ask Roxy to turn on the air-conditioning since she'd told her it was expensive.

'I was going to take you out and show you the town, but you don't look as though you're up for it,' Roxy said. 'Let's just be lazy slugs instead.' She stretched her arms above her head and exhaled loudly. 'So, tell me. What convinced you to get back on a plane? As much as I'd like to believe it's my irresistible personality and rapier wit, I've a feeling there's another reason behind this trip.' She glanced away. 'Since my wedding wasn't enough motivation for making the journey.'

Charlotte inhaled sharply. 'Oh, I can't—'

Roxy held up her hand. 'Hey, chill! I'm kidding. I think.' She stuffed a cushion behind her back. 'So, tell me more. You wanted to get away from normal, and experience bedlam?'

Normal. What must it feel like to be normal? Charlotte thought of Linda, her work assistant. Linda's life would be normal. Aerobics on a Tuesday, book club on a Wednesday, curry with her boyfriend on a Friday, family roast lunch on Sunday. Charlotte longed to be normal. To never have to overthink things or worry about her mother or listen to the running commentary in her head telling her she wasn't good enough.

Roxy interrupted her thoughts. 'Or did you just want a break from mother of the year?'

Charlotte sighed and leaned over to unbuckle her overnight bag. 'If we're going to talk about her, we need this.' She drew out a bottle of Ballantine whisky and waved it in the air. 'Duty free.'

'Oh, you wonderful woman, you!' Roxy whooped and scurried into the kitchen for glasses then poured a hefty nip into each. 'Now you're talkin' my language!'

Charlotte swirled her glass and clinked it against Roxy's. 'Let's toast to our reunion. And that I made it through a gazillion hours in a flying tube.'

They sipped the smoky liquid and the taste took Charlotte back to her college days. One of Roxy's boyfriends had brought a bottle to a party and the girls had quickly cultivated a taste for spirits. They'd agreed it would be in their cultural interests to indulge in good Scotch rather than the cheap wine they usually drank, and Charlotte should be the one to provide it since Roxy was always broke. For Charlotte, whisky later turned out to be more than just an interesting drink; it became a crutch for getting through the bad days.

'Hang on,' Roxy exclaimed. 'We can't drink without our theme song.' She scrambled to her feet and plugged in a small DVD player. The sound of Ke$ha singing *We R Who We R* blasted through the speakers. She hauled Charlotte to her feet, and the girls strutted up and down the small room, lip-synching, and bouncing up and down on the cushions.

'Bloody hell! It's been ages since I did that!' Roxy collapsed onto the couch and pulled Charlotte down next to her. 'Whoever said you were the quiet one had no idea what they were talking about.'

'Melinda.'

'Huh?'

'Don't you remember? That awful Miranda Bollard. The one who called us beauty and the beast and took great delight in telling me *you* were the beast.' Her face warmed. 'Idiot.'

Roxy clinked her glass on the edge of the coffee table. 'Fighting words, dear Charlo! And I'll never forget what a tiger you became.' She tossed back her head and laughed. 'I even remember your exact words. You said, "If you'd stop being such a sycophantic parvenu, you'd see Roxy has more beauty in her little finger than any of your prissy friends have in their entire aerobicized bodies". The twit didn't have a clue what *sycophantic parvenu* meant, so she had to shut her stupid mouth.' She set her glass on the floor and looked at Charlotte. 'You have more power than you think. You've let your mum walk all over you for years, but there's a quiet strength about you that's irresistible. Everyone knows it except one person.'

'And that would be?'

'You.'

Charlotte leaned back against a sequinned cushion. 'Now who's being mushy?'

She thought back to their childhood days when she would go to Roxy's home after school. Her mother would often pull her into the kitchen, tie an apron on, and put her to work. Sticky toffee pudding, treacle tart, chocolate cheesecake. Pastry after pastry covered the countertop of their small home—some for neighbours and friends but most contributing to the expanding waistlines of Roxy and her mother who understood Charlotte needed a distraction. For Charlotte, the memories lingered much longer than the taste of the pastries. Even today, whenever she passed a bakery, she was reminded of the comforting moments with Auntie Jilly and the rest of Roxy's family. Her own mother hadn't shared the same fondness. 'They're common folk, those Osbornes,' she'd commented one day. 'I've no idea why you spend so much time with them when you've got a lovely home just a few miles away.'

Charlotte knew her mother would never understand. She

had never been capable of seeing beneath any surface. If she had, she'd have noticed the hardness in her own perfectly made-up eyes, the tightness around her shiny peach lipstick. She would have seen a woman who repelled everything she used to attract—including her own husband. Charlotte often fantasised she would come home from school one day and find a mum who'd be baking apricot cheesecake in a messy kitchen. She'd wrap her arms around her and ask her about her day. She'd laugh and—

'Hey, dreamer!' Roxy's voice snapped her back. 'If I wanted to talk to myself, I'd invite Tnout to join me. I haven't seen you in three years. How about telling me what's going on in your world.'

Charlotte poured another tot of whisky and tucked her feet beneath her. Had Roxy read any of her messages? Where should she start?

'I'm waiting,' Roxy said. 'You're training to be a tightrope walker. You created a vaccine for cancer. You've had an affair with an Arabian prince.'

Charlotte shook her head. 'Things still suck. Probably more than ever.'

'More? How?'

She set her jaw and stared across the room. 'Long story.'

'I'm not going anywhere. Tell me.'

'Okay then. How about the day I came home to a kitchen filled with smoke?'

'That's it? What happened?'

'It wasn't long after you left. The fire alarm was going crazy and I couldn't find Mum. I freaked out and dashed from room to room like a crazy person—' Her voice quivered.

'Shit, Charlo.'

'She'd passed out in her bedroom. My fault because I came

home late. If I'd been there on time, I could have made dinner and she wouldn't have had to cook.' She took a large sip of whisky. It burned her throat and gave her courage to continue.

'That's what she said? What a bitch.'

'It gets better. About five months ago, I was called out of a client meeting for an urgent phone call—it was her, whispering there was an intruder in the house. I called the police and rushed home and when I got there, found an angry policewoman in the driveway. No intruder. And no Mum.' Her face warmed as the uncomfortable memory washed over her. 'It took me four hours to find her, Rox. Four hours! And guess where she was? In a pub with some bloke who lived across the street. The so-called intruder was a neighbour who happened to notice our front door was open. He was good-looking, so...' She shrugged. 'Then she called me an interfering brat.' She exhaled loudly. 'Why do I still get surprised when things like this happen?'

Roxy leaned over and topped up the glasses, her lips pressed tight. 'Because you're a good person and there's—'

'The best was right before Christmas,' Charlotte interrupted. 'You'll never guess what she decided to do. House-cleansing. And what do you suppose house-cleansing was? Dusting? Redecorating? Nope. It meant burning the photo albums with the photos...the only photos of—' Her voice broke.

Roxy leaned closer. 'Your dad?'

Charlotte nodded. 'Know what she said? She was exorcising bad spirits before Christmas. She called Dad a bastard, said he never cared about us, that we were better off without...' The words caught in her throat.

Roxy sucked in her breath. 'What a cow.' She squeezed Charlotte's hand. 'Your dad was lovely. I loved those cigars he smoked. They had a name that sounded like ice cream. Vanilla

Cream something.' She paused. 'Sorry, didn't mean to change the subject. So, what did you do?'

Charlotte stared at the ground. 'Went for a walk,' she murmured. 'I couldn't talk to her. But she realised she'd gone too far and got all weepy when I came home; begged me to forgive her in that annoying whiny voice she uses when she wants to have her way.' Charlotte mimicked her high-pitched speech. '*How could I be so mean when you're such an angel? Please forgive your silly mother.*' She snorted. 'All kind of rubbish she didn't mean. And what did I do? I caved. Again. Brushed it all under the proverbial rug and pretended everything was fine. You know, let's just all get on with our artificial little lives when nobody says anything meaningful to anyone.... blah, blah, blah...Then I sat back and waited for the next horrible thing to happen.'

Roxy stretched her legs out on the floor. 'She's jealous.'

'Of what?'

'Your relationship with your dad.'

'But I didn't—'

'Let me finish. She was never nice to you. I remember her making fun of you for being scared of the dark and for teasing you for being a neat freak. It made me so angry because you were so goddamn good to her. She didn't deserve you.'

'But I couldn't abandon her. I was all she had.'

'Bullshit! You were her scratching post. I always believed you stayed because your home was the only connection you had with your dad. You thought he might come back, and you were terrified of not being there. I'm right, aren't I?' She scrambled to her feet. 'Hold that thought! I'm gonna get us something to eat. Don't know about you, but I'm starving.'

Charlotte drained her glass as Roxy rummaged in the kitchen cupboard. Her mind flashed back to an evening just before her seventeenth birthday and the sound of voices yelling from the kitchen, followed by the smash of a window. No matter how loud she blasted Ke$ha over her headphones, she could hear every hateful word. She remembered pleading into her pillow, then holding her breath and thinking if she held it long enough her father would stay. It hadn't been the first time he'd had threatened to leave. He'd even walked out a few times. But he'd always come back. Until one day he didn't.

Roxy emerged from the kitchen, carrying a plastic bowl filled with brown rice crackers that were sprinkled with Parmesan. 'It's all I could find,' she said, shrugging. She handed the bowl to Charlotte and continued talking as though there had been no interruption. 'I never got it. Why you stayed.'

'I had no choice.'

'Course you did. She just manipulated you to think you didn't. Are you really still worried about what she thinks? Did she do that to you? Or did your dad?'

'What's he got to do with it?'

Roxy opened her mouth to speak, then took a deep breath. She looked Charlotte in the eye. 'Everything.'

Charlotte felt her face heat up. 'It wasn't his fault,' she murmured. 'He couldn't stay. She made it too hard.'

'Crap! You can't think he's innocent. He screwed up, too.'

'What do you know?' She glared at Roxy. 'You weren't there. If you hadn't left, I—' She stopped.

'You what?'

Charlotte stared at the floor. 'Nothing.'

'You can't dangle that out there. If I hadn't left, what?'

'I can't...there isn't—'

The door swung open.

'Hello,' said a male voice. 'You must be Charlotte.'

5

A long-limbed man stepped into the living room wearing baggy beige chinos and a short-sleeved shirt with sweat stains under the arms. A worn leather satchel dangled from his shoulder. Roxy bounded to her feet and wrapped her arms around him, knocking the John Lennon spectacles sideways on his face. She turned toward Charlotte, beaming. 'Charlo meet the man who inspired me to climb thirty-seven steps every day. Peter, meet the woman who flew a million miles to bring me a bottle of Scotch.'

The creases around Peter's almond-shaped eyes deepened as he smiled. He stuck out a hand and awkwardly shook hers. 'Happy to have you here. I've heard a lot about you from my lovely wife,' he said. 'She tells me you're more athletic than her, by the way, so perhaps *you* can haul her up the stairs now.' He ducked as Roxy aimed a playful punch toward his head.

The mood shifted from female intimacy to casual chit-chat.

'You do know that Charlo only came to Cambodia to check

I'd married a bloke worthy of me, don't you?' Roxy said with a coy smile. 'So, you'd better impress her, or she might convince me to trade you in for a newer model.'

'From what I hear, Charlotte's got better taste,' Peter replied. 'She chose *you* as a friend, didn't she?'

Roxy made a face. 'See what I mean? The guy's got class.' She sat on the couch. 'How was your day, gorgeous man?'

Charlotte noticed how Roxy's demeanour changed with Peter in the room. She was softer than her usual brash self, and her eyes sparkled when she looked at him. It was interesting to see how this quiet man had captured the heart of her friend who'd always sworn she never wanted to settle down.

Peter pushed the glasses higher up on his nose. 'Rough. As usual.' He sighed, then dropped the satchel on the floor and walked toward the kitchen. 'I'd love to join you in a drink, but I've got a report to finish and there's an early meeting tomorrow.' He poured a glass of water and came back to the living room.

Roxy patted the couch beside her. 'Just for a few minutes,' she said. 'We've been talking about you, and I want to tell Charlo about the amazing work you do to save the planet. And why you traded your home in Oz for a sweaty old city like Phnom Penh.'

He sat down next to Roxy, slipped off his sandals and folded his long legs beneath him. 'The Aussie lifestyle didn't appeal to me,' he told Charlotte. 'I was much happier with a backpack, a yoga mat, and some peace and quiet. My mates thought I was crazy to move here, but...' He shrugged. 'And now I don't have any of those things, except my yoga mat which I believe my wife has been made into a flying carpet. But I feel I'm doing something positive for humanity, and that's more important.'

Charlotte leaned forward. Peter was different from anyone Roxy had ever dated before. He appeared more serious-minded and was much better looking than the scrawny musician types that used to appeal to her. 'Why did you move here?' she asked.

'A combination of things. I wanted to do something useful. And then discovered I didn't like the way women are treated here.' He squeezed Roxy's hand. 'I've got three sisters and two nieces, and now a wife. They're all strong women and I'd never want them to be disrespected, so I became involved with the local community to see if there was some way I could help.' As he sipped his water, he told Charlotte how he'd founded a small local enterprise to support Cambodian women. 'Funny how things happen, isn't it?' he said. 'If I'd never stayed at the Home Karma guesthouse, I'd never have seen them.'

'Babe, you're being way too modest.' Roxy turned to Charlotte. 'Pardon me for interrupting, but he's referring to the women at the girlie bars.' She nudged him in the ribs. 'Tell Charlotte what you did.'

'Probably what anyone would do,' he said. 'They used to walk past every day looking so sad in their fancy gowns, so I asked the desk clerk about them. He told me their job was to flirt and buy drinks for men in bars. They also had to go home with them if they paid them. Many were abused but had no other way to earn a living. Ratha—the front desk clerk—gave jobs to a couple but there wasn't much more he could do. That's where I stepped in. Since I'm a foreigner, it wasn't easy, so I asked Ratha if he'd work with me, and we started an enterprise called Helping Hands.'

Charlotte took a deep breath. She had heard about girlie bars but didn't think she'd come into contact with them. Now she was learning her best friend's husband ran a social enterprise that rescued young women from prostitution. Why hadn't Roxy mentioned it before? 'How did you get started?' she asked. 'I had no idea you did anything like this.' She glared at Roxy, hoping she'd notice her irritation.

'First, I learned some Khmer, then I approached a couple of women who worked at the bar. I don't know who was more nervous—me or them. One of them—a girl named Sethya—knew Ratha because their mothers sold vegetables in a village a couple of hours from Phnom Penh. She'd come to the city to look for work and got a job at a garment factory, but the factory went out of business a year later, so she was unemployed. Since she's the oldest daughter, she provides support for her family and couldn't go back to her village or she'd be in disgrace. So, she did what other desperate women do: got a job in a karaoke bar.'

'Interesting,' Charlotte said. 'Doing what?'

'Actually, not interesting at all. Over here, karaoke bars aren't much different from brothels. Girls work as hostesses and bring alcohol and food to private rooms where groups of men go to sing badly, drink, and pick a girl.'

He took another sip of water, his frown deepening. 'Sethya and her friend had been sexually abused. So Ratha told them about Helping Hands.' He sighed. 'I knew they'd be nervous about talking to a strange man from Australia, but they trusted Ratha and he convinced them to come to a meeting. They were terrified someone would see them, but Ratha promised we'd watch out for them and they finally quit their jobs at the karaoke bar. Now they work with Roxy in her shop and they're able to send money home to their families.'

Roxy draped an arm around his shoulders. 'He's been such a source of strength to these women. And his work made it possible for us to stay in Cambodia since Ratha sponsored him. And me, of course.'

Peter's eyes misted. 'Not everyone was so lucky. Sethya's cousin was beaten by a rich businessman. He made sure she disappeared so he wouldn't have to pay her medical bills.'

'What?' Charlotte said.

'A couple of his bodyguards shoved her into a van. They said they were taking her to hospital, but she never arrived. It's been almost a year.' He took off his glasses and rubbed his eyes. 'Cambodia's a beautiful country, Charlotte. People are extremely kind, and you'll find most are friendly, unpretentious, and welcoming. But there's an undercurrent of scary stuff. Most people who come for a visit don't see it, but it's very real. Don't worry, it won't affect you as a tourist, but I see it all.' He pulled Roxy closer. 'That's why I love your crazy friend so much. She's a bright ray of sunshine in my life, even though she's totally insane and doesn't care she looks like a toucan.'

'Hey, hey, hey!' Roxy said. 'How about all the sensational things I do?'

'That's true, babe. You've been my creative muse.' He tousled her hair and turned to Charlotte. 'You must come to Helping Hands and watch her in action. Last week the girls made mobiles from pieces of driftwood, and the week before they spray-painted rice gold and silver. Roxy sells their work at her store and they adore her even though they've never seen anyone quite like her.' He set his glass on the glass-topped coffee table. 'Now I'm going to leave you two to carry on without me. I've work to do.' He picked up his sandals and went to the bedroom.

After the door shut behind him, Roxy raised her glass. 'Here's to the most wonderful man who ever crossed my path.'

Charlotte nodded. She hoped Roxy wouldn't resume the

conversation they'd started before Peter arrived. She saw the tender expression on her friend's face and figured she'd moved on. 'You're lucky,' she said. 'He's a big improvement on Dave the Rave.' Roxy pulled a face as Charlotte continued. 'Do you remember that hippy fellow with the skeleton earrings? And Randy Andy, who kept calling even after you told him you'd rather date a hippo.'

'Oh, you can talk!' said Roxy. "You had Tim whatsit, that weird American chap who made you recite poetry over the phone because he loved your *ahksennt?* And the bloke who wanted you to look after his dog when he went away, then stayed in the house when you came to feed it.'

Charlotte laughed. 'We've had our share of loonies, haven't we?' she said. 'Trevor told me I should write a book about them.'

'Who's this Trevor?' Roxy asked. 'Someone special?'

'Very. He's gorgeous, smart, funny, and caring. I love him dearly and he loves me too.' She sighed loudly. 'He's also gay.' She burst out laughing.

'That's better,' Roxy said. 'You look much better when you laugh. Perhaps you'll find your own Peter in Phnom Penh. Unless your mum flies over to haul you back.'

Charlotte gasped. 'Don't even joke about such a thing.'

'How did she feel about you coming here?' Roxy asked. 'I can't imagine she gave you her blessing. Specially since you were coming to visit the dreadful Roxy.'

'You need to ask? She played every trick in the book.'

'Like what?'

'Everything. First tears and words of dread. Something like '*How could you leave me? What would I do in this big house all alone?*' Then guilt: '*It's always all about you; you never think of anyone but yourself.*' Let's see, what was next?' She bit into a rice cracker. 'Oh yes, fear. '*What if something happens to you? You've never travelled by yourself before.*' And, like always, it ended with anger, '*You're just like your dad, leaving me all alone*'. Blah, blah, blah. I blocked it all out by picturing you at the other end. And feeling extremely grateful to my boss.'

She recalled the day in December when her manager had announced they were closing one of the agency's bureaus. All employees from that office would have to work in other branches, and the principals would assess who'd be placed where. In the meantime, everyone was instructed to take two months compulsory leave within the first quarter of the year. The thought had initially horrified her. Two months at home with her mother. Trevor had suggested something different. 'Go away,' he said. 'I mean, really away. Use this time for *you*, love. Take a safari. Go to a meditation retreat. Laze on an exotic island.'

'Fine for you to say,' she'd muttered under her breath. 'Who's going to make sure Mum doesn't burn the house down while I'm on a safari, meditating under a palm tree?'

Four days later, a phone call changed the direction of her life.

'You'll never guess what,' her mother said after she hung up. 'Your Uncle Alistair's being transferred to Brighton.'

Charlotte listened to her mother drone on about seeing her brother again, then retreated to her bedroom. She stared at the postcards Roxy had sent and made a decision. Alistair was nice enough, but she found him boring after a couple of hours. However, his moving here could be a blessing. She opened her laptop, googled 'Flights to Cambodia,' and, before she could lose her nerve, bought a ticket. She didn't tell her mother until the week before she departed, when it was too late to change her plans.

The voices of the Backstreet Boys jolted her back to the present and she suddenly remembered Rashid's letter. 'There's something I need to show you,' she told Roxy, jumping to her feet and heading toward her bedroom.'

'Hang on,' Roxy said. 'You didn't finish. You never told me what happened with you and Jonathan, 'I thought he was special.'

Charlotte called from the hallway. 'Nope.'

'Nope? What does that mean?'

'Nothing.'

'Nothing? Hey, it's me, Roxy. I know when you're avoiding something. Get back in here.'

'Doesn't matter,' she muttered, coming back into the room. She was tired from the journey and didn't want to deal with Roxy's questions.

'Course it does,' Roxy persisted. 'Is he still around?'

Charlotte took a deep breath. 'No, he's *not* around! He got tired of me, all right. Can we not talk about it?'

'Tired of you? Impossible. You're a—'

Charlotte burst in. 'It's not impossible, Roxy! He got fed up with me taking care of Mum.' Painful memories flooded back, threatening to spill over in tears, and she slithered down the wall and sat on the floor. She'd never talked to anyone about Jonathan and her feelings were still raw even though it had been more than six months since he'd left. At the time of the break-up, she had avoided mentioning it to Roxy, hoping she'd forget about it. How ironic her memory was sharp for the one thing Charlotte didn't want to discuss.

Roxy crouched beside her and touched her hand. Charlotte wrapped her arms around her knees and buried her face. Roxy held her, rocked her gently, and stroked her hair until the sobs subsided.

‘Sorry, Rox. I’m tired and emotional.’ Charlotte dabbed her eyes and inhaled deeply.

‘No need to apologise, hon.’ Roxy handed her a tissue. ‘I know it hurts. And I also know we need food. Too much whisky on an empty stomach.’ She scrambled to her feet and headed toward the kitchen door. ‘I wish I had some chocolate. I’ll get some tomorrow.’ She turned back to look at Charlotte. ‘Shit… Tomorrow. Sorry to bring this up now but I’ve got to work. Will you be okay till I get home?’

Charlotte blew her nose and nodded. As usual, Roxy’s attention span didn’t last long. It didn’t mean she didn’t care, but her mind always moved faster than the traffic on the M25. And it was typical she had nothing planned for her oldest friend who’d crossed the world to see her.

‘You can hang around the flat or explore if you’re up for it,’ Roxy said, switching on another pedestal fan. ‘I’ll ask the landlady to come up at noon if she hasn’t seen or heard anything from you by then. And I’ve told SomOn’s to watch out for you—he’s usually close by if you need him. I’m so sorry I can’t be here, but I got the dates muddled up—thought you were arriving yesterday.’

‘Yesterday? Did you go to the airport?’

‘Can’t hear you,’ Roxy shouted, her head buried inside the fridge.

‘I said, did you go to the airport yesterday?’

‘Why would I do that? I had a soap-carving class.’

‘You thought I was arriving.’

‘Nope. Found your schedule in the middle of my class.’ She peered around the fridge door. ‘I had to use my phone to take a photo and saw your flight info just in time.’ She pulled out a selection of Tupperware containers and lined them up on the kitchen counter. ‘I’m starving. How about you?’

Charlotte nodded, the growl in her stomach reminding her she hadn't eaten since the layover in Bangkok more than eight hours ago. Roxy set a couple of mismatched dishes on the dining room table and they shared a meal of warmed-up noodles and leftover chicken, still reminiscing about their early years. By nine thirty, Charlotte was exhausted, so she hugged Roxy goodnight and headed to the bedroom. She took a handkerchief from her pocket to wipe the sweat from her forehead and the initials on the cotton cloth rubbed against her face: *O.F.* Dad's hankie.

Memories of home flooded back and she thought of the long days without her father and how she'd spent her time: mostly rearranging the bookshelves and colour-coordinated her wardrobe, hoping external precision would bring the same order to her inner world. The animal shelter had been her refuge; the only place she'd felt safe and loved. There'd been nobody to complain or make demands, no one to hurt her, just a room filled with cats and dogs wanting a meal, a tummy rub, and a hug.

As she sat on the bed, a twinge of sadness caught in her throat. Roxy had a life here. The space Charlotte once occupied now belonged to Peter. She tucked the handkerchief under the pillow and lay down, hoping a good night's rest would smooth the sharp corners of her pain. The sharp edge of an envelope prodded her in the thigh. Rashid's letter. She'd forgotten to tell Roxy about it. Now it would have to wait until morning.

The *National Geographic* lay beside her on the bedside table. She picked it up and idly flipped through the pages, noticing some of the articles were highlighted with a yellow marker: Silk Island, the National Museum, the Phnom Penh riverside, Tuol Sleng, Kampot. She started to read but the words started to blur, and waves of exhaustion swept over her, so she dropped the magazine onto the floor.

From inside her bag, the ping of a text message sounded from her phone. She made a mental note to check it later, then slipped into a deep sleep.

6

Charlotte awoke with a pounding headache and fumbled for the clock on her bedside table. It wasn't there. She sat up and squinted at the table. Her stained-glass lamp was also missing. And the room was hot and muggy; not at all like most mornings in East Sussex. She reached up to the curtains behind her bed and felt a rough, unfamiliar fabric. Swivelling her head, she noticed the curtains were embroidered with fuzzy purple parrots. *Purple parrots?* For a moment she panicked. Then she saw her suitcase on the floor and took a deep breath. She was in Cambodia.

She lay back again, images from her dream buzzing in her head; the same one she'd had dozens of times before. In it, her father was riding a horse along a beach. Charlotte stood on the shore and watched him ride away. He looked back, waved, and called, 'Come and join me!' She shouted back, 'I can't. I'm afraid.' He rode into the water and disappeared into the distance.

She rubbed her eyes and groaned. Her head felt like a

throbbing drum. As she reached for a bottle of aspirin from her overnight bag, she saw a pile of papers on the end of her bed with a note from Roxy: *Arun sua s'day (that means good morning). I'll be home before the sun sets. Do something extraordinary today. Rx.* Bound to the note with a rubber band was a stack of promotional leaflets along with a map of the city and a discount coupon for a foot massage. Charlotte smiled. Roxy was doing her best to make her feel welcome. She swallowed a couple of aspirin and looked out of the window. There was nothing she had to do today. Nothing. No chores. No work. No managing her mother's moods. She didn't even have to get dressed if she didn't want to.

She watched a pair of women on bicycles and followed them along the street with her eyes. Somehow, they managed to pedal in long skirts and flipflops, and Charlotte gasped as they steered the bikes along uneven paths, bumping in and out of potholes. She couldn't remember the last time she'd taken a moment to watch the world around her. She'd always been too busy, too concerned about doing the right thing, too focused on getting from place to place.

Her stomach rumbled and she padded to the kitchen in bare feet, wondering if Roxy had any food in the flat. Perhaps now she was married, she'd be more practical. She opened the fridge and saw a half empty container of guava yogurt hidden behind a box of marshmallows and ate it all with a spoon. Then, she found a chunk of banana bread in a tin box on the counter. It looked mould-free, so she ate that too. Dirty dishes were piled in the sink, so she washed them and put them away, then tidied the living room, picking up magazines and socks from the floor and sweeping crumbs from under the coffee table and couch. She wondered how Peter felt about having a stranger under his roof for almost two months and guessed he probably didn't have much of an option once Roxy had made up her mind.

When everything was tidy, she checked the text from last night. *Sleep well. Your journey is about to begin.* She smiled. Another thoughtful touch from Roxy. Her phone was still on UK time, so she adjusted the settings and logged onto Wi-Fi. No messages from her mother, not even a response to the emails from last night. She started to write another, then stopped. She was in Cambodia to get away, and she was already obsessed with contacting her mother. She thought of the phrase Trevor came up with: *Emotional weeds.* 'You keep pulling 'em out, and they continue to grow back,' he'd told her one day after she'd broken down at work. 'We've all got them, love. We either rip 'em out from the roots or make friends with them.' She couldn't figure out how to do either.

She had battled for years, trying to tolerate her mother's manipulation, then berated herself for being too sensitive. But she didn't know how to do things differently. As long as she was around her mother, she was scared of doing something to upset her. She had considered moving out, but something always held her back. It had taken her a long time to realise the only way out would be to remove herself physically. But here she was now, thousands of miles away, still feeling guilty, and worried about doing the wrong thing.

Frustrated, she shook her head and put away her phone, then stood under the shower until the hot water ran out. It was almost mid-morning and she was curious to see Phnom Penh, but nervous about venturing out alone. So, she unpacked her clothes and folded them neatly, debating the pros and cons of going out. Roxy had said she would be fine, and she didn't have to stray far from the flat. She sat on the bed and looked through the brochures, then looked out the window again. This was ridiculous. She had to make a move.

She slipped on a pair of sandals, a knee-length skirt, and a short-sleeved cotton top. The guidebook had advised visitors to Cambodia to dress modestly, so she had left her tanks and halter tops at home. After scraping her hair into a ponytail, she slathered on a layer of sunscreen followed by a heavy spritz of mosquito repellent, holding her breath as she sprayed it onto her skin. She stuffed the travel brochures in her skirt pocket and wondered if she should tell anyone she was going out. The landlord, perhaps. Or a text to Roxy. A couple of colleagues had shared horror stories about foreign women who had been attacked, kidnapped, and trafficked in Asia. Perhaps it would be wiser to wait for Roxy.

She sat on the couch, willing the fear to pass then peered through the window a third time. Maybe SomOn would be nearby. A clump of trees blocked her view of the road, so she took a deep breath, wound the strap of her bag tightly around her wrist, and left the flat, locking the door behind her.

The midday sun hung high in the sky, so she tugged her floppy straw hat over her ponytail and jumped back onto the pavement when a chicken flew from a pile of vegetables on the edge of the road. Then, before she could catch her breath, an elderly woman thrust a plastic plate of sizzling fried dough toward her, saying. '*Num pong*?' Charlotte shook her head and stepped further back toward the building. Was the woman giving it to her or did she want her to buy it? She should have asked Roxy how to deal with vendors.

A pair of teenage girls walked past, arm in arm, staring. 'Hello,' said one. 'You so pretty,' then hid her face behind a hand and ran across the street, tugging her friend behind her. An aroma of barbecued meat mingled with the pungent odour of dust prickled Charlotte's nostrils. All her senses were aroused, her reactions hyper alert. A man wearing mirrored sunglasses waved from across the street. 'Hey, laydee! You want tuk-tuk?' She froze. This might be what her colleagues had warned her about. She wracked her brain for the word Roxy told her meant *no*.

'*Oh thay*,' she said loudly, hoping she'd said the right thing, then turned around and walked swiftly back toward Roxy's flat.

As she reached the entrance, a voice called out. 'Jallod! Hello, Jallod!' SomOn waved and pulled up beside her in his tuk-tuk. 'Okay, Jallod? We go now?' She hesitated. He revved the engine. 'We go now,' he repeated.

She tucked her skirt under her and climbed into the vehicle. Roxy must have told him to pick her up. His familiar face made her feel safe, so she leaned back on the cracked leather seat and gripped the metal bar on the side of the tuk-tuk, wondering where he was planning on taking her.

'You need Cambodia phone card?' SomOn asked. She nodded. That would be a good place to start.

The tuk-tuk swerved around the corner and her stomach leapt. She felt queasy from the heat, but there was something exhilarating about driving through Phnom Penh in a tuk-tuk. They bounced through a pothole and she grabbed the seat then remembered Rashid's comment about bumps in the road, and smiled.

The tuk-tuk left the main road and meandered through narrow alleys until SomOn pulled up in front of a shop with a glass counter displaying mobile phones. He jumped from the vehicle and sauntered into the shop, so Charlotte followed and found him talking with a salesperson. He pointed to Charlotte and babbled something in Khmer. The salesperson stared expectantly. Charlotte stared back.

'SomOn, I...' she stammered, hoping he'd give her some guidance. 'What do I do?'

SomOn beckoned. 'You come,' he said, then turned to the phone vendor and spoke again in Khmer.

'I don't understand,' said Charlotte. Part of her wanted to laugh and the other half felt frustrated in not knowing what was going on.

Finally, the vendor addressed Charlotte. 'Can help?' she asked.

'She want phone card,' SomOn said.

The woman smiled and nodded. 'Need passport,' she said. 'And two dollar.'

Charlotte looked around. 'I don't know.... I'm not—' She was the only westerner in the shop. Was this the right thing to do? SomOn stared at her. Roxy had said she could trust him, and she felt confident he wouldn't get her into trouble. With a shrug and a smile, she handed over two dollars and her passport, grateful she had it on her. Within minutes, her UK SIM card had been replaced by a Cambodian one and she had a local phone number.

'How much you want to buy?' the salesperson asked, staring at her.

Charlotte stared back, then looked at SomOn. 'What does she mean?'

'How much you want to buy?' SomOn repeated.

She looked around the store. She needed help. The salesperson spoke louder. 'You want to buy ten dollar? Twenty?'

'I have no idea what—'

'Excuse me, miss.' A man in a suit approached. 'She's asking how much money you want to put on your phone. If you're only making local calls, you'll probably be fine with ten dollars.'

Charlotte thanked him and paid the vendor. Five minutes

later, she was back in the tuk-tuk, sipping on a fresh coconut SomOn bought for her at a roadside stand.

'Where you go now?' SomOn asked.

Charlotte took the brochures from her bag. She was feeling more confident after her transaction at the phone shop, knowing SomOn was watching out for her and that people were helpful. She flipped through the leaflets. Should she go to the Killing Fields? Too intense and too far out of town. The Royal Palace? Not enough time. The Museum? Ditto.

SomOn was staring, clearly waiting for her to make a decision. She didn't want to keep him waiting so she shrugged and asked, 'Where do you think I should go?'

He started up the motorbike and pulled into the street. 'You go Tuol Sleng,' he said. 'Not far from here.'

Within minutes they were in front of a set of iron gates. Above the entrance was a large white billboard with the words *Tuol Sleng Genocide Museum*. Charlotte's heart pounded. Genocide museum? This was the spot she had read about; one of the awful reminders from the time of the Khmer Rouge. It wasn't a place she wanted to visit. Not now.

SomOn pointed toward the gate. 'I have customer now. Pick you up in one hour.' He seemed in a hurry to move on, so Charlotte climbed down from the tuk-tuk. She stood on the side of the road and watched a bus unload a group of people who walked toward the entrance. She didn't know how to get back to Roxy's flat, so unless she wanted to stand in the heat for an hour, there was no other option than to go inside. She thought of her dad's advice for visiting a new place: *Get to know the people through their history*. It would be a painful reminder of the country's horrifying past, but it would also be a way to learn more about Cambodia, so she walked through the gates of the former prison, determined to keep an open mind.

Rusted strands of barbed wire twisted around tall concrete walls surrounding the compound, and lines of tourists now stood where prisoners had been dragged inside in the 1970s. She paid the entrance fee and declined the offer of a guide, preferring to experience the museum alone. Above the entrance, a small sign showed a sketch of a smiling man with a large red cross drawn through it and the words: *No laughing or smiling*. Her heart beat faster. She'd learned about Pol Pot and the Khmer Rouge at school and it had horrified her to discover how many people had been tortured and killed while most of the world watched *Charlie's Angels* and listened to the Bee Gees. Now she was standing on the spot where hundreds had been brutalised before being dragged to the killing fields and slaughtered.

She walked into an open courtyard fringed with palm trees where a group of three monks in orange robes stood under a tree. She made eye contact with one, noticing with surprise he had blue eyes, then quickly looked away as he continued talking with the others. There was something comforting about his appearance and Charlotte felt a little more at ease, so she continued along the path. Three four-storey buildings framed the square, and she followed a couple of people into the first one under a sign that read *Building A*. Her hand flew to her mouth. Only two objects occupied the cavernous space: a rusted iron bedframe and a billboard-sized black and white photograph. The photo was of the room where she was standing pictured exactly as the Vietnamese had found it in 1979. It displayed, larger than life, a mutilated body of a prisoner chained to the bed.

She cast her eyes toward the floor. Dark blotches stained the tiles. She wheeled around, stomach churning, and caught the eye of the only other person in the room—a young Cambodian man in a grey business suit and glasses. His brown eyes were set deep into his brow, full lips drawn into a line beneath sharp cheekbones. She looked away and moved toward the door, dropping the museum leaflets in her haste to escape. The man picked them up and handed them to her. His gaze met hers and she mumbled an apology, embarrassed for a stranger to see her in a state of distress.

'Thank you for coming,' he said. She gave a quick nod, anxious to leave the room. 'My mother and uncle died during the Khmer Rouge,' he said, his jaw tense. 'I come from Battambang every year to honour them.' He lowered his eyes and walked away.

Charlotte's eyes welled up. She had never met anyone who'd experienced this kind of suffering and was shocked he'd be so ready to share his feelings with a stranger. For the next hour, she walked through the buildings, holding her breath each time she entered one. She gasped when she saw torture tools hanging on peeling yellow walls, and dug her fingernails into her palms when hundreds of faces stared at her from photographs in glass cases: a boy with a thick iron chain around his neck, a mother with a child's arm reaching into the picture, a westerner whose yacht had drifted into Cambodian waters. She saw the terror in their eyes and imagined them waiting for the horrific fate that awaited them.

The thump of her heart in her ears drowned out the sound of children playing in the street and the snick of her leather soles on the concrete floor reverberated on pockmarked walls as she walked from room to room. Across the room, a guide was talking to a group of visitors, his voice echoing around the stone walls. 'These rooms used to be classrooms, until the Khmer Rouge made them prison chambers,' he said, pointing to an exhibit. 'Prisoners were beaten and tortured with electric shocks or hot metal instruments until they confessed to whatever crimes they were charged with. Some were hung. Some were strangled. Women were raped.' He ushered his group from the room, and Charlotte heard his parting comment: 'Around seventeen thousand people came through these doors between 1975 and 1979. Only fourteen are known to have survived.'

She raced outside and down the steps and took a huge gulp of the hot afternoon air. Her head throbbed and her eyes stung. She dropped onto a bench near the exit gate and closed her eyes, images flashing through her mind like a revolving slideshow. What on earth had she been thinking? Why hadn't she listened to her inner voice and stayed outside? Even standing in the heat for an hour would have been better than this.

As she stared into the distance, trying to erase the haunting images, a long black sedan pulled up outside the gate and sounded its horn. A driver emerged from the front seat and opened the back door and a man walked to the car and got inside. As he bent down to get into the back seat, Charlotte caught a glimpse of him. He was slight and stooped, wearing a pale grey suit, with thinning hair neatly combed over a wrinkled brow, the sun reflecting off a gold bracelet on his right wrist.

Rashid.

7

Charlotte raced through the gates as the car pulled away. 'Rashid! Wait!' she shouted, waving frantically. The vehicle disappeared around the corner, so she scanned the street for SomOn, spotting him sleeping in his tuk-tuk. She ran over, jumped inside the vehicle, and tapped him on the shoulder. 'SomOn, can you please follow that car?' she asked, breathless.

SomOn nodded and pulled on his helmet, revving the bike into action. Speeding through rush hour traffic, he dodged cars and SUVs like an ant between elephants, trying to catch the vehicle ahead. As they turned the corner onto a narrow alley, a rubbish truck swerved in front of them. SomOn slammed on the brakes, and Charlotte grabbed her seat, catching her bag just before it flew into the street. The stench of rotting fish and putrid vegetables engulfed the vehicle and Charlotte slapped a hand across her mouth and nose.

SomOn pulled over to the side of the road and turned to Charlotte. 'Jallod, I not know where he go,' he said, then pointed to an ornate white building on the next block. 'Maybe Raffles Hotel. Many big cars go there.'

She climbed out of the tuk-tuk and ran toward the building and up a flight of white marble stairs. A plaque at the entrance read: *One of Asia's luxury hotels, Raffles-Le Royal Phnom Penh has been the iconic destination for celebrity guests such as Charlie Chaplin, Jackie Onassis, and Somerset Maugham since 1929.* She glanced down at herself. Would her dusty sandals and sweat-stained blouse be acceptable? She shrugged and pushed open a pair of glass doors framed by floor-length, white silk curtains. A chandelier the size of a small elephant twinkled above a gleaming teak table and a vase overflowed with an abundant arrangement of orchids, ginger blossoms, and birds of paradise. Piano music flowed into the room and Charlotte stepped aside as a couple of smartly dressed patrons with monogrammed luggage entered the hotel and walked toward the reception desk.

A doorman in a black silk suit approached her. 'Welcome to Raffles Hotel, madam.' He bowed. 'How may I help you?'

She bowed back. '*Sua s'day*. I'm looking for a man who may have come in here. Tall, elderly, Middle Eastern man, carrying a silver-topped cane.'

The doorman shook his head. 'I'm sorry madam, I have not seen anyone like that. Perhaps he is in another hotel? Would you like me to call the Sofitel? The Intercontinental?'

She declined and studied her surroundings. So, this was how the proverbial other half lived. In the lounge, three women wearing floral, linen frocks and shiny, high-heeled shoes nibbled on pastries from a multi-tiered afternoon tea platter. A Cambodian girl who probably weighed little more than Charlotte's suitcase presented a selection of teas in a sandalwood box, and two men in business suits tapped on iPhones at an adjacent table. She lingered in the doorway, eyes darting from table to table. It looked like the kind of place Rashid might stay. Perhaps he'd gone to his room or was having a meal in the dining room. She watched for a while, hoping for a glimpse of him, then realised the doorman would have known if he were in the hotel.

She went back outside and within seconds, SomOn drove toward her, waving. He handed her a folded paper. 'Jallod, I have this for you,' he said. 'Man from black car give to me.'

She took the paper and unfolded it. It was a promotional flyer for the *Plae Pakaa* dance show at the National Museum and read, *Our Traditional Dance Show showcases one of Cambodia's most famous arts, on a journey from the Angkorian palaces to villages of today. Special show this week for Seven Makara.*

'Who gave this to you?' she asked.

'Driver from big car you follow. He say it for you.'

Charlotte's brow furrowed. 'What did he say?'

'Nothing. He leave.'

Charlotte stared along the street, hoping the car would still be within sight. All she saw was a cluster of tuk-tuks and some expensive looking vehicles jockeying for position in the driveway. Her head still spun from the afternoon's experience and she was mystified by Rashid's appearance. She was also a little hurt he hadn't waited to talk to her. A sound behind her caught her attention and she turned to see SomOn motioning toward the tuk-tuk.

'I take you home?' he asked, buckling on his helmet. Charlotte climbed inside, realising she may be holding him up from another fare. When they reached the flat, she climbed the stairs, stopping halfway to catch her breath. It had been a challenging first day and she was eager to talk to Roxy. She found her in the kitchen, dressed in baggy, green shorts and a black Angkor Beer tank top, her hair poking out from her headband. She was tossing ripe tomatoes into the air and didn't turn her head when Charlotte came in.

'Welcome home!' she said, staring at the airborne tomatoes. 'I'm gonna to teach the girls to juggle.' She furrowed her brow in concentration. 'Remember when I won...Oops, hang...' She took a breath. 'That talent contest in Eastbourne? Just need to practice so I—Oh shit!' The tomatoes plummeted to the floor, one splitting open and seeds splattering across the room. Roxy bellowed with laughter then bent down to pick up another tomato from under the fridge. 'Well *that* worked well!' Want to help me?' She looked up when she didn't get an answer. 'Hey, what's the matter?'

Charlotte let out a loud sigh. 'I went to Tuol Sleng.'

Roxy's eyes widened. 'Are you mad? Why on earth d'you go there on your first day? I've lived here almost three years and haven't set a foot inside.' She took a bottle of wine from the fridge and poured it into two large glasses. 'You need a drink. So do I.'

'There's more,' Charlotte said, taking the glass. 'I saw the man from my flight.'

'The chap you were looking for at the airport? He was at Toul Sleng?'

'Yes. Rashid. But not at Toul Sleng. He was in a ...' She paused. 'I never told you the whole story, did I? Hold on a moment. I want to read you something.' She took the letter from her bag and read it out loud then folded it and put it back in her bag. 'See why I need to find him? It's meant for someone named Chris, who must be his son.'

Roxy set her wine glass on the counter. 'How d'you know it's for his son? And how d'you plan on finding someone in a country of sixteen million people?' She lifted her foot and wiped it with a paper towel. 'Rashid might be a dirty old man coming to Cambodia for a bit of fun. Happens all the time.'

Charlotte shook her head. 'He's no dirty old man. And the letter was signed *Baba*. I looked it up and it means *father* in Bengali.'

'But why did he write a letter if he's going to see him? It doesn't make sense.'

'No clue. But he also brought this.' She took the ring from the envelope and held it out to Roxy, then took a deep breath. 'Something else weird happened this afternoon. She drew the Plae Pakaa flyer from her pocket. 'Someone gave this to me. I think it was Rashid. But he disappeared.'

'Rashid gave you a flyer for a dance show?'

'Not Rashid, his driver. I think. In a black car. At Raffles hotel.' She noted Roxy's baffled look and pointed to the flyer. 'What does this mean—there's a special performance this Tuesday for Seven Makara?'

'Seven Makara? That's the seventh of January, the day when Cambodians celebrate Victory over Genocide Day.' She studied the flyer then raised her eyebrows. 'Sometimes you surprise me. Most people go to Plae Pakaa for the history, or the dance, or to support the culture. You want to go and find an old man. And I thought I was the crazy one.' She handed the flyer back. 'It's this week so I'll go with you. I wanted to show you something lovely, so this will be perfect.'

Charlotte leaned against the wall watching Roxy toss the tomatoes in the bin. Her first day in Cambodia hadn't been what she'd expected. She'd hoped to be lounging at a swimming pool or browsing an exotic market, and instead had become immersed in the country's tragic history and another peculiar encounter with a stranger. She took a deep breath and a dizzy sensation suddenly came over her—the same feeling she'd had at Heathrow airport the day she left home. At the time, she'd put it down to nerves, but today there was a sense of melancholy, as though someone had lost something. She shook her head, stuffed the flyer in her pocket, and headed for the shower.

8

For the next couple of days, Charlotte alternated between taking short walks near the flat, driving around town with SomOn, and reading in the café next door. The experience at Tuol Sleng had shaken her and she was nervous about venturing too far, so she decided to stay close to the flat, remaining safely inside the tuk-tuk whenever SomOn took her to other parts of town.

To her disappointment, Roxy had been tied up with work was only free in the late afternoons, so they spent evenings together, usually walking to local restaurants since Roxy wanted to help Charlotte acclimatise to the relentless heat. Peter was rarely around, and Charlotte had only bumped into him a couple of times in the morning as he'd headed to work. Roxy explained he was preparing a presentation for a humanities conference, but Charlotte wondered if her presence was keeping him away.

On the third day, Roxy cleared her schedule and told Charlotte to prepare for a day of surprises. When she wheeled her motorbike to the front of the building, Charlotte shook her head. 'I'm not going out on that,' she said.

'Don't be a wimp.' Roxy thrust a helmet toward her. 'Everyone rides bikes here.'

Charlotte shook her head. 'Not me. I'd rather walk.'

'In this heat?'

'Then let's call SomOn.'

'Why do that when we can use my bike?'

'I'll pay.' Charlotte looked along the street for a tuk-tuk. She had never been on the back of a motorbike and the traffic in Phnom Penh was horrible. Either she'd fall off the bike under a truck or get asphyxiated by exhaust fumes.

'Tell you what,' Roxy said with a sigh. 'I'll go slowly. We'll take Tnout with us and I'll stop whenever you want.'

'Promise?'

'Promise.'

Charlotte slid onto the seat and Roxy lifted Tnout and placed him in a yellow wicker basket between the handlebars. The dog wagged his stumpy tail and hooked his paws over the edge. 'Wrap your arms around me.' Roxy said. 'If they're long enough!' She laughed and slowly steered into the street.

Charlotte tensed as the bike wobbled around the corner and entered the inside lane of a busy road. Her palms started to sweat, and she gripped the sides of Roxy's blouse, curling her toes inside her flip-flops. Roxy stayed true to her word, staying in one lane, slowly following traffic, and after a while Charlotte relaxed her grip and looked around. Other passengers were talking on the phone, carrying bags of groceries, or sipping from cans of soft drink, and most of them weren't even holding onto the driver. If they could do several things at the same time, surely she'd be able to do one: stay on the bike.

She squeezed Roxy's arm and yelled into her ear. 'Keep an

eye out for Rashid. He's an elderly man who's probably wearing—'

Roxy shook her head. 'We're not gonna spend the day hunting for this new friend of yours. I've taken the day off and I'm not sharing you with anyone.'

She stopped the bike near a stretch of open-fronted stores where brightly coloured paintings and cardboard boxes stuffed with electronic gadgets were crammed onto wooden shelves. The sign outside read *Toul Tumpoung*. The Russian Market. Roxy climbed off the scooter, handed it to a security guard, and shoved her way through a crowd of people toward the entrance, Tnout scampering behind. 'Follow me,' she called, and disappeared behind a pile of teak statues.

The air was thick with humidity and Charlotte's blouse became soaked within minutes. All she could see of Roxy was a head of platinum hair bobbing in the distance through a swarm of shoppers. She mopped her face with a bandana, struggling to breathe in the heat, and pushed through the aisles. Tiny shops were piled high with exotic-looking trinkets and food that looked slimy and strange and she wanted to stop and examine them. But she was scared of losing Roxy, so she ploughed on, handbag wedged firmly beneath her elbow. The narrow passages were tightly crammed with people hauling plastic bags and Styrofoam containers and nobody moved to let her through, so she stood still and looked around. Across the way, she saw Roxy sitting on a bar stool with Tnout on her lap under a sign that read, *The Best Iced Coffee in Phnom Penh,* so she edged her way through the crowd and took a seat next to her.

Roxy grinned as she ruffled Tnout's ears. 'This place is famous. It's been here more than thirty years.' She waved at the stall owner and held up two fingers. 'I'm buying.' She peeled two dollar notes from a stack of bills and handed them to him. 'Cheap, eh? See why we come here. It's also friggin' delicious.'

The stench from a fruit stand smelled like a filthy gym bag combined with rotting potatoes and body odour. 'Durian,' Roxy said. 'It's banned from most hotels in Cambodia. Along with hand grenades and prostitutes.'

A narrow-hipped man with a broad smile plonked two glasses filled with crushed ice on the counter. Charlotte recoiled. 'Is this safe? The ice?'

'Don't panic. I drink here all the time. This guy's a legend.'

The man returned and poured a thick shot of expresso over the ice then drizzled an inch of condensed milk over the top. The dense, sweet liquid sank to the bottom of the glass, giving it the look of a parfait. Charlotte reached toward her glass, examined the rim, and wiped it with a napkin.

'Hang on!' Roxy said. 'There's more.' Ten seconds later, the man returned with two extra shots of espresso and plonked them on the counter. Roxy poured one into her glass and gestured for Charlotte to do the same. 'No nap for us today. We're on high octane!' Roxy drank back the chilled liquid then poured a gob of condensed milk onto a spoon and gave it to Tnout. Charlotte inspected her glass, wondering when it had last been properly cleaned. She reached inside her bag for hand sanitizer and poured a dollop into her palm. The coffee vendor stared at her, an expectant smile on his face.

Roxy nudged her. 'If you don't hurry, I'll drink it myself.'

Charlotte wiped the glass again and took a sip. Sugary crystals of condensed milk and the rich taste of espresso coated her tongue. Delicious. She drank it back and licked the sticky trickles of condensed milk from the edge of the glass. Tnout gave a short yelp and jumped from the stool onto the floor.

'Time to go!' Roxy slid from the stool and ran after the dog.

Charlotte followed, dodging shoppers with nylon bags stuffed full of vegetables, meat, and bags of rice. She swerved to avoid one, caught her foot on a wooden box filled with carved elephants, and crashed to her knees. Her bag fell open and the hand sanitizer flew across the aisle into a basket of bananas. She scrambled to her feet and brushed off the dust, hoping nobody had noticed. Across the corridor, she heard Roxy's laughter.

'So, I'm not the only clumsy one then,' she said, pulling Charlotte by the arm. 'Come on! I've another surprise for you.'

'Slow down.' Charlotte gasped. Her flipflops were dragging in the dirt and she wanted to sit down. 'I'm dying.'

'You'll be fine.' Roxy led her through a throng of tuk-tuks and moto drivers on the fringe of the market until they found her bike wedged between two cement pillars. Roxy nudged her onto the bike and drove down a back alley piled with discarded vegetables. For the next ten minutes, they skirted potholes and swerved around SUVs and buses spewing clouds of exhaust. Charlotte pressed the bandana against her nose and mouth, shrieking as they bounced over bumps. So much for Roxy's promise to drive slowly.

She was about to ask her to stop when they came to a wide, open road running alongside the Tonle Sap River. Gone were broken pavements and piles of rubbish on every corner, and in their place were spas, cafés, and souvenir shops standing side by side with glass-fronted restaurants, all facing a lush, grassy verge. Groups of western tourists sat at sidewalk tables where waiters dressed in white shirts and red bow ties handed out menus, and the sound of live jazz wafted from boats floating along the river. It was a calmer, more appealing side to the city than Charlotte had seen so far. This looked more like the Cambodia she'd been expecting. The next time

SomOn asked her what she wanted to do, she'd know what to tell him.

Excited at the idea of exploring this neighbourhood, she took one hand from Roxy's waist and waved at herself in a plate glass window. The sign over the window read *Happy Pizza*. She shouted in Roxy's ear, 'What's happy pizza?'

Roxy snorted. 'Phnom Penh's special treat,' she shouted back. 'Pizza sprinkled with pot. 'Is it legal? Heck, no. Does it matter? Nope. It's Cambodia.'

As they toured the city, Charlotte became accustomed to the motion of the bike. It was a good way to explore, even if it was a bit dusty and bumpy, and it was certainly the fastest way of getting through traffic. While they drove, she kept an eye out for Rashid, envisioning him in a nice neighbourhood, possibly even walking along the riverside. Would he be on foot or in a taxi? Would he be wearing the same grey suit? She tried to picture his son. He'd probably be tall, like Rashid. Would he look like a younger version of his father? She peered inside every café and looked down alleyways, hoping she might spot him. Instead, she saw elderly Cambodian women in patterned pyjamas waving their arms in exercise as though chasing away birds, and vendors squatting on sidewalks selling fried crickets, locusts, and spiders to tourists who strolled arm-in-arm along the promenade. The sights and sounds were entrancing, and she decided to return with her camera so she could capture it all. How good it would feel to have time to stroll alone, study her surroundings, and immerse herself in something new.

As they left the riverside road, Roxy swerved into an alleyway and stopped the bike outside a small shop with a sign that read, *Miss Bliss*. 'Here we are!' Roxy said, nudging her inside the shop and toward a padded armchair. 'Sit!' she said. Tnout scurried beneath the seat. 'Not you, Tnout, Charlo.'

Charlotte sat in one of the chairs and Roxy in an adjacent one, then two Cambodian women appeared carrying plastic bowls filled with water, flower petals, and slices of what looked like bark. The women set the bowls on the floor in front of the chairs.

'Lotus blossoms and lemongrass,' Roxy explained as Charlotte stared into the water. 'Take a whiff. It's gorgeous.'

Charlotte leaned over and breathed in the sweet mist emanating from the water. Gusts of air from the fan in the corner blew her hair and cooled the sweat on her arms. She closed her eyes and took a deep breath.

'Take off your shoes and relax,' Roxy said. 'It's pampering time.'

Charlotte slipped off her flip-flops and leaned back in the chair. One of the women picked up Charlotte's bare feet and slid them into the bowl of warm water. She washed one foot and calf then the other, then carefully wrapped each foot in a towel and elevated Charlotte's legs to a padded cushion, rubbing perfumed oil onto her ankles. Charlotte's head fell back onto the headrest as she immersed herself in the delicious sensations.

The next thing she knew, someone was prodding her arm. 'Wake up, lazybones,' Roxy said. 'They need this chair for someone else.'

Charlotte rubbed her eyes. 'That was amazing. Where do we pay?'

'All done. It's on me.' Roxy chuckled. 'Before you thank me, it's only seven dollars. Even I can afford that on my beer and noodle budget. Come on, let's go. We've another errand to do.'

They got back on the bike and five minutes later pulled up in front of the National Museum where Roxy bought two tickets to the Plae Pakaa show and stuffed them into Charlotte's pocket.

'Here you go. We're booked for tonight. Perhaps we'll find your friend, then you can stop searching for geriatric men and lost boys.'

She started the bike and drove through a market crammed with wilted vegetables and live fish in plastic bowls, then stopped in front of a small shop with a flickering neon sign. The words on the sign read *Boxy Wide Elephant.* Roxy jumped from the bike and ran toward the building.

"Now comes the highlight of the day,' she said. 'Hope you can handle it.' She pushed open a narrow glass door etched with a palm tree logo and beckoned to Charlotte who followed her inside. Roxy waved an arm. 'Ta-da! Welcome to my creation!'

Charlotte looked around. The walls were covered with enormous canvases painted with brightly coloured animal caricatures: pink elephants in blue striped trousers, spotted giraffes in veiled hats, purple rhinos in yellow Wellington boots. Curtains embroidered with parrots and dolphins hung from wrought iron railings, and silk scarves embellished with sequins and buttons were piled next to Lycra tights hand-painted with cartoon characters on gleaming pine shelves.

Roxy watched her, a huge grin on her face. 'How d'you like it?' she asked.

'I love it!' she said. 'It's like Andy Warhol teamed up with the Wizard of Oz.' Picking up a silk handbag embroidered with sequinned peace signs, she squinted at the label. 'Boxy Wide Elephant? How did you come up with that name?'

Roxy laughed. 'It's a Cambodian faux-pas.' She took the bag and dropped it on top of a basket of scarves. 'It was meant to be *Roxy's White Elephant*. The Cambodian sign maker got it wrong, and I ended up with a sign that said Boxy Wide Elephant. So, I decided to keep it. Much more original!' She waved at a couple of women looking through the window, then straightened a picture on the wall. 'It's been enormous fun putting it all together and people are starting to find me, even down this stinky old alleyway. I wish I were better at promotion, but I just want to design things.'

A painting of a purple iguana playing a saxophone caught Charlotte's eye and she reached out and touched the edge of the canvas. 'Have you been in touch with anyone back home?' she asked. 'Remember Geraldine? She's a journalist at the Herald now. I bet she'd write a piece about you. And how about doing a joint promotion with the elephant sanctuary? You could donate a portion of your profits from the animal paintings and—'

Roxy's chuckle stopped her. 'That's why I left this stop till last. Pump you full of caffeine, pamper you, then pick your brilliant brain. Worth every penny!' She took her arm and steered her toward the back of the shop. 'Come look around.'

In a small room at the rear, two young women squatted on the floor behind a glass partition, weaving straw baskets. Another woman stood at a counter embroidering a scarf, and one sat on a wooden bench bent over a pile of dog collars.

'What's she doing?' Charlotte asked.

'That's Chenla,' Roxy spoke in a low voice. 'Peter found her on the side of the road. Her stepfather had beaten her for years so we offered her a place to live and told her family we'd give her a job so they'd let her stay. She's putting sequins on dog collars.'

Charlotte stifled a giggle. 'Dog collars?'

Roxy held a finger to her lips and beckoned to Charlotte to follow her into the front of the shop where she closed the connecting door and spoke in a normal tone. 'They'd force her to go home if she wasn't making a living,' she said. 'She loves animals, so she came up with an idea to make collars for street dogs. The poor creatures will always be homeless and filthy, and they'll never let anyone put a collar on them. But Chenla wants them to look pretty, and we want her to feel safe and happy, so she can do what she likes.'

As they spoke, a woman entered the rear section of the shop. Tall and slender, a mass of curly black hair framed a suntanned face and pale blue eyes. She was dressed in pale green cotton slacks and a loose-fitting, white T-shirt and appeared to be in her sixties. She walked to Chenla, put her arm across her slight shoulders, and blew a kiss to the girls sitting on the floor.

Roxy waved to her through the glass partition. 'That's Annie,' she told Charlotte. 'She's my assistant, my shrink, my adviser, and the woman who keeps me sane.'

'What does that mean?'

'She's a friend of Peter's mum who arrived as I was putting my business together. Just so happens she was a psychiatrist in Brisbane, but she tossed it all in after her parents died and her husband walked out on her.'

The phone rang and Annie picked it up. She glanced through the glass and, noticing Roxy and Charlotte watching her, waved and smiled at them.

'Apparently her sixtieth birthday was a bit of an epiphany,' Roxy said. 'That's when she bought a ticket to Phnom Penh, closed her business, and sold all her stuff.'

Instead of sitting around feeling sorry for herself? Perhaps she could share those ideas with my mother. 'Did she come here to work?' Charlotte asked.

'She volunteered with street kids for a while, then knocked on our door. Good timing, don't you think? I needed someone to scrub floors and paint walls, and Peter was happy to know someone with a background helping troubled women. Perfecto!' She ran her finger across a bamboo shelf, absent-mindedly wiping off a speck of dust and smearing it on her sleeve. 'These girls are traumatised, Charlo. They're more comfortable talking to a woman, so Annie's been a lifesaver. She also doesn't mind I can't pay much.' She folded a silk scarf and dropped it on top of a wicker basket. 'You'll find most people you meet in Cambodia are either running away from something or running toward it.'

'Or here to do good,' said a gentle male voice.

They spun around. Peter stood behind them. He draped his arm across Roxy's shoulders and gave Charlotte a lopsided grin. 'Sorry to break up your party, but there's a problem and I need to drag you away, Roxy. Sethya didn't arrive home last night. Ratha's out looking for her and I need you to talk to the girls as they're a bit freaked out.' His brow furrowed. 'Charlotte, we'll drop you at home and meet you there later.'

Two hours later, after Charlotte had taken her third shower of the day, tidied her room, and read all the travel brochures, her phone rang. 'Charlo,' Roxy said, breathlessly. 'I'm really sorry, but things are bad. I need to stay with the girls so I can't go to the show with you tonight. I've asked Annie to go in my place and she'll meet you outside the museum at six forty-five.'

Charlotte hung up the phone and sighed, remembering all the times Roxy had altered their plans at the last minute or forgotten about them completely. She didn't want to appear uncaring, but it would have been nice to have had just one complete day with her friend.

9

Charlotte looked at her watch. She wasn't due to meet Annie for a couple of hours, so there was plenty of time to check her messages. She opened her laptop and an email from her mother jumped out at her. No subject or salutation, just two terse lines: *I can't find the remote for the TV in the living room. What have you done with it?*

A wave of anger swept over her. No response to any of her messages or photos. No concern about her safe arrival in Cambodia. How typical of her mother to think only about herself. She slammed the laptop shut, remembering the morning she'd left England and the not so subtle note from her on the hall table: *Bad headache. Sleeping late. See you in two months. P.S. If you decide to come back.* She took a deep breath and returned to the email in front of her. She should respond.

'Dear Mum,' she wrote, then paused. It had been her pattern to act immediately, and she had often regretted it. Trevor always advised her to take a moment and think about things first. Besides, it was still early in England and her mother didn't need an answer right away. There were better things she could do with her time.

She launched a browser and typed *Cambodia missing people* then ran her gaze down all the links: sites dedicated to missing children, pages about land mines, and people looking for relatives they'd lost during the Khmer Rouge era. Dismissing them all, she searched for *Bangladeshi people in Cambodia* and found a list of expat websites, information on visas for Bengalis, and Bangladeshi restaurants. She shook her head and tried again with a new message: *How can I find someone in Cambodia?*

The first was a link to a dating site, so she kept looking until one caught her eye: a Yahoo group for expats living in Cambodia which included such postings as, *Where can I find Greek yogurt? How much should I pay my gardener? Does anyone want a puppy?* It looked like a good place to start. After checking it was free and anonymous, she signed up for an account and posted a note of her own: *I'm looking for a Bangladeshi man from London named Chris as I have something that belongs to him.* She included her email address and looked at the clock. It was time to meet Annie.

❀

CHARLOTTE ARRIVED at the museum shortly after six and perched on a stone bench to wait. It always annoyed her when people kept her waiting, so she always arrived on or before a designated meeting time. She glanced down at her white, knee-length cotton dress, white sandals, and yellow silk scarf looped around her neck, wondering if she had dressed correctly for the occasion. When she last wore this outfit, Roxy had said she looked like a daisy in the dust, and now there were muddy specks on her shoes after walking from the tuk-tuk to the museum. She brushed them off and looked around, hoping nobody had seen her obsessing about the dirt.

Early evening was drawing in, and dozens of cars and motorbikes crowded the roads near the museum, the chatter of night vendors booming from the back of their wooden carts. She watched the scene, savouring a newfound comfort in her surroundings, and thinking back over the week. One person stood out as unconditionally kind: SomOn. The good-hearted tuk-tuk driver had become a special friend and always seemed to be nearby when she needed something. He'd taught her valuable lessons about Cambodian life and he'd introduced her to his tuk-tuk buddies: Mister Key, who constantly exposed his huge belly lifting up his shirt to keep cool, Poh, who had seven children and an eye for the ladies, and Tony, whose real name was unpronounceable and who giggled like a child whenever she spoke to him in Khmer. He'd also revealed his compassionate nature a number of times, such as the time he'd pulled to the side of the road and pressed a bundle of notes into the hand of an old woman squatting beneath a tree. When Charlotte asked him about it, he'd merely shrugged and said, 'My government not care about poor people. I must take care of those who have less than me.'

Another time, she'd mistakenly given him a twenty dollar note instead of the five dollars she owed him. The next morning, when she came downstairs, he was sitting outside the building, unwilling to start work until he returned the extra money.

She asked Roxy one day why someone who had so little gave so much. 'I told you you'd soon see the Cambodian way,' Roxy said. 'It's one of the reasons I stay here. People who have nothing almost always find something to give. Humbling, isn't it?'

After that, Charlotte made it a point to slip a few extra dollars into SomOn's pocket and often bought him a beer or a meal when they drove near a cafe.

As she waited for Annie, the honk of car horns blared around her. It was rush hour and everyone seemed in a hurry. Then, another sound, more harmonious and soothing: soft humming and tinkling bells. It seemed to be coming from a spot near the museum, in the direction of Wat Ounalom, the enormous walled pagoda whose golden spires dominated the skyline. There was still time before Annie was due to arrive, so she rose from the bench and walked through the gates of the pagoda.

Shimmering moonlight illuminated the route between enormous grey stone burial mounds and the shadowy trees. Charlotte followed the foot path to a cluster of yellow buildings where an elderly monk stood on the path, his head bowed. She took a quick step backwards, afraid she may have entered a sacred spot where she didn't belong. As she turned to leave, the monk looked up and beckoned to her.

'Welcome to our spiritual home,' he said. 'Please be happy to see around as you wish.' His wrinkles deepened as he smiled, then he asked, 'Would you like to learn about this special place?'

She nodded, and he told her some of the wat's history. There were forty-four buildings in the complex and behind the main temple was Chetdai, a five-hundred-year-old burial mound, or *stupa,* which stored the Lord Buddha's eyebrow hair. Hence the name *Eyebrow Temple.*

'Wat Ounalom is headquarter of Cambodia Buddhism,' he said, bowing toward the temple. 'And today for Seven Makara we have special chanting for peace and happiness in Cambodia. Please come and have blessing.'

She followed him into a tiny chamber at the side of the pagoda where he gestured for her to remove her shoes and kneel on a straw mat. Then, he sprinkled droplets of water on her head and asked her to stretch out her arm. When she did, he looped a long red thread around her wrist and tied it in a knot. 'For compassion and peaceful life,' he explained.

She bowed her head and inhaled the incense-scented air. Time seemed to dissipate into a haze of smoke and candlelight, and a sense of contentment settled in her chest. The gentle expression in the eyes of the monk transported her to her childhood, to a time when she felt safe, when her dad was there. A time of innocence when she thought the world was beautiful and everyone was good. She closed her eyes, emotions welling up as she was drawn into a place of complete peace. After a few minutes she rose, refreshed and grateful for the soothing presence of the monk. He still sat cross-legged on the mat across from her, so she fumbled in her purse and dropped a donation into a collection box before slipping on her sandals and leaving the room. It was almost six forty-five and she didn't want to keep Annie waiting.

Across the corridor, a door to an adjacent chamber was slightly ajar. She glanced into the room where a figure knelt on a straw mat enveloped in a mist of incense. Something about him looked familiar so she looked again and saw an elderly man dressed in white, a garland of orange flowers strung around his neck. As he bowed down, Charlotte caught the glint of a gold bracelet on his right wrist. She caught her breath and peered into the dim room to study his profile: whiskery eyebrows, a balding head, high cheekbones. Behind him, a silver-topped cane rested on the floor.

'Rashid?' The words slipped out in a whisper.

She took a step toward the room and a round-faced monk

appeared beside her 'Very sorry, lady,' he said. 'This room for man only.'

'But I know this man. I've been looking for him.' She pulled out Rashid's letter, fumbling with the folded envelope. 'This belongs to him. I have to give it to him.'

The monk bowed and gestured toward an adjoining room. 'Please to wait in that room. When he finish prayer you can see him. Not allowed in room for man when worshipping the Buddha.'

She looked at her watch. It was almost seven. Annie might be waiting for her. 'How long must I wait? It's very important I talk to him.'

The monk shrugged. 'Cannot say. This man guest of temple. Is possible he may stay for one day or two.'

She glanced toward the outer gate and saw Annie dismount her bicycle in front of the museum. It was beyond frustrating to be so close and unable to talk to Rashid, but she couldn't wait until he finished praying. She stuffed the letter in her pocket and looked toward the prayer chamber again. Rashid hadn't moved. Perhaps he would still be there after the show. She rummaged through her bag, found the Plae Pakaa flyer, and scribbled a note on the back: *This is Charlotte, the girl you sat next to on the plane. I have something that belongs to you. Please call me.* She included her phone number and handed the flyer to the monk. 'Please give this to him. It is very important,' she repeated, then walked across the courtyard toward the museum.

Annie strolled toward her, dressed in a long, floral skirt and white tank top. Her tanned face glowed as she reached out to grasp Charlotte's hands. 'Hello, my dear,' she said. 'Roxy's told me so much about you and it's nice to properly meet you.' She linked her arm through Charlotte's and led her into the open-air auditorium, pressing through a group of chattering tourists. Once they were seated, Annie turned to her and smiled. 'It's my first time seeing this show,' she said. 'I'm sorry Roxy can't make it but it's a privilege to be here in her place.'

Charlotte smiled back, fingering the phone in her pocket, and wondering if she should keep it on during the show. She didn't want to miss a call from Rashid, but she didn't want to be one of those annoying people who interrupts a performance with a ringing phone. She was about to tell Annie about her experience when a young Cambodian man strolled onto the stage and addressed the audience.

'Very many welcomes to Plae Pakaa,' he said, flashing a wide smile. 'Today is very special day for our country and our theatre. During the time of Khmer Rouge, much of Cambodia's culture was wiped out, and traditional dance was almost lost forever. Our organisation, Cambodian Living Arts, was created by a genocide survivor and is dedicated to preserving culture in our community.'

Charlotte switched her phone to *vibrate* as the announcer bowed to the audience. 'We are honoured to start this evening with a special blessing. Thank you for sharing it with us.'

A group of monks entered the amphitheatre and began to chant. They stood on the edge of the stage and drew handfuls of flower petals from the cloth bags strung across their shoulders, tossing them into the audience. Charlotte scanned the stage and wondered if they might have come from Wat Ounalom. Perhaps the round-faced monk would be among them. Had he given Rashid her note? She leaned forward to inspect them and noticed a young monk at the end of the line who looked familiar. It was the monk she'd seen at Tuol Sleng. The one with the blue eyes.

She nudged Annie. 'Look at the one at the end,' she whispered. 'He can't be Cambodian.'

Annie shook her head. 'Sometimes foreigners become monks for a while,' she whispered back. 'It's usually because they want to escape from something or start a new life. Pretty cool, isn't it?'

Before Charlotte could reply, the monks left the stage, the show began, and she forgot about Rashid. Caught up in a world of sequins, silk, and smiles, she clapped her hands in delight as dancers swirled, spun, leapt, and twirled in their re-enactment of traditional folk tales. Multi-coloured masks concealed faces as performers curved their hands and coiled their bodies into delicate and acrobatic poses, and musicians played haunting sounds from the early years of Cambodian culture. When the cast took their final bow, Charlotte and Annie were the first to rise in a standing ovation.

The presenter reappeared on stage. 'Thank you very much to everyone,' he said, after the applause died down. 'And we would also like to thank our sponsor, Monsoon Bangladeshi restaurant, which will have its grand opening this weekend. For everyone here tonight, there will be a special event at the restaurant if you show your Plae Pakaa programme. Have a good evening.'

People streamed from the performance, chattering about the show and dispersing in different directions. Annie took Charlotte's arm. 'That was gorgeous,' she said. 'And being with you makes me miss my daughter. You remind me a bit of her. Except for your accent, of course.'

'You have a daughter?' Charlotte asked. 'Is she in Australia?'

Annie nodded. 'We had a falling out when my marriage broke up. I think she needs time to heal, so I'm giving her space.' She smiled. 'We all need to find our own way, don't we?'

Charlotte looked at Annie. No wonder she'd been a source of strength to Roxy. There was a calm confidence about her that Charlotte found appealing and made her wish her mother were a bit more like her. She recalled Peter's words about people who came to Cambodia to do good things and her heart warmed that she'd met someone like Annie. She looked toward the pagoda and saw a faint light flickering coming from inside. 'Do you mind waiting a moment?' she asked. 'I have a quick errand to do.' She gathered her skirt and hurried across the lawn.

This time a different monk stood on the steps. 'Excuse me, please,' Charlotte said. 'I need to know if there's a man inside. I left a note for him. He was in the prayer room over there.' She pointed.

The monk looked at her with a kindly expression. 'Very sorry, miss. Everybody is no longer here.'

Charlotte's heart sank. She let out a loud sigh, hoping Rashid had received her note and would get in touch with her. After thanking the monk, she walked back to find Annie, constantly scanning the neighbourhood in case Rashid was nearby. But she only saw a crowd of westerners from the show, street vendors, and tuk-tuk drivers, so she returned to the museum grounds.

Annie sat on a bench outside the theatre, talking on her mobile. When she saw Charlotte, she stood and shut off the phone. Charlotte wiped the sweat from her upper lip and glanced down at her shoes that were now covered in dust. 'Do you have time for a drink?' she asked. 'There's something I'd like to talk about.'

10

Charlotte put down her wine glass. She leaned across the table at the sidewalk café where she and Annie had been sitting for the past hour. 'So, I have no idea what this means. If it means anything at all. But I think I met Rashid for a reason.'

Annie took a sip of tea and after pausing for a moment, took Charlotte's hand. 'It sounds as though you might need some advice,' she said. 'May I?'

Charlotte nodded.

'I'd like to share my experience as it might be helpful. These past few years have been difficult and there were times I felt my life was falling apart. Then I discovered Buddhism. It helped me get through the tough times and I believe that's what sent me to Cambodia and now to you. There were many things I learned, and one of the most important was this: there are two worlds in our universe: the world around us and the one inside us. I discovered I placed too much focus on the outside world. I'm guessing you might do the same.'

Charlotte fought the impulse to prod. She wondered what Annie knew about her and if Roxy had shared her secrets. Charlotte always fought to keep her personal life private, so she was disturbed to think Annie might know more than she wanted to share. She stared at her fingernails and took a deep breath.

Annie interrupted her thoughts. 'Can I ask you a personal question? Why did you come to Cambodia?'

'To visit Roxy,' Charlotte replied.

'Forgive my presumption, but I wonder if you might be running away from something. I believe things happen for a reason so you may want to consider what has already happened on this trip. And now you've told me about Rashid, I can't help but question your reason for looking for Chris.' She looked her in the eye. 'Whose wounds are you trying to heal? Rashid's or your own?'

Charlotte toyed with the stem of her wine glass. The conversation was making her uncomfortable. Annie held up her hand. 'No need to answer me. Do it for yourself.'

Charlotte took a breath, unsure what to say next. As they sat in silence, a red-haired man crossed the street and came toward them. His white T-shirt had dark stains under the arms and there was an angry burn on one of his legs. He stood next to their table and mumbled something under his breath.

Annie glared at him. 'Would you please leave us alone,' she said. 'I can't understand you.' The man swiped his mouth with the back of his hand, some of his sweat dripping onto Charlotte's shoulder. 'All the same, you are,' he muttered, shaking his head.

Charlotte tensed and held her handbag tighter, wondering if she should leave. But before she could move, a restaurant manager strode from the doorway and marched toward their table, grabbing the man's arm and ushering him from the patio. The man turned, glared at Annie, and scurried away.

'What was that about?' Charlotte asked after the manager had apologised and gone inside.

'No idea.' Annie shrugged. 'Just some weirdo.' She gestured to the waiter for another cup of tea. 'I'm sorry if I'm making you uncomfortable. I was hoping to give you a few things to think about. Annoying professional habit, I guess. After my parents died and Ken walked out, I learned I'd been living my life for other people and not so much for myself. It was Buddhism that helped me move on. I discovered there was only so much I could control, and I found a way to trust everything would work out for the best.'

. 'I used to feel that way,' Charlotte said. 'But after Dad left...'

Annie interrupted. 'Try to think about what *you* want, darling. Figure out what makes you happy and how you can be true to yourself. If your search for this man and his son helps you find what you're looking for, perhaps it's a good enough reason for you to be here. Just don't get too hung up on someone else's problems. We're all on our own journey. Focus on yours.'

Charlotte drained her wine glass. 'I'm not sure I know how to do that,' she said. 'I spent so much time taking care of Mum that I lost my identity. This is the first time I've had for myself in years, and I'm spending most of it thinking about *her*.' She stopped talking when the waiter padded up with a new pot of tea. 'I keep wondering if I'm doing the right thing,' she continued after the waiter left the table. 'She doesn't reply to my messages and I'm afraid I've upset her even though I know I've done nothing wrong. I think she likes knowing she has a hold over me.' She chewed on her bottom lip. 'I try to think of a time when she was nice to me. But for as long as I can remember, she was egocentric and self-absorbed. I used to watch Dad and wonder how it felt for him. He can't have been happy. Even when he left, she played the victim.'

'So, how did you and your mum manage alone?' Annie asked.

Charlotte fidgeted with the napkin. 'Mum made sure we were fine, financially. She's not stupid. Thing is, everything else had to be on her terms. I'm sick of putting her needs first but I don't know how to do things differently.' She tore off a piece of napkin and twirled it between her fingers.

'Be gentle on yourself, love,' Annie said. 'You can't control what anyone does or says, but you *can* control how you react to it. One more piece of advice: find a way to let go of those negative feelings. You came here for a reason and that may become clear if you let things unfold.'

She signalled to the waiter for the check and Charlotte reached for her wallet. 'This one's on me,' Annie said. 'I'm going to sit here a bit longer then walk home. No need to wait.' She wrapped Charlotte in a warm hug and bid her goodnight.

Charlotte hailed a tuk-tuk and climbed on board, thinking about the conversation with Annie. She turned to wave goodbye and saw the red-haired man had returned to the table where Annie was sitting. She was about to tell the driver to turn around, then realised Annie was deep in conversation with him. Confused, Charlotte turned her focus back to the road ahead.

⁂

CHARLOTTE OPENED the door to the flat. 'I'm home!' she called. 'It was fabulous.'

Silence.

She went to the living room, expecting to find Roxy curled up in a chair or sprawled on the floor with a magazine, but the room was empty. A whimpering sound came from outside, so she went to the glass door leading to the balcony and opened it. Roxy leaned on the railing, her chest pressed against the metal barrier, shoulders shaking. Charlotte pushed the door open and rushed over to her. 'What happened?' she asked, grabbing her arm and turning her around to face her.

Roxy's eyes were ringed with smudges of mascara; her cheeks flushed and streaked with tears. 'Sethya. They found her.' She clutched a wet tissue. 'Those fucking bastards.'

'Sethya? Is she—?"

Roxy shook her head and Charlotte stood quietly, waiting for her to speak. Eventually she squeezed out the words. 'Dead. Beaten. In the pond.'

Charlotte reached for her hand. 'How did you hear?' she asked softly.

Roxy pushed her hand off and turned away. 'Her cousin's husband,' Roxy said. 'He's a moto driver. Rode here to tell us. Fucking, disgusting bastards.'

Charlotte took a deep breath. 'I'm so sorry.'

'He said she'd...' She clasped her hand over her mouth. 'Those...those assholes. They forced her into prostitution.' She swallowed, her words coming faster. 'She wasn't making money for them, so they...It's not—' She paced up and down the balcony. 'Fuck this country. It's a shithole. These people are monsters and don't give a damn about anyone. What the hell am I'm doing in a place like this?' She buried her face in her hands.

Charlotte drew her into her arms. 'It's horrible. I'm terribly sorry.'

Roxy pulled away and rubbed her face with the back of a hand. 'I must tell the girls before they hear it from someone else.'

Charlotte reached for her bag. 'I'll come with you.'

Roxy squeezed her hand. 'Thanks, hon, but I need to do this alone.'

Charlotte sank into a wicker chair and watched her leave. As the door slammed shut, she took a deep breath. Her heart ached for Sethya and she realised this was the seedy side of Cambodian life Peter had referred to. She thought of Roxy having to break the news to the other girls and sighed. It was one of the things she admired about her friend; she'd always been gutsy, and full of strength and creativity and passion. She wished she possessed even one of those qualities. There'd been many times when Roxy had scolded her for being timid. 'You've gotta stand up for yourself,' she'd told her when they were teenagers, clearly frustrated by Charlotte's lack of self-confidence. 'Don't let the turkeys of the world sit on you.' One birthday she'd given her a book called *How to be a Feisty Woman* which Charlotte never read. Roxy was feisty enough for both of them.

These next few days were going to be tough and Charlotte wondered how she could make things easier for Roxy. Perhaps she could iron her clothes, take her for a foot massage, cook her a nice dinner. She stood up and her phone pinged with a new email—another message from her mother: *I still can't find the remote. Do you ever check your emails?* She cursed, shut off the phone, and went to bed.

STREAKS of early morning sunlight filtered beneath the curtains. It was 6 a.m. and Charlotte had been awake more than an hour. She'd heard Roxy and Peter arrive home sometime after midnight and since then had tossed and turned, unable to sleep thinking about Sethya, then fuming over the messages from her mother. A truck rumbled past on the street below so she brushed strands of hair from her face and sat up. There was no point in staying in bed. She rose, dressed, wrote a quick note to Roxy, and slipped from the flat.

An early morning fog hung over the Russian Market and a rubbish cart rumbled along the pavement, dragged by an elderly man in baggy trousers tied at the waist with a piece of rope. Inside, a sleeping child perched on a mountain of rags. Charlotte's heart melted as she watched the child stir in her sleep then noticed a Styrofoam container and rotten banana topple onto the road. Within seconds, a boy ran from behind a building, grabbed the banana, and disappeared. Charlotte watched the scene unfold, wondering whose plight was worse, the child, the old man, or the boy. She'd never realised how much she had before this trip to Cambodia, and she was struck by the privileged life she led.

As she gazed along the road, her phone beeped with a new email. *Come to the Garden Café on Street 344 before 9 a.m. Ask for Hasan. I can help you find Chris.*

She stared at the message, taking a moment to realise it was a response to her internet posting. Someone knew Chris. Her heart raced as she fingered Rashid's letter in her pocket, then looked at the address on the text: *Garden Café, Street 344*. She'd been paying no attention where she'd been walking and had no idea how to find Street 344. She started to call Roxy then noticed it was 6:42 a.m. Roxy would be furious if she called at this hour. She walked another block and looked up at the rusted sign partially hidden behind a tree: *Street 322*. It was only a few blocks away.

A few minutes later, she stood in front of a building with a faded brown awning and a sign that read, *Garden Café*. Knee-high grass poked between a battered fence, and broken bottles littered the alleyway. She kicked a cardboard box and jumped back as a chicken ran from it, flapping and squawking, then she tapped on the dusty glass door to the café. No reply. She knocked again and waited, deciding to give it a few more minutes before she left. Then, just as she was about to turn away, the scraping sound of a bolt stopped her and a man's face peered through a crack in the door.

'What d'yer want?'

'I'm here to see Hasan. About Chris.'

The door creaked open and a middle-aged man wearing boxer shorts and a soiled white tank top stared out at her. His short, muscular frame was covered in dark hair, and there was a faded dragon tattoo on his left forearm with the mouth of the dragon spreading onto the back of his hand. 'That's me.' he grunted. 'I'm havin' breakfast.' Crumbs flecked the stubble of his pockmarked face and he wiped them away, gesturing toward the door and grunting again. 'Come in, then.'

Charlotte took a step forward and peeked inside the café. The smell of cigarette smoke and burnt coffee wafted through the open door and paper napkins littered the tiled floor. Most of the walls were covered with beer posters, their edges curled and yellowing.

'Come on, then.' Hasan swung the door open and patted himself on the chest. 'I'm from Bangladesh too. Like Chris. Want coffee?'

She lingered in the doorway, pondering her options. If she left and Hasan knew Chris, she'd miss her chance of finding him. If Hasan were lying or if something weird happened she could make an excuse and leave, or call Roxy. Her mother's voice echoed in her head: *You're such a little fraidy-cat.* What had Annie said? *Things happen for a reason. Trust things will work out for the best.* She drew back her shoulders and stepped inside.

Hasan lit a cigarette and pointed to a chair. 'Why you lookin' fer Chris?' he asked.

'I have something for him.'

'It's gotta be the fella who works 'ere.' He flicked ash onto the floor. 'He's the only Bengali I know named Chris. Crazy, crazy Chris, that's what we call him.' He grinned, flashing two gold teeth. 'Hang on; I'll get 'im. He'll be real happy to know there's a pretty girl lookin' for 'im.' He walked into a back room.

Charlotte lingered near the doorway, unwilling to go any further until she knew what she was getting into. Muffled conversation drifted from the next room then Hasan returned with a younger man wearing boxer shorts and a black T-shirt stretched tightly across his chest. He stared at her through heavy lids.

''Ere he is,' Hasan said. 'What d'you have for him?' He leered. 'You got some for me too?'

She took a step back, starting to feel uncomfortable. 'It's not here. I'll go and get it.'

'No need to rush, beautiful.' Hasan pointed to the chair. 'First have a coffee with your new Bengali pals.' He took three cracked mugs from a shelf, filled them with water, and placed them inside a countertop microwave.

As he did so, the other man circled behind Charlotte and tapped her on the shoulder. 'Got somewhere to go?' he asked. The stench of body odour was so strong that Charlotte moved sideways to avoid making contact with him. He reached out and touched her cheek, winking at Hasan. 'From what I recall, you were the one who wanted something, weren't yer, Charlotte?' He licked his upper lip as he pronounced her name. 'Hasan said yer were looking for Chris. You've found him.'

Charlotte backed against the wall. The radio was playing a Kanye West song in the background and Hasan turned up the dial, bobbing his head in time to the music. She dipped her hand into her pocket, fingers trembling, and pulled out her mobile phone. 'I'll call my friend,' she said. 'She can bring it... the thing for Chris.' She flipped open the phone, hoping the men wouldn't notice her trembling.

The man in the boxer shorts grabbed her hand and held onto it. 'I'll call 'er. What's 'er number?'

Charlotte gripped her phone tighter. 'No. I will. I need to go...' Trickles of sweat ran down the back of her neck and she looked around the room, searching for another way out. The windows in the rear appeared to be rusted shut, and there were metal bars on the outside. The only exit was through the front door. She inwardly cursed herself. Her mother was right. She *was* an idiot.

She noticed movement in the corner and a small furry creature scampered across the floor and disappeared under a wooden box. She gasped and jumped back, jerking her hand away from the man in the boxer shorts. 'What's that?' she asked.

Hasan guffawed and the other man banged the table with his fist, sending paper napkins flying onto the floor. 'Probably a rat,' he said, grinning widely. 'Wouldn't be the first time, would it? They're everywhere in this shithole country.' He shook his head. 'You scared of rats? Hasan and Chris will look after you.'

Hasan smirked at Charlotte. 'Wanna get a closer look?' He got down on his knees and reached under the box, his hands swiping around on the grimy, tiled floor. Then he reached into the corner and pulled out something furry that was wriggling frantically. He thrust it toward Charlotte and laughed when she backed away.

'Please,' she whimpered. 'I don't...' She turned her head away from the creature squirming in Hasan's hands, her stomach in knots. The creature let out a yowl and she forced herself to look. It was a black and white kitten. 'It's a cat!' she said. 'What are you doing to it?'

Hasan dropped it onto the table, one hand pinning it down. 'We're looking after him, aren't we? His name's Toyota. 'Cause we found 'im under a Toyota!' He bellowed and grabbed the cat by the scruff as it tried to scramble away. 'Say 'ello to Charlotte, Toyota!' He dangled it in front of her face. 'We've been feeding it rice so it can get nice and fat and make a good meal. The last one was *real* tasty. We've developed quite a taste for kitty meat, haven't we, Moh...I mean Chris...oh, whatever.'

'Moh?'

Hasan slapped a hand across his mouth. 'Shit! Oh well.' He slapped Moh on the back. 'He's every bit as good as Chris, though.' The men roared with laughter.

The scraping of a key in the lock sounded from across the room and the front door swung open. A young Cambodian woman walked into the café carrying a bucket, mop, and vacuum. '*Sua s'day*, Mister Hasan,' she said. 'I come early because I take daughter to school.' The woman turned to close the door behind her.

Moh stepped toward her. 'Not today, Nara.'

Nara put down the bucket. 'I sorry. But Mister Hasan he say...' She stared at Hasan.

Charlotte took a couple of sideways steps toward the door, her back pressed against the wall. Moh stepped toward Nara. 'Leave. Now.'

Nara bent to pick up the bucket and as she leaned over,

Charlotte ran across the room and shoved her away from the half-open door. Moh lunged toward Charlotte and grabbed her arm. She pulled away, ripping the sleeve of her jacket as Moh held on, the sound of Hasan's laughter ringing in her ears. She wriggled from his grasp and raced onto the street, sprinting along the road, and across two lanes of cars whose drivers honked and shouted as she ran in front of them. Her throat burned. Sweat soaked her back. She turned the corner towards Roxy's flat and saw her sitting on the pavement with Tnout.

'Thank goodness you're here!' she said, racing up to her, gasping for breath.

'Where the heck d'you go so early? Fed up waiting for old lazybones?' Roxy stared as she flopped down onto the pavement beside her. 'Bloody hell. What on earth happened?'

'I just had—' She took a rasping breath. 'Hold on, I can't—' She wiped her face on a sleeve. 'These men—'

'Slow down. I don't know what you're saying.' Roxy handed her a bottle of water and Charlotte gulped thirstily. In between sips, she told her about Hasan and Moh and the cat and the café, expecting sympathy and concern from her friend.

'I should've called you,' she sighed.

Roxy's eyes flashed as she turned like an enraged panther. 'No, you bloody well shouldn't. You should've stayed the hell outta there. What did you think you were doing? Trying to find a fictional person named Chris in a city of three million people? It's Cambodia, sunshine. People disappear here.'

'But he contacted me. He saw my note.'

'A message on a website from a stranger? And you go flitting off without telling anyone. Then you're *surprised* when it goes pear-shaped? Are you bloody insane?' Tnout licked Roxy's ankle and she pushed him away. 'Don't you realise some people care about you? Like me, for instance. What would I do if something happened? Call your mum and tell her I'd lost her daughter? Put another message on a website?' She stood. 'We've just been through a nightmare with Sethya and I don't ever want to deal with something like that again. If you want to play detective, go ahead. But remember you're not in Brighton anymore. Can't you just enjoy your bloody holiday like a normal person?'

Charlotte's face heated up. She clenched her jaw as hot tears burned her eyes. The fear that still flickered from her encounter with Hasan turned to anger, ignited by Roxy's incendiary words. She erupted. 'You think this is just a holiday? You think I'm here only to have fun? You don't have a clue, do you? You have no idea how much I hate my life. How I want to run away from everything. I thought I was doing something helpful. Something...nice.' Her cheeks burned. 'Since I can't fix my own screwed up life, I thought maybe, just maybe, I could help someone else. And now you tell me I'm an idiot? And you're—you're saying... d'you think I don't already *know* I'm useless. That I can't do anything right?' She paused for breath, angry tears burning her eyes. 'I'm no good to anyone.' She sprinted up the stairs to the flat.

A GENTLE TAP sounded on the bedroom door then Roxy peered inside holding a white sock in one hand and a large can of tuna in the other. 'I come bearing gifts,' she said. 'Couldn't find any flowers or chocolates, and it's a bit early for Scotch, so this is it.' She tiptoed across the room and sat cross-legged on the floor next to the bed. 'Look, I'm sorry for flipping out. Losing Sethya hit me hard. And I was worried when you weren't here.' She inhaled loudly. 'I apologise for shouting at you, but I'm not sorry for calling you insane. What the hell were you thinking?'

Charlotte slammed her book shut. 'Did you come up here to yell at me again?'

'Relax, won't you? I'm not your mother. It's also not my job to babysit you. But sometimes you need guidance, especially in a place like this.' She shook her head. 'In case you haven't noticed, you happen to be gorgeous. Men look at you.' She sighed. 'You don't have a clue, do you? You're too naïve. And you did something stupid today.'

'I don't want to hear it. You're preaching.'

'Oh, knock it off, Charlo! It's me, Roxy.' She sighed. 'Maybe I should've warned you better, but I thought the episode with Sethya would have been enough for you to see there are some scary characters around. Some of them look for gullible women like you. So, either knock off this search for Chris, watch your back, or take Tnout with you next time.' She took a deep breath then pulled a face. 'He'd be useless, wouldn't he?' She got down on one knee and held out the can of tuna. 'Will you just accept this offering, and forgive me for scolding you?'

Charlotte put down her book. She didn't want to be angry at Roxy, but her reprimand reminded her of the way she'd constantly felt back home. Awkward. Embarrassed. And wrong. She wasn't proud of what she'd done at the café, but she'd taken a chance on doing something good. At least she'd thought so. Maybe Roxy was right, and she'd acted irresponsibly. Maybe she should just go home.

'Charlo?' Roxy moaned. 'Say something soon or my bloody knee's gonna give out.'

Charlotte looked down at Roxy clutching a can of tuna and a giggle bubbled up in her throat. She'd never been able to stay angry for long and she'd run out of angry words. 'Apology accepted.' Charlotte picked up the can of tuna that had rolled under the bed. 'Just don't make me open this. Knowing you, it's probably been in your cupboard since you moved in.' She lowered her voice. 'You're right. I *was* stupid. I didn't think I'd get into trouble...thought I could take care of myself.' She wrapped her arms around her knees. 'Know what I heard when I went into that café? My mum's voice, telling me I couldn't get a better job because I didn't promote myself. I heard her criticising me for being afraid of the dark...I heard her say I couldn't...'

Roxy clasped Charlotte's hand. 'I want you to hear this. You are not stupid. You're perfect the way you are, no matter what your mother or anyone else tells you. And I know you better than anyone in the world. So, let's never let anything or anyone to come between us, okay?'

Charlotte nodded. But something still bothered her. There were unspoken words between the two of them and Charlotte didn't want to be the one to bring them up.

11

The following morning, Charlotte clung onto Roxy's waist as they drove across town on the motorbike. They passed the Russian market and wove through a neighbourhood where groups of old men sat on the street playing cards, then turned a corner onto Street 322. Suddenly, Charlotte gripped Roxy tighter and shouted in her ear. 'Roxy! Toyota!'

Roxy slammed on the brakes. A tuk-tuk swerved around them, missing them by inches. 'What the fuck!' Roxy pulled to the shoulder and planted a foot on the ground, looking around. 'Where?'

'The cat. Toyota the cat.' Charlotte climbed off and stood on the pavement pointing toward the Garden Café. 'He's in there! We've got to get him.'

Roxy leaned the bike against a railing and took a deep breath. 'Jesus Christ! Don't ever do that to me when I'm driving' She shook her head and gestured to a driver to continue when he glared at her through the window. 'So, what d'you propose we do about this cat? Call an animal shelter that doesn't exist?'

Charlotte unbuckled her helmet. 'I saw him in the window,' she said. 'We've got to do something.'

'How about we don't? How about we go for coffee instead? Or a pastrami sandwich? Or I leave you here and you walk home?'

'Could you live with yourself if something happened to him?'

'You're not gonna drop it, are you? Come on, then. But if those men come anywhere near you...' She pushed the bike two doors away from the café and stared at Charlotte. 'So, what d'you want to do now?'

'Let's wait and see,' Charlotte replied. 'Maybe they're just getting ready to open.'

'More likely sleeping off hangovers.' Roxy mopped her forehead with a bandana. 'Shit, it's hot. I'll give you ten minutes, then it's *hasta la vista* Toyota. I'm gonna get an iced coffee. Want one?' She crossed the road to a coffee cart and returned with two plastic cups. 'The girl told me the Garden Café never opens in the morning,' she said. 'She says it only sells booze, and there are strange people who go there at night. Finish your coffee. Let's get out of here.'

Charlotte looked toward the café. It was clear Roxy didn't want to stay, but the cat had looked terrified, and it was up to her and Roxy to save it. As they stood on the street drinking coffee, the café door opened and Hasan emerged, shirtless, a faded towel stretched tightly around his hairy stomach like a skirt. He hauled a rubbish bag to the pavement and dumped it with a crash onto the street. Minutes later he returned with two more. Empty beer bottles tumbled out and rolled into the gutter. Charlotte watched, hoping he wouldn't see her, then noticed something move near his ankle. It was Toyota. The cat slunk toward the pile of rubbish and Hasan turned and kicked it. It squealed and darted behind a bin.

Charlotte gasped. 'Oh, God!' She handed her empty cup to Roxy. 'I'm going to get him.'

Roxy grabbed her arm. 'No, you're not. Gorilla-man might recognise you, then it won't be just the cat who's in trouble.' She sighed. 'I can't believe I'm doing this.' She tossed the coffee cups into a bin then stomped down the street, waving her arms and shouting. 'Hey! Hey! What are you doing with that cat?'

Hasan glared at her. 'Who the fuck are you?'

'I'm the Phnom Penh representative for...' She fumbled for words. 'Animals being...treated by...ABTABI! Animals Being Treated Awfully By Idiots.' She stood, hands on hips. 'We rescue horses from circuses and promote elephant rights in tourist attractions. We're about to start a new branch. For pigs. Wanna be one of the founding members?'

Hasan glowered like an angry bull. 'Look, lady, I don't know what you're preaching, but you can get the hell outta my place.'

'Only when you stop mistreating that cat, or I'll have to call the animal brigade to take further action. Besides, logistically, I'm not actually *in* your place. I'm on the pavement, which is public. So, you've no legal control over what I can do here.'

Hasan stepped toward the rubbish bin and shoved it aside. He seized the wriggling Toyota by the scruff of the neck and thrust him toward her. 'Take it! It's a filthy creature anyway.'

Roxy grabbed the cat and tucked him inside her duffel bag. 'I'll make sure ABTABI knows about you,' she said. 'And if I hear about you mistreating any other animal, I'll be back with the rest of our squad.' She stomped back to the motorbike, handed the bag to Charlotte, and started the engine.

'You were amazing!' Charlotte shouted as they sped down the street, laughing.

'Just one more idiot to add to countless others I've taken on. I'm not afraid of a thug like him. I just hope he never sees me around town!' She glanced behind her. 'And I hope Peter doesn't mind we've adopted a cat.'

THAT EVENING, Charlotte pushed open the door to Monsoon restaurant, ready for a girls' night out. She'd asked Annie to join her and was looking forward to getting to know her better. Besides, it would be good for Roxy and Peter to have some time alone.

She spotted Annie standing under a shiny *Opening Night* banner, a paper plate in one hand and glass of wine in the other.

'I thought you might forget,' Charlotte said, walking toward her.

'How could I, when you were so excited about coming?' Annie pointed toward a platter on the buffet table. 'These pakoras are delicious,' she said. 'But I think you need to sign the guestbook first.'

Charlotte went to the folding table near the door and pulled out her Plae Pakaa programme as proof of admission. Since the show, she'd thought a lot about Rashid and wondered if the monk had given him the note and if he might make an appearance tonight. A man in a floor-length yellow robe waddled over, flashing a set of brilliant white teeth. He stuck out his hand.

'Very welcome to Monsoon, madam. I am Bikram, the owner. It is my honourable pleasure to greet you.' He glanced at her programme then stroked his beard and gestured toward the guestbook. 'Please sign our book and enjoy our complimentary feast.' He handed her a blue fountain pen. On the handle were three initials: *RCF*.

She stared at it then looked up at Bikram. 'Can I ask where you got this?'

Bikram waggled his head. 'I do not know, madam. Perhaps it belonged to a customer.'

'Is he here now?' Charlotte held her breath.

Bikram shrugged. 'Anything possible.'

Charlotte signed the register, then hastened back to Annie who was standing at the food table. She grabbed her wrist and whispered, 'I think Rashid's here.'

Before Annie could respond, Bikram tapped a glass with a serving spoon and called for silence. A group of monks filed into the room and knelt on a long straw mat at the head of the room. Everyone sat on the floor and crossed their legs, so Charlotte did the same.

'Do this,' Annie whispered, pressing her palms together. 'It's called a *sampeah*. It's a sign of respect.' Charlotte put her hands together and the monks started to chant, sending gentle vibrations throughout the room. It reminded her of her time at the pagoda and how peaceful the chanting had made her feel. The monks dipped their fingers into small bowls of water and sprinkled droplets onto the people sitting in front of them, then plucked handfuls of flower petals from another bowl and scattered them onto the congregation. Charlotte lowered her eyes, wondering how long this would last. Her stomach growled. She should have eaten something.

Annie touched her hand. 'It's a tradition for new restaurants,' she whispered, wiping a droplet of water from her forehead. 'They do it to bless them.'

The sonorous voices of the monks filled the room and Charlotte noticed everyone had closed their eyes. She did the same then felt something plop onto her lap. She squealed and flung it from her knee, sending it flying across the room. She opened her eyes and watched in horror as a frangipani blossom landed in a tray of pomegranate seeds on the buffet table. She clasped her hands over her mouth, and glanced around the room, hoping nobody had noticed.

A faint giggle came from the front of the room and she sneaked a look at the line of monks. One of them glanced her way and when she met his gaze, he looked away and resumed chanting. It was the young monk with the blue eyes. She closed her eyes again, forcing herself to relax and prayed nothing else would fall on her or cause her to create a commotion.

Once the blessing ended, she made her way to the buffet table leaving Annie talking to one of the guests. Steam wafted into the air from a large metal bowl and she bent to inhale it. A mound of saffron rice dotted with almonds and raisins was piled high in a silver chafing dish, and chunks of seasoned chicken were arranged on large platters.

She picked up a warm piece of *nan,* dipped it in a mound of hummus, then scanned the room for Annie, wondering if she should wait before filling a plate with food. It was hard to spot her in the crowd since many of the patrons were westerners dressed the same way, in crisp linen or casual chinos, so she scooped a forkful of chicken onto her plate and turned to look around. As she did so, she bumped into a slender man in a long orange robe standing next to her at the table.

'Oh! I'm so sorry!' she exclaimed, dropping her fork on the floor. Piercing blue eyes looked back at her and her face heated up as she put her hands together in a *sampeah*. 'Oh, goodness! I really don't—I mean I won't—' She bent down to pick up the fork and cracked her knee on a wooden stool. 'Ouch! Shit! Oh, I'm so sorry—I didn't mean to say...'

The monk picked up the fork, a bemused look on his face. He placed it on the table and turned back to her. 'I think you might need a new fork,' he said. 'And I'd probably stay away from the bowl of pomegranates if I were you.'

'Oh! I'm so sorry about that. I thought it was a bug on my leg, so I—' She grimaced. 'I'm apologising for everything, aren't I?'

The monk smiled. He was a few inches taller than she was and his robe was snugly wrapped around his slender body. A pair of gentle eyes deeply set in a handsome face the colour of coffee and high cheekbones which accented his wide grin.

'Is that an English accent?' she asked.

He nodded. 'It's impossible to hide. I don't talk a lot during the day since I live in the pagoda and my Khmer isn't very good.' He shrugged and pulled a face. 'It's nice to speak English again.'

She laughed. There was something about him that made her think of Trevor: a warmth in his voice and a sense of humour that shone through his unassuming exterior. 'Where are you from?' she asked. 'And how does an Englishman become a monk? How did you end up in Cambodia?' She shook her head and smiled. 'Am I asking too many questions?'

'No problem,' he said. 'I'm from the London area and I've been in Cambodia almost a year.' He glanced across the room to the other monks. 'Long story. How about you?'

'Long story for me too.' She reached across the table for another piece of *nan*. 'I'm visiting my friend, Roxy.' She gestured toward Annie who was walking toward them. 'That's Annie. She's been in Cambodia a couple of years and has been studying Buddhism.' She thrust out her hand. 'I'm Charlotte, by the way.'

He took a short step back. 'It's a pleasure to meet you, but I can't shake your hand. Monks aren't allowed physical contact with women.'

'Sorry. I had no idea. I don't know much about Buddhism. Just what Annie told me.'

'And what's that?'

Charlotte shrugged. 'That I shouldn't worry so much and that I should pay attention to my thoughts. Also, that things happen for a reason.'

He tilted his chin. 'That's a good start.'

'I guess there's probably more to it than that.'

'Just a bit. Do you want to know more?'

'I'm not sure. Do I?'

'It's up to you. I teach basic Buddhist principles at the pagoda every Friday evening at five if you want to come along. Drop in anytime. It's free.' He glanced over his shoulder at the monks collecting in the doorway. 'I need to leave now.' He bowed and raised his hands in a *sampeah*. 'I'm Samnang.'

Annie slid next to Charlotte as he walked away. 'Isn't that the monk from the dance show?' she asked.

'It is. His name's Samnang.'

'Samnang,' Annie echoed. 'What a lovely name. It means lucky'.

AFTER A COUPLE of hours at Monsoon, Annie went home. Charlotte decided to stay longer in case Rashid showed up and she offered to help replenish bowls of curry so she didn't feel awkward being on her own. Once the food was almost gone, she climbed up a narrow, metal staircase to the rooftop terrace where a small group of people leaned against a low wall on the flat roof, sipping wine from plastic cups. She observed them for a few seconds, envious of their carefree demeanour and speculating what their lives must be like. She gazed across the city, wondering how it would feel to live in a place like Cambodia. Her father would love it, with its mysterious, third-world rough edges, and the hidden charm of a developing city. Her mother would hate everything about it.

A sliver of moon reflected on the river, and the ornamental spires of a pagoda glimmered in the distance. At night, it looked like a shimmering jewel; all the dirt and rubbish from the day hidden beneath a blanket of light.

Her phone buzzed and she flicked it open, expecting to see a message from Annie saying she'd arrived home. Instead, the text read, *Let me know when you want to see Chris again.*

Her heart pounded. It could only be from Hasan. The rational voice in her head told her he was a jerk and she could change her phone number. But the timid voice reminded her she was in a Bangladeshi restaurant and he could be here, too. Since he was the last person she wanted to see, she picked up her bag and started toward the staircase.

Suddenly a shrill voice screeched in her ear. 'How the fuck can anyone call this chicken korma?'

Charlotte wheeled around as a tall, heavyset woman in a clingy, white mini dress dangled a forkful of food, her mouth puckering as though she'd sucked on a lemon. She looked to be in her late twenties and reminded Charlotte of a B-grade actress in an English soap opera: brash, uncivilized, and to be avoided at all costs. She cast her eyes downwards and took another step toward the stairs.

'Hey, I'm talkin' to you.' The woman sidled up to Charlotte, blocking her path and pointing to the bowl of food in her hand. 'I'm from Bangladesh so I know what a real korma tastes like. I've never made one in my life, and never plan to—way too much dirty work. But I'm more of a food expert than the trainee who put this together.'

Charlotte shrugged, assuming the woman had no real interest in anyone else's opinion. The woman picked up a samosa and bit into it, sending trickles of grease down her chin. She flashed a gold tooth and pulverized vegetables as she opened her mouth wider, then stuck out her hand. Long scarlet nails with chipped polish on nicotine-stained fingers reached toward Charlotte.

'I'm Christal,' she said. 'Like the champagne, just spelled different. Both bubbly and expensive, and everso intoxicating.' She batted her eyelashes. 'So I'm told.'

'Charlotte.'

Christal pinched Charlotte's cheek with her greasy fingers and emptied her wine glass. 'Boring event, innit? I only came for the food and because my cousin had to work. I'm staying with him so Christal's all on her lonesome tonight.' She spooned a forkful of rice from a chafing dish and shovelled it into her mouth. 'Thank God there's free booze. But the food sucks, and the men are fat and dreary.'

Charlotte leaned away, wondering why Christal had picked her to talk to.

Christal gestured toward a couple of elderly men at the bar and lowered her voice. 'See what I mean? You shoulda been at The Buck Bar last night.' She winked. 'The guys were smokin'. And they were falling all over yours truly. Took one of them home with me I did; showed him what a Bengali babe can do.' She wiped a hand across her mouth and tossed her long, black hair, releasing an aroma that reminded Charlotte of the Primark perfume display. 'So, what's your story? Why are you here?'

Charlotte held her breath. 'I came to visit my—'

'Great,' Christal interrupted. 'Hasan says I'm hotter than most of the women in this city. And he should know since he's my cousin. I've gotta say, men are more attracted to me than these skinny little Cambodian girls with no boobies.' She let out a loud hoot of laughter.

Charlotte recoiled. Had Christal said *Hasan*?

Christal thrust out her chest. 'Now I'm stuffed with samosas and free booze, so I'm ready to do the fandango. Time to find a man to shower with my bubbles. Wanna join me?'

Charlotte tightened her jacket around her shoulders and made a deliberate display of looking at her watch. 'I'm, er, meeting my friend here and I...' She scanned the terrace in search of someone who might save her, but there was no need. By the time she turned back around, Christal was halfway down the stairs, lurching toward a couple of businessmen at the bar. She leaned against a brick wall and took a deep breath of the night air, now infused with the aroma of curry and jasmine. The group on the terrace had dwindled and there was only one couple left, both of whom were perched on wooden stools, smoking. One tossed a cigarette butt over the edge of the roof and Charlotte looked down to see where it would land. On the pavement below, an elderly man was climbing into a tuk-tuk, a leather briefcase tucked under his arm. It looked like Rashid.

'Rashid?' she shouted. 'Doctor Farouk?'

He didn't respond so she sprinkled a handful of cashews over the edge, hoping it would get his attention. He didn't look up, so she grabbed her phone, zoomed in, and took a couple of photos as he stepped into the vehicle. One captured the top of his head, the other a profile as he turned to speak to the driver, and the third an image of him looking up when he hooked his walking stick over the tuk-tuk's canopy. It was definitely Rashid. And now she had a picture of him, perhaps she might find someone who would recognise him.

12

Roxy clutched her mug as she spoke into the phone. 'I understand, Chenla. I don't think—' She took a sip of coffee. 'No, I can't tell you if—' She stared at Charlotte, a deep frown furrowing her brow. 'There's not much I—' She walked into the bedroom and closed the door behind her.

Several minutes later she reappeared. 'I don't know what to tell her,' she said to Charlotte. 'They're scared. Sethya was like their big sister and now they want Peter and me to look after them.' The phone buzzed in her hand. 'It's Chenla again,' she said, looking at the screen. 'I'd better go.' She pointed toward the kitchen. 'Behind the bag of cat biscuits, there's a menu for a noodle restaurant that delivers. I'm not sure what time I'll be home. Sorry.' She picked up her bag, hugged Charlotte, and left the flat.

Charlotte lay back onto the couch and stared at the ceiling. For the past few days, Roxy and Peter had been consumed with work, and she'd hardly seen them. Forced to occupy herself, she'd indulged in foot massages, visited Annie at the shop, and explored local markets hoping to familiarise herself with her surroundings. She'd never spent this much time alone and, after an initial nervousness, discovered she was enjoying her own company. There was no schedule to adhere to, nobody to answer to. It was the first time she'd had the chance to relax without feeling obliged to do something or guilty for taking time for herself. And if she got lost or felt lonely, she could call SomOn who'd hasten to pick her up and show her something new.

She'd overheard some of Roxy and Peter's discussions with police officers and human rights' organisations, as well as phone calls that came in at all hours from Sethya's friends and family, and it gave her an immense admiration for the work they did, showing her a new side of her childhood pal. She did her best to keep out of their way, tiptoeing from the flat if they were in meetings and doing all she could to keep their place tidy. She spent a lot of time thinking about her mother's message and pondered how to respond. Then after receiving another, she'd sent a brief response saying, *The remote is in the drawer under the telly,* and minutes later felt guilty for being so brusque.

In the middle of the week, Roxy and Peter went to attend a funeral ceremony in Sethya's village, and Charlotte realised she was bored. She'd explored the neighbourhoods near the flat, visited tourist attractions with SomOn and spent hours wandering around local markets. She'd started reading *The Buddhist Way* which she'd borrowed from Annie and realised why she was feeling edgy. She didn't want to spend the rest of her holiday inside a third-floor flat with a stray cat; she needed to get outside. Rashid's *National Geographic* was on the coffee table in the living room, so she flipped through it and looked at the locations he'd marked. She'd already been to some and didn't want to make another mistake by going to a place of torture; something scenic would be nice. As she pored over the magazine, a picture of *Koh Dach,* Silk Island, caught her eye. Tall palm trees fringing sandy paths. No cars, high-rises or busy roads in sight. Only rice paddies, wide-open fields, and oxcarts.

She read the accompanying article and discovered Koh Dach was across the river from Phnom Penh, so she'd have to take a ferry. She also read it would be helpful to have transportation to explore the island, so she flipped through the materials for ideas. One of the flyers had an advertisement for bicycle tours of Koh Dach. that read: *Rent a bike and cycle this beautiful little island if you want a true taste of rural Cambodia.* Just what she needed.

She opened her laptop to research bike rentals, and a buzzing sound came from the machine. It was her mother calling on Skype. Charlotte groaned. The last thing she wanted to do was talk to her. If only her mother had called a few minutes later, she would have left the flat. But she couldn't ignore her now. With a heavy sigh, she clicked *Answer.*

Her mother's whiny voice reverberated through the speaker. 'Thank goodness you're there. Alistair's coming tomorrow, and I can't turn on the telly.' Her face appeared. 'Are you there?'

Charlotte nodded. 'Yes, mum. I sent you a note and I—'

'You'll never guess what,' she interrupted. 'I'm going to be on the afternoon news. The local station filmed me talking about the handbag exhibit. I need to know where you put the extra batteries so I can turn on the TV.'

Charlotte fanned herself with the map, trying to identify the way she felt. Was it disappointment or anger? Frustration or impatience? Her mother hadn't once made eye contact with her; she'd only talked about herself. 'Remember me?' she wanted to say. 'I'm your daughter and I'm on the first holiday of my life. How lovely of you to express such interest in my trip.' Instead she muttered, 'Perhaps you should look in the bottom drawer of my bedroom dresser. Or on top of my wardrobe.' She swallowed hard, resentment burning in her chest. Couldn't her mother just buy new batteries? She took a deep breath. 'How exciting you'll be on TV,' she said. 'Maybe you can tape it. Let me know if—' The screen went blank.

She closed the laptop, cheeks burning. Her mother had hung up on her. Angry tears burnt her eyes. She had to get outside.

Once downstairs, she spotted SomOn in his usual spot sitting in his tuk-tuk chatting to another driver. He would know where to rent a bike. He did, and after he took her to the rental shop, she cycled along the riverside road with a small backpack strapped to her back. Most of her childhood had been spent riding bikes, so she was comfortable navigating the flow of traffic, even though she often had to swerve out of the path of cars that meandered onto her side of the road. She pulled her bandana around her mouth and nose to block out petrol fumes and dust, and tugged the helmet low on her head until she reached the ferry landing.

A rusted double decker boat was tied up at the edge of the river and two skinny Cambodian youths in flip flops cranked a metal ramp for arriving passengers. First went the cars and motorbikes, and once they had boarded Charlotte pushed her bike up the ramp, paid the attendant, and wiped the sweat from her face. A slight breeze rustled her hair as the boat left Phnom Penh and drifted toward the opposite shore, the muddy brown water of the Tonle Sap changing to brilliant green when it met the Mekong.

Once docked on the other side, she followed the stream of

passengers and vehicles up a steep, sandy incline and climbed onto the saddle. She pedalled along bumpy dirt roads into the heart of the countryside, sweating through her thin cotton T-shirt, and laughed out loud with delight. This was what she needed. It was only fifteen minutes away from the city, but it felt like a different country. There were no cars, and the only buildings were ramshackle wooden huts and tiny shops selling beer and soft drinks from ice chests. Occasionally, a motorbike or tuk-tuk buzzed by, churning up clouds of dust, and the general pace was bucolic and relaxed.

As she cycled farther into the countryside, the narrow path turned into a wide gravel road, fringed on both sides by lush paddy fields. Roxy had told her she'd be safe in rural areas, so she waved to the cows, and rode in circles around potholes, happy to be away from traffic. The only people she saw were villagers who all seemed surprised to see a foreigner, so she smiled at everyone, wondering if they spoke English. As she bumped through a mango grove, a group of barefoot children ran from a house shouting, 'Hello, hello!' so she greeted them with a broad smile, giving a thumbs up as she wobbled past. Vast fields of lemongrass, tomatoes, and herbs surrounded her, and a host of delicious smells assaulted her nostrils: the aroma of freshly cut rice, the fresh scent of leafy foliage, and mouth-watering scents of fried garlic and ginger from roadside stands.

She soon came to a wooden gate surrounded by tall bamboo stalks bearing the sign, *Silk Farm. Please Visit*, so she steered her bike through the gate, excited to explore somewhere new.

A young Cambodian woman in a brilliant green dress strode toward her, smiling. 'Good morning,' she said. 'I am Nita. I'm very happy to meet you and pleased to show you our shop.' She tucked her arm in Charlotte's, handed her a small porcelain cup filled with jasmine tea, and escorted her to the rear of the property where the chirping of cicadas, and twittering of birds echoed from the trees. Three women and two men squatted on the floor, each turning wooden spinning wheels with callused, sun-baked hands. They shifted pedals with a gentle *clack* and pushed shuttles across taut, brightly coloured yarn, weaving threads of raw silk thread into intricate designs.

'My family has been making silk for many generations,' Nita said. 'Would you like to try?' She ushered Charlotte toward a stool and encouraged her to sit next to an elderly woman with missing teeth. The old woman giggled and lowered her eyes until Nita said a few words in Khmer then she guided Charlotte's feet onto the pedals. She took her hand and held onto it as the shuttle *whooshed* across the strands of silk and giggled again as Charlotte's feet slipped from the pedals.

'Wow. Not easy.' Charlotte laughed. 'It's like a dance routine.'

Nita took her arm. 'Come. I will show you our production,' she said, guiding her away from the spinning wheel. 'We have many mulberry trees and worms. Would you like to see?'

Charlotte nodded. 'I'd love to,' she said, and followed Nita to a wooden building with a green tin roof and chicken wire strung around the perimeter. Row after row of wooden shelves were stacked with cardboard containers crammed with caterpillar larvae. Charlotte peered inside one, then looked around the room to see dozens of large, rattan baskets wrapped in netting and overflowing with caterpillars that were wriggling among fresh, green mulberry leaves.

Nita pointed to the baskets. 'These caterpillars are like gold for us,' she said. 'They produce the threads to create beautiful things. Our colours are made from vegetable dyes and the weavers sometimes spend a month or more making tablecloths and bed covers.'

A pile of square, silk handkerchiefs lay on one of the shelves. On top was a pale yellow one, like the handkerchief Rashid had on the plane. Charlotte picked it up, rubbing the soft silk between her fingers. 'Have you had many visitors this week?' she asked.

Nita shook her head. 'It's been very quiet. Tomorrow we had a small group of foreigners from a bus, but nobody else since before the holiday.'

'Tomorrow? Do you mean, yesterday?'

'Ah, yes. Yesterday.' Nita giggled and hid her mouth behind her hands. 'We had small group. One man who arrived is our new volunteer, Chris. He is going to help us with our shop.'

Charlotte stopped examining the handkerchief. 'Chris? Is he here?'

'No. He work in fields with my father today.'

'Will he be back later?'

Nita nodded. 'Of course. Not able to work many hours in field. It is too hot.' She beckoned. 'Now I will show you our shop.' She led Charlotte through the open-air workshop into a small hut.

Charlotte followed, her mind spinning. Perhaps today would be her lucky day. She hoped the new volunteer would return from the field soon as she was impatient to meet him. It invigorated her to think she may be able to find Chris and reunite him with his father. Even though Roxy thought she was crazy, it gave her a mission and made her feel useful.

Nita was explaining the history of the farm, so Charlotte forced herself to pay attention. Around the room, straw baskets brimmed over with ruby red, shimmering blue, iridescent pink, and emerald green silk scarves. Tables were draped with intricately designed tablecloths, and boxes stuffed with an assortment of silk purses and jewellery. Charlotte sorted through the basket and picked out a purple and pink scarf for Roxy, a silk wallet for Annie, and a yellow mobile phone case for herself—all for less than ten dollars. There was a scarlet scarf she knew her mother would like, but she still stung from the earlier conversation, so instead she bought a chequered scarf for SomOn and learned it was called a *krama*. Then she sat in the overgrown garden and watched the birds as they flitted from tree to tree, waiting for Chris to return.

As she sipped her tea and ate pieces of fresh mango that Nita brought to her in a sparkling white bowl, a herd of water buffalo ambled past the gate. She sat back and took a deep breath, inhaling the warm damp air until Nita returned to replenish the mangoes and pointed to a man banging nails into a wooden hut. 'That is Chris,' she said.

Tall and gangly with long, sinewy muscles glowing with sweat, the man crouched in the garden, pulling broken beams from beneath the shed. Charlotte walked toward him. 'Excuse me,' she said. 'You're Chris?'

He straightened and wiped the back of a filthy hand across his brow. '*Ja*.' He spoke with a German accent. 'Christof. My wife and I just arrived.' He reached out a callused hand. 'Very hot, isn't it? You are working here, too?'

Charlotte shook her head, trying to conceal her disappointment. 'I just came to say hello,' she said. 'I hope you enjoy your visit.'

She stuffed the paper bag containing the scarves into the bicycle basket, said goodbye to Nita, and steered the bike back onto the dirt path. Her thoughts flitted from Rashid's letter to the conversation with her mother to her encounter with Samnang, and before long she realised she was lost. She thought she'd been retracing her path, but she was surrounded by a cluster of thatched huts on a road that didn't look familiar. A couple of old women studied her with unblinking stares, so she pulled over and said, '*Sua s'day*. Can you help me, please?' The women's gaze bore into her. One chuckled, revealing blackened teeth in a face creased with deep wrinkles. The other muttered words Charlotte didn't understand. Charlotte pointed along the road. 'River? Where is river?' she asked. The women continued to gape, expressionless.

'River!' she repeated, raising her voice. The women cackled, and Charlotte laughed along with them. She'd done exactly what she'd often criticised in others—spoken louder to people who didn't speak her language. Two boys strolled down the path, their short black hair fashionably coiffed with matching side-swept fringes. Roxy had told her to look for young people if she needed help since they usually spoke English, so she waved to them and shouted. 'Hello. Do you speak English?'

'Can me help you, please?' said one of the boys.

Charlotte suppressed a giggle. 'I need to find the ferry. The boat. To Phnom Penh.'

One of the boys beamed and nodded. 'Please to follow.' He disappeared for a few seconds then reappeared pushing a motorbike and beckoned her to follow. She hesitated, not sure if she could trust him. She had no choice if she wanted to find her way home, so she mounted her bicycle and followed him. Pedalling furiously to keep up, she kept her gaze fixed on the boy as he wound around curves, passed a field of cows, and bounced through potholes, frequently looking behind to make sure she was still there. Before long she saw the river and the boy pointed. 'Here is ferry,' he said, handing her a plastic water bottle that he took from his satchel. 'Please to enjoy our country.' He drove away and Charlotte rode onto the ferry.

As the enormous iron vessel left the riverbank, she wedged her bike between a rusty car, two motorbikes, and a food cart selling sticky rice and packets of crisps. The hot wind blew through her hair and she drank deeply from the water bottle as she watched small wooden boats float past, groaning under the weight of a day's vegetable harvest. She wiped her face with the back of her hand, catching the eye of a bare-chested Cambodian man in baggy trousers who seemed amused to see a tall, foreign woman in mud-spattered shorts. She grinned self-consciously and he smiled and moved to the other side, exposing a group of men who were leaning on their motorbikes, smoking cigarettes. A loud laugh bellowed from one of the men bending over the railing, an arm dangling over the side. As he raised the cigarette to his lips, his sleeve fell back, uncovering a dragon tattoo.

Charlotte took a quick step backwards into the shadows, her heart beating faster. She peeked around the edge and saw the man with the tattoo gesturing to a girl with a basket of mangoes who came over to him. He said something to her, bellowing with laughter when she ran away, then turned back to his friends and took a deep drag on his cigarette. As he did, Charlotte got a good look at his profile. She also recognised the laugh. It was Hasan. She pushed her body closer to the side of the ferry as Hasan opened a can of beer and belched loudly. She wished she had the courage to say something, but it would only get her into trouble. That was Roxy's style, not hers. She stayed in the shadows until the ferry docked in Phnom Penh then waited until Hasan threw his leg over the motorbike, revved the engine, and sped away from the ship. Once he was out of sight, she pushed her bicycle onto the shore and rode in the opposite direction.

Now rush-hour, the roads teemed with traffic. Horns

honked and the putter of tuk-tuk engines competed with the screeching of tyres as cars sped through the city. Bicycles seemed invisible to everyone, so Charlotte decided to return hers, then started walking toward Roxy's place. It was Friday night and there were people all around, dressed for a night out. Peter and Roxy would still be away and their flat would be empty. A pang of loneliness hit her. This was just like Friday nights back home.

The sound of chanting drifted from a street nearby and she remembered Samnang's invitation. His Buddhist class was on Friday nights. So, she followed the sound of chanting and purposefully started walking toward the pagoda.

13

Samnang sat cross-legged on a straw mat in a small room at the pagoda. His face lit up when Charlotte entered. '*Sua s'day*,' he said. 'I'm so happy you came.' His English accent seemed out of place on a man with a shaved head dressed in an orange robe. He gestured toward two young men sitting opposite him. 'Meet Vannat and Sideth. I'm teaching them Buddhist principles and they're helping me with my Khmer. Please join us.'

The men giggled and sneaked a peek at Charlotte. She nodded a greeting then sat down beside them, amused at how they scooted sideways away from her. Samnang continued talking. 'Buddhism teaches us to be sceptical of our feelings as they're not always truthful guides to reality,' he said. 'Remember, nothing is permanent.' He looked at one of the men. 'Vannat, you say you're afraid to embarrass your family because you're not ambitious. I believe the Buddha would tell you to do what feels right as long as you don't hurt anyone. Don't forget our lessons from last month.'

Vannat nodded vigorously then he and Sideth scrambled to their feet. 'Vannat and Sideth are security guards and they need to get to work,' Samnang told Charlotte. 'Please stay.'

The young men bowed to Samnang and put their hands together in *sampeahs* to Charlotte, then left the room. Charlotte looked around and studied the small space. The wooden ceiling was painted with vividly coloured frescoes depicting the life of Buddha, and straw mats covered almost every inch of the tiled floor. At the front of the room, stone sculptures were draped with garlands of orange blossoms, their sweet floral aroma scenting the air. She tucked her feet beneath her, remembering to keep her soles pointed backwards. Roxy had told her it was an insult to point your feet toward a monk and she didn't want to make any mistakes. She sensed Samnang watching and turned her attention back to him.

'I don't think anyone else is coming tonight,' he said. 'So, I'd like to begin with a meditation.'

Her throat tightened. She'd never meditated before and didn't know what to do. She also didn't know if it would be all right to ask questions or if she should wait for Samnang to speak. Should she close her eyes? Would she need to tell him what she was thinking? How long would she have to sit still?

Samnang's voice cut through her thoughts. 'Have you ever meditated before?' he asked, as if he'd read her mind.

She shook her head.

He smiled. 'Don't worry. It's easy. First, get into a comfortable position and close your eyes. Then focus on your breath. Don't think about how to do it. There's no right or wrong way.'

That much she could do. She wondered if she needed to think about anything as well.

'You might find your mind begins to roam,' Samnang

continued. 'That's normal. Just keep bringing yourself gently back to your breathing.'

Her brain buzzed with activity. There was too much on her mind and she'd never be able to silence the voices in her head.

'It may be easier to focus on a mantra,' Samnang said. 'Something like *peace* or *calm* or *silence*. Perhaps visualise a peaceful place—a quiet forest, or a tranquil lake.' He closed his eyes and tapped a bundle of reeds against a small gong. 'Let's begin.' The chime reverberated through the room and Charlotte observed him for a moment wondering if he would know if she didn't close her eyes. She took a deep breath. Annie had said Buddhism had helped her. She should give it a chance.

She inhaled the warm air, closed her eyes, then opened them again. Samnang sat still, eyes shut, hands upturned in his lap. Once again, she closed her eyes. Birds twittered in the trees outside the window, and the sound of children laughing and shouting echoed around the pagoda grounds. Her legs felt numb. The room was hot. Samnang began to chant, and she told herself to relax. There was nobody around, no reason to be self-conscious. Her mind started to wander. Had her mother found the batteries? Was she cooking meals for herself? She forced her mind back to the present. Breathe. Focus on a lake. What lake? Maybe the pond at the bottom of the garden. Or the swimming pool at their old house. She suppressed a giggle and cracked open her eyes. Samnang still sat motionless; eyes shut. She closed her eyes again and breathed deeply. Was Trevor going to yoga classes without her? Did he miss her?

A plane flew overhead. Where had Rashid gone after he left the airport, she wondered. Stop thinking. Recite a mantra. *Peace.* She inhaled and immediately saw images of Roxy, Peter, and Annie and thought of all the experiences she'd had since leaving England. She was far from everything that could hurt her; surrounded by people who accepted her. An image of her father popped into her mind. She could almost smell the aroma of his aftershave and feel the softness of his cashmere sweaters. Her breathing deepened as she imagined the comforting feeling of his arms around her. A tear slipped from her eye and rolled to the corner of her mouth. Samnang continued to chant. She opened her eyes, brushed the tear away, then closed them again, soothed by the memory.

After a few minutes, Samnang tapped the gong. 'Now bring your mind back to the room,' he said. He laid the gong on a table beside him and smiled at Charlotte. 'How was that for you?' he asked. 'I bet you're feeling a bit uncomfortable.'

Charlotte straightened her legs and let out a deep breath. 'I've done yoga for years, but never held any position that long, especially on a hard floor. And it's impossible to think about nothing. How do you do it?'

'That's our first lesson.' He lit a stick of incense and blew on it before inserting it into the neck of a glass bottle on the floor beside him. 'Life is suffering. It's the first of the Buddha's Four Noble Truths.' He picked up a book and opened it. 'According to Buddhism, there are three kinds of suffering,' he read. 'The first is the obvious suffering caused by physical discomfort, whether it's from stubbing your toe, hunger, lack of sleep, or chronic disease.' He paused. 'Or from sitting on a hard floor. It's also the emotional suffering you feel when things don't go your way. Or when you're worried about money or meeting other people's expectations.'

Charlotte sighed loudly.

'The second is the suffering caused by life's constant changes. No single moment is reliable because the next comes along fast on its heels. So, the mind never finds a place to sit back and enjoy life without fear.' He closed the book and placed his hand on the cover. 'The third is all-pervasive suffering. That's the fear which constantly exists, no matter what's going on in our lives. In Buddhist literature it's compared to a fatal disease that hasn't fully ripened, since its presence is always there and growing every minute.'

Charlotte stretched her arms above her head and arched her back. 'Are you're saying I'm always going to have problems, no matter what I do with my life? That I can never relax?' She frowned. 'Why would this appeal to you? Or to anyone?'

'In the Buddha's first sermon, he said *I teach one thing and one thing only: suffering and the end of suffering*,' Samnang said. 'That doesn't mean physical pain. It refers to the mental suffering we have when our tendency to hold onto pleasure comes upon the fleeting nature of life, so our experiences become unsatisfying and uncontrollable. The idea of suffering is a central thought in Buddhist practice. In Pali, the word is *dukkha*, roughly translated as *suffering*. It's sometimes translated as *unsatisfactoriness* or *stress*—words we can relate to better.'

Charlotte furrowed her brow. 'I don't get it. Why would anyone study a doctrine that's about suffering? I thought Buddhism taught acceptance, and non-attachment, and peace? Isn't it stressful to immerse yourself in something dealing with unsatisfactoriness? And who uses words like that anyway?'

Samnang smiled. 'I don't, usually. I didn't study many seven syllable words at school. But I bet there are plenty.' He closed his eyes. 'Let's see. How about telecommunications. And decriminalization.'

Charlotte grinned, up for a challenge. 'Onomatopoeia. Industrialisation.'

'Individuality,' Samnang said with a grin. 'And familiarisation. Those are words we can use in a Buddhist context, and I bet you can relate to them. I'm guessing you're on a path of individuality that brought you to Cambodia. And something has made you want to familiarise yourself with Buddhism.' He looked her in the eye. 'Am I right?'

It was as though he knew her. Had she told him anything about herself when she met him at Monsoon or was it so obvious she was searching for something? She was about to speak when she remembered Annie's guidance to call monks *Bhante,* a title that meant *venerable sir*, and took a deep breath. 'Bhante Samnang, I don't know if I'm on a path,' she said. 'I just feel stuck. I keep meeting people and landing in situations that feel as though they're happening for a reason, but I don't have a clue what that might be.'

'Tell me more.'

'There's a lot going on and I'd rather not go into it. But when Annie told me about Buddhism, I thought it sounded interesting. Then I bumped into you—literally.' She exhaled. 'Everyone keeps telling me things happen for a reason. I don't know if I'm buying that. And I don't want to study something that's all about suffering.'

'There's more than that,' Samnang said. 'I've studied Buddhism for years and at the time I was attracted to it for many of the same reasons you are. It *is* gentle and forgiving. It *is* about acceptance and letting go. But it's also about looking inside yourself.' He fingered a string of wooden prayer beads. 'Attachment is the root of suffering. Think about that for a minute. It took me a long time to realise I was attached to my own sense of right and wrong. I grew up with judgement and anger, so I was resentful, and determined to do things my way. Once I learned how to let go of that attachment, the world seemed a different place. It wasn't, of course. But it was different inside me.'

Wisps of incense hung in the air. A bird flew through the

window, fluttered around the room, then settled on the sill as Samnang spoke.

'In the *Dhammapada*—that's one of the Buddhist scriptures —it says, *Better it is to live one day wise and meditative than to live a hundred years foolish and uncontrolled.* We must take one step at a time. You're not going to learn everything about Buddhism in one hour with me, you know, as much as you might like to.'

Charlotte wrapped her arms around her knees. Samnang's words made sense and she felt she could trust him. 'I met a man recently who said the same,' she said. 'He told me most things weren't predictable and advised me to keep an open mind.'

'And how do you feel about that?'

She shrugged. Her shoulders were starting to tense again. This wasn't what she'd expected from a Buddhist lesson. Wasn't she supposed to be listening to Samnang, not the other way around? It had been such a long time since anyone had expressed interest in her that she suddenly felt awkward and reluctant to say more. Then she remembered a tip her father had given her: When you feel self-conscious, ask questions.

'Can I change the subject?' she asked. 'I'd like to know more about you, if you don't mind. What was your name before you became a monk? How did you end up in Cambodia, teaching Buddhism to people like me?' She took a breath. 'Are you allowed to tell me?'

Samnang rested his hands in his lap. 'Of course. My name was Robin. Like the bird.' He gazed through the open door into the leafy courtyard. 'My path into Buddhism was partly by design and partly by chance. If you believe in Fate, it was preordained.'

'How so?'

'When I was seventeen, a friend took me to a meditation

class. It wasn't my cup of tea since I was more into self-loathing and victimization. I only went because it was next door to a pub, and I figured I could sneak out for a pint while everyone had their eyes closed.'

'You weren't always spiritual?'

Samnang chuckled. 'My idea of spiritual was watching *The Sixth Sense* with a few cans of beer. I was an angry teenager who blamed everyone else for what went wrong in my life. My friend, Harry, worked in the newsagent where I bought my cigarettes and I agreed to go to his *medication* class for a laugh —that's what I called it. I thought he'd like me more if I shared his interests.' His eyes clouded over as he smoothed his robe. 'I hated it. My back hurt, and I spent the entire time thinking about someone who was making my life miserable and plotting how to get back at him. Instead of getting relaxed and reflective, I became irritated and revengeful. I couldn't even sneak to the pub because Harry insisted we sit right at the front.

'After the meditation, a woman came to give a guest lecture. She was a tiny little thing with a shaved head and a face like a Botticelli angel. I didn't think much of her at the time; just figured she was some guru with a message to push.' He glanced toward the statues at the head of the temple and took a deep breath. 'Her name was Ani Pema. I thought Ani was her first name, then found out it meant *nun* in Tibetan. She told us she'd been a heroin addict in London and stole money to buy drugs. She tried to commit suicide twice, and both times she was saved by a stranger. Her voice was so soft I could hardly hear her. But when she talked, she stared right at me. It felt weird at first, but I got caught up in her story, then in her gentle energy. There were more than forty people in the class, and she didn't pay attention to anyone else. It was as if she knew. So, when we left the room, I didn't go to the pub. I went to the park and cried.'

SAMNANG WATCHED Charlotte as she left the room. Not long ago I was like her, he thought, his mind slipping back to one of his first days in Cambodia when he was trying to adjust to his surroundings. He had been sitting cross-legged on the pagoda floor, sweat running down the back of his neck and clouds of mosquitos swarming around his face. He remembered how his skin had prickled with perspiration and waves of nausea washed over him, no doubt brought on by the lukewarm rice from that morning's food donation. Every day had brought new challenges. Some small, such as how to cross busy roads, how to address senior monks, and where to buy sandals. Some complex and demanding, like how to sleep on a stone floor, how to communicate, and how to conduct himself as a western monk in an Asian country. Even though he'd studied Khmer for three months. his limited knowledge of the language was virtually useless unless he needed to ask for food or directions.

Other novice monks had helped him settle in. They'd showed him where to sleep (in a tiny alcove with a straw mat), where to shower (outside, in a concrete enclosure), and where to gather for Morning Prayer. He'd learned that almost every Cambodian male over the age of sixteen spent time as a monk —some for less than a year, some for life—and many chose monkhood as a path out of poverty and a way to become educated.

Since he'd practised Buddhism for five years before he came to Cambodia, he was used to the social hierarchy and precise rules for practicing monks. Never carry money or sleep in a comfortable bed. Don't participate in any form of entertainment such as singing, dancing, or watching TV. Don't eat or touch food between noon and dawn; the right time to eat begins when the day is light enough to see the lines on the palms of one's hand. Always chant after eating. Never ask for anything without it being offered unless you are sick. But it was different being here, far from home. The rules were no longer in a book; they were his reality.

It had been a long, difficult road, and it was now hard for him to relate to the person he used to be. The early years of pain and self-recrimination were distant nightmares. His present way of life had taken hold in the same easy way he had slipped into his Buddhist name. He was no longer Robin, he was Samnang—a name selected to describe his character and journey.

Not long ago, his life had consisted of sleeping till noon and waking with a hangover. In England, he'd spent most of his days as a short-order cook in the *Smiling Cow* vegetarian restaurant, then drinking in the pub until midnight. Now his days began at four in the morning with two hours of meditation and chanting. At 6 a.m. he joined the other monks to walk barefoot through the city with a battered aluminium bowl to receive food offerings from local people who wanted spiritual blessings. His feet were often blistered and cracked from the heat of the street, and his back throbbed from nights spent on concrete floors. But he was the happiest he'd ever been.

Something about Charlotte reminded him of himself. Perhaps it was her loneliness and the critical way she looked at herself. Or maybe it was the desire she had to be a better person. Either way, he was determined to help her.

14

Roxy looked up when Charlotte walked into the flat. 'You hungry?' she asked, waving an open bottle of nail varnish. 'There's leftover fish soup in the fridge.' She went back to painting her toenails.

Charlotte dropped her bag, and grimaced. 'I don't think so,' she said. 'That's been there since last Sunday. I'll make myself a sandwich.'

'First, call Alistair. He's trying to reach you.' Roxy dragged her laptop from beneath the couch and pushed it toward her. 'He sent me a message on Facebook. Said he sent you one, too.'

'Alistair?' Charlotte's heart sank. The tranquil feeling she had brought from the pagoda evaporated. 'What does he want?'

'He wants to send you ten million dollars to create a sanctuary for rare orchids.' Roxy shook her head. 'How the heck would I know. He's *your* uncle.'

Charlotte's mind raced. She had been hoping for a quiet night at home with Roxy and wasn't ready to handle family issues. If Alistair wanted to reach her, it could only be about her mother. She sighed. 'Can't I ever have a moment to myself?' she muttered, frustrated.

'Sounds like your Buddhist lessons were successful,' Roxy said with a smirk.

Charlotte ignored her then paused as she eased the laptop open. Any engagement with Alistair could only be unpleasant. 'Self-flagellation,' she muttered, and snapped the laptop shut. She tapped on the cover with her fingertips and chewed on her lower lip. A few seconds later she sighed, opened it again and launched Skype. Best to get it over with. She clicked on her uncle's number and watched the images spin on the screen. No answer. With a groan, she flopped onto a cushion on the floor, balanced the laptop on her lap, and dialled again. Still no reply. She went to the kitchen, took a bottle of water from the fridge then returned and tried one more time. Again nothing. So, she closed the lid and put the laptop back on the coffee table. She'd done her duty—three times with no answer.

Roxy screwed the top back on the bottle of nail polish. 'He'll call back if he needs you,' she said.

'What if something has happened?'

'As I said, he'll call back if he needs you. What've you been up to? I've missed you.'

'Not much. Actually—' She paused. She wanted to keep her conversation with Samnang to herself for a while. Even though she had only spent an hour with him, there was something calming about him that made her feel different, more aware there were other ways to see the world. She'd never met anyone like Samnang, and she wished she could ask him what to do about the feelings that were bubbling up in her now. She had just started to forget about home and now this, another reminder of the shadow that always hung over her.

'Hello?' Roxy called from across the room. 'You still here? I asked what you've been doing while we were away. Surely you found an adventure or two in this insane city.'

Charlotte reached into her bag. 'Actually, yes,' she said, pulling out a silk scarf and holding it up. 'For you. You've probably got dozens, but...' She shrugged.

Roxy took the scarf and draped it around her neck. 'It's my colour.' She sighed. 'I'm sorry you got caught up in this trauma. I feel badly leaving you alone so much when it's meant to be your holiday.'

Charlotte leaned back on the cushions. 'No need to worry about me. I worry enough about myself.' She grimaced. 'I wish I could be more like you.'

'Are you mad? Why?'

'The way you deal with things. You're so brave and I'm afraid of everything.'

'Like your mum?'

'Like her, and flying, and getting sick, and saying stupid stuff. And doing the wrong thing, and putting on the wrong clothes...' She exhaled, then let out a short laugh. 'D'you remember when you did that? Went out wearing two different boots?'

Roxy ran a hand through her spiky hair. 'I had more on my mind than what I was wearing that day. I was worried to death about you.'

Charlotte's mind flashed back to a time that haunted her. It had been an early evening in October, the year she had turned eighteen. Her mother had accused her of plotting to have her sent to a rehab facility, then thrown a glass decanter. Charlotte had run from the house. The wind had been frigid and dark clouds were gathering, but she hadn't noticed or cared. All she'd wanted was get as far away as possible. She'd found herself on the seafront, dressed only in the light cotton dress she'd been wearing in the centrally heated house, and kept walking along the shoreline, hands buried in pockets, cheeks burning with hurt and resentment. She was never going back. That would show her. Her sandal had caught on a rock and she'd tripped, cutting the side of her foot on a piece of glass buried beneath the pebbles. Blood trickled from her ankle and she'd tumbled onto the pebbly ground where she remained, arms wrapped around herself trying to keep warm. She wasn't sure how long she'd stayed, staring at the waves, her mind numb with misery. Then, the sound of shouting. A beam of light and Roxy's voice calling her name as she clambered across the pebbles and pulled her into her arms.

A voice snapped her back to the present. 'That's what did it for me,' Roxy said.

'Huh?'

'I thought you'd given up.'

Charlotte swallowed a lump in her throat. 'I don't really want to...Rox, can't we move on?'

Roxy picked a speck of lint from her blouse. 'We all have shitty things in our past, you know,' she said, softly. 'One day I'll tell you mine. I guarantee it's much more memorable.' She bit her bottom lip and looked away. 'Just not now.'

There was something in Roxy's voice Charlotte hadn't heard before. A tone that sounded as though she had something to share and didn't know how to. It only lasted a brief moment, then the same old Roxy was back, eyes flashing and a crooked smile on her face.

'Hey, how about you acknowledge yourself, for a change,' she said, taking a sip from a bottle of water then handing it to Charlotte. 'It took guts for you to get on a plane to come here, you know. Or maybe you don't. But you got the hell out of England and you no longer sit at home with the cat when I go to work. You also don't seem so neurotic.' She ducked when Charlotte threw a pillow at her. 'By the way, you forgot to wipe that water bottle before you drank from it.' She pulled a face. 'Now, if you can just ease up on that bug spray—it's suffocating me.' She chuckled. 'Anyway, tell me how you've been managing without me. Met any more handsome monks? Saved any more wild critters?'

Charlotte told her about her day trip across the river and described the Silk Farm and the Cambodian boys who helped her. 'People have been so kind,' she said. 'I've had so many experiences and I'm falling a little bit in love with this country.' She stopped. 'Oh! But I saw...' She inhaled deeply.

'You okay?'

'Hasan.'

'Who?'

'Hasan. The man with the cat. Where we rescued Toyota, remember. I saw him on the ferry.'

'So? Did he see you?'

'I don't think so. Do you think he's still looking for Toyota?'

'No way in hell,' Roxy said. 'He's probably looking for the fat blonde who threatened him with a bike helmet. He doesn't give a shit about Toyota.' She nudged Charlotte with her elbow. 'You care more about a cat than your best friend, don't you? Come on, admit it, or I'll pelt you with mothballs!'

Charlotte pushed her away. 'I'm serious Rox. I never want to see that horrible man again.'

'Then, don't,' Roxy said. 'However, you might. It's weird how often people bump into one another here. I'm always seeing the same people. And I'm not the only one. Peter tells me he's constantly—'

Charlotte interrupted. 'Do you think Hasan has family here?'

'Family? How would I know. Why d'you want to know?'

'There's a woman. Someone I met.'

'What d'you mean?'

'In Monsoon, the other night at the party. She's Bangladeshi and she told me she had a cousin named Hasan. I was just wondering......?'

'If it's the same Hasan?' Roxy laughed. 'Don't be daft. Does she have hairy arms and tattoos?'

'Now that you mention it!' Charlotte grimaced. 'More like a female Godzilla, really. Enormous breasts, long greasy hair, mouth as foul as a West End hawker. She thinks she's God's gift to men. I can't remember her name.'

'A Bengali chick with a filthy mouth and enormous boobs?' Roxy said. 'That can only be one person. I think her name's Chris. Or Chrissy. Or whatever she's calling herself.'

Charlotte nodded. 'That's it! Christal.' She pouted and tossed her hair, imitating Christal's voice, *Bubbly, expensive and intoxicating like the champagne*. It must be the same one. How do you know her?'

'She flounced into my shop a couple of weeks before Christmas, reeking of hairspray and Gloria Vanderbilt cologne. Told me she wanted to buy something gorgeous to make her more appealing. Yup, she actually said that. Made me want to puke into my soy latte. But I needed the business, so I sold her a fabulous red silk skirt. She could barely squeeze her bum into it, but she insisted she liked the voluptuous look and waltzed out with it.' Roxy stood up and paced across the living room. 'Would you believe she brought it back five days later? Her fat backside burst the stitching. And madam wanted a refund. Know why? *Badly made merchandise*. I told her very nicely I couldn't give her money back because she'd worn it and it was her stupid fault for ripping it—no, I didn't say stupid—'

'That doesn't sound like you.'

'Yeah, right. But you'll never guess what she did. Threatened to phone one of her boyfriends. The one who's Minister of Commerce. Said she was gonna report me for running a shoddy business and have mister boyfriend close me down. Told me Cheng or Feng or whatever his name was wanted to keep her happy so she wouldn't tell his wife about him. What a bitch.'

'What did you do?'

Roxy's eyes blazed. 'What could I do? Gave the witch her money back. I just hope I never see her ugly, pockmarked face again or I won't be responsible for the outcome.' She shook her head and grunted.

Charlotte grabbed Roxy's hand and pulled her onto the couch beside her. 'Rox—I don't suppose—You don't think—?'

'Don't think what?'

'You called her Chris.'

'Yup. Stupid bitch. Egotistical monster. Christal's too fancy a name for that tart. If I ever see her on the street, I'll go and—'

'Chris? From Bangladesh. You don't think....?'

Roxy stared at Charlotte. 'I have no idea what you—'

'Chris,' Charlotte repeated. 'Roxy, think!'

Roxy's eyebrows rose a notch. 'Cripes, Charlo. You're not thinking...not that she might be *the* Chris?' Her eyes widened. 'You said Chris was a man.'

'I assumed it.' Charlotte ran to the bedroom, grabbed the letter from under her pillow, and dashed back to the living room. She unfolded the pages and breathlessly read out loud. *'You were no longer my child.... You weren't the child I had hoped for....'* She stared at Roxy, dumbfound. 'He didn't say *son*. He said *child*. What if this awful creature turns out to be the Chris I'm looking for?'

15

As Charlotte stood and stared at Rashid's letter, the sound of an incoming Skype call broke the silence. It was Alistair. She pulled a face and Roxy put a finger to her lips and tiptoed into the kitchen.

Charlotte pressed the talk button. 'Charlie?' Alistair's voice echoed through the room. 'Yer there, lass? I canna see your face.'

She turned on the camera. 'Hello Alistair. Is everything okay?' It had been more than a year since she'd seen his jowly face and mess of sandy hair, and he looked more frazzled than usual.

'Ah there you are. Gorgeous as ever. Ah've only got a minute as I'm aboot to lose service.' His gravelly Scottish accent was more pronounced than she remembered. 'No need ta worry. It's all okay. Just wanted ta let you ye know—'

'Let me know what?'

'Yer mum. She's in the hospital, love. No need fah concern. It's all okay.'

Charlotte was suddenly alert. 'What happened?' How many times was he going to say it was okay?

'She fell. Broke 'er wrist. They wanta check her oot so I'm on my way to see her now. No need to worry. It's all—'

'I got it, Alistair—it's all okay!' Charlotte echoed, wishing he would get to the point and stop placating her. 'How did she fall?'

'Climbing on something in yer room, she said. She dinnae want to stay at the hospital, but the doc persuaded her to stay fer a couple of tests. Ah just went to your hoose to pick up some things.'

Charlotte's heart sank. Her mother had fallen while looking for something in her bedroom. It must have been the batteries, and it had to have been her fault. She was always the one to blame. When the washing machine broke down, it was because Charlotte had been the last one to use it, when the electricity got shut off it was because Charlotte had forgotten to pay the bill (even though she'd never paid it before), and when the bus broke down on the way to work it was because Charlotte had told her this had been the best route to take. She held her breath, expecting to hear a snarky remark courtesy of her mother. Instead, Alistair lowered his voice and spoke in a gentler tone. 'There's more, Charlie,' he said 'Something about you...you need to know. I think there's—what ye might—found them in...' His voice broke up then faded away completely. The screen went black and Charlotte immediately redialled, anxious to hear what Alistair was about to tell her. No answer. She'd lost the connection.

'Damn it!' she shouted, grabbing a pillow from the couch and throwing it across the room.

Roxy appeared from the kitchen. 'What's up?' she asked. 'I

tried not to listen, but I did. Just didn't hear it all 'cos I dropped the cat food behind the fridge.'

'It's Mum.' Charlotte stared at her phone. 'She's in hospital.'

'Is she—?' Roxy paused. 'Hang on a minute. You sure? D'you think it's a trick to make you go home?'

Charlotte shrugged. 'That was Alistair. He wouldn't lie.' She sighed. 'Don't worry. I'm not going home. He said she's fine. But I don't know what to do.'

'What to do? Are you insane? You do exactly as you've been doing these past two weeks. Enjoy your bloody holiday. That's why Alistair's there, so you don't have to be her nursemaid.'

'I think there's something else. Alistair tried to say something, but we got cut off.'

'So, what does that mean?'

'What if something bad has happened? What if mum's worse than he said? What if—?'

'What if she's decided to have a sex change? What if Toyota's a Russian spy? What if Alistair's in love with Tom Cruise. Get a grip, Charlo. Enough what-ifs.' She grabbed Charlotte's arm and tugged her toward the kitchen. 'I've got a what-if for you. What if you don't eat anything and disappear down the drain on the balcony? There's nothing you can do till you hear from Alistair, so let's open a bag of cheese balls and roll them in peanut butter. Peter bought some last night and I've been dreaming about them all day.'

Charlotte pulled away. 'I'll be with you in a sec. Just need to get something.' She went to the bedroom and shut the door behind her. Her mother was in hospital. It was her fault. She sat on the bed and closed her eyes, tears welling up. She'd done it again. She'd created a problem, without even being there. Her gaze fell on her open suitcase in the corner of the room. A couple of colourful, cotton blouses were neatly folded inside—blouses she'd bought for her mother. A tear trickled down her cheek. She should never have come. Even far from home, she was on edge. Her mother's silence had felt like punishment and as hard as she tried to ignore it, it was always on her mind. She was twenty-four years old and still felt accountable for her every action. There must be a way to loosen the emotional cords that strangled her.

For years, she had wavered between depression, anger, and resignation. Some days she'd felt compassion for her mother as she watched her battle with alcoholism. Other times she'd resented her for making her life miserable. But she had always done what her mother wanted, then despised herself for being spineless.

She could hardly remember the time when they had been a happy family. It felt like a million years ago. She smiled as she pictured her mum and dad singing along with musicals on the telly. They had both known the words to every song from *The Sound of Music* and her dad's favourite had been *My Favourite Things.* Charlotte chuckled as she remembered the lyrics she'd made up with him one wintery afternoon.

Raisins on tables and chocolate on mountains.

Beards on mothers and tutus on fathers.

Monkeys that fly through the air like a jet.

These are some things that I'd like to forget.

'You okay?' Roxy yelled from the living room. 'The cheese balls are almost gone!'

Charlotte splashed water on her face, smoothed her hair, and went to join Roxy. As she entered the kitchen, a tapping sound came from the entrance to the flat. The front door swung open and Daro, the landlord, peered inside.

'Hello Miss Roxy,' he said, stepping into the room. 'And hello to you too, Miss Jallod.' He tucked his shirt into wrinkled trousers. 'Very sorry but have to speak about something.'

'What is it, Dara?' Roxy asked.

He stared at his shoes and stuck his hands deep into the pockets of his trousers. 'My wife,' he mumbled. 'She not happy. With cat. Bad luck for Cambodian. Dangerous for childrens so my wife not like cat to be here.' He stagger-stepped back and caught his shoe on a beanbag. Stumbling, he grabbed the edge of a wicker chair and knocked it to the floor with a clatter. As he reached out to steady himself, he caught his elbow on a shelf and knocked over a jar filled with peanuts, sending them flying. His face scarlet, he knelt and scooped up the nuts, dropping them back into the jar one at a time.

Charlotte glanced at Roxy whose face was turning pink with bottled-up laughter. She looked away before she too started to laugh.

'So very sorry, Miss Roxy,' Daro stammered, propping himself against the wall with one arm as he positioned the jar on the shelf. He giggled nervously then looked at his watch. 'Must to go now.' He pushed open the door and vanished.

Roxy slid down the wall onto the floor, tears running down her cheeks. 'Oh, that poor man,' she wheezed between hoots of laughter. 'He'll probably never set foot in this place again!' She clutched at her stomach. 'Ouch...my sides.' Her eyes widened. 'Shit...I hope he's gone!' She cracked open the door and peeked outside. 'All clear.' She wiped her eyes. 'Poor Daro! His wife's got him around her finger. Women call the shots in Cambodia, so she probably sent him up here. I bet he was dying from embarrassment before he even knocked on the door.'

Charlotte sat next to Roxy, chuckling. Then she grabbed her arm. 'He told us to get rid of Toyota. What do we do now?'

Roxy picked a peanut from the edge of the rug. 'I had a feeling this might happen. It sucks they're weird about cats, doesn't it?' She rolled the nut across the floor toward Toyota. 'Sorry, kitty. You'll have to find another home.'

Charlotte reached out and pulled the cat to her. 'Roxy! We are not getting rid of Toyota.'

'So, what do you propose we do? I'm not moving out. Neither's Peter. I'm sorry, the cat's gotta go.'

'Don't you have any friends who'd take him?'

'Seriously? Like any of them would risk losing their lodging. He'll be fine. He's a street cat.'

Charlotte held Toyota closer. 'He won't be fine. If you're not going to ask your friends, I'll find him a home.'

'Among the hundreds of people you know here? How d'you propose to do that?'

'I'll ask Samnang. There are stray cats at the pagoda. He'll know what to do.'

Roxy flopped onto a chair. 'Actually, that's not a bad idea. They probably *will* take him there. Top marks in figuring it out. Let's go now before Daro comes back with an exterminator.'

They bundled Toyota into a canvas bag and drove across town to the pagoda where Charlotte dismounted. Roxy revved the engine. 'I'll go home in case Alistair calls,' she said. 'I don't want to hang out with monks tonight. Call when you're ready to leave.'

CHARLOTTE WALKED UNDER A STONE ARCHWAY, gripping the bag with Toyota inside. The cat wriggled frantically so Charlotte held it tightly against her body, whispering words of reassurance as she walked down the path. She approached the room where she had first seen Samnang and peeked through the window. It was empty. A sweet scent of incense filled the air, and dozens of miniature Buddha statues stared at her in the gloomy light. She continued along the alley connecting the pagoda buildings, passing tall, leafy plants standing like shadowy sentries in the dark. A pair of elderly monks sat on a wooden bench, and a young monk splashed water over his face and arms from a water pump. Sonorous tones of chanting drifted from a nearby building so Charlotte walked toward the sound, using the glow from her phone to light the way.

Toyota mewled from inside the bag and she reached down to stroke his back. The chanting stopped and a group of monks emerged from the building. One walked alone, head bent. As he grew closer, he raised his head and looked her way. It was Samnang. She raised an arm and gave a small wave.

'Hey! What a nice surprise,' he said as he approached. 'I get to speak English again.'

Toyota wriggled and let out a loud yowl from inside the bag and Charlotte lunged for it as it started to slip from her grasp. 'Oh God! Toyota—Oh, Samnang. I mean Bhante Samnang. I'm sorry. I didn't mean to say God—It's just this cat...' She stammered, her face warming with embarrassment.

'Looks like you've got something interesting in there.' he said. 'And don't worry about saying God. It's allowed. Let's sit out here for a while, and you can let the cat out of the bag.' He chuckled. 'There are plenty of people around, so we won't be alone.' He smoothed his robe and sat on a wooden bench. 'So, what brings you here?' he asked.

'It's this cat. Nobody wants him.' She sat down and told him how she and Roxy had rescued Toyota from the Garden Café and how he had now been banished by their landlord. 'I can't abandon him after all he's been through,' she said, eyes glistening. 'I don't know what to do.'

Samnang reached out to Toyota. 'He's quite welcome to stay with me. It'll be nice to have another friend to speak English to. Unless he's been spending time with Khmer streets cats and doesn't understand my Cockney accent.'

Charlotte gripped the bag, reluctant to hand it over. The little cat had been good company and there had been many times she'd curled up with him on her bed, whispering endearments in his ear. It had made her feel safe and loved and she would miss his presence. She noticed Samnang looking at her with a puzzled expression and ran a hand through her hair. She hadn't intended to become emotional but there was something about letting go of Toyota that made her want to cry. Samnang's gaze swept from the cat to Charlotte's face. 'It's not just about the cat, is it?' He said gently. 'Something's troubling you.'

She chewed on her lower lip. The longer she stayed, the greater the chance she might reveal too much. Outside the pagoda walls, a car backfired, and Toyota leapt to the ground. Charlotte stood and shoved her hands into her pockets. 'I'd better go,' she said. 'Roxy's waiting. And I need to call my uncle.'

'As you wish. I'm here if you want to talk.' Samnang smiled tenderly, and Toyota rubbed against his leg. Charlotte looked at the cat, then at the monk. His gentle way touched her heart and reminded her how rarely she experienced genuine warmth and concern. Perhaps it would be okay if she stayed a while. That way she could spend time with Toyota, and delay talking to Alistair. She sat back down on an upturned urn and tried to speak, but no words came out. Tears sprang to her eyes and spilled down her cheeks as she pressed a hand over her mouth.

Samnang sat quietly, hands clasped in his lap. Two monks walked by carrying candles, and a warm breeze blew through the grounds of the pagoda. Charlotte took deep gulps of the warm night air, willing the feelings to subside. After a few minutes of silence, she lowered her chin and spoke in a whisper. 'Things are a bit of a mess.'

'Tell me.'

Words poured from her like lava from a volcano. She told Samnang about her mother being an alcoholic and her father leaving home. She described how alone she had felt after Roxy moved away, and talked about her boring job, her fear of leaving home, her desire for adventure, and her lonely existence in England. Eventually she took a deep breath and stared at her hands. 'There's so much I want to do, but I don't know how to do it.'

'How do you mean?'

'I want to travel like Roxy, but I don't have the courage, I want to leave my job but I need the salary, I want a relationship but I can't meet anyone. I'm just...' the words caught in her throat.

'What's holding you back?' asked Samnang.

'Everything,' she whispered. 'I spend all my time at work or at home with Mum and I don't have the chance to do what I want.'

'And why is that?'

'I feel badly leaving her alone.'

'For what reason.'

'I'm afraid.'

'Of what?'

'That she might hurt herself.'

She'd said it. She'd told a stranger something she'd never

allowed herself to articulate to anyone, not even herself. She wasn't sure what her mother would do if she wasn't there. That was the real reason she hadn't left with Roxy, or gone away, or held onto a relationship. She'd never known if her mother's threats had been made because she was drunk or because she wanted to hold onto Charlotte or if she would really harm herself. So, Charlotte had shouldered the burden.

Samnang kept eye contact as he asked in a gentle voice. 'She's your mother, Charlotte. You're the child.'

Charlotte stared, unblinking. 'But I had to—'

'You are not responsible. Not to her or for her. She's an adult and no matter how damaged you think she may be, she is only responsible for herself.'

'I'm all she has,' Charlotte said in a small voice.

'What happened to your father?'

'He left.'

Samnang slowly nodded. 'What happened?' he repeated.

'He didn't want to live with us anymore.' She paused. 'It was my mother's fault.'

'How so?'

Her throat tightened. 'Because she's a drunk and made life horrible for him. I didn't want to be there either—not without Dad—but I couldn't go. I wasn't strong enough. She ruined both our lives.' She glanced at him. Had she said too much? She'd had these thoughts many times before and never shared them with anyone except Roxy. But the way he listened, the way he asked questions and looked at her; somehow it felt safe, so she continued. 'I'm stuck,' she said. 'I don't want to stay at home. But I don't know where to go.' She wiped her eyes. 'I came here to get away. I wanted to visit Roxy and forget about home. Then my uncle called today. Mum's in hospital. I don't want to talk to her, but I can't ignore her if she's hurt. I'm *not* going home. Not yet. But I can't stay here forever.'

'It sounds as though you're dealing with a lot,' Samnang said. 'Perhaps I can help. First, you need to know you're never responsible for another person's actions, only your own. Second, guilt is a useless, destructive emotion. And third, seek tools that ground you.'

'Tools? Like earphones to block out her voice?' She pulled a face, embarrassed at her outburst. 'She never takes any interest in *my* life so why should I bother doing anything for her?'

'Tell me about a time you've dealt with a challenging situation,' Samnang said.

'What do you mean?'

'There must be other times when you've felt badly, not just with your parents.'

She leaned back and exhaled. 'I lost my best friend.'

'Tell me about it.'

'She was more interested in travelling the world than staying home. I can't say I blame her; I'd have done the same thing. But she didn't even keep in touch even though she knew I —' She looked away. This wasn't the time to talk about Roxy 'That's in the past. I don't want to talk about it.'

'You don't have to. I just wanted you to think of something that upset you and how you dealt with it.' Samnang sat forward. 'Every challenge provides an opportunity to grow. And, just as important, anything or anyone who troubles you can become your teacher.'

Charlotte sighed. How had she dealt with Roxy's leaving? She hadn't. She hadn't had the courage to speak to her best friend in case she upset her, but she'd resented her for leaving her behind. After she'd left, she'd cried a lot, and every time she'd received a message from Roxy telling her what a wonderful time she was having, she retreated a little further inside herself. But she never said anything to anyone—not even Trevor. Instead, she wrote light-hearted emails to Roxy telling her all about work and the animal shelter and movies she'd seen and the rotten weather and all kinds of inconsequential nonsense. Then she'd wallowed in her misery and beaten herself up for being a coward. She swallowed a lump in her throat. Her mother was right, she was useless at everything. Perhaps she *should* go home.

A beeping sound interrupted her thoughts, and Toyota leapt from her lap onto the ground. A vibration buzzed in her pocket and she pulled out her phone. 'It's Roxy,' she said, looking up at Samnang. 'Should I answer it?'

'Do as you wish.'

She punched the reject button then turned back to Samnang, an awkward expression on her face. 'I shouldn't have done that. She might worry about me.' She sent a quick text message: *Be free soon* and tucked the phone back in her pocket.

'So how *did* you deal with challenges in the past?' Samnang asked.

'I waited for them to go away.' She glanced down at her lap, wondering if she'd said too much. Nobody had ever asked her questions like this. 'I can't keep doing that, can I?'

'You can if you choose to. But I have a feeling you want to do things differently. May I offer a suggestion?'

She nodded.

"Follow your instincts and listen to your soul. When you can do that, you'll start doing more of the right things—just do them with confidence, not fear of consequence. Find a way to mentally separate yourself from issues and people that upset you. Then, take a deep breath and breathe peace into your heart. Slow things down and become grounded before you respond to anything, and you'll find you will know the right thing to do.'

Charlotte shook her head. 'There are too many voices in my head,' she said. 'I don't know which to listen to.'

Samnang picked a flower from beneath the bench and held it in his hand. 'We take our challenges with us wherever we go and the only way to escape is to face them head-on.' He said. 'Imagine you're floating in a pool. If you move your hand through the water, what happens?'

'You create ripples?'

'Exactly. But you don't create just one ripple, do you? You create many. It's the same thing in life. The ripples you produce go out into your universe and return as feedback.'

'I don't follow you. My actions create ripples, so the same things keep coming back?'

'Not really. Everything we do makes an impression, so it's important to be aware of our actions and to spread ripples of love, kindness, and acceptance, because that's what will come back. If you project fear, you'll receive the same in return. If you send out love, it will come back to you. You can't control what you get in life, but you can control how you deal with it.'

Charlotte took a deep breath. 'How do I learn to do that?'

'Practice. It took me a long time to discover how not to let other people's actions affect me.' His brow furrowed. 'Years ago, I had an experience that hurt me deeply. I walked away from someone I loved. Over time I forgave them, but I had a much harder time forgiving myself.'

'What happened?'

'This isn't the time to share it.' Samnang brushed a leaf from his robe. 'Buddhism doesn't celebrate revenge. Hatred and pain don't disappear easily so the only way through suffering it to let go of those emotions and move on.'

'I don't know if I can. I just want Mum to disappear. Then I won't have to deal with her.'

Samnang paused and rested his hands in his lap. After a few seconds, he spoke. 'Is that really what you want? Do you want her to disappear or do you want to get someone back who exists in your memory? Chances are, you won't be able to do either, so you'll need to make a choice: Create an existence that doesn't include your mother or find a way to keep her in your life. There's no right or wrong, it's up to you. Discover a way to accept her for what she is. Not to condone or condemn, but to find compassion for the path she's chosen. She has her own form of suffering and she's obscuring it with alcohol.'

'But that's not *my* problem.'

'Correct. It's not your problem. But remember, punishing the broken by pushing them away only keeps them broken. Be the stronger one. Find a way to deal with your pain. Then do what makes *you* joyful, wherever and whatever it may be. I have a feeling you won't find happiness until you do.'

Charlotte took a deep breath. She had never been given guidance in dealing with her challenges. But she'd never talked to anyone about them either. She'd always believed she should keep them to herself, and she'd done a good job at hiding them.

She sensed Samnang was waiting for her to say something, so she stood up. 'I need to go,' she said. 'Roxy's expecting me.' She checked her watch, then hoisted her bag onto her shoulder and put her hands together in a *sampeah*. 'I'll think about what you said. And thank you for looking after Toyota.'

As she turned to leave, she heard a scratching sound from the alleyway between the pagoda buildings. 'Toyota! Here kitty,' she called, peering down the dimly lit path. Nothing moved so she took another step, catching her sleeve on a nail sticking from the wall. She reached to unhook it and noticed a shadowy figure walk toward one of the stupas near Samnang. He looked familiar so she squinted to get a better look, then Toyota darted from a shrub and ran across her foot, diverting her attention. She turned back toward the stupa, but the man was no longer there. And all that remained in the alleyway was a silver-topped walking stick leaning on the wall.

16

Charlotte and Samnang walked through the gate and found Roxy perched on her scooter. She leapt up and the sudden shift of weight made it crash to the ground. She hauled it upright and brushed her hair back from her face. 'Well, hello,' she said, hauling the bike upright. 'Nothing like making an entrance, eh?' She turned to Charlotte. 'So, where's the kitty?'

'He's got a new home," Charlotte said, gesturing to Samnang. 'Roxy, this is Bhante Samnang. He's going to look after Toyota.'

Roxy bowed her head and put her hands together in a *sampeah*. 'Honoured to meet you, Bhante. Thanks for being a friend to Charlo and her adopted kitty.' She started the bike and nudged Charlotte toward the seat. 'Your uncle's trying to reach you and I said we'd be home in ten minutes.'

Charlotte's smiled evaporated. She said goodbye to Samnang and climbed on the bike, dreading the conversation she was about to have. The moment she walked through the door, her laptop made a loud buzz, so she slipped into the bedroom and closed the door behind her.

Alistair's face came into view on the screen. 'Is it too late ter talk?' he asked, pushing his spectacles up on his nose. 'Did ah keep you up?'

'Of course not. It's only ten o'clock. What's going on?'

'I'm here with yer mum, love. She want ta say hello.' He lowered his voice. 'Then ah'd like to talk to yer alone.' He passed the phone to Charlotte's mother who sat on a bed dressed in a pale green hospital gown. Her long, black hair fell limply on her shoulders, red-rimmed eyes like berries in a snowbank in her pale face.

Charlotte forced herself to smile. *Breathe. Remember Bhante Samnang's words. Be kind.*

The phone quivered in her mother's hand. 'Hello, darling girl,' she said. Tears glinted in her eyes as she ran a shaky hand through her hair. 'I miss you.'

Don't fall for the drama. Stay grounded. 'Hi, Mum. Are you okay?'

Her mother reached for a tissue and blew her nose. 'Of course I'm not okay. I'm alone, and I had a bad fall. If you hadn't hidden those batteries on top of your cupboard, it never would have happened.'

Here it comes. It's all my fault. Don't buy into it. Alistair said she's fine. 'I'm sure they'll give you something for the pain,' she said.

'Obviously. I'm in a hospital. But these nurses are useless. They never come when you need them. And there's nobody at home to help me.'

Charlotte took a deep breath. She had been expecting this,

but it was still hard to take. She forced a lightness that she didn't feel. 'What happened with the TV programme?' she asked.

Her mother stared blankly. 'I don't know what you're talking about.'

'The TV programme. The one you told me about, with the handbag exhibit. Did you see it?'

'You're kidding, right? How could I watch anything when I'm laid up with a broken ankle? There's no television in this ghastly room.'

Charlotte groaned. She couldn't say anything right. 'I'm sorry you're struggling, Mum. I wish I could help, but Uncle Alistair said you haven't done anything serious. I know you're going home in a couple of hours so—'

Her mother snorted. 'To an empty house.'

'How about I arrange for meals to be delivered? There's a service I heard—'

'Don't put yourself out. You seem to be having a wonderful time with your new friends and that Roxy girl.' She tightened the hospital gown around her neck and narrowed her eyes. 'D'you have any idea how hard it's been since you left?'

Charlotte's face heated up. Here we go again; all about her. And how dare she refer to her oldest friend as *that Roxy girl.* She looked away, focusing her gaze on the electrical wires outside her window and wishing she were anywhere other than on the phone with her mother. 'I'm sorry to hear,' she said. 'But I was hoping to hear from you. Did you get my other emails?'

'Of course. I replied to every one. You must be too busy to read them.'

Lies. She's defending herself again. Don't take the bait.

'Well, let's just make a better effort to keep in touch, shall we? I'm always available if you need to reach me, and Uncle Alistair's right there.'

'How lucky I am. He's my angel; the only thing that keeps me going.' She glanced away, looking at something across the room. 'I need to go. The nurse just arrived to discharge me. It'll be a struggle to move, so I need to save my energy.' She grimaced. 'The next four weeks will be really, really hard till you get back. I hope they pass quickly.'

Charlotte found herself looking at the hospital floor then at the bottom of an armchair as the mobile phone dropped from her mother's hand and landed with a thud on the ground. *I guess she's finished talking to me. Not a single question about how I'm doing. Not even a goodbye.* Anger and disappointment welled up in her chest. There had been so many conversations like this, she could practically write the script. *How are you doing? No, how am* I *doing? Did you forget to get in touch with me? What have you been doing to keep you so busy that you couldn't call?* She recalled Samnang's advice: *Punishing the broken by pushing them away or walking away only ensures they remain broken.* She's hurt. She's alone. She's an alcoholic.

The next minute she heard someone pick up the phone, then Alistair's face reappeared. 'Hang on a minute, love,' he said. 'Yer mum's getting dressed and ah want to talk to yer. I'm gonna walk to my car so we can have a chat.'

What now? Was he going to ask her to come home? She couldn't—wouldn't—consider leaving Cambodia yet. She needed more time. More time with Samnang and Roxy. More time to figure out what to do with her life.

She caught sight of the car park as Alistair walked outside, then the screen steadied when he settled into his car. 'Okay then. Sorry aboot that.' He swiped a lock of hair from his eyes and met her gaze. 'She's really fine, you know. Just needs ter be dramatic.' He made a face. 'She's gone downhill since ah was here last, hasn't she? All she wants tae do is drag me to the pub. But ah don't drink anymore so she thinks ah'm boring.'

So much for the devoted brother, the angel.

'But there's somethin' ah want to discuss with yer.' *Here it comes. She needs you. You have to come home.*

'Ah found something yer need to know aboot.' Alistair's gaze drifted, as if uncomfortable with the conversation.

Charlotte's pulse quickened. Was her mother hiding alcohol again?

'When yer mum learnt she had to stay in the hospital she asked me ter pick up some of her things from home.' He scratched behind his ear as his voice faltered. 'Ah couldna find her overnight bag, had to search all over the hoose for it.' His tone changed to a more casual pitch. 'It's quite messy since you left, by the way. Ah dinnae think she does much in the way of cleaning, and there's a pile of laundry outside the kitchen door.'

Charlotte fidgeted. She had no interest in what he was saying and wanted to get to the point. 'What are you trying to say, Uncle Alistair?

He cleared his throat. 'Ah started poking aroond to find a bag or somethin' I could put her clothes in. There are lots drawers filled with makeup, and bags of shoes. Some of the makeup's old so I was thinking of tossing it oot and makin' a wee bit of space, but figured she might—'

Charlotte interrupted, recalling her uncle's penchant for boring people with details nobody cared about. 'Uncle Alistair, *please.* What do you want to tell me?'

His eyes darted away. 'Ah found somethin' under her bed,' he said. 'Somethin' that's been there a long time.' He rolled down the car window. A puff of steam came from his mouth as he breathed in and out in the cold air. He cracked his knuckles, shivered, and wound the window back up again. 'It was a box of letters,' he said, then paused and adjusted the rear-view mirror. 'They were addressed tah you.'

'Me? Why me?'

'They're from yer dad, love.'

Charlotte gripped the phone tighter. Her mind went blank. 'I don't understand.'

'Ah didnae read them. Just glanced at a couple ter see what they were aboot.' His voice picked up speed. 'They were written years ago. Your dad started writing tae yer when he left home.'

Confusion pulled her into a mental vacuum. Alistair was wrong. She'd never received anything in the post from him, not in all the years she'd been waiting to hear something. There hadn't been any letters. Not for her.

She realised she was holding her breath and that Alistair was speaking her name. 'Charlie? Yer there?' he asked.

She wanted to tell him to stop talking; that she didn't want to hear any more of his lies. 'You're wrong,' she whispered. 'I didn't get anything. They're not for...' A lump caught in her throat, preventing her from speaking.

'I'm sorry, love,' Alistair said quietly. 'I know what this means.'

'It's not...I haven't...' Charlotte struggled to form a sentence, then realisation sunk in. Waves of shock intensified into a tsunami of rage as she put the pieces together and understood. Her mother had lied to her. All these weeks and months after her father had left, when her mother had moaned about being left alone, and taken out her bitterness on anyone who would listen, she'd been a fake. A liar. She had hidden the letters. She'd told Charlotte her father had forgotten about her. Anger shot through her chest like an electric current as her mind spun with infinite scenarios. She clutched the phone in her hand, unshed tears glistening in her eyes.

Alistair cleared his throat. 'There's more, love,' he said, softly. 'Roxy knows.'

17

The blood rushed to Charlotte's head as Alistair's words sank in. 'What do you mean?' Her voice trembled.

Alistair removed his glasses, breathed onto the lenses, and rubbed them with a handkerchief. 'Ah dinnae want ter tell ye anything out of context. All I know is yer dad mentions yer friend Roxy. Ah'll scan the letters and send them to yer. I'm going to the office now, so ah'll get them to ye this afternoon. By the way, I didnae tell yer mum I found them.' His eyes darted toward the parking lot. 'Dammit, it's started raining. Ah hope it doesn't last long because I...'

Charlotte tuned out. She was aware of his voice in the background and waited for a break in his monologue to say goodbye and hang up. Her mind reeled as she replayed his words. *I found a box of letters...addressed to you*. Then his parting remark: *Roxy knows.*

She heard voices and realised Roxy was in the next room. Charlotte edged open the bedroom door, eager to tell her about the call with Alistair, then realised Roxy was on the phone. 'She's acting weird again,' Charlotte heard her whisper. 'Better not tell her yet.' Charlotte half expected Roxy to turn and see her in the doorway, but she was too engrossed in the conversation to realise anyone was listening.

Charlotte grabbed her bag and stuffed her feet into her shoes. Roxy was talking about her. This wasn't the time to speak about her father. She scribbled a note on a scrap of paper: *Going for a walk. Don't wait up,* dropped it on the coffee table, and slipped through the door. As she stepped onto the street she shivered despite the warmth of the evening. A tuk-tuk driver shouted out, 'Tuk-tuk, lay-dee? You want ride?' She shook her head and quickened her pace, hoping he'd go away.

Tramping down one road and up another, she paid no attention to where she was going. She walked on and on, into the maze of streets crisscrossing Phnom Penh, leaving the neighbourhoods she knew and stumbling into new ones. Here, the uneven pavements were cracked, and discarded Styrofoam containers littered the road. A rat crept from a pothole; she flinched and kept on walking. Her eyes burned from crying and for the first time since arriving in Cambodia, she felt completely alone. She couldn't turn to Roxy, Samnang would be asleep, she didn't want to bother Annie. There was nobody.

As she stood on the edge of a street, a shrill female voice yelled, 'Charlene! Over here!' She glanced in the direction of the voice, wondering who could be calling. Through the window of a dimly lit saloon, a plump, suntanned arm waved in her direction. The woman called again. 'Charlene! It's Christal. Come have a drink!'

Charlotte looked away, pretending she hadn't heard. Then the wooden shutters on the bar window crashed open as Christal leaned through it, flashing her breasts to anyone who passed by. 'Hey! Remember me? From Monsoon?' she yelled before Charlotte had the time to walk away. 'Get your arse in here!'

Charlotte grimaced. Typical that Christal would show up now. And it was clear she wasn't going away. She took a deep breath. Maybe a night in a bar was what she needed. Something to take her mind off her mother and Roxy and Alistair and the letters. A drip fell on her head and she looked up. Another fell into her eye, followed by more. It was raining. That wasn't typical for this time of year, but she didn't want to get wet and she didn't care to linger on the street, so she decided to take her chances in the bar. Maybe just one drink.

She pushed open the door and recoiled at the scene in front of her. A young Cambodian girl wearing skin-tight satin shorts, a bikini top, and shiny platform shoes sat on the edge of a bench fondling the thighs of two obese western men sitting next to her, while the men took turns pinching her cheeks and rear end. Standing next to them, a petite brunette in a mini skirt poured beer from a cracked brown jug into the men's glasses. Every few minutes, the men peeled dollar bills from a wad of cash and stuffed them down the girls' bras, and everyone screamed with laughter.

Charlotte turned back toward the doorway. She opened the door to leave then jumped back inside when torrents of rain poured from the roof into the gutters.

'Charlene! Over 'ere.' At the counter, Christal was straddling a barstool, dressed in clingy, white trousers and a see-through black top exposing a lace bra the same scarlet as her lipstick. Her arm was draped across the shoulders of a deathly-pale, emaciated woman with closely cropped, jet-black hair and painted-on eyebrows. On the bar were four empty shot glasses. Charlotte slowly walked toward them. Bon Jovi blasted from a jukebox, and the plank floor was sticky beneath her feet. Dingy lights shone onto beer posters with pictures of scantily clad women, and male customers huddled in dim corners with bar girls draped across their laps. She glanced down at herself. Dressed in a modest, knee-length denim skirt, pink cotton top, and linen jacket, she felt like a baby dove in a basket of vipers.

Christal summoned the bartender with a wave of her arm. 'Borey, another tequila shot! Fuck it, make it three.' She patted the stool next to her as Charlotte approached. 'Plonk yer backside here, darlin'. Flippo just arrived, so I'm showing her the seedy side of town. When in Asia, start with the ladyboy bars, 'ey?' She snorted with laughter at Charlotte's bewildered expression. 'Did yer think they were girls, babycakes? So do those assholes over there, panting to get them back to their hotel rooms. It's the best entertainment in town when they find out their beautiful little girlies are really beautiful little boys!'

The bartender placed three shot glasses in front of them. Charlotte remained standing, unsure if she wanted to stay. Her phone beeped so she glanced at it and saw a text from Roxy: *R U Okay?* She replied with one word: *Fine*, then switched off the phone and shoved it to the bottom of her bag. Christal and Flippo looked at her expectantly, their glasses poised in mid-air, so she forced a smile and picked up her glass. Roxy's message had convinced her; she was staying.

'Cheers!' Christal shouted over a blast of loud music. 'Or *sokhapeep la'aa*, as they say in this part of the world!' She clinked her glass against Charlotte's then Flippo's, drained the tequila, and slammed the glass on the bar.

Charlotte took a deep breath. '*Sokhapeep la'aa* back to you,' she mumbled, and drank the shot. It tasted sweet and the alcohol burned her throat. A tingling sensation spread across her chest. It felt good.

Flippo tucked her black tank top into tight, leather shorts. 'One more, Borey. Keep 'em coming!' She winked at the bartender then squeezed Christal's thigh. 'Great first night innit? My Christal always shows me the bubbles.' She kissed Charlotte on the cheek. 'Cool to meet you, Charlene.'

'Charlotte,' she murmured, then realised nobody was listening and she didn't really care. She wasn't interested in making new friends, she just wanted to stop thinking about Alistair's call. Alcohol had always been a good solution when she'd wanted to block something out and she was already starting to feel better. She thought of all the times when she'd sat in her room with a bottle of Scotch (or Drambuie or Baileys or gin), listening to music on her headphones, drifting away to a peaceful place where numbness took over, and realised she could do the same here. So, she held out her glass every time the bartender returned to fill it and tried to forget what had driven her here.

An hour later, her head was spinning. Her cheeks blazed, and her throat felt like sandpaper. She leaned against the bar and glanced down at her jacket, crumpled in a puddle of beer on the floor. She bent over to pick it up but the room swam in circles, so she sat back on her stool, leaving it on the ground.

Draping one arm around Christal, she slammed a fist on the counter. 'I'm having a ferry fun time with my new friends.' She lurched across the bar, waving a ten-dollar bill at the bartender. 'Next round's on me! Who needs friends when you...when you have friends?' She raised a beer mug above her head and tossed her hair back over her shoulders. 'I mean, who needs old friends when you have new friends? *Soccer peep la haa*!' She giggled.

'New friends are the best, innit?' slurred Christal. 'Here's to new friends. My new family! Ackshulee my only family since my real family sucks.' She burst out laughing, spraying a mouthful of beer across the bar.

How sad, Charlotte thought, then she sighed. *My family sucks too*. Her mind suddenly flashed onto Rashid's letter. There was a way she could make things better for Christal; let her know there was someone in her family who cared. She squinted at her watch. Midnight. She picked up a pint mug, splashing beer onto the bar. 'Happy new day!' she clinked her glass against Christal's. 'Here's to a fabulously wonderfilled day of new friends and old preeblums. I mean probleems. No, I mean...prahblems!' Giggling, she leaned toward Christal. 'I have something speshull to tell you, my byootifol new friend. But first, I really, really have to pee.'

She wobbled in the direction of the bathroom in her bare feet. Her flip-flops had slipped under the bar and the soles of her feet picked up crumbs and fragments of dirt on the sticky floor as she crossed the room. Shoving open the door to the ladies' room, she lurched inside, then leaned against the counter where she stared at a poster which was taped to the wall. The edges were curled and the tape coated with dust, but the words were large and easy to read.

To find the lotus, go to the mud.

Jump in the mud.

Swim in the mud.

You will find you were the lotus all along.

She leaned on the sink, fighting waves of nausea as she looked at herself in the mirror. Wisps of hair stuck to her forehead and one of her earrings had disappeared. She read the poster again and the words swum before her eyes. All of a sudden, Samnang's words echoed in her head: *Every action you make causes ripples. You can't control what you get in life, but you can control how you deal with it.* She turned on the tap, cupped her hands and filled them with water, splashed her face and ran her tongue over her cracked lips. This wasn't the solution. It was only making things worse. Her hand slipped inside her bag and she touched Rashid's letter. Not the time or the place.

She walked back into the bar where Christal and Flippo spun around the tiny dance floor, arms wrapped around one another's waists. Christal's blouse was unfastened, exposing a lace bra and jiggling breasts, and the two women screeched with laughter every time they crashed into something. At a nearby table, three Cambodian men were pouring tots of Johnny Walker into plastic cups and beckoning to the women to join them. It wasn't going to end well, and Charlotte didn't want to be around when the inevitable scene happened, so she went to the doorway and out onto the street.

She nervously looked around, unsure how to find her way to Roxy's flat. On the corner, a tuk-tuk driver snored loudly inside his parked vehicle, oblivious to music blasting from a karaoke bar and women prancing past in high heels. Neon signs flashed names like *Whisky Gogo, Supergirl Bar, Golden Bunny Bar,* and a couple of western men sat in their cars, beckoning to young Cambodian girls. Charlotte stepped across a muddy puddle and tiptoed around a pile of broken beer bottles to the tuk-tuk. She stuck her head inside. 'Hello...Um... Excuse me—' The driver stirred and glared at her. 'Excuse me, sir. Can you take me home?'

'I sleeping. No work now.' He rolled over and closed his eyes.

She pulled out her wallet. 'I'll pay you ten dollars.'

Grunting, the driver slid his feet onto the ground. He snatched the money from her hand and revved the engine, leaving his helmet on the seat inside the tuk-tuk. Good money for a trip, she muttered, knowing she'd given him more than three times the fee for a single fare.

Seven minutes later she was at Roxy's flat. Her stomach churned from the motion of the tuk-tuk and she felt queasy. Stumbling up the stairs, she clutched the handrail, tripped up the last step, and fell onto the door, banging her knee with a thud. A tube of lipstick toppled from her bag, rolled down the concrete stairs one at a time, and landed with a clink at the bottom. She suppressed a giggle. She mustn't wake Roxy and Peter. Once inside, she tiptoed to her bedroom and flung her bag onto the floor. Rashid's letter fell out and Charlotte picked it up, tears prickling behind her eyes as she read it again. Someone named Chris might be waiting to hear from his father the same way she'd been waiting to hear from hers. She couldn't give up looking now.

18

Mid-morning sunlight streamed into the room when Charlotte finally awoke and eased her body into an upright position. Beads of sweat prickled her forehead, and wisps of hair stuck to her neck from the heat in the room. Swarms of insects furiously batted their wings on the window and sounds from the street announced the constant stream of relentless traffic. She swatted a fly from her arm then looked at her watch and grimaced. She had slept almost eleven hours.

The events of the night before flooded back, and she lay down again, remembering her conversation with Alistair. The letters! Alistair had said he'd send the letters. She sat upright and hefted her laptop onto the bed and logged on, heart pounding. There was nothing. She checked her spam filter—nothing there either—so she climbed out of bed and pulled on her clothes, gingerly lifting a foot and grimacing at the sole which was caked with layers of grime and beer. At the bottom of the bed was a note from Roxy: *Guess U had a good night. See U after work.* She left it on the bed and slipped on her flip-flops, pleased to know Roxy had already left. She wanted to ask her about Alistair's statement, but something was holding her back.

She walked around the flat, opening all the windows and switching on the overhead fan until her stomach growled and she remembered all she had eaten last night was a bowl of peanuts at the bar. So she devoured three slices of toast, half a melon, and a banana, washing a couple of Tylenol down with three cups of coffee. From what she could recall of last night, it had been a disaster. Instead of making her feel less stressed, it had made her feel worse, both physically and emotionally. Her body felt battered, her mind numb, and she had made no progress in finding out if Rashid was related to Christal.

For the next ten minutes, she scrubbed her feet and stood under the shower until she felt clean. Then, she washed the dishes, swept the balcony, reorganised her wardrobe, and checked email five times. She got a text from Christal, *Great night, innit!! Let's do it again soon,* and an email from Trevor telling her about his new boyfriend. She didn't reply to either. By early afternoon, she'd heard nothing from Alistair and could barely sit still. She ironed a pile of shirts and dusted the shelves in the living room, meticulously wiping between the pages of every book, then polished the bottom of every tealight. She tried to read couldn't concentrate on the words, so she swept the balcony again. Anxiety intensified her hangover. Hours dragged by with agonizing slowness. The flat was too confining; she had to get out.

After spraying herself with mosquito repellent and rubbing sunblock on her face, arms, and chest, she walked down the street, unsure about where to go. Sightseeing held no interest, it was too hot to walk far, and she was too jittery to sit in a café. She stood on the edge of the road hoping inspiration would strike, then jumped back as a moto carrying a couple of monks almost hit her. Suddenly she knew where she'd go: to find Samnang. She started walking toward the pagoda, her pace quickening. Samnang would know what to do. He'd advise her how to talk to Roxy.

As she walked through the gate, a cat came over and rubbed against her leg. 'Toyota!' she breathed, picking him up and holding him against her face. 'I miss you. Where's your friend?' She walked over to a young monk in the courtyard. 'Excuse me. Do you know where I can find Bhante Samnang?' she asked.

'He go to Kampot today,' the monk replied. 'Go to work in pagoda for two weeks.' He smiled and walked away.

Kampot. That was in the south of the country. She couldn't wait two weeks to see him. She ran after the young monk. 'Sorry, Bhante. Can you help me, please? How do I get to Kampot?'

'Bus to Kampot very easy,' he said. 'Only three or five hours. But expensive. Five or seven dollars.'

Charlotte grinned. His reply was typically Cambodian. 'What time do the buses go, Bhante?'

'All the time. Sometimes go to Kep first. Sometimes to Kampot. Sometimes on time.'

Clear as mud. But she wanted to see Samnang, so she made a decision—she'd go to Kampot, whether it was three hours or five, on time or not. Roxy had been urging her to see more of Cambodia, so she wouldn't be suspicious if she took off for a few days. And that way she could avoid an awkward conversation with her. She hurried back to the flat and stuffed a duffel bag with three cotton shirts, a pair of shorts, sandals, underwear, cosmetic bag, laptop, and a travel guide, hoping Roxy wouldn't come home early. There was a travel agency a few blocks away where she could find out about bus tickets to

Kep, so she sent a quick note to Roxy: *Taking a bus to Kampot. Back in three days*, then added *All is well* in case Roxy was concerned about her, and left the flat, locking the door behind her.

As she waited to cross the road, a tuk-tuk drove toward her. In the back seat a tall western woman with curly black hair was talking on her phone. It was Annie. Charlotte waved. Annie would know about buses to Kampot and she might even want to come with her. The tuk-tuk drew closer and Annie made brief eye contact then looked away. Charlotte ran toward it, calling her name. Surely Annie had seen her. The tuk-tuk drove past and stopped on the opposite corner. A red-haired man climbed in and the vehicle sped away. Charlotte stood staring as it disappeared. It looked like the man they'd seen at the café. Why hadn't Annie waited? She stood for a while, expecting the vehicle to return, then called Annie's number. There was no answer, so she resumed her journey to the travel agency and bought a ticket.

A fifteen-seat, white minivan was parked on the edge on the road with a group of people standing next to it clutching bags, boxes, and backpacks. She approached a backpacker and asked where to queue, but he tossed his blonde dreadlocks and shrugged, so she dropped her bag beneath a tree and waited. Half an hour passed. Three more people arrived. A woman tried to open the rear door and was shooed away by the driver, so she joined Charlotte on the pavement and fanned herself with her bus ticket. Another half hour went by. Charlotte's back was wet with sweat. Her head throbbed, and she was feeling nauseous from the heat. Four-thirty—the designated departure time—came and went. At four forty-two, the driver unlocked the doors. Sixteen people boarded.

Charlotte squeezed into a window seat and watched with a

combination of irritation and amusement as passengers scrambled for seats and places to store their bags. Having a ticket seemed no guarantee you would find a spot. At four fifty-eight, after waiting for latecomers who seemed to be related to the driver since he welcomed them with hugs and smiles, the bus finally pulled into rush-hour traffic. Horns honked, buses spewed clouds of filthy fumes, and motos and tuk-tuks merged into congested streets. Pedestrians scuttled between them, dodging vehicles as they darted across the road, clutching plastic bags and small children in their arms. As they left the metropolitan area, the roads became wider and Charlotte saw a different side of Cambodia. Open-air markets were packed with rickety stalls selling plasticware, kitchen tools, fruit and vegetables, cheap clothing, and electrical parts. Makeshift shacks propped up by wobbly wooden posts displayed merchandise beneath faded plastic awnings. Rubbish piled high on street corners and the smell of rotten vegetables wafted through the tissue Charlotte pressed to her nose.

The change in scenery was startling. The congested streets of Phnom Penh, packed with concrete office buildings and billboards, were replaced by rice paddies with water buffalo dragging sturdy iron ploughs. Men and women wearing kramas and baggy trousers wielded sickles in the fields, bent like apostrophes under the searing sun. The cloudless sky was bluer than it appeared in the city and soaring palm trees stood like sentries guarding the horizon. Inside the bus, hot blasts of air crept through cracks in the windows, mingling with the inefficient air-conditioning. The vehicle bumped and rolled over potholes with its load of passengers, luggage, cardboard boxes, and a crate of smelly chickens. A video screen at the front of the bus played an old Bruce Lee film. The motion was hypnotic, and Charlotte was soon lulled to sleep by the heat and the gentle buzz of voices around her.

Suddenly, the bus swerved, and she woke with a start, knocking her head against the window and dropping the packaged sandwich she'd brought for the journey. A young man sitting next to her leaned over and picked it up. 'Very important you have food,' he said, handing it back with a smile. 'Where are you from?'

Charlotte thanked him, taken aback by his direct query, and studied him before answering. He was about her age, slim, with neatly combed hair, dark brown eyes, and a cracked front tooth. He was dressed in a navy suit, crisp white shirt, and blue and white striped tie. He stared, waiting for her reply.

'England,' she answered.

His smile broadened. 'Oh, you so lucky. I want to travel. My dream is to be architect, so I must work to save much money. Then I can help my family and also follow my dream.' He stuck out his hand. 'My name Saran. I very please to meet you.'

She introduced herself and spent the next hour answering questions: How old was she? Where did she work? How much money did she make? Did she have a husband or a boyfriend? When Saran asked why she had come to Cambodia, she gave him the abbreviated version: she was visiting a friend in Phnom Penh, interested in exploring Kampot, and looking for a monk who was staying there. In return, he told her his entire life story. He was twenty-five and worked in a bank in Phnom Penh. Most of his family were farmers and he was on his way to Kampot to visit his parents. He told her how much he earned (three hundred and seventy dollars a month), explained he sent most of it to his family, and described the single room with limited electricity above a motorbike shop that he rented for eighty dollars a month. He proudly told Charlotte he'd been the first in his family to go to university and had worked for three years in an air-conditioned office in the city.

As he talked, Charlotte smiled to herself. Where else would anyone disclose their salary to a stranger or ask about the details of their life? As she had discovered, Cambodians had a way of divulging even the most personal details within minutes. It was an endearing quality and seemed to show a great deal of trust on behalf of the young man, but it wasn't a custom she was used to, and she hoped he wouldn't ask her about things she didn't want to discuss.

In between spurts of conversation, he offered slices of mango from a plastic bag. She declined, thinking it wouldn't be wise to eat fresh fruit if she hadn't peeled it herself, so she pretended she was allergic to mango.

Saran stuck his hand into the bag of fruit. 'I very happy,' he said, dipping the mango in a blend of chili and salt at the bottom of the plastic bag. 'I take care of mother and father and little sister and see my family four times every year. I am oldest boy, so this is my duty.'

After a while he stopped talking and Charlotte spent the rest of the journey looking through the window until after four hours, a rest break, and a brief stop in the seaside village of Kep, the bus pulled up at the depot in Kampot. She stood to retrieve her bag from the overhead compartment and noticed Saran lingering in the aisle. 'You have hotel in Kampot?' he asked.

'No. I mean yes. I mean...I don't know.' She had heard about scams where Cambodians enticed tourists into expensive hotels that were allegedly owned by someone's 'father' or 'brother' or 'uncle', so she was guarded about giving too much information to someone she'd just met. Saran seemed delightful, but she didn't know him.

'My father, he work as tuk-tuk driver,' Saran said, ignoring her hesitation. 'I ask him to help you. We find hotel then you come to our home for dinner.'

Her face grew hot. 'I, er…I think I have plans. And you haven't seen your family for a long time, so I don't want to intrude.' She pulled her bag from overhead. 'It's kind of you to offer, but I think it's probably not a good idea.'

His smile vanished. 'You not want meet my family? Why you busy today?' He stared, waiting for a reply.

She took a deep breath. Now, she had insulted him. She didn't want to be rude, but she needed to protect herself. And she didn't know the Cambodian culture enough to understand what would be acceptable and what might be considered insulting.

Saran put his hand into a pocket and pulled out an ID tag attached to a red lanyard. On it was a headshot, his name, and the name of a bank. 'See,' he said, thrusting it toward her. 'No need to worry, Jallod, I am good employee and honest man.' He turned and walked toward the door. 'Come, we go now.' He climbed down from the bus into a sea of tuk-tuks waiting to sell their services for passengers who might want transportation. Charlotte followed, and a driver grabbed her arm before she had even stepped off the bus. She pulled away, and another man thrust a leaflet into her hands. A third grabbed her bag and carried it toward his vehicle.

'Hey! What are you—?' she shouted.

Saran thrust himself between her and the driver, retrieved the bag, then took her arm and guided her outside the throng to an elderly man sitting in a tuk-tuk. 'This my father,' he said. The man smiled and squeezed Saran on the arm. Saran spoke to him in Khmer, then turned to Charlotte. 'It is settled. My father, he take you to small hotel near river. Very cheap. We come back tomorrow morning, and you have lunch at my home. Then we will find for you Bhante Samnang.'

She opened her mouth to object, then stopped. She was exhausted, flustered, and overheated. She needed a shower and a cold drink. Most of all, she needed to trust someone. So, she stepped into the tuk-tuk and leaned back against the seat.

Saran grinned as he climbed up beside her and loosened his tie. 'My father say it is honour to drive you. His name Kosal. He tell me today is good day because he make seven dollars.'

She took a deep breath. While she'd been worrying about being scammed, this man was just trying to make a living. And he was just one of many. She looked back with a sympathetic gaze toward the drivers swarming around the bus. How would it feel to have to compete for work every day? And to have a family to support? No wonder they were competitive. She realised she had spent more that morning on a couple of coffees and a sandwich than Saran's father had made in a day, and immediately felt guilty. Saran and his father didn't know her, yet they'd invited her to lunch and were welcoming her as a friend, not just as one more fare for the day. She sighed and put on her sunglasses, wondering why her first instinct had been one of suspicion. Living in England had made her sceptical about trusting people, particularly since her mother always doubted everything. Charlotte wanted to be more like her father; open to new experiences and ready to trust a stranger.

As they drove, she scanned the landscape and noticed Kampot seemed to move at a slower pace than Phnom Penh. Roads were narrower and many were fringed by small leafy shrubs and brilliant pink oleanders that burst from stone planters on the centre partition. Rows of old French colonial houses and stately mansions no higher than two floors tall stood side by side with small open-air cafés and bakeries.

They came to a large roundabout in what seemed to be the middle of town where an enormous round stone statue loomed in the centre. 'What's that?' she asked Saran.

'Durian,' he replied, grinning. 'Cambodia's smelly fruit. Kampot is the durian capital of the entire world. You like?'

She pulled a face. She had no intention of eating durian. The smell was bad enough; she couldn't imagine how it would taste.

Saran tapped his father on the shoulder, spoke into his ear, then pointed to Charlotte and laughed. She leaned forward, feeling light-hearted at being in the countryside and felt herself relax. After a few minutes, they drove away from the city centre and past a cluster of shops, then Kosal swerved off the main road onto a long dirt path. Rows of palm trees fringed the barren track and there was nothing in sight other than a group of men working in a distant field. No buildings. No houses. Just a long, bumpy sand road and dozens of goats. Charlotte's palms started to sweat as she recalled Roxy's warning about trusting strangers. Maybe she had been too quick to accept Saran's offer.

She was about to ask Kosal to stop when they came to a wooden fence and Kosal climbed off the bike, opened the gate, and drove through. A young woman walked toward them, carrying a glass jug and a large smile. She chatted with Kosal in Khmer for a few minutes and poured a glass of ice-cold juice for Charlotte. Then, Saran lifted Charlotte's bag from the tuk-tuk and dropped it on the ground. 'This your hotel,' he said, pointing to a low wood building fringed with oleander shrubs and fig trees. 'My father, he do many work here so they give you a room for only twenty dollar. It have shower and free breakfast and free Wi-Fi. We go now. See you tomorrow morning at ten o'clock.' He jumped onto the tuk-tuk and sped away before Charlotte could respond.

The lodging turned out to be perfect. It was a charming Cambodian guesthouse on the Kampot River, and Charlotte's room was a small bungalow with a thatched roof, small patio, and a bed draped with mosquito netting. Other than the twittering of birds, it was completely silent. Once she'd showered, changed into shorts and a tank top, and ambled down to the river, dusk was starting to fall. The water shone with phosphorescence, and hundreds of fireflies glimmered in the leafy trees that fringed the property and hung over the riverbank.

A beeping sound cut into the silence and she took her phone from her pocket to see a message from Roxy: *Happy u r exploring Cambo. Bring back some Kampot pepper.* Charlotte didn't want to be reminded about yesterday, so she pushed the off button. But before the phone closed down, there was another beep, this time from an unknown number: *Getting closer.* It was from the same number as the other mystery text messages.

She sent an immediate reply: *Who is this?* There was no response, so she dialled the number. The call didn't go through, so she sent another text message: *Please reply.* Seconds later there were five consecutive beeps, each message containing a single letter. First *T*, then *R*, then *U*, then *S*, then *T*.

19

Charlotte settled into her bungalow and logged onto Wi-Fi, amazed that such a desolate place had a signal. Here she was, tucked away in a bamboo hut on a river nobody had ever heard of, on the edge of a mysterious country in Southeast Asia, and the connection was stronger than she often had in London.

She opened her email and a headline jumped out at her: *Letters from home.* Her chest tightened and she stared toward the window. A moth flew into a naked lightbulb. It dropped onto the floor at her feet, flapping its wings in desperation. For a moment she watched it struggle, then she gently picked it up and placed it on the windowsill, thinking of the email she was about to read. What if the letters contained something she didn't want to know? What if her mother had been right all along? Perhaps it would be better to leave the memories undisturbed.

She left her room, walked across the lawn, and sat by the edge of the river. The ripples on the water were mesmerising and she stared into the blackness. It had been seven years since she'd had any contact with her father. And while part of her longed to know what he'd written, another part was terrified to read his words. She had spent so many hours wondering about him, cursing him for leaving, praying for him to return, but she'd finally accepted the truth: he wasn't coming back. A dim light glowed from her room. The warm evening attracted mosquitos, so she went back to her cabin. Maybe she'd just take a peek.

She took a deep breath and clicked on Alistair's note: *Here are some of the letters I scanned. Thinking of you.* There were eleven attachments. She opened the first, dated October 14, 2013, five days after her father left. *Darling Charlie-horse. There's more space between us than I would ever want. I miss you terribly.* She stopped, tears blurring her vision, then swiped the back of her hand across her face and continued. *I've tried phoning, but you never answer. I came to see you on Tuesday, but your mum said you were at the animal shelter. Phone me when you get this letter.* At the bottom was a London phone number.

She dug her fingernails into her palm. He had tried to reach her. But something didn't sound right, so she read it again: *I've tried phoning, but you never answer.* She slammed the laptop shut and raced to the river. Memories from the day he'd left washed over her: her mother's yelling, the slam of doors, revving of the car engine, the pressure on her chest as she'd held her breath, waiting. Then, the panicked feeling when she'd tried to call Roxy and hadn't been able to find her phone. She remembered scrambling beneath the covers, crawling under the bed, searching every pocket, finally having to confess to her mother she'd misplaced it. It had been odd that her mother hadn't yelled at her that time; hadn't criticised her for being stupid or careless or foolish or useless. And strange that her mother had mysteriously produced a spare phone, almost as though she knew it would be needed. But now Charlotte knew the truth: she'd stolen her phone.

Grief replaced by rage, she paced the riverbank and waded knee-deep into the water. Then a realisation: there were more letters. She went back to her room and read them all, hoping one would reveal her dad's whereabouts. Each contained messages written with increasing concern about her silence, but nothing explained where he'd gone or why.

Then came the tenth letter, written sixteen months after his departure: *I'm anxious, Charlie-horse. It's unlike you to not respond and I can only think it's because of my encounter with Roxy. I know how close you are, and that she tells you everything, so I'm sorry you had to find out this way. I hoped it might help you understand why I left your mother. I should have told you a long time ago, but I was afraid of losing you. I was scared you might despise me or think less of me. Please give me a chance to explain.* It ended abruptly. No details. Just an appeal for her to hear his explanation; one she'd never received. Her hand trembled as she folded the laptop and reached for a cardigan, shivering despite the warmth of the evening.

Alistair's voice echoed in her head: *Roxy knows*. But Roxy had never said anything. She'd been a shoulder to cry on and a safe place for Charlotte to vent her feelings. She'd never let on there might be something else, something more important.

She sat at the window, staring into the darkness. On the other side of the lawn, a waitress waved as she went home for the night, but Charlotte didn't have the energy to respond. A tear trickled down her face as she rocked back and forth, waves of sadness washing over her. She felt alone and lost and needed a friend, no matter what she might have done. She reached for the phone—she had to talk to Roxy. But as she punched in her number, she remembered her comment on the phone in Phnom Penh: '*Better not to tell her yet,*' and paused. She walked onto the porch and sat on the step, wishing she were somewhere else. Hours crawled by, how many she didn't know or care, and once darkness fell, she went back inside and lay on top of the covers, scrunching a sweaty pillow beneath her head. The ticking of the bedside clock mirrored the sound of her heartbeat, and she stared at the moon through the glass partition in the door. On the bedside table, a trail of ants marched across the surface, so she reached for the bug spray, knocking the water glass to the floor where it smashed into dozens of jagged shards. She cursed and flung the can across the room.

Voices shouted in her head. *Roxy knows. My mother lied.* Her mind raced and she couldn't sleep. She squeezed her eyes shut and tried to think of something peaceful, but nothing came. All she could see was Roxy's face. What did she know that she hadn't told her? The voices screamed louder as she tossed fitfully and finally checked her watch. 4 a.m. She hadn't slept a wink.

From across the lawn she heard hotel employees arriving at work, rattling plates and clanging pans in the kitchen, chattering loudly as they began another day. On the other side of the river came the sound of chanting from a pagoda. She pulled the pillow over her head to muffle the noise and fell into an exhausted doze.

The aroma of cooked bacon wafted through the cracks in the window, finally coaxing her from an uneasy sleep. Rays of sunshine filtered through the thin curtains, casting spiral patterns on the wooden floor. Her eyes burned and she rubbed them and looked at the time: 10 a.m. She sat upright with a start. Saran was picking her up in thirty minutes. All she wanted to do was crawl back under the covers, but she couldn't let Saran down, so she scrubbed her face, dressed, and stumbled across the hotel grounds.

Saran stood in the shade of a bougainvillea bush talking on his phone. He hung up as Charlotte approached. 'Hello Jallod,' he said, smiling. 'We go now. My father waiting outside.'

She followed him and climbed onto Kosal's tuk-tuk, hoping she wouldn't have to talk much. Being in the presence of strangers wasn't something she relished at most times, and today it required more effort than she could muster. Perhaps nobody in Saran's family would understand English so she could stay quiet.

Kosal started the engine, handed her a bottle of cold water, and donned a helmet. As they drove along the bumpy road, Saran babbled in broken English about the weather, his family, and his job. Charlotte nodded politely, realising after a few minutes she had no idea what he'd said. They passed through fields of flowers, near herds of goats, and across tiny creeks. Charlotte stared straight ahead, giving brief responses to Saran's endless questions about her family. His chatter was background sound, and when he asked about her friends, she smiled as though she didn't understand.

After driving almost an hour, they turned onto a sandy trail that meandered through emerald paddy fields abundant with lush rice stalks into a small village. Clusters of women and children stood outside huts, stirring pots over open fires. They waved to Kosal, who pointed to Charlotte and Saran with a broad smile. Saran waved back, clearly excited to show off his new friend. Charlotte gave a half-hearted wave, her usual good manners suppressed by the anxiety in her head.

The tuk-tuk stopped in front of a small wooden hut supported by sturdy timber posts, where an elderly Cambodian woman bent over a blackened cooking pot, her bare brown feet callused and covered with dirt. Chickens pecked around her feet and she occasionally gave them a hefty kick, sending them squawking and flapping into the bushes. When she saw the tuk-tuk approach, she stopped stirring and flashed a smile revealing several missing teeth.

'Is my mother,' Saran said to Charlotte. 'I think she happy to meet you.'

The moment Charlotte stepped from the tuk-tuk, she was surrounded by people who seemed to materialise out of nowhere. A wrinkled man with rheumy eyes reached out and gripped her arm with bony fingers, a group of brown-eyed children peeked shyly from beneath a cracked stone table, two old women with shaved heads hobbled toward her on crooked sticks, and a pretty, teenage girl giggled and waved. Charlotte greeted them with the only words of Khmer she could remember, intrigued by the interest they expressed in her and uncomfortable at the attention. Everyone was smartly turned out—men in white, starched shirts with vibrantly coloured full-length kramas wrapped around their lower bodies, women in long-sleeved floral blouses above mismatched flowered skirts or vividly patterned trousers, and children with neatly combed hair. Saran's mother wore a pink and white striped cotton blouse over a flowered skirt that trailed in the dust above her bare feet, and a tarnished necklace dangled around her throat. Despite the heat and dust, everyone looked fresh and clean. Charlotte suddenly became aware of perspiration stains on her blouse and the wrinkled skirt she'd pulled on in a hurry that morning.

She met Saran's mother's eyes and smiled at the teenage girl. While the children seemed overwhelmed by her presence, everyone else was incredibly welcoming to the tall English stranger. But as much as Charlotte wanted to join in, her heart wasn't there.

Saran stepped from the tuk-tuk holding a plastic bag filled with bottles of water. 'You are special guest, Jallod,' he said, handing her a bottle. He gestured toward the group of people. 'My father, he tell everyone they can meet *baraing* lady. We very happy today.'

Baraing? Charlotte struggled to remember the meaning of the word, then recalled Peter talking about the *baraings* who visited his organisation. Foreigners. Literally translated as *French*, the term had become synonymous with a foreign person. She was the foreign lady.

Everyone was staring at her with bright smiles and a lump came to her throat. This had been planned for her. While she'd been irritated at being inconvenienced, Saran's family had been arranging something special for their lunch guest. Putting her hands together in a sampeah, she bowed to them. '*Sua s'day. Akun*,' she said.

Everyone laughed.

'Oh, you speak such good Cambodian,' Saran said, ushering Charlotte toward his house. 'Me the only person in family who speak English. My sister, she speak a little but she shy.'

His mother stepped away from the cooking pot and gestured to the only unbroken chair.

'Please to sit,' Saran said. 'It our pleasure to have you visit our home.'

'Oh, no. I couldn't.' Charlotte held up a hand in protest.

'Yes, Jallod. This your seat today.'

He shooed a chicken from beneath the chair. It fluttered across the path in front of the young girl, who ran to Saran and grabbed his trouser leg, holding tightly to the fabric and looking up at him. 'This my sister, Bopha,' Saran said, resting his hand on the girl's shoulder. 'She never meet *baraing* lady before.'

Bopha gazed at Charlotte with enormous brown eyes as she clung to Saran's leg. Dressed in an orange cotton blouse and a yellow and white knee-length skirt, her straight black hair fell to her waist. She was stunning, with a raw, natural beauty and dark sparkling eyes. She stared at Charlotte for a moment, then darted inside the wooden hut. Kosal remained in the tuk-tuk drawing on a cigarette, his scrawny chest rising and falling with each inhalation. Deep wrinkles ran from his sunken cheeks to a whiskery chin, his thin grey hair mostly covered by a Nike baseball cap.

Charlotte turned to Saran. 'What about your father? Isn't he going to join us?'

'Is hard for him to walk. He break legs escaping from Angka. Angka beat him. They kill his sister. He happy in tuk-tuk.'

Charlotte's mind reeled. *Angka?* Angka was the name they called the Khmer Rouge. This soft-spoken, unassuming man whose definition of success was a day that earned him seven dollars was a survivor of the Khmer Rouge.

20

Saran's mother ladled a scoop of brown liquid into a cracked porcelain dish and set it next to a bowl of rice on the folding table in front of Charlotte. Floating in the steaming broth was something with spiny bones and eyes. Charlotte scooped some onto her spoon and moved it to another plate, her stomach churning. She was already feeling queasy, so she'd just eat the rice and ignore the rest.

Everyone's eyes were on her. Saran's mother grinned and nodded, gesturing for her to eat. Kosal sat in the tuk-tuk a few yards away, shovelling rice into his mouth with a plastic spoon and occasionally glancing in her direction. Nobody else had food. Charlotte wiped her fork with a paper napkin and glanced at Saran. Something in his expectant smile made her realise this was special, so she took a deep breath and lifted her fork. 'Looks good,' she said with a smile and a nod. Even if they didn't speak English, they'd probably understand.

Saran's mother hovered, just like Charlotte's headmistress

from primary school had done with the daily portions of rice pudding. She'd hated the stuff and had learned how to spread it around her plate so it looked as though she'd eaten most of it. She'd do the same now. She spooned the brown liquid—bones and eyes and all—onto the rice, burying the bones beneath the rice and stirring it all together. Then she took a forkful and held her breath, expecting it would make her gag. But it was delicious—a blend of spicy, sweet, and bitter flavours on fluffy rice. Suddenly, she realised she was hungrier than she thought. It had been hours since she'd last eaten and she hadn't had much of an appetite since arriving in Kep. She dug in for another forkful. Saran's mother padded back to the cooking pot, apparently satisfied her guest was enjoying her meal. She filled another bowl and handed it to Saran, who squatted on the ground and slurped it noisily.

'My mother buy this food with my money,' he said to Charlotte. 'She use the rest for medicine for father. He old man. Not very healthy.'

She glanced at Kosal. Dark mahogany skin and a face scarred with deep furrows, his body gaunt and bony. He must have had children late in life as he looked almost as old as her grandfather before he died. She thought of her own father and wondered what he would look like now. He'd always been proud of his appearance, so she guessed he'd probably still be trim and fit. And age wouldn't have dimmed the sparkle in his green eyes that had drawn people to him all his life. How he would have loved this experience: sharing a meal with foreigners who'd opened their home to a stranger. It was just one more thing he and her mother disagreed upon—the idea of bringing anyone new into their home. She had never hidden her disapproval when he'd invited people for dinner, so her father had stopped the invitations. And Charlotte had stopped meeting interesting people.

Everyone sat in silence, wolfing down spoonfuls of rice. The meal seemed to be the focal point of business, so conversation took a back seat till the food was finished. Every once in a while, Bopha peeked from the hut, giggling and hiding her mouth behind her hand.

After Charlotte finished her stew, she turned to Saran. 'Why is everyone eating rice?' she asked.

He scraped the last morsel of food into his mouth and put his bowl on the ground. 'Not enough meat for everyone. You our special guest.'

A lump caught in her throat. They'd gone to all this trouble just for her. She scraped the bottom of her bowl, holding her breath as she swallowed a piece of gristle, determined to finish it all.

As she wiped her mouth with a faded towel, Saran jumped up and wedged a machete into his belt. 'Come. Now we go for walk.' He took his bowl to the outdoor sink, picked up two bottles of water, and ushered Charlotte to the nearby path.

They strolled through the village, greeting neighbours who seemed to have heard about the visitor. Each time she met someone new who bowed and smiled politely, Charlotte wanted to cry. She'd felt fragile when she'd met Saran that morning, now she felt even more so, having been treated like a valued guest by people she'd just met. Nobody spoke English but it didn't matter. They communicated with their facial expressions and some gave her a bunch of bananas or a bottle of fizzy drink when Saran introduced her in Khmer. She heard a couple of words, *baraing* and *mitpeak,* which she'd learned meant *friend,* and wished she'd brought a gift of her own. Next time she'd be more thoughtful.

Saran plucked a flower from a bush and thrust it under her nose. 'This *bophana* in my language. It mean flower.' He handed it to her. 'My sister Bopha named after auntie—sister of my father. She die under Angka. My father tell me she beautiful. Like flower.'

As they walked, he told the story of his family. Kosal had been fourteen when the Khmer Rouge seized power in 1975. His sister, Bophana, was three years older. Before the invasion, they had lived with their parents in Battambang, Cambodia's second largest city, but were later forced to evacuate to work camps in the countryside.

Charlotte did a quick calculation. That made Kosal fifty-nine years old. He looked at least seventy.

'My grandfather was teacher,' Saran said. 'He very smart man. But Pol Pot want to kill all smart people, so grandfather must pretend he is farmer and that he not know how to write. He throw away spectacles and tells wife and children to make hands and feet dirty and hard so they look poor. They have no food – just work for Angka in rice field. No talk to anybody in the village – too many spies. They so hungry they eat insects and dirt, and every day afraid they may be killed.' He held open a gate for Charlotte as they crossed into a field.

'My grandmother, she die from hunger,' he continued. 'She give her food to her children so nothing left for her.' He paused. 'Bophana, she taken away one day. Never return. My father hear from a neighbour that soldiers rape her. They keep her two weeks—maybe three—then kill her. My father find her body under a tree when he working in the field. He cannot show sadness or tell anyone he know her or he will be killed too.'

Charlotte stood still. 'How awful,' she said. 'I can't even imagine.'

'But my father very lucky, Jallod. He play the flute and learn

Khmer Rouge songs. All other young boys killed except my father because soldiers like his music. He beaten many times. They hurt his legs, but he not killed. When he sixteen, he escape from camp. He lie down under dead bodies in truck so get away. He run fast on damaged legs and become hurt very badly. So today is hard for him to walk.'

He stopped talking and looked around, then sprinted toward a tall palm tree on the other side of the path. 'Now I get you coconut,' he said. He slipped off his shoes, grabbed hold of a rope dangling from the tree and pulled himself up the trunk.

Charlotte watched him, amazed how fast he'd shifted his mood. One minute he was talking about tragic death in his family, the next up a tree picking coconuts. Roxy had been right when she'd said Cambodians had an amazing capacity to accept their challenges. It must be their Buddhist faith that gave them strength. She thought how Saran had treated her from the first moment they'd met. He'd been gracious and friendly, and so had the rest of his family, despite all their personal difficulties. They all showed incredible tolerance—almost an acceptance—in the way they talked about their lives. Saran hadn't expressed bitterness or anger, just stated facts and moved on. Perhaps she could learn to do the same.

A shout interrupted her thoughts. 'Jallod! Look!'

Hanging from the top of the tree, Saran was twisting a large green coconut and chopping at it with the machete. The enormous fruit jerked loose from the branch and Saran flung it to the ground where it fell with a thud a few feet from her.

'Jallod. Please to be careful!' he shouted. A few seconds later, another thud when a second coconut fell, then he slid down the trunk and landed beside her. A smile flashed across his face. 'You like drink coconut? I cut for you.' He sliced off the top with the machete and handed it to her. She took it from him, tilted her head back and poured the sweet liquid down her throat. Saran gave a thumbs up and sliced the top off the other coconut. 'Kampot best coconuts in Cambodia. I get some more for you.' He strode toward the tree.

Charlotte held up her hands. 'Oh no! I don't need any more. It's very generous, but they're too big to carry. And your family has already been so kind to me.'

Saran's brow furrowed. 'But you bring good luck to us, Jallod. My father been very sick and unhappy. Today he have reason to be happy.'

They walked back to the house, the clatter of dishes and shrill laughter ringing out as they approached. Charlotte handed the coconut to Saran's mother who sliced it and arranged it on a plate. As she nibbled on a chunk, she realised she hadn't thought about her father or Roxy for several hours.

At the stone basin, Saran's mother, sister, and two other women scrubbed dirty pots while another swept the ground with a straw broom. Bopha ran from the house carrying a plastic bag filled with mangoes, rambutans, and bananas and approached Charlotte. Smiling shyly, she handed her the bag. 'These fruit from our field,' she whispered. 'We berry happy meet you.' She giggled, covering her mouth with both hands, and rapidly backed away, catching her foot on a plastic stool and knocking it to the ground.

Saran picked up the stool then gestured toward the tuk-tuk. 'We leave now. Go to pagoda to find Bhante Samnang.'

Charlotte fumbled in her wallet and handed him a ten dollar note. 'I'd like to contribute to the meal please, Saran.'

Saran backed away, raising his hands. 'Please no. This is our delight.'

'Will you give it to your father for driving, then?'

'No need.'

She climbed beside him in the tuk-tuk and turned to bid farewell to his family. Thirteen people stood outside the wooden hut, waving. Bopha blew a kiss and Saran's mother leaned against her cane as she flashed a toothless grin. Charlotte quickly turned away so they wouldn't see her tears.

21

Kosal drove beneath a stone arch and along a path leading to a pagoda. As he pulled up in front, Saran jumped from the tuk-tuk and raced up the steps. He stopped to speak to a monk, then ran back to the vehicle. 'I find out!' he exclaimed, breathless. 'Monk with blue eyes not here. He stay at Wat Sambor. Is near your hotel, Jallod. We go there now.'

Charlotte wiped the sweat from her forehead. Saran was trying to help but she was exhausted. She didn't want to appear ungrateful, but she'd rather see Samnang when she felt like talking. 'Thank you, Saran,' she said. 'But I...I mean, I think there's...Actually I'd like to have a rest.' She bit the inside of her lip, hoping he wouldn't be upset.

Saran hopped onto the tuk-tuk and tapped his father on the shoulder. 'No problem, Jallod,' he said cheerfully. 'Go back now.'

They returned to the hotel and Charlotte said goodbye to Saran and Kosal then walked across the lawn to her bungalow.

As she collapsed onto the bed, her phone vibrated with a new text: *One more*. She looked at it and groaned, then remembered Alistair's earlier email. He'd said there were eleven attachments; she'd opened only ten. She picked up her laptop and opened the last letter. It was dated October 4, 2014—almost a year after her dad had left.

Darling Charlie-horse, I'm afraid I've lost you. It hurts too much to be in the same country, so I'm going back to Belgium. You can find me through my friend, Patrick Jansen. Here's how to reach him. I love you. The letter ended with an address and phone number.

She slowly closed the laptop. Who was Patrick? Was her dad in Belgium? She left her bungalow and walked through the closely cropped grass across the gravel trail bungalow, hardly noticing the sharp stones under her feet. She thought about Saran's family with their tiny wooden house and their collection of farm tools and oil lamps. They didn't have any of the comforts she'd always taken for granted; things like electricity and running water and air-conditioning and plumbing. But they had something she'd never experienced: a tightly knit family where everyone watched out for one another.

She walked over to the bar, expecting to see people gathering for happy hour. But other than a couple sitting on the patio, there was nobody. So, she bought a bottle of wine and carried it back across the lawn to her bungalow. Once inside, she locked the door behind her, and filled a glass to the rim.

THE SUN WAS SINKING below the distant mountains when Charlotte arrived at Wat Sambor and she wondered how to find Samnang. From a distant spot, the gentle buzz of voices drifted across the courtyard, so she walked toward it and saw Samnang sitting with another monk under a tree. He was speaking Khmer, so she lingered in the shadows watching how his brow furrowed when he pronounced the words, and how often he tossed back his head and laughed at himself. A smile spread across Charlotte's face. She needed someone like Samnang right now; someone who would listen without judgement.

After a few minutes, she heard Samnang ask in English if they could take a break. The other monk nodded and walked away, leaving Samnang alone. Charlotte hastened toward him and gave a small wave. 'Bhante Samnang, I found you,' she said.

Samnang looked up and smiled. 'Charlotte! What are you doing in Kampot?'

'I need to...I mean I want to...I don't know how—' Her voice broke off, and she stared at her feet. 'I'm sorry. Are you free for a few minutes?' She dropped her bag, bent to pick it up, and her hat fell off. 'Oh dear. There I go again,' she said, her cheeks warming.

Samnang suppressed a grin. 'Let's sit out here and have a chat. What's going on and why are you here?'

She pulled a tissue from her pocket and wiped beads of sweat from her lip. Then she told Samnang about her mother's accident, her father's letters, and Alistair's comment about Roxy. She stumbled through it in a flurry of jumbled, emotionally charged words, peppered with a stream of tears. 'So, it feels like my life is a total disaster,' she said in a breathless voice.

'Why do you say that?' Samnang asked. 'Nothing has changed. All that's different is you now know about it. You couldn't have done anything to change it.'

'I thought my mother...' She broke off.

'Needed you?' Samnang asked.

Charlotte nodded, balling the tissue in her hand. 'I even convinced myself she appreciated me. But now I know she's a selfish, lying bit— Oh, sorry—' Sorry seemed to be the word that punctuated most of her sentences these days. She pulled at the tissue, peeling off strips and shredding them. 'She lied to me. She hid my father's letters...told me he'd...' She took a deep breath.

'Take a minute,' Samnang said.

'I can't.' She stumbled on. 'I'm so angry. I could've left home years ago. Do you know why I didn't? I felt guilty. She said she'd be lonely if I went away. So, dutiful, infantile, *stupid* Charlotte stayed home, cooking meals, cleaning the house, paying rent, holding her hand when she was hungover.' Her face reddened. 'I gave up any chance of being a normal teenager. And *this* is how she repays me? *This*? She builds this...this dishonest little web and weaves her daughter into it.' She took a deep breath, trying to control the tears. 'My dad didn't walk away from me. And now I'm going to...I'm going to —' She shredded the scraps of the tissue. 'Oh, I don't *know* what I'm going to do.' She ran a trembling hand through her hair.

Samnang sat on the bench, hands folded in his lap. For almost a full minute, he looked at her and said nothing, then he got up from the bench and sat on the grass. He crossed his legs and placed his palms together. 'Close your eyes,' he said in a soft voice. 'Listen.'

Charlotte stared at him. She'd just had an emotional breakdown, and this was his response? Listen to what? She sat on the bench, clutching the fragments of torn tissue, unsure how to respond.

'Listen,' Samnang repeated. 'It's only when we silence our minds that we hear our feelings.'

She huffed loudly. She knew what she was feeling: hurt, sad, and angry. This wasn't a time to be quiet, she needed to talk.

Samnang continued to sit still with his eyes shut. Charlotte glared, willing him to look at her and pay attention. He remained silent, so after a few minutes she closed her eyes and sighed again, hoping he'd get the message. Her back hurt, her neck was stiff, and her eyes burned from crying. She didn't want to be silent. She opened her eyes and looked around.

A few seconds later, Samnang opened his eyes and reached into a small cloth bag strung around his waist. 'Perhaps you need something more tangible,' he said. 'This bracelet's for luck and protection. It's also a reminder to show compassion.' He pulled out a ball of red thread, cut off a short section with a pocket-knife, and tied it around her wrist.

'But I—'

He placed a finger on his lips. 'Just listen. When your mind's buzzing with confusion and anger, it becomes numb. Only a silent mind can be alert and alive and sensitive to its surroundings. Do you know why?' He met her eyes.

'No.'

'A silent mind doesn't judge or reject so easily.'

She watched him through half-closed eyes. She'd sought him out for advice, but he was preaching. If Roxy were here, she'd understand. She'd join her in condemning her mother. Charlotte needed a friend, not someone to tell her how to act.

'Take a minute to be mindful,' Samnang continued. 'When you become aware you're judging something, the judgement will stop. And once you stop judging, you start to see things as they are.'

'But I *do*.' she burst out. 'My mother lied and my father...' Her cheeks burned. 'I don't buy it. How can being silent or mindful, or trying not to judge help anything? I don't mean to insult you, but you've got no idea ... I can't just sit under a tree and be quiet.'

Samnang nodded. 'I'm sorry if I'm taking you somewhere you don't want to go, and it doesn't insult me at all. I've been there myself.' He shook his head and smiled. 'I didn't think it would work for me, either. I just wish I'd known then what I know now. We all learn at our own pace. Mine was slow. And I know I still have a long way to go, and a lot to learn.' He fingered his wooden beads. 'But once I stopped judging, my relationships improved, with other people and with myself. There's nothing you can do to change others, Charlotte, you can only change the way you react to them. Once you do that, you'll notice how things improve. Not because *they've* changed but because *you* have.'

'But I'm not a monk or a nun,' Charlotte replied. 'I can't be sweet and passive and forgiving. I'm so angry that I just want to disappear. I want to scream at everyone and—' She tossed the tissue onto the grass.

'Then why did you come here? Why seek me out?'

She leaned down and rested her head in her hands. 'I just want it all to go away.'

'We both know it isn't going away,' Samnang said, softly. 'The only way out of pain is through it.' He looked into her eyes as she sat up. 'Do you know the story of the lotus?'

She shook her head.

'The lotus is a beautiful flower that begins its life underwater, buried in mud. As it grows, it slowly rises above the water where it opens its petals to the sun. The dirty water rinses it clean so when it opens to the air, the mud is all gone. You don't have to be Buddhist to understand we're all like the lotus. Some of us stay below the murky water and never make it to the surface. Others push through the dirt and become more beautiful.'

Like the poster, Charlotte thought. The one in the pub.

To find the lotus, go to the mud.

Jump in the mud.

Swim in the mud.

You will find you were the lotus all along.

For a moment, she reflected on Samnang's message. Then, she remembered her mother's betrayal and pictured her father waiting for a letter that never came. She thought of all the nights she had lain awake, wishing she could turn back time. She jumped up, knocking her hat to the ground. 'I'm sorry,' she blurted out. 'I can't do this,' than bolted from the garden and ran beneath the stone archway onto the street.

22

Samnang's words dominated Charlotte's thoughts as she walked along the riverside until dusk. Strolling past families playing ball, couples on benches, and the regular collection of exercise buffs going through their daily regimens, she searched the rippling water for lotus blossoms. It would be a sign if she saw one, a beacon of hope to give her a sense of direction. But she only saw tangles of water hyacinths and strands of weeds clogging the banks.

She diverted into a convenience store and bought a bottle of cheap wine then took it to the road next to the river where she sat and drank from the bottle. A western couple walked by and Charlotte's head snapped in their direction as the woman's words drifted her way, 'appalling drunken girl...' Embarrassed, she tossed the half-empty bottle into a bin and started walking.

She strode quickly, seeking distance from the couple's steely glares, and her gaze fell on a brightly lit row of shops a couple of blocks to her left. She drifted into the neighbourhood and discovered a string of bars and cafés draped with fairy lights and large open-air patios. Every restaurant had a set of enormous speakers and music blared from each—jazz, funk, reggae, each different to the one next door. The pavement was crowded with people chattering in French and German and tables were piled high with bottles of beer. Charlotte recoiled and kept walking until she found a tiny, dimly lit café tucked away on a side street and slipped inside. There was an open table in the back, so she sat down and placed an order for fried spring rolls, a banana flower salad, and a large vodka tonic. She downed the drink as soon as it arrived, then ordered another.

As she waited for her second drink, a young man appeared next to her, brandishing a knife. 'You want coconut, lay-dee?' he asked, waving a coconut beneath her nose. She shook her head and picked at a spring roll.

A waiter approached and set a martini glass decorated with a paper umbrella in front of her. Charlotte stared at him with a blank look on her face. 'I didn't order this,' she said, handing back the glass.

The waiter nodded and pointed across the room. 'From men at bar. You no pay.'

She looked toward the bar and a middle-aged Cambodian man caught her gaze and winked. Next to him was another man. They both grinned, leering toothy invitations. One wore a black suit with a striped tie that hung loose around his collar. The other was in jeans and a tight-fitting black T-shirt, his stomach bulging over his belt. A small mountain of mobile phones rested on the counter in front of them—the tell-tale sign of affluence in Cambodian society. Charlotte let out a sigh, hoping they'd get the hint now she'd sent back the drink.

Mr. Business Suit beckoned and the man in jeans gave a thumbs-up. Charlotte looked the other way. She wasn't in the mood for making small-talk and these men looked as though they might not be used to being ignored. She scanned the room for an exit. It was at the other side, so she'd have to pass the two goons if she wanted to make a getaway. She took her phone from her bag and pushed a few buttons, pretending to make a phone call, then heard a voice at her shoulder. 'I think you like cocktail, yes?' It was Mr. Jeans. He dragged over a chair and sat down. 'Not good for pretty girl to drink alone.'

Mr. Business Suit sauntered over, belched, and gestured toward the bar. 'Three more drinks, *oun*!' he said, dragging another chair to the table. As he did, he raised his arm and Charlotte saw a leather strap stretched tightly across his chest and something bulging under his jacket.

'I'm sorry but I have to go,' she said, pushing back her chair.

A waiter scuttled over with a bottle of Johnny Walker, placed it on the table and bowed before backing away. Mr. Business Suit thrust a glass into Charlotte's hand, gold teeth flashing in the light of the Angkor Beer sign. '*Jul Mouy*! You drink!'

'I said I have to go,' she repeated, trying to keep the fake smile on her face. 'I have an appointment.'

'Just one drink,' Mr Business Suit said. 'I see you look sad. We make you happy.' He grunted and pointed to her glass.

Not again, Charlotte thought. She leaned over to pick up her bag and blood rushed to her head. 'I need to go to the toilet,' she said. 'I'll be right back.' She stood and backed away from the table into the middle of the room. Once she reached the counter, she turned toward the exit, caught her foot on a broken tile and stifled a yelp of pain as her ankle twisted over. She glanced back at the men, relieved to see they were drinking and slapping each other on the back, then stumbled outside.

Neon signs flickered from the bars, and scantily clad girls

lingered in doorways. Her ankle throbbed and she realised with dismay she hadn't paid her bill. Hopefully, the waiter would understand why she'd bolted. She'd go back tomorrow and settle up.

As she leaned against the wall, a man sidled up to her and breathed in her ear. 'Want marijuana, lay-dee? Something stronger?'

She shook her head and limped away. The girls glowered in her direction, an unwanted intruder on their prime turf, so she turned the corner and walked away from the town centre. Within minutes, she found herself on a concrete road that became narrower and darker as she progressed. The glow from a few small shops cast scant light on the alley. Then, footsteps behind her. She glanced over her shoulder as a dark shape grew near, and felt a sharp tug on her elbow when her bag was wrenched from her arm. She screamed and lurched toward the assailant, toppling to the ground, and smashing her elbow on the pavement as she fell. Her head bounced off the unforgiving curb and pain shot through her temple. Blurry images of strangers' faces swam before her eyes. The sound of leather soles on the pavement, a shadowy silhouette of a tall man walking down the alleyway toward her.

Heart pounding, she pressed herself against the wall. *Don't let it be the thugs from the bar.* Next to her, something moved. *Please, no rats. Not now*. Then, a cough in the darkness, a figure standing near her head. Someone spoke. A hand grabbed her shoulder. She thrashed out. Her arm struck a walking stick, a soft male voice said, 'Help her.' Strong arms wrapped around her, lifting her from the pavement. She let herself go and fell back onto cool leather of an airconditioned car, inhaled the aroma of Tiger Balm. Then, everything went dark.

CHARLOTTE ROLLED OVER AND GROANED. Deep searing pain, a throb that resonated from the bruise on her forehead to the back of her head. She forced her eyes open, afraid of what she might see. Through blurry eyes, she saw her laptop on the bedside table, her clothes folded on the dresser, her door key on the counter. She breathed a sigh of relief. She was back in her hotel, lying on the bed in her room.

She sat up abruptly and caught her breath as a sharp pain shot through her temple. Memories from the previous night washed over her and her heart raced as she remembered what had happened. Someone had stolen her bag. She swung her feet onto the floor and looked for her shoes, frantic to get to the lobby and find someone to help her. On the chair next to her bed, her jacket was draped over a small lumpy item with a long strap hanging down. It was her bag. She grabbed it, unzipped it, and tipped the contents onto the bed: her passport, then her wallet, Rashid's letter, and a collection of knickknacks essential to her life. Relief flooded over her. Someone had rescued her from the alley, and someone had found her bag.

She put everything back in her bag and zipped it tightly. It was four o'clock in the morning, so she pulled on her pyjamas and lay under the ceiling fan watching the blades go round. The whirring sound was soothing, so she closed her eyes, feeling the tension drain from her. A door opened in the next bungalow, then the sound of faint music from a distant radio as she drifted off to sleep.

All at once, she was on a beach. Her dad was riding a horse and pointing toward the ocean. Her mother was thrashing in the waves. Charlotte shook her head and shouted into the wind, 'I can't help you anymore. You'll pull me under.'

Her father yelled. 'Come and join me, Charlie horse!' This time she took his hand and leapt up next to him.

'Where are we going?' she asked. The roar of pounding waves drowned out his reply.

She didn't know what awakened her. The annoying buzz of mosquitos? The throbbing in her head? She lay in the dark until faint shimmers of light cracked the blackness and morning sounds crept through the cabin's thin walls, then rose and limped to the bathroom. She looked in the mirror and gasped. Staring back at her was a face drained of colour. Dull, straggly hair damp with perspiration, and bloodshot eyes ringed with black mascara. This was a face she recognised. She'd seen it before but hadn't realised till now who it reminded her of. It was her mother.

She looked away. Perhaps she should brush her hair and put on makeup. Or take a shower. Her shoulders slumped. Who was she kidding? No amount of makeup or grooming would make a difference. She was turning into something she dreaded.

A muffled thud from outside interrupted her thoughts. She dashed into the garden where a small bird lay on the grassy verge below the sill, its tiny wings fluttering weakly. She ran back inside, grabbed a tissue box from her bedside table, and went back to the garden where she squatted next to the bird and scooped it up, remembering her training at the animal shelter. Birds that flew into windows usually hit the glass with their beaks, forcing their heads up so their chests took the brunt of the impact. It was crucial to turn them right-side up or they'd probably die.

She turned the bird over and cupped her fingers around its motionless body, then gently placed it inside the tissue box, propping it upright with folded tissues. She sat cross-legged on the ground, her back against a tree, with the box balanced on her knees. Please don't die, she whispered. Please don't leave me. Drawing the box closer, she leaned her head back and closed her eyes. A warm breeze wafted through the leaves and the rhythmic chirping of cicadas echoed in the background. Her body started to droop, and the box slipped lower down on her lap.

Suddenly a high-pitched voice rang out. 'Waiter! I want a bottle of water!'

She jumped. She had fallen asleep and the box on her lap was empty. She scrambled to her feet and looked around, frantically searching for the injured bird. Then, a twig dropped from the tree onto her shoulder. She looked up as a small bird hopped along the branch and flew across the river. It was her bird; she knew it. This was the first good thing to happen in a long time.

The voice rang out again. 'Hey! Charlene!' and a figure came toward her: a tall, thin woman with closely cropped jet-black hair and painted on eyebrows. It was Flippo. Charlotte groaned. If Flippo were here, Christal wouldn't be far behind.

Flippo strode across the lawn, waving. 'Fancy seeing *you* here,' she said, yanking Charlotte to her feet. 'Bubbles figured a few days away from the shitty city might give me a better impression of this country. We came down in a private car last night. How 'bout you?' She tightened the sarong around her waist and kept talking before Charlotte could respond. 'We roped Hasan into paying for the car. He's the only one working these days, innit?' She yawned and stretched her arms above her head. 'Yer haven't seen either of them, have you? They're probably sleeping off last night. Come get coffee?' She raised her eyebrows. 'Looks like you could use some too.'

Charlotte's smile froze. Not Hasan as well. She clutched her bag closer and pointed to the gate. 'Sorry, but I've got to—I'm about to—'

A bird flew across her path. Charlotte squared her shoulders and looked Flippo in the eye. 'Actually, I have an appointment.' She walked away, then stopped and looked back. 'And by the way, my name's Charlotte.'

23

Charlotte closed the hotel gate behind her and hobbled along the sandy path. Her ankle throbbed and she'd been in such a hurry to escape from Flippo that she hadn't paid any attention to where she was going. She wanted to see Samnang, but she had no idea how to find Wat Sambor again.

Up ahead, two young men stood next to a motorbike leaning against a brick wall. Charlotte walked up to them. 'Excuse me—*Sua s'day*—can you please give me a ride?' she asked, hoping they spoke English. She took two dollar bills from her wallet and held them out.

One of the men nodded. 'Where you want go?' he asked. He handed her a helmet and pointed to the leather seat, ignoring the money. 'I not moto driver but I take you.'

Her heart sank and she scanned the street to see if a tuk-tuk or a taxi might be coming down the path. But she was far from a main road and there were no vehicles in sight. It had been a struggle walking with a sore ankle, and she couldn't go much further so she took a deep breath. She had to have faith in someone. She strapped the helmet under her chin, climbed behind the driver and said, 'Please take me to Wat Sambor.'

The motorbike driver turned out to be a pleasant young man who refused to take any payment and only wanted to practise his English. When they arrived at the pagoda, he reached into his satchel and handed her a mango. 'Many thank yous for helping with speaking, lay-dee,' he said. 'I hope you holiday nice.' He sped away, leaving her on a grassy verge near Wat Sambor.

She wasn't ready to face Samnang, so she bought a bottle of cold water from a sidewalk vendor and looked for a place to sit. It was a hot morning, but the slight breeze made it bearable, so she sat on a bench under a tree and pulled her hat down to shield her face. Fanning herself with a large leaf, she considered her options about what to do next. The first decision was easy. She had sensed it coming for weeks, perhaps months, but last night's experience had made up her mind. It was time to stop drinking. Her reflection in the mirror this morning had shown what she might become, and she didn't like it.

The encounter with the bird had shifted her attitude and made her feel calmer than she had felt in a while. It had been a message; she was sure of it. She wasn't useless. She *could* make a difference, and she didn't need anyone how to show her how. Her shoulders relaxed and she took a deep breath as she considered her situation and reached three conclusions: one, her mother had deceived her, two, her father had tried to connect with her, and three, Roxy was hiding something. She took off her sunglasses and rubbed her eyes, speculating what she might do. She could go home—no way. She could call Mum—again, no way. She could ignore her—a strong possibility. She could do nothing. She smiled wryly. Wasn't that what Samnang had suggested?

A wisp of smoke floated toward her from a passer-by's cigar. She inhaled the rich, buttery aroma, recognising the scent of Vanilla Cream, her dad's favourite flavour. She thought of how she used to bury her face in his cardigan after he'd left home, hoping the scent would linger forever. As she pictured him, one of his sayings popped into her head: *Courage is looking fear right in the eye and saying, get the hell out of my way, I've got things to do*. She thrust out her chin. She could do that. But where should she start? His letters. There was an address for his friend in Belgium.

Her mind flashed to Rashid and the futile attempts to track down Chris. Perhaps she'd been crazy thinking Christal might be Chris and that Rashid was here in Kampot. She drained the water bottle and stood up, bringing her thoughts back to the present. It was time to find Samnang.

As she walked into the courtyard, she spotted him talking with another monk, so she waited until they'd finished their conversation, then gave a small wave. Samnang bowed to the other monk and walked toward her. 'I was hoping you'd be back,' he said, smiling. 'I think—' He paused. 'Something's changed.'

She pushed a lock of hair behind her ear. 'Rough night.'

'That's not what I mean. You seem calmer.'

'Really? I think I owe it to a little bird who almost broke my window and—' She broke off, noticing Samnang's confused expression. 'Never mind. I'm going back to Phnom Penh, but I wanted to apologise before I left.'

'For what?'

'I was rude yesterday. You were trying to help, and I insulted you. I'm sorry.'

'As I said before, there's no need for apology. It's my job to help you pursue a new path. The rest is up to you.'

'I was thoughtless,' she said. 'I also wanted to ask you something. You said that you understood what I was dealing with. What did you mean?'

'Are you sure you want to know? Your challenges belong to you, so my experiences shouldn't affect the way you lead your life.'

Charlotte nodded and Samnang gestured toward a bench. 'If you want to hear my story, I'm happy to tell you. It just might take a while.'

IT TOOK an hour for Samnang to explain his personal history and reasons for becoming a monk. He finally paused, and Charlotte took a deep breath. 'Perhaps we're both in Cambodia for a purpose,' she said. 'So, what happened next? After you arrived.'

'It wasn't what I'd expected. The man who picked me up at the airport didn't speak any English and the car had no air-conditioning. That night I slept on a straw mat on a concrete floor in a hut in the middle of nowhere. It was rainy season, and everything was soaked. I didn't expect luxury and I thought I was prepared, but I really had no idea...and I didn't sleep a wink the first night.' He grimaced. 'Mosquitoes. The next day, they gave me robes and an alms bowl and introduced me to the Venerable Tep Chhim—*Lokru*, they called him. Then I got sick. Twenty-four hours of diarrhoea and vomiting almost made me go home. I was too stubborn to quit but I won't kid you, it wasn't easy.'

'Sounds awful,' Charlotte said, frowning. 'But what about

the person you mentioned the other day? The one who made your life miserable?'

'I prefer not to share that. It's in the past and I can't change it.' His expression softened. 'Lokru got me through the hard times. He became like a father to me. And when he told me he was moving to Phnom Penh, I asked to go with him. That's how I ended up getting ordained there. Lokru was the one who chose my name. He'd seen me struggle and heard how much I'd changed. He said my coming to Cambodia was good luck: for him, for his country, and for me. And that's how I became Samnang.'

24

The sound of children splashing in the river greeted Charlotte as she walked onto the hotel grounds. Across the lawn, a couple of hammocks were strung between tall palm trees. Christal lay in one, snoring loudly through her open mouth. Rolls of fat flopped over her emerald green bikini and a bottle of Angkor beer had spilled onto the grass beneath the hammock.

Charlotte trod softly across the lawn, trying not to wake her, then suddenly a voice rang out. 'Hey, Charlie!' Charlotte hadn't noticed Flippo dangling in another hammock, her scrawny frame wrapped in a skin-tight blue swimsuit and an enormous hat pulled low on her head.

Flippo clambered from the hammock and tiptoed across the hot gravel in bare feet. 'Fuck, that's hot!' she squealed, scampering to a patch of lawn where she flapped her arms and yelled. 'It's beer o'clock, innit?

Charlotte decided to be polite for a few minutes then make a quick getaway, hopefully before Christal woke up. Flippo ran over and grabbed her arm. 'Sorry 'bout calling you the wrong name,' she said. 'Bubbles has a useless memory unless it's for a man or a drink.' She led Charlotte to the open-air lobby, flopped onto a padded wicker couch, and patted the seat beside her. 'As penalty for screwing up, let's make her buy the next round of drinks.' She yelled across the lawn. 'Bubbles! Get yer fat arse over here. Cocktail time!'

Charlotte quietly groaned as Christal jerked awake, grasped the side of the hammock, and tumbled onto the grass. As she fell, she grabbed the bottom of her bikini, hoisted it over her ample derriere, then scrambled to her feet. 'Shit, Flippo! Lower yer voice, willya?' She walked across the lawn and sat on the couch next to Flippo. 'Well, look who's here!' she said, looking at Charlotte. 'What the hell happened to *you* last week? We looked for hours. Thought you'd been abducted or gone home with one of those assholes from the bar.'

'Bullshit, Bubbles. Don't make our beautiful friend feel bad,' Flippo said. 'Truth is, we had no idea you'd left, Charlie. We were too shitfaced to remember our names, never mind worry about you, sweet cheeks. Besides, there were a couple of blokes who showed up and paid our bar bill.' She winked at Christal and banged on the glass tabletop. 'Let's get some cocktails, shall we? It's way past noon.' She waved her arm and a thin strap slipped off her shoulder. Tugging it up, she yelled to the waiter. 'Boy! Bring me a Long Island iced tea!'

Christal nodded. 'Make that two. Charlie, wanna make it three?'

Charlotte shook her head. She didn't want to hang around Christal and Flippo but realised this might be an opportunity to find out if Rashid was Christal's father. So, she smiled politely and replied, 'Nothing for me. I'm on the wagon.'

'The wagon?' Christal snorted. 'What wagon? The one loaded with beer?' She nudged Flippo with her elbow.

Charlotte shrugged. 'Lemonade's fine.'

As the waiter set the cocktails on the table, Charlotte scanned the other occupants of the patio. There were two elderly women drinking tea, a family playing cards, and three boys gawking at their phones. She wondered if Rashid might be here, too, and if he *were*, would he be lounging in the lobby, sitting at the bar, or swimming in the river? She realised she didn't know much about him other than he was Bangladeshi, used to work as a surgeon, and had an English wife.

Flippo and Christal lounged back on the couch, their cocktail glasses almost empty. Neither seemed inclined to move and while Charlotte wanted to get away, there was something she needed to do. She reached inside her bag for Rashid's ring and slipped it onto her middle finger. Bending her knuckle to make sure it didn't fall off, she placed her hand on the table next to the cocktail glass. Christal picked up her glass with a brief glance at Charlotte's hand and finished her drink. Charlotte twisted the ring around her finger, hoping to attract Christal's attention, but there was no reaction. So, she took it off, twirled it in her palm, and dropped it onto the floor where it rolled near Christal's foot.

'Watch where you're dropping yer stuff.' Christal leaned down and picked up the ring. 'Nice ring. A bit big for you, innit?'

Charlotte nodded. 'It's a gift from my dad.'

'Lucky you.'

Charlotte took the ring from Christal's outstretched hand. 'Did *your* dad ever give you anything special?' she asked.

Christal raised her eyebrows and sneered. 'You're kidding, right? My dad wouldn't give me a blanket from his bed if I was freezing to death.' She hesitated. 'Actually, he did give me something special.'

'What's that?' Charlotte held her breath.

'A bloody good sex drive!' She roared with laughter, spurting liquid across the table. 'That's what got him in trouble in the first place, innit?' She glanced up as a man approached the patio. 'Hello, darling. About time you joined us!'

Charlotte looked around to see who Christal was addressing, and her mouth went dry. Hasan was walking up the steps, dark glasses covering his eyes. His paunch drooped over a pair of baggy swim trunks and his hairy chest was sprinkled with sand. A pair of binoculars hung over his bare shoulder.

She put on her sunglasses, tugging her hat low on her head, and pulling strands of hair over her forehead. As she did so, Christal leaned across her and yanked the binoculars from Hasan's arm. 'Put those away, you depraved freak,' she teased. 'We were just talking about your charming uncle. Charlie here was asking if he ever gave me anything special.'

Hasan tilted his glasses down and peered over the top. Lowering his chin, he looked Charlotte up and down, then lit a cigarette. 'Charlie? Isn't that a man's name? You look all woman to me, babe.' He blew a smoke ring toward her.

She sank lower into the seat, inwardly recoiling. The last time she had been this close was when he and Moh had been leering at her in the café. She prayed the sunglasses and hat would disguise her identity.

'What was you askin', Bubbles?' Hasan said, turning his attention away from Charlotte. 'Your dad give you sumthing special? Sure, he did: a big bum and a big mouth. Haha! That's a good way to describe *him*, isn't it? A big bum with a big mouth!'

'Don't be a shithead,' Christal replied, sneering. 'We're

related, whether we like it or not.' She turned to Charlotte. 'My dad was married five times. Mum was his third wife. She was gorgeous when she met him, and now she's a manic-depressive crackhead.' She took a cigarette from Hasan and lit up. 'My old man's a friggin' fireman, for fuck's sake, you'd think he'd have some respect for human life. But he doesn't put out fires, he ignites them, if you get my drift. Whaddya think he uses those ladders for?' She inhaled deeply. 'He doesn't have bedroom eyes, he's got gutter eyes. Any woman who meets 'im ends up in the gutter.' She flicked ash onto the floor and took another puff of the cigarette. 'So little Christal flew far, far away, and I don't give a shit if I never see his ugly face again. That answer your question, babycakes?'

Charlotte stared at Christal, unsure how to respond. Then her phone buzzed inside her bag and Christal nudged her. 'You gonna answer that?'

Charlotte glanced at the phone. It was Roxy. She pressed the reject button and turned it off. Her conversation with Christal hadn't turned out the way she'd hoped. But, as distasteful as the contact had been, she now knew Christal wasn't Chris. She placed a couple of bills on the table and stood up. 'That's for the lemonade,' she said. 'Enjoy your afternoon.' She slunk away, eyes downcast, hoping Hasan wouldn't stop her.

Glancing at her watch, she saw it was 1:50. The bus left at three o'clock so there was enough time to make the bed, wash the shower, and wipe the bathroom counters before returning the key to reception, indulging her manic obsession to leave a place cleaner than when she arrived. After she finished her tasks, she waited at the front desk, the sound of clinking glasses drifting across the lawn, accompanied by shrieks of laughter from Christal, Flippo, and Hasan. Hoping they wouldn't see her standing at the other side of the lobby, she opened the guestbook, wrote a brief review, and read comments from some of the guests. She flipped back to the previous page, and a signature jumped out at her, written in the swirly script of a fountain pen: Dr. Rashid Farouk.

25

The bus trip from Kampot was long and uncomfortable. This time there was no friendly Cambodian to chat with, only a barrage of questions marching through her head. Charlotte stared through the window, watching the lines in the middle of the road as the thump of music from the radio pulsated in her head.

Nobody at the hotel could remember seeing an elderly Bangladeshi man, even though Rashid's name was in the register. She had asked the cleaning lady and the bartender and the receptionist but none of them recalled anything. She'd even asked some of the hotel guests, but no-one had seen him. Finally, she'd asked to speak to the manager, a middle-aged Frenchman who ran the hotel with his Cambodian wife. He'd listened patiently as she'd described Rashid and pointed out his name in the guest book, then merely shrugged and said, 'I'm very sorry, madam. We do our best to remember all our guests but sometimes they are very private, so we don't want to intrude.'

A group of chattering American teenagers on the bus made sleep impossible so Charlotte tried to block out their voices. Then, as they approached Phnom Penh a bouncy brunette leaned across the aisle and prodded her friend in the ribs. 'That's the café!' she squealed. 'The one with the sexy new waiter named Chris. He's got the most delicious English accent you ever heard.'

Charlotte tuned out of the rest of the conversation and craned her neck to see the name of the café. A bright yellow awning hung over the front door and the name emblazoned in orange read, *Jinjerbread.* Minutes later, the bus arrived in Phnom Penh and Charlotte threw her bag over her shoulder, making a mental note to return to the café another time, and set out for the long walk to Roxy's flat. She wanted time to rehearse what she was going to say.

'Roxy,' she muttered under her breath,' What do you know about my father?' Too blunt.

She tried again. 'Hi Rox. You were right about Kampot, it's lovely. Anything new going on in your world?' Too insincere and weird.

The third try felt better. 'I missed you in Kampot. We would have had fun together. By the way, I had a message from Alistair and there's something I need to talk about.' She took a deep breath, realising the right words would come when she saw Roxy. She never liked to plan things in advance, anyway. If she rehearsed a speech, she always forgot what she was going to say.

When she reached the apartment building, dusk was falling and barbecues on street corners were starting to simmer. She stood in the doorway, fingering the red string around her wrist, and hoping Peter wasn't there. It would be impossible to present a façade of normalcy and act as though nothing was wrong if someone else were around. In the living room, a mosquito zapper crackled and hissed as insects flew into the coils. The only movement came from a pedestal fan that turned the yellow curtains into winged butterflies. She walked through the flat, listening for sounds. There was nobody in the living room or kitchen, just the ticking of the wall clock. It was almost ten o'clock. Perhaps everyone was asleep. Or maybe they'd gone out. She padded through the kitchen, trying to be quiet, then spotted a note taped to the fridge: *Roxy's in Apollo hospital. Call me or meet me there. Peter.*

CHARLOTTE RAN THROUGH THE HOSPITAL, wincing each time she stepped on her sore foot. At the end of a corridor, Peter sat on a wooden bench, hunched over his mobile phone. She limped toward him and his brow furrowed.

'What happened?' she panted. 'Is she okay?'

He uncrossed his legs and ran a hand through his hair. 'How did...?' He paused and took a breath. 'Your phone must be switched off,' he said, curtly.

She tossed her bag on the bench beside him. 'What happened?'

'She came off her bike.' The muscles in his face tightened.

Charlotte gasped. 'What? How?'

'An SUV hit her.'

'Oh no! Where? Is she all right?'

'Seems to be, but they're keeping her here. She hit her head when her helmet came off. She was on her way back from Annie's. I think there was oil on the road, but I don't know the details.'

'How did she get here?'

'Waiters at a café called for help. She was unconscious. Someone called the last person she'd phoned. That was me. Damn driver didn't even stop.'

'What!'

'Just left her there like an animal.'

Charlotte took a deep breath. 'What did the doctor say?'

'She's got to have a CT scan. I'm waiting to see if I need to stay here or take her home.' He leaned against the wall. 'A lot's been going on since you left. She needs you.'

Charlotte stared along the corridor. Her friend was hurt, and she'd ignored her phone calls because she'd been wrapped up in her own misery. Tears pricked the back of her throat. This was Roxy. Her best friend. A baby's cry echoed along the tiled corridor as a woman walked past carrying a child wrapped in blankets. A surgical gurney rattled at the end of the hallway, and a desk phone rang in an adjacent office. Peter's voice resonated in her ear. 'Charlotte? You listening? I asked if you wanted to see her.'

She took a deep breath. 'Of course I do.'

She pushed open the door to the hospital room, nervously peeking inside. Roxy lay in a narrow bed, a tube running into her arm from a bag of saline above the bed. She was covered with a thin blue blanket and her feet poked out at the bottom, her toenails painted with purple nail polish. Strands of pink hair poked from beneath a white bandage that was wrapped around her head. Charlotte eased the door shut behind her.

A voice came from the bed. 'Martha.... it's you,' Roxy said, lifting her head off the pillow and weakly waving an arm. 'You came...'

Charlotte froze. 'Roxy? It's me, Charlotte. I don't know who—'

Roxy chuckled, then groaned loudly. 'Shit, Charlo! Fooled

you, didn't I? Ouch! My bloody ribs. That hurt so fucking much, but it was worth it to see your face.'

Charlotte stood motionless near the door. Couldn't Roxy ever be serious? She'd just been in an accident and was acting like an idiot. Her mind went blank. For the first time in their relationship, she didn't know what to say.

Roxy fell back into the pillows. 'When did you get back? Did you bring pepper?'

'Pepper?'

'You went to Kampot, didn't you? Home of the world's best pepper.' She winced as she tried to move. '*That* was painful! I feel like I fell under a bulldozer. Bloody reckless driver coulda killed me.' She rubbed her head. 'You didn't bring pepper?'

Charlotte shook her head.

'How was your trip?'

'Fine.'

'That's it? You go on a solo adventure, and all you can say is fine? You okay?'

Charlotte dug her nails into her palm. Anything she'd say would give away her feelings. 'I said everything's fine. I'm just tired.'

'Well, you picked a jolly old time to go away. Did Peter tell you?'

'About your accident?'

Roxy tucked a pillow under her arm as she shifted her position. 'That's just part of it. I feel like crap and I'd prefer to forget about it all. But I'm so pissed off.' She groaned. 'For goodness sake, sit down.' She gestured toward a folding metal chair next to the bed.

Charlotte sat on the edge of the seat and stared at a framed picture of a waterfall hanging on the wall. Maybe if Roxy did all the talking, she wouldn't notice Charlotte's lack of participation.

'It's Annie,' Roxy said. 'She cheated me.'

Charlotte stared back. 'Annie? What do you mean?'

'She's a phony. It was her fault I came off my bloody bike... too busy thinking how she screwed things up.'

Charlotte stiffened. 'What are you talking about? Annie's lovely. She's a Buddhist. I don't—'

'She's not lovely at all. And I don't buy her Buddhist bullshit. Wait till you hear this.' She propped herself up on an elbow, groaning as she raised her shoulders. 'Remember her story about coming here to start a new life? Total crap. Know why she came to Cambodia? To hide.' Her cheeks reddened. 'She's a junkie. Her husband walked out because she drove him away. And she didn't close her business. She ran it into the ground.'

'Where did you get *that* idea?'

'Chenla.'

'And you believe her? Over Annie?'

'Just listen to me, will you? She saw Annie take money from a customer and stick it in her pocket. Annie told her she was keeping it for me, and Chenla believed her. Why wouldn't she? But it happened again so Chenla told the other girls. Nobody said a word to me, of course. Cambodians don't question anyone who's from a higher social order—especially an expat.

'But a few days ago, I was doing inventory and noticed some tapestries were missing. I asked Chenla where she'd put them—figured they didn't get onto the shelves yet. She looked like she'd seen a ghost. Eventually, she told me Annie sold them and kept the money.'

'No way. Annie wouldn't—'

Roxy held up her hand. 'Hear me out. I called Annie and asked her to meet me. She didn't show up. Then she didn't come to work the following morning. Or the next. So, I went to her hotel. Not to accuse her of anything; just to talk about it. And guess what? She'd checked out without paying her bill. The hotel manager's an Aussie, so he didn't have any trouble telling me how *he* felt. Said she'd been stoned most nights; had some strange visitors. Heard her yelling on the phone to her ex-husband about money.'

Charlotte stood and pushed the chair back. 'It's a mistake. Chenla probably misunderstood. Maybe the hotel manager had an axe to grind.'

Roxy narrowed her eyes. 'Why are you defending her? I already told you I know what's going on.' She reached for a cup and took a sip of water. 'I got in touch with Peter's mum in Sydney. She did some poking around and gave me the whole story.'

Charlotte crossed her arms. 'I want to hear Annie's side of it.' She hadn't meant the words to come out as they did, so tough and harsh. But there had been something about Annie she'd felt she could trust; an older woman who'd inspired her to believe in herself. And now she was defending her to her oldest friend, which made no sense at all. A lump came to her throat. It wasn't in her nature to mistrust people and now she was doubting everyone.

An awkward silence settled over the room. Roxy lay back on the pillows and closed her eyes. 'I'm tired. Let's talk tomorrow.'

Charlotte left the room and leaned against the wall in the corridor, relieved to get away. She had been anticipating an awkward encounter with Roxy, but not this. A cough behind made her turn around. Peter stood in the corridor, dangling the door keys.

'She told me to go home,' he said. 'Test results won't be

ready till morning, so she's stuck here another night.' He walked to the door and Charlotte followed him into a waiting tuk-tuk. They sat in silence for the first few minutes as the vehicle drove through the city, then Peter turned to her. 'Where the hell were you? I called a million times.'

She caught her breath, taken aback by the tone of his voice. 'I didn't know. I—'

'Why didn't you answer your phone? I was worried sick about Roxy, then started thinking someone might've abducted you or something? Couldn't you have bothered to call?'

'I'm sorry but...I feel so—'

'You should! Roxy's turning herself inside out for you, and you disappear on her. I'm surprised at you. Don't you care?'

She looked down at her hands. She wouldn't cry. It had been a tough day and now she had upset Peter, too. They rode in silence until she was able to speak. 'I'm sorry,' she muttered. 'I didn't know.'

Peter held up his hand. 'Say it to Roxy, not me.'

The tuk-tuk jolted as it picked up speed. They passed a police station and Peter shook his head. 'By the way, they caught the bastard,' he said, curtly.

'Who do you—?'

'The man who killed Sethya.'

Charlotte gasped. 'What did they do with him?'

'Nothing.'

'How could they do nothing? He—'

'He's a big wheel in the military.'

'So, what does that mean?'

'It means the police won't do a damned thing.' He took off his glasses and rubbed his eyes with the palms of his hands. 'Big shots get away with murder here. Literally. Buy their way out of everything.' He exhaled. 'I heard about a guy who ran someone over, backed up, and ran them over again. Roxy's lucky to be alive.'

'What?' Charlotte's eyes widened.

He pressed his lips together. 'With some of the bigshots, it's cheaper to throw money at a dead person's family than foot a doctor bill. I know, it's fucked up. Sometimes I wonder—' His voice drifted off as he took out a handkerchief and wiped his brow. Neon signs flickered on each side of the street and people lingered outside nightclubs smoking cigarettes. The tuk-tuk stopped at a traffic light and Peter turned to her. 'She's wanted this forever, you know,' he said, softly.

'Wanted what?'

'You, here.' The light changed. 'She wouldn't stop talking about it. Shoulda seen her when she found out you were coming. She gets lonely. You're probably the only real friend she has.'

'Hardly,' Charlotte said, sighing. 'She's the popular one. Always has been.'

'Quantity's not quality,' he said. 'She knows lots of people but they're not real friends. Don't let her down, okay?'

She started to speak, then paused. Better to keep quiet until Roxy was home.

'You do realise she's envious of you, don't you?' he said.

'That's a laugh. I'm the one who's envious. I've always wanted to be more like her.'

'She told me you're the only person who really listens. I'd hoped to meet you at our wedding, but it seems you had better things to do.'

The tuk-tuk stopped outside their building. Peter paid the driver and strode upstairs, two steps at a time. Charlotte scurried behind him. Once inside the flat, he turned his head and spoke over his shoulder. 'I'll be leaving early for the hospital tomorrow then going to Boxy Wide Elephant till Roxy's back on her feet,' he said, then disappeared into his bedroom.

She went to the kitchen and opened the fridge, hoping to find something to eat. Something comforting. Peter's words still echoed in her ears. *Roxy is envious of you. You're the only real friend she has*. Perhaps she had been wrong to judge her friend without knowing the details. Maybe there would be a rational explanation. A packet of fudge fell onto the floor. She picked up a piece and nibbled on it, then put the box back in the fridge. The flat felt empty without Roxy, so she leaned against the wall, her appetite gone, then noticed a book leaning on a bag of biscuits, *Twisted Roots Under Solitary Trees.*

'Peter,' she called, hoping he'd hear her from his room. 'Where did this book come from?'

He stuck his head through a crack in the door. 'Thought it was yours,' he said, and shut the door behind him.

She picked up the book, flipped through it, and slipped it into her bag. The tiny flat suddenly felt very hollow and large. She went to her room and stood by the window, staring across the city. A sliver of moon hung in the sky and the roads were deserted. She had nobody to talk to, nobody to share her concerns with, and no one to keep her company. There had been many times when she had felt lonely back home. But she'd never felt so alone as she did right now.

26

The creaky front door woke Charlotte when Peter left for work the following morning, so she rolled out of bed and got dressed. A text flashed on her phone: *Coming home today. No need to visit me.* She didn't reply. She'd been hoping Roxy might stay in hospital another day so she'd have longer to pluck up her courage for their conversation but now she realised she'd have to find the words.

She looked at the clock. Roxy probably wouldn't be home until later in the day so there was plenty of time to put her plan into action. She opened her laptop and reread her father's letter: *You can always find me through my friend, Patrick Jansen. Here's how to reach him.* The letter was dated 2014 and Patrick's situation might have changed since then, but it would be a good place to start.

She opened a browser and typed *Patrick Jansen, Belgium,* into the search engine, then groaned when more than fourteen thousand results showed up. Which Patrick Jansen was he? The alpine skier, the soccer player, or the author? Did he go by the name of Pat? Did he still live in Belgium? She could search for hours and never know if she'd found the right one. She stared at the screen, read some of the profiles, and decided none of them sounded like the kind of person her father would befriend. His friends would probably be professionals, and have similar interests, like opera or tennis or horseback riding. There must be an easier way to track him down.

She found a ream of computer paper in Peter's office and began to write. *Dear Mr. Jansen. My name is Charlotte and my father is Olivier Fontaine.* Too formal. She tried again, *Dear Patrick. This letter may come as a shock out of the blue.* Too expressive.

The third attempt felt best. *Dear Mr. Jansen. My father, Olivier Fontaine, told me I could contact him through you. I hope this is still the case and would greatly appreciate your assistance.* She wrote about her discovery of the letters and the desire to reconnect with her father. *As you can imagine*, she ended, *I'm extremely anxious to hear back, and would be grateful if you would contact me as soon as possible.*

Her heart raced as she dropped the letter at the post office. Patrick Jansen could have moved. He might not respond. The post from Cambodia could take forever, or never reach its destination at all. She also had no idea how this man knew her father. All she could do was be patient—and trust. It was late morning and she didn't want to be home when Roxy arrived, so she headed to Jinjerbread, hoping to find nourishment and a waiter named Chris.

*

JINJERBREAD WAS CRAMMED with people slurping bowls of noodles and munching on sandwiches, so Charlotte scanned the room, looking for non-Cambodian staff. In the back corner, a young western man was removing an apron, his shoulder-length black hair tied back in a ponytail and his tanned face peppered with freckles. As he walked from the counter, a co-worker waved and called out to him, 'Bye, Chris. See you tomorrow.' That was easy. With any luck he'd be receptive to a stranger with a weird request.

She walked toward him. 'Excuse me. You're Chris?' she said.

He grinned playfully and pointed to his chest. 'As the name tag says.'

She stuck out her hand. 'Charlotte.' A firm handshake and a warm smile. Dark eyes that reminded her of Rashid. 'I think your father was on my flight from London.' She dropped his hand. 'Is he a doctor?'

'Yeah. He got here a couple weeks ago.'

She took a deep breath. 'He left something on the plane. I've been looking for him.'

Chris laughed. 'Sounds like something he'd do.'

A middle-aged blonde woman approached and draped an arm around Chris's waist. 'Hi Mum, this is Charlotte,' he said. 'She's trying to find Dad.'

The woman smiled and shook Charlotte's hand. *She must be Rashid's English rose.*

'Do you live here, too?' Chris asked Charlotte.

She shook her head. 'I'm here on holiday.'

'Charlotte was on Dad's flight,' Chris told his mother. 'She said he left something behind.' He turned to Charlotte. 'What'd he forget this time?'

Charlotte held out the envelope. 'This.'

Chris glanced at it. 'It's addressed to me,' he said, and reached out his hand. 'I'll take it.'

She clutched the envelope, reluctant to part with it. 'Could I give it to him myself?' she asked. 'He was very kind to me, and I'd like to see him again.'

'Suit yourself. He's here somewhere.' He looked around, then pointed across the café. 'There he is.'

Charlotte looked in the direction of his pointed finger and saw a thin, balding man sitting at a table facing toward the window. His shoulders were stooped, and he wore a pale grey suit jacket a little too big for him. Charlotte's pulse quickened and she stepped toward him. As she did so, a stocky man with a moustache cut her off.

'Bloody hell, Chris,' he said. 'How d'you manage to work in this ghastly heat?' He glanced at Charlotte and smiled. 'Sorry. Didn't mean to interrupt.'

Chris unpinned his name tag and stuck it in his pocket. 'Dad, it's Charlotte. From your flight.'

The man wiped his face with a handkerchief and stuck out a sweaty hand. 'Nice to meet you. Hope you're enjoying yourself as much as we are.'

Charlotte's cheeks warmed. She glanced across the room as the man pushed back his chair and stood, revealing a beard and pale complexion. She turned to Chris. 'Oh. I don't think...It's not' She stumbled over her words. 'Never mind. I don't... Different flight. Gotta go.'

She dashed into the street, disappointment washing over her. Chris and his parents probably thought she was weird, but Roxy was right; her quest was absurd. Then she thought about her encounter with Rashid and how he'd planted seeds of hope when she'd been afraid. He'd probably had no idea the effect he'd had on her, and there was a chance she might be able to pay him back. She couldn't give up now.

She contemplated posting another notice on the Cambodian forum, then her phone buzzed with a message: *Just got home. Hospital food sucks. Pick up a pizza with everything on it. Pizza shop is 119 steps from fruit market.* Five seconds later, a second text arrived: *Not happy pizza!* She hesitated. As much as she wanted to trust her friend, she felt guarded. Then she remembered the quote, *Solitary trees, if they grow at all, grow strong*, and took a deep breath. If there were a time to talk to Roxy, this was it.

❦

SHE FOUND THE PIZZA SHOP, placed an order, and stood in the shade to wait. Since she was going to face Roxy, she needed something to distract her: a double mushroom three cheese pizza with olives and garlic should do the trick. As she debated whether to pick up beer, a voice called from across the street. 'Jallod! Hello Jallod!' It was SomOn. He did a U-turn in the tuk-tuk and drew up next to her. 'Jallod, I see man,' he said, beaming.

'What man?'

'Man from black car.'

She stared blankly.

'He give you paper and you look for him at hotel.'

She stepped into the street and leaned against the tuk-tuk. 'Where did you see him?'

'Take to airport. I think he leave Cambodia.'

Her heart sank. Rashid had left.

'Must go now,' SomOn said. 'Have customer.' He pulled away from the kerb and into traffic.

The pizza shop manager called her name, so she collected her order and walked to Roxy's flat, her mind buzzing. She still had the ring and the letter, and she wouldn't ever see Rashid again if he'd left Cambodia. Deep in thought, she climbed the steps to Roxy's flat, clammy and exhausted. Balancing the pizza box on one hand, she pushed open the door with the other and slipped off her shoes, leaving them in the entryway.

A voice called from the next room. 'I'm in here! Only eleven more steps to go.'

Roxy was in her bedroom, lying in a hammock that hung from the ceiling. Gauze pads were taped to her shoulder and leg, and a large adhesive plaster stuck on her forehead. 'Isn't this brill?' she said as Charlotte entered the room. 'Peter hammered some hooks into the ceiling and rigged it up for me. I hope the nails hold.' She pointed at the plasters on her head and body. 'This is all that remains from my adventure. Happily, I haven't damaged my brain—no more than I've done in the past twenty years, that is. Now, get over here and bring me that pizza.'

Charlotte stood next to the hammock, nerves fluttering in her chest. Roxy seemed to be back to her usual chipper self and didn't seem bothered by last night's awkwardness. Or if she did, she was choosing to ignore it. Charlotte inwardly sighed; that was usually her style, not Roxy's. She put the pizza box on a chair. 'I'll just leave it for you,' she muttered. 'Not hungry.'

Roxy hoisted herself into a sitting position and winced. 'Hey! I'm not eating alone. Sit down.'

'It's okay,' Charlotte said, backing away. 'Another time.'

Roxy wedged a pile of scarves under her hip and lowered her voice. 'Please wait,' she said. 'I know when something's wrong. And I didn't really want pizza.' She paused. 'I'm not very good at this.'

Charlotte's heart hammered. 'I'm not sure what—'

Roxy raised her hand. 'Don't say anything. There's something I have to tell you. I was planning to last night but then you became all weird, so I decided to wait till today.' She winced as she touched the plaster on her face. 'I'm crap at communicating, so I need you to just listen, okay? But first I've got something to give you. Don't open it now—just stick it in your bag. In case you don't want to talk to me later.' She handed Charlotte a spiral notepad covered in silver foil. On the front were two raised words made with tiny shells that read, *History Book*. She took a deep breath as Charlotte put it in her handbag 'D'you remember when Arfer died and you wrote me that note?' she asked.

Charlotte nodded. Arfer was the rabbit she had when she was ten. *R is for rabbit. Let's call him Arfer. Arfer rabbit, get it?* When Arfer died, Roxy went with her to the vet and helped bury him in the tomato patch at the bottom of her garden. Later, Charlotte had written her a letter: *You are the best friend a girl—and a bunny— could ever have. I will love you forever.*

'Of course. Why are you telling me this?'

''Cos there are some things I'm proud of and being there for you and Arfer's one of them. It's not much, but it's the best I can come up with.'

Charlotte leaned against the wall, staring at the floor.

'That's not all I have to say. It's a bit more intense.' She swallowed. 'When you were in Kampot, I had a note from Alistair. He wanted to know if you were okay, and he told me... about your dad's letters.'

Charlotte tensed.

'He said there was something about me in one of them,' Roxy's voice trembled. 'I panicked. I realised you might read things that...' Her gaze drifted to a stain on the wall and she took a deep breath before continuing. 'I wanted to talk to you before you...before you read them. But you never answered your phone.'

A car backfired on the street and Charlotte jumped. Roxy

continued without taking a breath. 'I've been a mess since I heard from Alistair. That's probably why I wiped out on my bike. Then you came back and acted strange, so I figured...' She dislodged a scarf from beneath her hip, and nervously wound it around her arm. 'I screwed up. I'm deeply sorry, and I've despised myself for years.' She looked toward an open window. A bird fluttered on the sill then flew onto an adjacent building. 'I should have told you.'

Charlotte held her breath. *She* was meant to be doing the talking. What about the words she'd rehearsed? 'What're you talking about?' she muttered.

'Didn't Alistair tell you?'

Charlotte shook her head.

'Shit. Then I need to start at the beginning. It was all so long ago, at a party in London, just after my seventeenth birthday.' Her voice was quieter than usual. 'I was with that American guy I met at a Pearl Jam concert who ditched me for a Swedish bimbo.' She took another breath. 'I was shattered. And I was also stoned which wasn't a good combination. So, I turned into a snivelling wreck in a corner. That's where...where he found me.'

'Who?'

'Your dad.'

Charlotte froze. 'My dad? You saw—'

Roxy nodded. 'I know. I'm sorry. I didn't know why he was at a party for art students, but I didn't give a shit. He was so kind and lovely and gave me a hug and stroked my hair—told me I'd get over it. He looked so gorgeous in his brown suede jacket, with that delicious Vanilla Cream Flake aroma, and I just—' She chewed on her ragged fingernails, face flushed.

'You just what?'

'I—well, I—Shit, Charlo, I can't do this.' She closed her eyes. 'It was a long time ago. I didn't—'

'Tell me, Roxy?'

'I...I kissed him.'

'You *what*?'

Roxy buried her face in her hands, words tumbling out faster. 'I was a stupid, teenage idiot. I hate myself for being such a jerk and I'm horribly embarrassed. If it's any consolation, he was horrified. He pushed me away, told me to go home and sleep it off. Said it'd be our secret.'

Charlotte's voice came out as a whimper. 'Your secret?'

'I didn't—'

'Your secret?' Charlotte interrupted, this time louder and with more emphasis. She took a step back.

'I wasn't—'

Charlotte glared. 'Shut up, Roxy. I don't want to hear it.' She choked back a lump in her throat. 'What else happened?'

'Happened? Don't be ridiculous. Nothing else happened.'

'You've kept quiet all this time. You didn't say a word and then—' She paused. The words caught in her throat. 'You left.' She shook her head.

Roxy stretched out her arm. 'I said I'm—'

Charlotte's eyes narrowed. 'That was why, wasn't it?'

'What the—?'

'Why you left. You didn't have the guts to tell me, so you went. What a spineless thing to do.'

'Spineless?' Roxy's eyes widened. 'Don't be ridiculous. Why d'you think I didn't say anything, Miss Prissypants? Because I know how you idolise that man. Because I didn't want you to think badly of him. Because your mum had already messed you up enough.' She exhaled loudly. 'Gimme a break. I was being considerate of *you*. As for leaving the country, I left because I wanted to. It had nothing to do with you. Or your father. I left because I actually dared do something with my life. Not like you, who never had the guts to speak up for yourself.'

Charlotte fought back tears. How had this become *her* fault?

'If you want to accuse someone of being spineless,' Roxy continued. 'Look in a mirror. Ask yourself why you didn't come with me. And why you didn't have the balls to get on a plane when I got married. What was the reason for *that?*' Her face reddened.

For a moment nobody moved. Charlotte's temples throbbed and the thrum was deafening. She couldn't tell Roxy the truth now—that she'd been scared and lonely and that she'd missed her every day; that Roxy's absence had made her feel even more abandoned and alone. Her heart raced as she struggled to find words. Then she heard her mother's voice in her head: *Hard day at work, darling? Have a cocktail.* A six-pack of Angkor beer sat on the counter and she took a step toward it, longing to open one. Then she stopped herself. She marched across the room, picked up a potted plant, and smashed the ceramic jar against the tiled windowsill. Clumps of soil flew across the floor.

'There!' she shouted, tears spilling down her cheeks. 'See what a mess I can make. How fast I can ruin everything I've always kept so neat and tidy? Like our friendship.' She rubbed the back of her hand across her face and glared at Roxy. 'Stupid me for thinking you understood me. And for thinking you wanted me to visit. You only wanted me to come here so you could rub it in my face...show me how useless and pathetic I am, and how wonderful your life is. Admit it!'

'Oh, stop being a victim. It's not the end of the world I kissed your father or that you discover he's not the saint you think. Grow up!'

Charlotte spun on her heel, fire burning in her eyes. 'Know

what? I'm glad I didn't come here before. You with all your new friends and wonderful husband, hiding on the other side of the world and pretending you were my best friend. I bet you had fun laughing about me and my pitiful existence, didn't you?'

'What the hell're you going on about? I'm owning up to something, and you turn it into—'

'Save it for someone who believes you. I've been here four weeks, Roxy! You've had plenty of time to talk to me. Why now? Because Alistair called? Would you have said anything if you hadn't heard from him? What else do you want to tell me?' She glared. 'Like where my father is?'

'What're you talking about? That was the last I—'

'Alistair said you knew. And Dad said it in one of his letters.'

'Are you insane? I don't have a clue where he went. Is that what this is about? D'you really think I'd keep something like *that* from you?'

'You had plenty of secrets. What's one more?' She kicked a piece of ceramic pot across the floor, shattering it into shards. 'I don't know you anymore. I'm—' A door creaked open behind her and Peter entered. He took a step backwards and looked at Roxy then at Charlotte. 'Looks like I've come at a bad time,' he said.

Charlotte glared at him, grabbed her backpack, and sprinted down the stairs two at a time.

27

Charlotte stood on the street, paralysed. Everything had backfired. She'd planned on asking Roxy about the letters and, instead, Roxy had turned on her. The phone buzzed with a new text. She took it out of her bag expecting to see an apology from Roxy and planning to ignore it. Roxy couldn't speak to her like that and expect to be forgiven so fast. But the message contained a single word: *TRUST.*

She dropped it back in her bag and walked toward the riverside, finding herself at Jinjerbread. She wasn't in the mood to deal with obscure messages or be around other people, so she went inside and looked for a quiet place to sit. Students perched at small wooden tables, resting coffee mugs next to their laptops while they chatted on Facebook or worked on assignments. A group of businessmen pored over spreadsheets, and three western women nibbled on a plate of muffins. It was too crowded for Charlotte's liking, so she started toward the door.

Then, she spotted a small room with a sign that read

Private Work. There were two women inside reading newspapers, so she ordered a large coffee and a slice of chocolate cake and found a seat inside the room. She opened her laptop, still burning from the confrontation with Roxy and hoping to find something that might distract her. There were three new messages: one from Trevor, one from Alistair, and one from her mother. She groaned and opened Trevor's message first: a gossipy note with snippets about his shower installation and photos of his new boyfriend's cat. Next, she read Alistair's note *Your mum's doing fine. She managed to get to the supermarket and stock up the fridge. It's all okay.* He didn't mention the letters.

She finished the chocolate cake and ordered a cappuccino and a cinnamon scone, putting aside the message from her mother. Then she browsed Facebook, skimming over posts from work colleagues, and watching animal videos. The door opened and closed as one of the women left the room. The other checked her watch. An air conditioner leaked onto the corner of Charlotte's table. She watched every drop as it fell, each thumping like a heartbeat. *Drip. Drip.* Finally, she drained the coffee and stared at the remaining email. She couldn't ignore it any longer. The message was brief, typical of her mother's demand for attention. *Hello my darling girl. I'm counting the days till you get home—only twenty-seven to go*. Another woman entered the room. Charlotte stared at the screen and chewed on the inside of her mouth. *I miss you. It's really hard being injured and alone. I haven't been out for days, and nobody bothers with me. Alistair's so busy working that he can't visit so I'm living on boiled eggs and toast.*

The air conditioner dripped on the keyboard. *Drip. Drip.* The drops came faster.

I'm sure you're having a wonderful time with your friends, and don't think about me. I think of you all the time and can't wait till you're here.

She bit into her bottom lip. More lies. More victimization. A flash of anger flared in her chest. Samnang would advise her to detach from her feelings and to forgive. But this time she couldn't let it go. She took the elastic band from her hair and wrapped it around her wrist. It was time to speak up. She glanced around the room to see if the women were observing her. One was listening to something on her iPod, the other still reading the newspaper. So, she inserted her headphones and clicked the Skype logo on her laptop. She'd keep it short and with a bit of luck nobody would mind if she spoke quietly. Heart pounding, she waited for her mother to answer.

After almost a minute, a face came into view and Charlotte watched as she wiped a smear of pink lipstick from her mouth and stared at her.

'Oh. It's you. I just got up.' She yawned widely. 'What time is it?'

'Three o'clock in the afternoon. It's six hours later here, remember?'

Her mother ran a shaky hand through her long hair, eyes darting to a spot beyond the screen. 'Is there a reason you're calling at this unreasonable hour?'

Charlotte tugged on the elastic band on her wrist. She had to speak now, or she'd never find the courage. 'Mum, I know.'

Her mother kept talking. 'How come you're not with Roxy or doing something with your new friends? I'm in a lot of pain with my wrist today. I think I—'

'Mum, I said I know.'

'Of course, you know. I sent you an email. Don't you read?' She inspected her nails then glanced toward a sound coming from the kitchen. 'Can you call back later?'

With a rustle of papers, the woman sitting next to Charlotte stood up. Charlotte watched her leave, oddly comforted by a stranger occupying the same space. She took a deep breath, twisted her fingers through the rubber band and uttered a word she rarely said to her mother. 'No.'

Her mother's eyes widened. 'No? Why not?'

Charlotte heard a man's voice in the background. Her mother glanced away and fiddled with an earring. 'That's the plumber. Bloody tap froze again.'

A plumber? At nine o'clock on Saturday morning?

Charlotte leaned closer to the screen. She snapped the elastic band, leaving a red welt on her wrist. 'Please listen to me, Mum. I said I know. About the letters.'

If tension had a sound it would be the sound of breathing. The thump of a heartbeat. The surge of blood through veins. If shock had a face it would be her mother's. Eyes frozen open in a stony stare. Shoulders held rigid in motionless anticipation. The air-conditioner continued to drip onto the table, the only sound in the room. Nobody spoke.

Finally, Charlotte broke the silence. 'Do you have anything to say?'

Her mother became an injured tiger protecting her den. She pounced. 'What are you telling me? You know *what*? That your father was a useless sonofabitch who deserted us? That he didn't give a shit about us? I hope you also know *I* was the one who took care of you. *I* raised you and sacrificed my own happiness to give you a decent life at great expense to myself, I'll have you understand.' She narrowed her eyes. 'What else is there to know?'

'What about the letters, mum.'

'I don't have a clue what you're talking about?'

'The letters Daddy wrote. After he left. You lied to me. You had me believe—'

'I don't remember any letters. And if there were any, they were probably full of lies. Why should you care about it now?'

'Because they were for *me*! You never even told me they came. Daddy thought I didn't answer because I was upset with him.'

Her mother leaned closer toward the computer screen, her eyes tearing up. Her voice took on the syrupy tone Charlotte knew well. 'Oh darling, don't be daft. You know I'd never do anything to upset you. I was just trying to protect you. You were so young and naïve.' *Drip. Drip.* 'I didn't want you to leave me. I was watching out for you. You should be thanking me.' She shook her head slowly. 'Silly thing. You've got it all wrong. Come home and we'll figure it out.'

Charlotte leaned back and pressed her back against the chair. How many times had she seen those manipulations? How well she could anticipate what her mother would say under pressure. She toyed with the elastic band on her wrist, snapping it back and forth. Then, with a single motion, she ripped it from her arm, sending it flying it across the table. 'Mother,' she said in a firm, clear tone. 'I'm not buying it,'

She looked around, hoping her outburst hadn't been noticed, then lowered her voice. 'I don't think you want to protect me,' she said. 'I think you want to keep me to yourself.' She paused. She'd never spoken this way. But the miles between them gave her a voice and a strength that surprised her.

Twenty seconds passed and her mother didn't say a word. 'Mum? Are you still there?' Charlotte asked. She took a deep breath, waiting for the backlash. Her mother continued to stare at the screen, blinking quickly as though she had dust in her eyes. Or as though she'd suddenly discovered her daughter had a voice. For a moment, Charlotte felt a flash of pity, then she dug her nails into her palm and reminded herself there was no need for sympathy. This had been building for years, the back and forth, the power struggle where her mother held all the cards and Charlotte felt all the guilt. The fight with Roxy had enflamed her enough to realise it was time to stand up for herself.

She stared through the glass door into the café, reassured to see everything looked the same. People were coming and going, meeting friends, drinking coffee, nothing had changed from the moment she'd walked in other than her attitude. As she closed her eyes, waiting for her heartbeat to slow down, she felt a sensation she rarely experienced: relief. She'd spoken up to her mother and, to her surprise, was no longer concerned about her reaction. She couldn't take back her words, wouldn't even if she wanted to, but she felt lighter and more centred than she'd ever felt. As her pulse returned to normal, she spoke in a calm, quiet voice. 'What did he do to make you so angry?'

Her mother's eyes blazed. 'What could *you* know? You were a self-centred sixteen-year-old. You didn't understand a thing about life.' She swept a lock of hair from her forehead. 'Who's been filling your head with all this nonsense?' She closed her eyes, then huffed loudly. 'Oh, I get it. Roxy. That's why she wanted you to go to that stupid country, so she could poison your mind against me. Her and her common family, always pretending they could give you more than I could. And now she's trying to take you away from me.' Her eyes filled with tears.

'No, Mum, you've got it wrong,' Charlotte said. 'Roxy and her family were always there for me.' Her voice faltered. Even though she'd just had a blowout fight with Roxy, she knew she'd always been her greatest ally. 'And I did know a little about life. Actually, I knew quite a lot—Daddy taught me. But you never paid attention. You were so wrapped up in yourself that you never noticed...you never noticed *me*.'

She reached across the table to brush away a fly. As she did so, she caught the eye of one of the women who smiled at her. Perhaps she'd been listening, after all. Charlotte felt a sense of confidence in knowing a stranger might have witnessed a new side to her personality.

'I've been happy since I came to Cambodia,' she told her mother. 'I've met some wonderful people. People who *like* me. I'm starting to discover more about myself, and I've been doing a lot of thinking. About what I want.' Her mother started to speak, but Charlotte carried on. 'I like it here, Mum. I like who I am. The only thing that's been hard has been thinking about *you* and wondering if you approve.' She shifted in her seat. 'Do you have any idea how much your opinion means to me? Do you ever notice how much I try to please you? I'm twenty-four years old, and I'm still worried about what my mother thinks. It's those stupid emotional weeds—'

'The what?'

'Nothing. I'm trying to tell you—' She took a deep breath, surprising herself at her boldness. 'I can't take care of you, anymore.'

'Are you drunk? What's going—?'

Charlotte drew back her shoulders and sat up straighter. 'I need to figure some things out for myself.'

'What are you talking about?'

'I don't know how long it will take, but I'm sure you'll be fine. If you have a problem, I'm sure you can ask Alistair.' She narrowed her eyes. 'Or the plumber.' Her words tumbled out faster as her confidence grew. 'I can't come home and forget everything.'

'Stop being such a child. You have responsibilities. You can't just disappear like your irresponsible friend.'

'Responsibilities? Like what? A job I don't like?'

'How about a mother who needs you.'

'For what? To cook for you, clean up your empty bottles, wait for you to notice what I've given up for you? You're an adult, Mum. You're forty-six years old and you're acting as though you can't manage without me. How about what I want?'

'What *you* want? How very selfish. You're just like your father.'

'I hope so.'

'I can't let you—'

'I have nothing else to say. I'll keep in touch, so you'll know I haven't disappeared, but you've got to stop counting the days till I come home. And now I need to go. I'm in a café and shouldn't be disturbing other people.'

She clicked *End Call* and rested her forehead against the laptop, then pulled out her earplugs and wiped the sweat from the back of her neck. *Well done*, an internal voice whispered. *Idiot,* whispered another. *Breathe*, a third voice said. It was Samnang's voice. She replayed the conversation in her mind and how she'd defended Roxy to her mum. Perhaps she'd been unreasonable shouting at her friend, but Roxy's confession had shocked her, and she still didn't know what else she knew about her father. She felt a little embarrassed for acting so impetuously, but she also realised the fire burning inside her from the argument had fuelled her to call her mother.

As she stared into the café, a woman entered, her floral dress stretched tightly across broad hips, and shiny high-heeled pumps clicking on the tile floor. She walked across the room, pulled out a chair, and sat down next to a petite woman with long hair piled on top of her head. After they hugged and chatted for a few minutes, the petite woman came over to Charlotte's table. 'Jallod, hello!' she said, nervously fingering a short, beaded necklace. 'Remember me? Chenla. I work at Boxy Wide Elephant with Miss Roxy.' Her smile disappeared. 'I hear she get hurt. Is she okay?'

Relieved to shift the focus away from her mother, Charlotte described Roxy's accident. Chenla expressed great concern and asked Charlotte to send her love, then pointed toward her companion. 'I have lunch now with Piggy. She live in Thailand and she my father sister cousin daughter.'

'Peggy?'

'Piggy,' repeated Chenla. 'She called Piggy because she fat and because she snort when she laughs.'

Charlotte swallowed a giggle. Not only did many Cambodians possess a lack of personal boundaries, they could also be unwittingly funny.

'Also, she tell me something to say to you.' Chenla glanced nervously at her friend then back to Charlotte. 'She say she seen you somewhere before.'

28

Charlotte stayed in the café long after Chenla and Piggy had left. She rested her elbow on the sill, stared through the window, and mulled over the day. When dusk fell and the sky morphed from brilliant blue to smoky grey, she gathered her things and got ready to leave. As she zipped her laptop case shut, a man in a business suit sat down at a table across from her. He took an armful of books from his satchel and stacked them on the table next to him. She noticed their titles: *English Language for Government Institutions, Understanding Acronyms,* and *How to Deal with Difficult People.* She smiled. She could teach *him* a thing or two about difficult people.

The man caught her eye and nodded a greeting. 'Good evening,' he said. 'You are working too?'

'Not really. And I'll be leaving soon.'

He reached into his briefcase, drew out the *Phnom Penh Post* and offered it to her. 'You would like something to read? I finish with newspaper.'

'That's kind, but I have something.' She pointed to the copy of *Twisted Roots under Solitary Trees* on the chair next to her.

'Ah, I like that title,' said the man, nodding. 'I work with organisations where we talk about acronyms. Your book is good one for that.'

'Acronyms?'

'*Twisted Roots Under Solitary Trees*. Acronym is TRUST.'

❦

AFTER SHE PACKED up her laptop and books, Charlotte stood at the door of the café and paused. The conversation with her mother had exhausted her; she couldn't face another with Roxy. It would be better to find a guesthouse for the night and have some time to think.

As she pushed open the door, she heard someone call her name. She turned around and saw someone waving to her. It was Hasan, perched on a stool, wearing the same tank top he'd worn in the café and a pair of tight black jeans cinched at the waist with a huge brass buckle. Her stomach tightened, and her instincts told her to ignore him and leave right away. He might still recognise her from the Garden Café.

'Charlie!' he shouted again. 'Someone 'ere wants to see you.'

Sitting next to him with her back toward the exit was a tall woman with curly, black hair whom Charlotte recognised right away. Annie. It was too late to brush Hasan off and she wanted to find out about the situation at Boxy Wide Elephant, so she walked over, planning to say a quick hello then leave.

As she got closer, she heard Annie whisper, 'I need to go.'

Hasan shook his head. 'Hang on a minute.' He addressed Charlotte, 'Charlie, baby, you know Annie, don't you? She's leaving Cambodia and going back home.' He looked around. 'Let's find you a seat.'

'No thanks. I'm on my way to an appointment.' Charlotte tried to avoid making eye contact and looked at Annie. 'Are you okay? Roxy said you left the shop.'

Annie kept her back to Charlotte and fumbled in her bag, knocking her sunglasses onto the floor. 'Fine,' she said curtly. 'Gotta get back to Oz.'

Charlotte bent down to pick up the glasses as Annie swivelled around and looked into her eyes. Her pupils were dark pinpricks, and the whites were riddled with red. She snatched the glasses from Charlotte's hand. 'Hasan and I—we're having a private conversation,' she snapped. 'Were you listening?'

Charlotte frowned. This wasn't the same Annie she'd spent an evening with. 'Of course not,' she said, taking a step back. 'What's going on? I didn't know how to find you when I came back from Kampot and we had such a good time that evening, so I thought—'

Annie gave a twisted smile. 'At the dance show?' she said 'Yeah, it was nice.'

'And at Monsoon. When we met Samnang. Remember?'

'I've been busy.' She twisted around and flashed a smile at Hasan. 'Are we done yet?' she asked.

'Don't be a jerk, Annie,' Hasan said. 'Charlie's a pal.' He winked at Charlotte. 'We was in Kampot together, weren't we, babe? By the way, Christal and Flippo took off for Ho Chi Minh City yesterday. Crazy broads said there ain't enough excitement in Phnom Penh. You're different, though, aren't you, Charlie? You're a good girl.'

Charlotte looked at her watch. 'I have to go. Nice to see you Hasan. Bye, Annie.' She walked out of the café and down the street. Something was going on with Annie that she couldn't put her finger on. It had been hurtful to see her so standoffish and Charlotte wasn't sure what she could have done to upset her. Their time together had felt special, and now Annie was acting as though she didn't care.

She sent a text to Roxy: *Staying in hotel tonite,* and walked toward a neighbourhood which was known for its cheap guesthouses. As she crossed the street, she noticed a beggar squatting on the pavement. His legs had been amputated at the knee, and there were deep wrinkles etched across his face. On the ground next to him was a small bathroom scale and a handwritten sign that read, *I weigh you. Only 100 Riel.*

She wondered how her mother would react if she saw him. She'd always crossed the street to avoid homeless people and used to instruct Charlotte never to give to beggars. 'You never know what they do with the money,' she'd cautioned. Her dad had been the opposite. He'd always reached into his pocket and made sure to touch every beggar and homeless person on the arm or shoulder despite his wife's protestations. 'They're people too,' he'd say. 'And they're worse off than we are. Besides, when you're feeling down, there's no better remedy than doing something good for someone else.'

Charlotte stepped onto the scale and handed two dollars to the beggar, aware it was about forty times the amount he charged. He reached up and grasped her hand, a wide smile lighting his face. 'Kind lady,' he said. 'You will bring joy to many because you give of yourself.' She held on and looked into his eyes, touched by the gentle penetrating gaze that appeared to see right into her heart.

Less than an hour later, after a couple of stops to inspect a few lodgings, she booked herself into a room at the *Sleepy Gecko* guesthouse that came with Wi-Fi, a miniature TV bracketed to the wall, and a tiny patio with rusty wrought iron railings. She went up to her room, took a bottle of cold water from the mini fridge, then squeezed onto the balcony and leaned on the railing. The smell of petrol fumes mingled with the aroma of dust from people walking down the alley, and the tinny crackle of music floated up from a transistor radio. She stood for a few minutes, watching the street life, then went downstairs to the pool and crumpled onto a lounge chair. Immediately, a front desk clerk appeared at her side. 'Very welcome, madam,' he said, placing a tray on the table next to her. 'This week we do promotion with Klang Beer. Free drink with every room.' He smiled and walked away, leaving an open bottle of beer and a large glass.

'Wait! I don't—' Charlotte called, but the man had disappeared. She sighed. It had been a challenging day. She picked up the bottle and poured the amber liquid into the glass, then wiped her hand against the glass and smeared droplets of icy water on her forehead. She closed her eyes, inhaling the fruity aroma as her thoughts drifted to her mother. What would she be doing now? Would she tell Alistair about their conversation? Would she call her? She took a deep breath. It was time to stop speculating on her mother's life.

A bird chirped loudly above her head, startling her from her reverie. One hand still wrapped around the glass, she stared at the open bottle of beer. Alcohol wasn't the answer. It never had been. It had been a prop to get her through the dark days—and there had been many—and it had dulled the pain when she'd felt lonely and desperate for a way out. There were other ways—better ways—to deal with those feelings. It suddenly it dawned on her: she'd been the classic victim. She'd fallen apart when her father had gone, then allowed her mother to mistreat her. She hadn't spoken up when her boss required lengthy hours of her time. Then, when Roxy left the country, she'd complained about being abandoned.

She put the glass down and imagined what it would be like back in England. The weather would be cold and dark. So would her mother's mood. Work would be stressful. Her days would be boring. The only thing she missed was Trevor, but he'd jump at the chance to visit Cambodia. Her heart raced with excitement at the idea of staying in Phnom Penh. Roxy was here, so was Samnang. She was getting used to the heat and would find a way to deal with the bugs. Maybe she could get Toyota back and...She paused and took a breath. She'd told her mum she wasn't coming home but she didn't have any idea of what she'd do here or how she'd support herself.

Suddenly, a cloud of mosquitos swarmed around her ankle and she scrambled in her bag for bug spray, her fingers touching the hard edges of *Twisted Roots Under Solitary Trees.* She pulled out the book, and a slip of paper fell from the pages onto her lap—a receipt from the WH Smith bookshop at Heathrow. On the back, a few lines had been scribbled in a barely legible scrawl: *One doesn't discover new lands without consenting to lose sight of the shore for a very long time. You are my special messenger Ch*—The edge of the paper had been ripped away, cutting off the rest of the word. She read it again. *You are my special messenger Ch*— It must be meant for Chris. From Rashid.

Butterflies fluttered around the garden. The scent of jasmine lingered in the evening air. She took a deep breath and her head fell back against the chair as she drifted off to sleep. She was transported to a beach with two horses; she rode one, her father the other. A young boy sat on the saddle in front of her father. He was crying and her father was consoling him.

'We'll find him,' he reassured the boy. 'You just need to trust.' Charlotte looked at her father and nodded. 'I'll help,' she said.

A loud crash awakened her. The patio door had blown shut and a strong wind had swept her hair across her face. She looked around, confused, until she realised where she was. Then, the message from her dream flooded back and she suddenly realised its meaning. Somewhere in this city was a young man who'd walked away from his father and didn't know he was looking for him. It wasn't Rashid who needed to find his son; it was Chris who needed to find his father.

She scrambled through her bag for Rashid's letter and wrapped her fingers around the envelope. It felt less bulky. She ripped it apart, panic rising in her chest. The ring was gone.

29

Charlotte turned the backpack inside out, checked all her pockets, and searched the hotel corridors. No ring. Heart racing, she retraced her steps along the riverfront, frantically scanning the pavement, and ended up back at Jinjerbread where she ran to the room where she'd been sitting. There were crumbs under her table, and a discarded napkin below the chair leg, so she crouched down and ran her hands across the tile floor, then looked in the corner in case the ring had rolled away.

A waitress watched from the door, an amused look on her face.

'I was here earlier,' Charlotte said, breathlessly. 'Have you seen a ring?'

The young woman shook her head. 'No, madam. Very sorry.'

Charlotte walked through the café inspecting the floor while trying to stay calm. Perhaps the ring had fallen out when she'd picked up Annie's glasses.

'Well look who's back,' a voice boomed from across the room. It was Hasan, still seated at the counter drinking coffee. 'Come over 'ere,' he said, waving his arm. A couple of customers glared, clearly irritated by his loudness, so she walked over, intending to examine the floor near him. He winked at her and burped. 'Took yer time, didn't yer?' he said, then thrust a closed fist toward her. 'If yer can guess what's in my hand, you get a date with me. And if yer don't, yer still get a date with me. What'll it be?'

Charlotte took a step back.

'Don't be daft. I'm just havin' yer on! Figured you might be looking for this.' He opened his fist to reveal Rashid's ring.

She gasped and reached for it, but he pulled his hand away. 'Didn't notice when Annie swiped it from yer bag, did yer?' He twirled it around his finger. 'It fell onto the stool and she snatched it when you picked up her glasses.' He rolled his eyes. 'She's not my type, that one. Too old. Too intense. Thought she could buy some blow with this ring, but I don't do business with thieves. 'Specially thieves who steal from friends.' He held out the ring. 'We *are* friends, aren't we?'

She took a deep breath. Hasan was playing games and she didn't have time for them. 'Thanks, Hasan,' she said. 'I'm really grateful but I need to go now.'

He pulled back the ring and placed it on the edge of the counter. 'Now you owe me one,' he said. 'And how come yer haven't come back to my café?' he asked. 'Not fancy enough?'

She froze. Hasan snorted and slapped his thigh. 'There ain't many chicks look like you, yer know. D'ya think I didn't recognise yer?' His eyes bored into her as he drained his coffee. 'Too bad you missed Moh. He skipped town.'

'Moh?' Charlotte's voice came out as a whisper.

'Stole some cash from me on his way out. Asshole. Only

smart thing he did was fish for women online. How we met you, innit? But I can't be bothered with jerks and I've had enough of his tricks.' He picked up the ring and dangled it in front of her. 'Here, you want this or not?'

'So, what did you mean?' she asked. 'That I owe you one.'

He sniffed loudly. 'Enough, already! This one's on me. But I'm not getting all soft, all right. I just thought this bauble might be something special. Saw you show it to Bubbles and figured you mighta wanted it back. It ain't my style. Specially with that inscription.' He handed her the ring and waved her away. 'Go on then. Get outta here unless you want to spend the rest of the night with me.'

She hurried from the café and slid the ring from her finger. She hadn't seen any inscription and was eager to know what it said. Holding it up to the streetlight, she saw the words, *What goes around comes around*, and underneath, three tiny letters that read, *L.I.F.*

ONCE BACK AT THE HOTEL, Charlotte put the ring back inside the envelope, stuffed it in a zippered pocket in her bag and went to bed, quickly falling into a dreamless sleep. Hours later, the sound of pans in the hotel kitchen awakened her and she lay still, thinking. It had been more than a month since she'd arrived, and here she was, alone in a hotel room, avoiding the friend she'd come to visit. It hadn't been her intention to come to Cambodia and change her life. But, then again, maybe it had. Perhaps there'd been something deeper at work; something that subconsciously realised this would be her way out. She rolled over, thinking about the interesting people she'd met, each one who'd taught her a lesson. Life had become more enriching since she left England, and it had all begun with Rashid.

She picked up the phone on the bedside table and dialled reception. 'I'd like to stay another three nights, please,' she told the clerk, then glanced at the clock. It was already nine o'clock, and she wanted to resume her search for Chris

For the next two days, Charlotte tried everything she could think of. She returned to Monsoon and talked to Bikram— 'No, lady, I have not seen your friend with the fountain pen. Nor do I know of anyone named Chris.' She walked into two Bangladeshi restaurants that she saw while walking through the city— 'So sorry you lost your friend. I am not knowing anybody with this name'—then visited the British Embassy and told a clerk she was looking for a British national who might have disappeared in Cambodia— 'Miss, we have so many people to look for. Leave your number and we'll call if we find your friend.' She searched online for someone named Chris Farouk, finding a Chef Farruk, a blogger named Christopher Fouk, and a rapper named Fuuk-Kriss, amongst hundreds of others who also sounded unlikely. She posted a note on the *Bangladeshi Community in Cambodia* Facebook page that was written mostly in Bengali script, and joined a website called *Bangladeshi Expatriates in Cambodia,* combing through the names of all their members. None sounded like the son of a British Bengali doctor.

To her relief and surprise, she heard nothing from her mother, and she responded to Roxy's frequent messages with one-word replies. Several times a day she checked email, anxious to hear from Patrick and growing more frustrated and distressed when she heard nothing. After three days, she was tired. Tired of walking the streets. Tired of the hotel's breakfast buffet. Tired of making no progress.

Every night she dined in the noodle bar at the hotel before retreating to her room, dejected. On the third night she turned on the tiny television set, craving the familiarity of an English-speaking programme, but only found Khmer soap operas, Cambodian political commentary, and dance performances. She flipped through all the stations, finally finding an English-language cable station showing a programme about the Southeast Asian striped rabbit. She was about to turn it off when the announcer showed a picture of a group of western teenagers with adopted rabbits. One of the rabbits looked like Arfur and her mind flashed to Roxy. She'd forgotten about the *History Book.*

Drawing it from her backpack, she stared at the shiny silver cover before opening it. On the first page was a photograph of two young girls, one a plump blonde sitting in a wheelbarrow wearing striped shorts and a polka dot top, the other a neatly dressed redhead in a white cotton sundress, holding the handles of the barrow. She turned to the next page which displayed a photo of the same two girls, now wearing blue and white school uniforms, Roxy's frizzy hair sticking out from under a straw hat, and Charlotte dressed in crisply ironed clothes with shiny shoes. There was a naughty grin on Roxy's face and Charlotte smiled, remembering that moment when Roxy had told her she hated biology because the teacher smelled of cat food. On the next page was a photo of their high school dance, Roxy dressed in a purple satin miniskirt, Charlotte in knee-length yellow chiffon. The last picture had been taken on the day Roxy left England. The girls had their arms wrapped around one another, Roxy giving a thumbs-up and Charlotte wearing a frown. That had been a miserable day. Roxy had said she'd no plans to come back, and Charlotte was dreading her going. She'd guessed Roxy would be a bad correspondent but hadn't realised how quickly she'd drop out of communication. The messages had been sporadic at first, usually when Roxy found an internet café or had time to kill in a railway station. But, as time had gone by, weeks or months had passed between messages and Charlotte was left wondering what her friend was doing.

Her eyes filled with tears. She'd depended on Roxy too much. And while she'd been hurt at the lack of contact, she'd been surprised beyond belief when she'd received an invitation to Roxy's wedding. She'd had no idea Roxy had found someone special. Charlotte had been too hurt to respond. Then, when Roxy asked when she'd be arriving so she could order her a traditional Cambodian outfit, Charlotte stayed silent.

For a couple of days, she'd considered going, then decided against it. It was too far, she couldn't afford it, she wouldn't get the time off work, and her feelings were hurt. What she didn't admit was that she'd feel like a failure. Roxy would have a new group of smart, cosmopolitan friends in Cambodia, and Charlotte would feel awkward among them. Better to stay home and use her mother and work as an excuse. Her eventual response had been simple and short: She just couldn't make it.

Returning to the photo album, she noticed a scrap of folded paper pasted inside the front cover with a message scribbled in a childish scrawl: *You are the best friend a girl – and a bunny- could ever have. I will love you forever.*

She lay back on the bed and cried.

30

The phone buzzed with a new text: *I miss you.* Charlotte rolled over and took a deep breath. It had been more than a day since Roxy's last message and she missed her, too. As she sat on her bed wondering how to respond, another text came through: *Where are you? I'll come to you.* This time she replied: *I'm at the Sleepy Gecko. 186 steps from the National Museum on Street 174.*

For the next ten minutes she tidied the room and worried what she'd say: '*Who the hell d'you think you are?*' Too strident. '*I'm sorry, I'm such a fool.*' Too wimpy. She didn't want to appear needy or apologetic, and she felt sad that she'd had no contact with her friend, but she still hurt from Roxy's comments. There were unanswered questions about Charlotte's father, and she'd have to tread carefully if she wanted to coax the relationship back to normal.

She watched the clock until there was a tap on her door. Roxy stood in the dimly lit corridor dressed in striped pyjama bottoms and a navy tank top. Her hair stuck out like bristles on an old toothbrush and a long strand of gold ribbon was twisted around her wrist. Attached to the ribbon was Tnout. When Charlotte opened the door, he bounded toward her, leaping up and grabbing her shorts in his teeth. Roxy yanked him back. 'I had to bring him,' she said. 'My bike's messed up and SomOn was busy so I had to find another tuk-tuk. Tnout kept running after me, so—' She shrugged and let go of the ribbon then leaned on the wall, breathing hard. 'There are thirty-two steps up to this room. I just can't...' She looked around the small space with its single bed and tangle of electrical wires hanging from the ceiling light fixture, then took a deep breath. 'This is weird,' she said. 'But I'm glad you told me where you were. I was worried.'

Charlotte shut the door behind her. She didn't want to start another argument but there were things she had to say. 'I'm sorry,' she said. 'For my part, for overreacting. I've spent a lot of time thinking and I know I can be emotional sometimes so—'

'Sometimes?' Roxy interrupted. 'You're always emotional.'

'Well, I had good reason for it this time. My dad—' Her thoughts flashed onto the argument and Roxy's confession. She'd planned on keeping a level head, but angry tears pricked her eyes and she glared at Roxy.

'It's always about your dad, isn't it?' Roxy said. 'Grow up. You're twenty-four years old.'

Charlotte felt her face heat up. Roxy wasn't listening; she was off on her own tirade as usual. 'Actually, this time it *is* about my dad,' she said. 'And it's also about you, if you'd give me a chance to talk. I'm fed up with you interrupting and pointing out all the things I do wrong. You're not so perfect either, you know.'

'Never said I was, Miss Prissypants! But I'm not the one who blames everyone else when my life sucks. And, by the way, I don't give a shit about being perfect. That's *your* obsession, not mine. And just so happens you're the one who stormed out and checked into a guesthouse when you couldn't handle what I had to say. You've been ducking my phone calls for two days and now you say *I'm* angry with *you.* Why did you invite me up here? To get in my face all over again?'

'As a matter of fact, I wanted to tell you I was sorry. Silly me for thinking you might care enough to feel the same way. All you care about is your own little victory.'

Roxy's face reddened. 'Oh, so that's it, is it? You want me to grovel. Well I'm not made of that kind of stuff, sister. That's your programme!' She walked to the bathroom, stuck her hands under the tap and wiped them on her forehead. Then, she walked back into the room and took a deep breath. 'Now you mention it, I believe you're right. I am angry with you.'

Charlotte opened her mouth to speak but Roxy kept talking. 'I'm angry because you didn't listen to me when I said I was sorry about kissing your dad. I'm angry because you act like a victim. I'm angry because you didn't come to my wedding. And I'm angry at you because...' Her eyes glistened. 'Because you just don't get it!'

Charlotte glared back. 'What, Roxy?' she asked, 'What exactly is it that I don't get?'

Roxy took a deep breath. 'Everything! You don't get me. You don't get yourself most of the time. You don't get...' She shook her head. 'You don't get how much you mean to me,' she said, quietly. She sat down on a folding chair and leaned forward, resting her head in her hands. After a moment, she looked up. 'You have everything I've ever wanted,' she said. 'Beauty, intelligence, kindness, an ability to draw people to you...and you don't even know it. You are so bloody special that it breaks my heart when you think you're not good enough. You've let your mum belittle you for so long I'm afraid you're starting to believe what she says. And you've been buried in that bubble of yours for so long that...' She wiped beads of sweat from her upper lip. 'I missed the crap out of you.'

Charlotte slid to the floor and pulled her knees toward her chest. 'Why didn't you keep in touch?' she asked.

'Why didn't you join me?'

Charlotte closed her eyes. How could she explain to Roxy that life had been miserable without her? It wasn't in Charlotte's nature to quit her job and fly across the world. That was Roxy's style, not hers. 'I figured you'd moved on,' she said, opening her eyes. 'And I didn't want to see you with your new friends. I knew I'd be awkward and strange.'

'Awkward and strange!' Roxy laughed out loud. 'Jesus Christ, Charlo. That's not exactly how I'd describe you. I'm the one who's awkward and strange. You can be a total idiot sometimes, y'know. How on earth could I move on from the one friend I've had since kindergarten? You're like my sister. I told Peter so much about you he thought I'd made you up and he was super excited to meet you at the wedding. Then you blew me off like some casual acquaintance that you didn't give a shit about.'

'I couldn't. It was a busy time at work and Mum wasn't well.'

'Total crap. And you know it.' She glared. 'You just didn't want to come. You made it very clear when you didn't reply to the invitation till the week before.'

Charlotte closed her eyes. She'd known this would come back to haunt her. It never been because of her mother or her work or her schedule. She'd been scared. Scared of flying to Cambodia, but mostly scared of being in a situation that would intimidate her. 'I didn't think...'

'Didn't think what?'

'You'd miss me. You had everyone else, so it wouldn't matter if I wasn't there.'

'Everyone else? You knew my family couldn't afford to come, so who's everyone else? The girls in my shop? Annie? A group of tuk-tuk drivers?' She shook her head. 'There were eleven people at my wedding. Two of them were SomOn and his wife. So yeah, you're right. My oldest, dearest friend would totally have been in the way.' Her eyes welled up.

'I didn't realise…' Charlotte reached out to take her hand.

Roxy pulled away. 'I half expected it to happen. It's all part of your pattern of running away.'

Charlotte dug her nails into her palms. How could she explain what she'd been afraid of—how it had been easier to remain where she was? She'd never have imagined Roxy would have needed *her*. 'You're right,' she said. 'I didn't think. I had no idea you'd care if I wasn't there. And I thought about you every minute on your wedding day. I don't blame you for leaving England. If I were you, I'd have left too.' She paused. 'I can't explain why I was so upset at you for going.'

'I can,' Roxy said.

Charlotte raised her eyebrows. 'You can?'

'It doesn't take a genius. I was one more person who deserted you.'

A silence settled over the room, broken only by the ticking of the clock and the sound of traffic on the street outside. 'I was hoping you might learn to do stand up for yourself after I left,' Roxy said. 'I really wanted you to travel with me, but most of all I really, really wanted you to get away from your mum.'

Charlotte let out a loud sigh. 'I'm sorry. For getting so angry with you,' she said. 'I'm a fool.'

'Sometimes,' Roxy said. 'But there's always hope. Maybe if

you stop thinking about what you left behind, you can focus on what you're doing here. In Cambodia. With me. Just stop doing things for other people, all right? There's not much time left.'

'There might be,' Charlotte said. 'I told Mum I'm not going home.'

Roxy spun around. 'You what?'

'I told her I knew about the letters. And I said I wasn't coming home.'

'You didn't!"

Charlotte nodded.

'Well done, you!' Roxy beamed. Then a shadow fell across her face. 'What about your job? Where will you live?'

'I don't know. Haven't got anything figured out. I just want to do things differently now. I'm not sure if it's because of Samnang, or Cambodia, or the bird in Kampot—'

'The bird in Kampot?'

'Never mind.' She opened the mini-fridge and took out a bottle of water. 'I also stopped drinking.'

'Hallelujah,' Roxy said. 'I was a bit worried so I'm glad I don't have to be the one to raise the subject.'

Tnout scampered over and Charlotte rubbed him behind the ears before turning to Roxy. 'We need to finish,' she said. 'About my dad. Where is he? Why did he leave? Can't you just tell me?'

Roxy perched on the edge of the bed and stared back at her. 'I have no idea,' she asked. 'D'you really think I'd have kept quiet if I did?' She lay back on the bed and stared at the ceiling. 'But there is something.'

Charlotte's throat tightened. It was never a good sign when Roxy didn't look at her.

'What?'

Roxy sat up and looked at her. 'About your dad. At the party.'

'Yes?'

'He left with Patrick.'

'Patrick?'

'Our art professor.' Roxy bit her bottom lip. 'It was the first time I'd seen him with anyone, but I just couldn't—'

'What do you mean?'

'Patrick's gay,' Roxy said quietly.

Charlotte's mouth went dry. What was Roxy talking about? Who was Patrick, and what did he have to do with her father? Roxy must have misunderstood. Her father didn't have a friend who was an art professor. She was about to tell Roxy she must be wrong when it struck her. She'd heard the name Patrick before. In her father's letters.

She collapsed onto the bed next to Roxy. 'Did you—?' She couldn't get the words out. She rolled over, closed her eyes, and heard Samnang's words in her head: *It's only when we silence our minds we hear what we're feeling.* A thousand thoughts flew through her head, so she looked at a speck on the floor, and forced herself to take a breath. Roxy was staring, waiting for a response. Tnout was lying on the floor chewing the edge of the rug. She raised her gaze and looked at Roxy. 'Why didn't you tell me?'

'I couldn't.'

'But you're my friend.'

'It wasn't my place. I hated keeping it a secret, but it wasn't up to me to say anything. Then the longer I stayed quiet, the easier it became to pretend it never happened.' She picked at her cuticles. 'I also wanted to tell you to your face. That's another reason I wanted you to come.'

Minutes passed, and neither spoke. Music boomed across

the street from the adjacent nightclub. Tnout raced around the room, sniffing every corner. Finally, Roxy spoke. 'Talk to me, Charlo. Say something. Tell me to get lost if you want but say something.'

Charlotte took a breath. She'd spent the past seven years wondering why her father had left, hoping he'd show up at the door. And all that time she'd had no idea he'd been leading another life. 'I need a minute,' She said, then walked into the bathroom and closed the door behind her. Her thoughts rushed back to her childhood. She'd never questioned why her parents had moved to separate rooms, or why her mother spent so much time with her girlfriends. The blood pounded in her ears. How dare he. How dare he make her waste so many hours missing him, resenting her mother, questioning herself. She didn't care he was gay. She cared he didn't trust her enough to tell her.

She turned on a tap and ran the water to hide the sound of her sobs. After a few minutes, she dried her face and cracked open the door. Roxy lay on the floor with Tnout licking her toes.

'Charlo?' Roxy said in a quiet voice.

'I'm okay,' Charlotte replied, then took a deep breath. She looked at Roxy whose brow was knotted in a worried frown. 'Thank you,' she said. 'For telling me.'

Roxy ran a hand through her hair. 'I'm sorry, darling. It's a lot to take in. And I do love you, y'know.' She glanced at the *History Book* on the bedside table. 'Did you see those photos? Thought it might give you a laugh.' She paused. 'Actually, I thought it might remind you of our childhood.'

'I know,' Charlotte said. 'I know why you gave it to me.' She tucked it into her duffel bag, then looked at Roxy. 'Since we're being honest with one another, I have to ask you something.'

Roxy raised her eyebrows.

'Who were you talking to on the phone that day?' she asked.

'Huh?'

'On the phone. You said I was acting weird.'

'I haven't a clue what you're talking about.'

'The day Alistair called. You were on the phone in the other room. I heard you. Who were you talking to?'

'Charlo, I really don't know—Oh, for goodness sake!' She laughed.

'What?'

'You thought I was talking about *you*? I was talking to Peter. About Annie. She'd been acting strange, and I wanted him to know. And you thought...Jesus Christ, I'm not that stupid. If I want to talk about you, I'll wait till you leave the flat!'

Charlotte's face warmed. 'So, I got that wrong too, did I?'

'You sure did. I know you think Annie's the best thing since truffle popcorn, but you may want to reconsider—'

'I know,' Charlotte interrupted. 'I'm learning things aren't always what they seem.' She sat for a moment in silence, waiting for a sarcastic retort which never came.

'Are we okay?' Roxy asked.

Charlotte nodded. 'Always.'

Roxy got up from the chair and tied the ribbon around Tnout's collar. 'What d'you want to do now?' she asked.

'Go home.'

'But your mum—?'

'Not that home, doofus. Your place. If that's okay with you. I'll deal with the rotten tomatoes on the counter and dirty dishes in the sink.'

'I cleaned them. Felt so shitty about all this crap, thought it'd give me something to do. Then I felt even shittier 'cos I smashed Peter's margarita glass.'

Charlotte grabbed her hand and planted a kiss on her palm. 'You're a nutter. But I love you.'

Tnout raced across the room and Charlotte picked him up and followed Roxy down the narrow staircase.

'By the way, I told the tuk-tuk driver to wait,' Roxy said, with a twisted smile. 'I figured you might be coming back with me.'

31

When Charlotte got up late the following morning, she found a bunch of roses on the coffee table with a note, *Happy Valentine's Day to the bestest friend in the world. Popping to a doctor's appointment.* Attached to the flowers was a five-dollar gift card to Jinjerbread.

She took the roses into the kitchen, filled a plastic jug with water, and arranged the flowers in it. There was nothing planned for the day, so she took a long shower, then washed her clothes in the sink and hung them over a chair on the balcony before going downstairs for a walk and coffee. Across the road, a makeshift booth was piled high with Valentine's Day bouquets. White, fluffy teddy bears were dressed in T-shirts with sentimental slogans and silver Mylar *I love you* balloons were tied to every corner. She walked further and saw two more flower booths that seemed to have popped up in the past few days and a crowd of young men standing outside the Swiss chocolate shop. She pushed through them and continued down the street to Jingerbread where she settled into an armchair near the window.

As she studied the menu, there was a tap on the glass next to her and a young woman in a business suit and dangly earrings waved at her through the window. She entered the café and walked over to Charlotte. 'Hello Jallod. Remember me?' She nodded enthusiastically. 'Piggy. Cousin of Chenla. We meet yesterday. Happy Valentine Day.'

'Oh, hello, Piggy,' Charlotte struggled to keep a straight face.

'Sorry to interrupt, but I want to tell you something.' She wriggled into an unoccupied chair next to Charlotte and placed her patent leather bag on the table between them. 'I remember where I saw you,' she said, breathlessly. 'It was on the plane from Bangkok. I remember because you so beautiful. Also, because you lucky in having so much space to sit.'

Unblinking, Charlotte stared at her. 'What do you mean?'

'On the plane. You have two seats. Everybody else very squashed.'

'Oh no, that wasn't me.' Charlotte shook her head. 'I was sitting next to an old man.'

'I very sure it you,' Piggy insisted. 'You were in front of me. And nobody next to you.'

'He was Bangladeshi,' she said. 'Wearing a grey suit and very bushy eyebrows. He carried a stick with a silver top. Don't you remember?'

'Oh no, Jallod. Not see any man. I remember thinking, "Why this baraing have no handsome man. She beautiful and skinny like supermodel"'. Piggy giggled. 'I see you drink many glasses of wine. It bumpy flight. Not usually that way.' She picked up her bag and stood. 'Very sorry to disturb you. I go now.'

Charlotte watched her walk away and reached for her

phone. She typed *Dr. Rashid Farouk* into the search engine, hoping to find a photo to show to Piggy. Six thousand and forty-seven results showed up. The first was a news item dated January 5 headlined, *Renowned brain surgeon suffers fatal heart attack at Heathrow*. She flashed past it, scanning for something with a photograph. She was about to go to the *Images* section when she paused. Brain surgeon? Heathrow? She went back to the first headline and clicked on it.

Eminent neurosurgeon Dr. Rashid Farouk died after suffering a massive heart attack at Heathrow Airport yesterday afternoon. Dr. Farouk, 77, suffered the fatal attack hours before he was scheduled to board a flight to Phnom Penh, Cambodia. He collapsed after leaving the WH Smith bookshop in Terminal Five.

Her heart pounded. Doctor Rashid Farouk. That was her Rashid. The date must be wrong. She reread it. January 5. The day of her flight. She read the rest of the article.

'I noticed him sweating heavily and shaking, then he fell on the ground,' said Anne O'Connor, manager of WH Smith. Paramedics were unable to resuscitate him.

Dr. Farouk recently retired from St Bartholomew's Hospital in London where he worked for 30 years as a neurosurgeon. He was recognised for his research in epilepsy and pioneering work in the field of peripheral nerve surgery. He was a Fellow of the Royal College of Surgeons (FRCS) and listed in the register of top fifty UK doctors. He was believed to be travelling to Cambodia to visit his son. Dr. Farouk is survived by his wife, Rose, and his son, Chris.

Her mind raced. The article said he died *before* the flight. It had to be another Rashid Farouk. At the bottom of the article was a photo of a dark-skinned man wearing a suit and tie, his arm draped around the shoulders of a petite, blonde woman. The man in the picture was younger than the man she'd met on the plane, but he had the same whiskery eyebrows and empathetic expression. The caption read *Dr. Rashid Farouk (53) on his wedding day to Rose Bradford (34).*

My English Rose.

She tipped the contents of her bag onto the table sending a cascade of lipstick, hand sanitiser, pens, tissues, home key, and scraps of paper tumbling out. She scrambled through the papers, found her crumpled boarding pass, and flattened it out so she could read the date: January 5. Shoving the contents back in her bag, she leapt up, and dashed from the café. She ran along the street, ignoring calls from tuk-tuk drivers and dodging pedestrians on the pavements. Her bag bounced up and down on her chest and her scarf fell onto the pavement, but she ignored it and kept running. She had to find Roxy.

She arrived at the flat, raced up the stairs two at a time, and shoved open the door. Roxy!' she shouted. 'You here?'

Roxy was on the phone in the kitchen. She hung up when Charlotte burst through the door and pointed to the roses. 'Good use of plastic jug,' she said. Her eyes opened wide. 'What happened?'

'Rashid,' Charlotte panted. 'Look!' She thrust her phone toward her and stabbed at the story with her index finger. 'It's him! My Rashid. What on earth? I don't understand—' She struggled to catch her breath.

Roxy grabbed her arm. 'Slow down, will ya?' She took the phone, read the story, and handed it back. 'This man's dead,' she said. 'It's obviously not Rashid.'

'It *is*! I know it's him.' She pointed to the article. 'Look at the date he died. The day I arrived.' She slid down the wall and sat on the floor. 'Shit, Roxy. This freaks me out.'

Roxy squatted beside her. 'Did you have a few drinks on the flight?'

'Jesus, Rox, I did *not* imagine him. I talked to him. I told you...Remember the—?' She jumped to her feet. 'Wait! I've got a photo— the one from the rooftop.' She swiped through the pictures on her phone, flashing past photos of her and Roxy and the countryside and Toyota. 'It's here somewhere. Where'd it go?' She flipped to a collection of photos from Monsoon. 'Must be right here. Hang on. Here we go...this is the one.' She stared at the phone and paused.

'Let's see, then.' Roxy took the phone from her hand. 'This one?' She held it toward her, frowning. 'It's a tuk-tuk.'

Charlotte shook her head. 'Something's wrong.' She zoomed in on the photo with her fingers. The tuk-tuk driver was visible, as were people on the street and vehicles driving by. In the background, a bicycle leaned against the wall next to the restaurant. But no Rashid. 'He was there,' she wailed. 'I know he was.' She flipped through the pictures again. 'Did I delete it? Am I going mad?'

Roxy grasped her arm. 'You sure you didn't imagine him? Maybe he had a similar name to this fellow who died. Or he just looked like him. Your Rashid's probably walking around somewhere.'

Charlotte pushed her away. 'I filled out his customs form. I know his name.'

'Maybe someone's pretending to be him.'

'Don't be ridiculous. He told me he was a doctor. And he married an Englishwoman. I know he went to WH Smith to buy a book.' She paced the room, hands clenched into fists. Suddenly she stopped walking. 'How did I get his letter? And the ring? I should do something—notify the police...get in touch with his wife—'

'You're kidding, right? What would you say? "I was sitting next to your dead husband on the plane"? Maybe just let it go.'

'Let it go? How can I? A man died, and I sat next to him on a plane that same day. I couldn't possibly have dreamed it all up.' She took a deep breath. There was something mysterious going on; something beyond her comprehension that had begun the moment she'd met Rashid. And this new revelation confirmed the suspicions she'd been having for quite some time: Rashid had come into her life for a reason.

32

Charlotte stood at the kitchen sink scrubbing each dirty dish with a frayed cloth. She polished a tarnished pewter pan till it shone, then put all the silverware away, without caring if she was putting it in the right place. It had been four hours since she'd read about Rashid, and she couldn't sit still. Maybe she should check with the airline and find out if his name was on the flight manifest. There must be a record of him entering the country.

She could hear Roxy's snoring from where she sprawled on the couch, so she hung the dish towel on the hook and slipped into her bedroom. For the second time that day she typed Rashid's name into Google. An updated headline jumped out: *Wife of surgeon seeks missing ring.*

Mrs. Rose Farouk, widow of Dr. Rashid Farouk who died last month at Heathrow airport, is appealing for help in finding her husband's gold ring. According to Mrs. Farouk, Dr. Farouk had been wearing it on his journey to Cambodia. When he was found by paramedics, the ring was missing.

'It's a family heirloom and I appeal to anyone who might have seen it,' said Mrs. Farouk. 'My husband's wish was to give it to his son, and I will be extremely grateful if it is returned to us.'

At the end of the article was a contact number so Charlotte grabbed her phone and punched in the number. A recorded voice spoke in Khmer, followed by an English translation: *You are unable to make international calls from this number.* She stared at the phone, then flung it onto the bed. Stupid service! She lay back on the bed, mulling over what to do next, and saw a pile of old newspapers on the windowsill. She reached for her laptop. The reporter who wrote the article would know how to reach Rashid's wife.

She logged on to search for the journalist's name and noticed a new email in her inbox. *Sender: Martin Jansen. Subject: Your father.* Her pulse quickened. Martin Jansen? She clicked on the message, forgetting all about the reporter, and read his note.

Dear Charlotte. Your letter arrived today. I hope you don't mind I opened it, even though it was addressed to my brother. Since it was postmarked Cambodia, I thought it might be important. Patrick is away, so I scanned your letter and sent it to him. I am cc'ing him on this email so he can respond directly to you. Good luck with your father.

Her eyes welled with tears. She'd found someone who could help her. And now she had Patrick's email address so she could contact him directly. She hit 'reply', omitting Martin from her response.

Dear Patrick, I hope you've read the letter Martin forwarded so you know why I'm writing. I would greatly appreciate it if you would get back to me with any information you have about my father. Best Regards, Charlotte.

She peeped through the living room door, eager to share the news with Roxy but she was still asleep, so she went back to her emails. The next one was from her boss, entitled *Return to work*. She gasped. Her office was expecting her back in three weeks. She started to compose a reply, then stopped and stared at the screen, contemplating how to respond. Samnang's voice popped into her head: *Breathe. Slow down.*

She closed the laptop, went to the window, and looked outside. A woman on a bicycle was pedalling past, ringing a bell and calling *pong tia koon* in a high-pitched voice. Charlotte watched two women approach the bicycle, and realised the vendor was selling fertilised duck embryos. Charlotte grimaced, imagining the smell and taste of the so-called delicacy. She'd grown to love much of Cambodian street food but couldn't stomach the idea of eating unborn baby ducks. She continued to watch as the bicycle vendor handed a bag to a customer, tugged a floppy cotton hat on her head, and pedalled down the street. Wisps of smoke from street-side barbecues filled the air, mingling with exhaust fumes from cars and Charlotte watched as Tnout ran onto the street and ran after a motorbike, Daro chasing after him. She laughed out loud, realising these scenes had become normal and familiar. The idea of being in England no longer held any appeal. She turned from the window, picked up *The Buddhist Way* and read a few lines.

Buddhism inspires us to take responsibility for our lives, without moralizing, by understanding cause and effect—karma. Like gravity, the law of karma functions everywhere and always.

She stared at the page, pausing to consider the difference between karma and coincidence and which one applied to her, then continued reading.

In Buddhism, there is no such thing as pure coincidence, for the universe is naturally governed by the laws of cause and effect. Nothing happens by chance. Everything is ultimately due to our own influence—whether intentional or not. Coincidence is an illusion. The word karma is the Sanskrit term for action. Karma is not meant to make us feel helpless or hopeless. It reminds us we have full autonomy in the shaping of destiny.

She closed her eyes, breathed deeply, and felt her shoulders and neck muscles relax. Her mind started to drift, and she wondered how long she should wait to hear from Patrick, and what to do it he didn't contact her. Then she nudged her thoughts back to the present. *Stop. Breathe. Empty your mind.*

She heard a door open in the next room. The sound of muffled voices filtered through the thin wall. She closed her mind to the noise and sank deeper into meditation. She sensed Roxy's presence in the next room and the scamper of a gecko's feet as it ran across the ceiling above her. The window vibrated slightly as a rubbish truck drove past the building. She took another deep breath and leaned back onto the pillows.

The next she knew, it was 6 a.m. and there was a spasm in her neck from falling asleep against the wall. She immediately thought of Patrick and grabbed her laptop. There was a new message. *Subject: Re: Your father. Sender: Patrick Jansen.* She sat up, suddenly alert.

Dear Charlotte, I was happy to receive your letter via my brother. Your father and I have been friends for many years, so your message brings great joy. I'd prefer to discuss the situation by phone rather than communicate via email, so I'll call you if you send your number.

33

After she replied to Patrick, Charlotte couldn't sit still. Roxy and Peter were still asleep, so she slipped out and walked toward the riverfront, one hand clutching the phone in her pocket. Her stomach was in knots, fear and anticipation making her queasy with nerves and excitement.

A family crossed the road in front of her, and she watched as the little boy clasped his father's hand and gazed up at him. A horn blared so she leapt out of the way as a car swerved around her. All she could think about was Patrick's message and how long it would be before she heard from him. While she hadn't expected much information in an email, there'd been something about his note that worried her: *I'd prefer to discuss the situation by phone.*

Lifting her gaze from the pavement, she realised she was in front of the Royal Palace. Enormous golden spires pierced the cloudless blue sky, and a group of Japanese tourists scurried toward the gates, chattering loudly. Charlotte followed them, almost bumping into a young man standing at the entrance.

'Good morning, lady,' he said. 'You would like guide? I go now with small group if you wish to join.' She was about to refuse then reconsidered. Being anonymous among a group of tourists might be a good place to be. So she nodded, paid her admission fee, and followed him into an enormous hall.

The guide pointed to the walls. 'Observe how the building is mostly yellow and white,' he said. 'Yellow is symbol of Buddhism, white is Hinduism. These were the two main faiths of Cambodia until they were combined in the twelfth century by King Jayavarman the Seventh.' Charlotte's mind raced as she pretended to pay attention, unable to focus on anything other than Patrick's message.

The guide continued. 'The Royal Palace was built in 1866 after King Norodom moved the capital from Oudong to Phnom Penh. About one hundred years later, the palace became a prison when the king and his family were held by the Khmer Rouge.'

Usually, Charlotte would find this interesting, but today there were other things on her mind. She calculated the time difference between Cambodia and Belgium. It was five hours earlier there. Too early for anyone to be awake.

As they moved to another section of the palace, the guide pointed at the floor. 'We're now entering the Silver Pagoda,' he said. 'The floor is made from more than five thousand silver tiles, and each one weighs more than one kilogram.'

Charlotte jiggled back and forth on her heels, then nudged her way to the front of the group. Slipping two dollars into the guide's hand, she muttered, 'Thank you, sir. I need to get some air,' and walked toward the exit. When she reached the road, the edge of her sandal caught on a cracked paving stone. She stumbled and steadied herself against a wall.

'You okay, miss?' a man called from a tuk-tuk.

She waved. 'Fine. Just fine.'

Fine? She was anything but fine. She was a million miles away from a home that no longer felt like home, in the middle of a bizarre mystery, waiting for an email from a stranger. And one of the pieces in the puzzle was a woman named Piggy. So much had changed in such a short time. Monks and stray cats and tuk-tuks and people with weird names. She shook her head and continued walking.

A sound from behind caused her to jump, and a tuk-tuk pulled up next to her, clanging a bell. The driver thrust a flyer into her hand then drove off. She glanced at it: *French Cake Shop Opening Soon. Free coffee with first pastry*, then tossed it into a rubbish bin and walked away.

She turned the corner toward Roxy's flat, then stopped and stood for a moment. She could still hear the distant jingle of the tuk-tuk, so she went back to the rubbish bin and rummaged inside it for the brochure. Roxy could do a promotion like that. Not with pastries and coffee, but with artwork. The girls could make the cards and Roxy could give away a hand-painted postcard with every purchase. And if she wanted to branch out further, Trevor had a friend in Brighton who owned a craft shop and he'd probably sell her products.

She stared at the brochure, wondering why she was thinking about Roxy's business when there was so much else on her mind, then she flagged down a tuk-tuk and headed to the flat.

❀

PETER AND ROXY sat at the living room table, poring over a pile of documents. They glanced at Charlotte as she entered so she went into the kitchen, poured a glass of water, and sat onto the couch with a magazine, waiting for them to take a break.

Finally, Peter pushed back his chair. 'I'm done for today. Let's get back to this tomorrow, shall we?' He looked at Charlotte. 'Everything okay?'

Charlotte put down the magazine. 'Actually, there's something I'd like to talk about. Do you have a minute?'

Roxy glanced at Peter. 'There's something we want to discuss with you, too,' she said. 'You first.'

'I had an idea,' she said, tucking her feet beneath her. 'Now that Annie has gone, I thought you might need help.' She paused, unsure if they'd be receptive. Then she imagined how it would feel to return to England, and continued. 'I love what you're doing,' she said. 'You're helping people and you've got some unique designs like *rice-fetti* and those wonderful animal pictures. I don't want to go home, and I'd like to stay here to help you with your business, so here's what I've been thinking.' For the next fifteen minutes, she outlined her ideas about ways she could help Boxy Wide Elephant, then took a deep breath and asked, 'What do you think?'

Roxy and Peter exchanged glances. *Why aren't they saying anything? They don't want to insult me.* Charlotte laughed uneasily, fearful that she'd overstepped boundaries. They had their own way of running their business and she'd been presumptuous in thinking she could contribute.

Roxy spoke first. 'What do I think?' She pushed a pile of papers aside. 'I think we're on the same wavelength, my friend. Peter and I had the same conversation before you walked in. We need another pair of hands. And someone with business skills.'

'We thought of you right away,' Peter said. 'But we didn't know if you'd want to stay in Cambodia for—'

'We can't pay much,' Roxy interrupted. 'But you can stay

with us till you find a place. And I'll pay you commissions on any sales you bring in, of course.'

Charlotte finally let herself exhale. 'What? You kidding me?'

'Dead serious.'

'Oh my God, you two are the best.' She beamed. 'You've no idea how much this means to me.'

Roxy picked up a handful of silver paper stars and threw them at Charlotte. 'Consider yourself initiated as the newest member of Boxy Wide Elephant! We'll have no problem getting you a work visa, so I'll start working on it today. You've gotta come to the British Chamber meeting with me on Thursday. I'm lousy at networking. And how about we create a new logo with—'

Peter put his hand on Roxy's shoulder and pressed her down in the chair. 'Slow down, woman. You're gonna scare her away before she starts.' He ran a hand through his hair. 'I also wanted to apologise for being grouchy at the hospital. I was worried, and I'm afraid I took it out on you. Forgive me?'

Charlotte nodded and for the rest of the afternoon, the three of them created a working agenda. Charlotte would work in Boxy Wide Elephant two mornings a week overseeing the staff. She'd spend three mornings in the office designing public relations materials and implementing a marketing plan. One afternoon a week she'd teach yoga to the girls, and the other afternoons would be spent networking with local organisations, brainstorming ideas with Roxy, or getting a massage, compliments of Boxy Wide Elephant. As they worked, Charlotte constantly glanced at her phone, wondering when Patrick might call. Everyone in Belgium would be awake by now. She didn't want to say anything to Roxy and Peter until she knew more, so she hoped they wouldn't notice her obsession with time.

When she went to bed it was almost midnight—early evening in Belgium. Her eyelids drooped as she drew the curtains and turned out the light. But there was still one thing left to do. She started a new email to her boss. *Dear Jim,* she wrote, *I regret to inform you I won't be coming back.*

34

A wave cascaded over a mound of pebbles, washing a lotus blossom onto the shore. It landed at the feet of a young girl playing on the beach who carried on building a sandcastle. Another wave washed over the castle, knocking it into a shapeless heap of wet sand. The girl began to cry then saw the flower half-buried in the sand. She brushed it off and held it up to her father, who took it from her and tucked it behind her ear. Then his phone began to ring. 'Just a moment,' her father said. 'I need to get this.'

Charlotte awoke with a jolt, the sound of ringing in her ears. She scrambled beneath the sheets and grabbed her phone. 'Hello,' she said in a croaky voice.

'Charlotte?' A man with a heavy French accent. 'Is this Charlotte?'

'Who's this?'

'It's Patrick.'

'Patrick, I—' She swung her feet onto the floor, rubbing the sleep from her eyes.

'Sorry if I woke you,' he said. 'I thought you'd be eager to hear from me.'

'I am. I'm so happy to hear your voice.' She swallowed a lump in her throat, anxious to hear more. 'Is my dad with you? Can I talk to him?'

There was a long pause, then Patrick spoke. 'Actually no.' The sound of a siren echoed down the phone. 'It's a long story. He's had many...problems.' He cleared his throat.

'What do you mean?' She tried to remember to breathe. Patrick was a stranger and she didn't know anything about him or what he meant to her father. While she wanted to trust him, she wanted to feel him out first.

After a moment, Patrick replied. 'It's his health,' he said.

'Is he okay?' Silence, then sounds of scuffling in the background. 'Patrick? Are you there?'

'My apologies. I'm now in a quiet room.'

'What's going on? Can I talk to him?'

'He's not well. I don't want to upset him.'

A wave of anger swept over her. Who was he to speak to her this way? He was *her* father. 'Patrick,' she repeated. 'Please tell me. Why can't I talk to him? What happened?'

'A lot of things, *cherie*.' Charlotte heard him sigh. 'It started when he moved to Belgium with me.'

'When was that? I had no idea...'

'He thought you didn't want to see him and so—'

'But that was years ago. Why didn't he try to contact me?'

'He couldn't.'

'Of course he could. He could've called, or come to visit, or —' Her voice broke.

'He couldn't, *cherie*,' Patrick repeated.

'I don't understand.' She wanted to reach down the phone and shake him, tell him to speak faster, explain what was going on.

'Just a minute.' He spoke to someone in a low voice then returned to the phone. 'My apologies,' he said. 'I can tell you now. Your father was unhappy in Belgium. He wanted to stay with me, but his heart was in England—with you. He returned to London after a few months and I was planning on joining him. But things changed.' He cleared his throat again.

'What do you mean?'

There was a long pause, then he replied. 'He'd been having headaches. Bad ones. We thought it was from stress. Then the day he arrived in London, he collapsed.'

'What? Where?'

'I don't recall. On his way into the city. Someone called me.'

'What are you saying?'

'It was a ruptured brain aneurysm.'

Charlotte inhaled sharply. She was afraid to ask the next question and waited until Patrick spoke. 'He survived,' he said. 'He was lucky. A team of brain surgeons saved his life. But he was in a coma for four weeks and he...' His voice trembled. 'He has not returned to normal.'

In a small, ragged, barely inaudible voice, she asked, 'What does that mean?' Then she held her breath, waiting for a response.

'His sight was weak, and he couldn't speak well for almost two years. He's able to talk now, but he can't...' He paused.

'Can't what?'

'Remember,' Patrick replied. 'He can't remember who he is. Or who I am, some of the time. So, I'm afraid, *cherie*, there's a strong chance he might not remember you either.'

Charlotte walked to the window and pushed it open. She needed air. A small glass candleholder tumbled from the sill and smashed on the tiled floor.

A voice came from the phone: 'Charlotte? Are you there?'

Her throat was too dry, and she couldn't form words.

'I know this is hard,' Patrick said. 'But the doctors say there's a high chance of improvement. I think it would be good for him to see you. And I know you must be anxious to see him after all this time.' Another siren sounded in the background. 'But you're so far away in England,' he said. 'And I don't know when we'll be back in Europe.'

Charlotte's mind snapped back. 'What d'you mean? Aren't you in Belgium?'

'We left Europe,' Patrick said. 'The surgeon who operated on your father told us about a procedure before he retired. He was the most experienced neurosurgeon in Europe and we trusted him, so we came here three months ago to—'

'Where?' Charlotte interrupted. 'Where are you?'

'Thailand. We're in Bangkok.' The phone beeped. The battery was fading. 'Did you hear me? We're in—'

The phone died. Charlotte flung it onto the bed. Stupid bloody idiot! How could she forget to charge it? She searched the room until she found the plug hidden under a pile of clothes then plugged it into the wall socket and stared, willing it to regain power. Daddy was in Thailand. Only an hour away. She clutched the phone, her mind spiralling. Ten minutes later, as it began to charge, there was a loud beep and a text message: *Sorry I lost you. At the hospital. Will call later.*

She played over the conversation, recalling the sequence of events Patrick had described. Her father collapsed in London, brain aneurysm, emergency surgery. His surgeon had retired and was one of the best in Europe. A chill ran down her back. With a shaky hand she replied to the text. *What was the name of dad's surgeon*?

An immediate reply: *Dr. Rashid Farouk.*

35

Charlotte was still clutching the phone when there was a tap on the bedroom door. Roxy peered inside, holding a basket filled with fabric swatches. She marched into the room. 'Let's make a patchwork quilt. We can call it Elephant Patches. Maybe you can—' She dropped the basket on the floor when Charlotte didn't reply. 'You okay?'

Charlotte shook her head. 'It's Dad. I know where he is.'

Roxy fell onto the bed beside her. 'Your dad? Shit, Charlo. Did Alistair...?'

'He had nothing to do with it.' She exhaled. 'I don't know where to start.'

Roxy gently removed the phone from Charlotte's hand. 'Who called?'

'Patrick.'

'You've gotta start at the beginning, love. I've no idea who Patrick is.'

Charlotte poured out the story, telling Roxy all she knew. An hour later, after three cups of tea, a bag of cheese balls, and two-thirds of a bar of Toblerone, she rubbed her eyes. 'He's an hour away. Can you believe it?' She glanced at her watch. 'Samnang gets back today. I need to tell him.' She tossed the rest of the chocolate bar to Roxy. 'Take this. I'll be back later.'

Clouds shrouded the early afternoon sun as she walked across town. It had been only a few weeks since she'd first discovered Samnang's pagoda, and now she felt a sense of belonging. While Kampot had been more beautiful and less populated, there was something about this structure that spoke to her. It had been the first sacred spot where she'd meditated, the first place she'd learned about Buddhism, the first space where she'd encountered genuine acceptance from a stranger. Her feelings for Samnang were strengthening every day and she felt gratitude to the young monk who'd introduced her to a new way of life and taught her how to see the world differently.

Once she arrived, she approached a monk and asked for Samnang.

'He return from Kampot today,' the monk replied. 'Will find him now.'

She waited in the courtyard, watching a flock of birds fly through the trees, until Samnang came into view. She jumped to her feet. 'I'm so glad you're back. I need to talk with you.'

A shadow flickered across his face. 'I just received news from home so I'm a little distracted today, I'm afraid.'

Her hand flew to her mouth. 'Oh! I'm sorry for interrupting. Is everything okay?'

'Not really.' He fingered a strand of wooden beads. 'It's my father. He died. A few weeks ago.' His eyes clouded over. 'News travels slowly when you don't want to be found, doesn't it?'

She caught her breath. 'I'm so sorry. Were you close?'

Samnang glanced down at his hands. 'My father wanted a son like him. That wasn't me.'

Charlotte perched next to him. 'What happened?'

He gazed into the distance. 'Nothing,' he said in a monotone voice. 'That was the point. We didn't have a relationship. But his rejection shaped my destiny.' He looked toward the stupas. 'If it hadn't been for him, I wouldn't have found Buddhism, or come to Cambodia, or looked for something meaningful. I needed something different or I'd —' Deep furrows formed across his brow. 'So, I'm grateful to him for that.' He inhaled. 'But I left without saying goodbye.'

They sat in silence. The sound of chanting drifted from the pagoda. Toyota crawled onto the bench and curled up on Samnang's lap where the monk stroked him gently as he gazed across the courtyard. Eventually, Charlotte asked 'Do you want to talk about it?'

⁂

SAMNANG NODDED and took a deep breath. 'I'll never forget,' he said. 'The day I got the call.' He continued stroking Toyota as he talked. 'It was just before nine on a Tuesday morning and I was waiting for a bus. Then my phone rang, so I let the bus go past and took the call. It was Ghandivita. Telling me it was time.' He paused.

'For what?'

'To leave. Time to go to Cambodia.' His eyes shone. 'It was the moment I'd been waiting for.'

'Why Cambodia? And who's Ghandivita?'

'My teacher, the head of the Buddhist community in my town.' He smiled. 'I couldn't have done it without him. He spent hours with me—counselling me, teaching me about the Four Noble Truths, the Eightfold Path, and the Stages of the Path to

Enlightenment. He also supported me when everyone else turned away.'

'Turned away?' Charlotte asked.

'I didn't fit in. My father wanted me to study, and my friends wanted me to get stoned.' He closed his eyes and inhaled deeply. 'I was a disappointment to my father, and the Smiling Cow was the only place I could escape to. Until I met Ghandivita. Then, I had four years of studying, meditating, and practising Buddhism.' He paused as a group of people walked through the grounds. 'I learned how to walk on my own path and I know they had to walk on theirs. Only my mum understood what it meant to me. She even went with me to a couple of meetings and loaned me money for a retreat in Wales.'

'When did you decide to be a monk?'

'July tenth, almost four years ago.' He shrugged. 'I'm good at remembering dates. It was also a month after my twentieth birthday.'

She looked away, trying to recall what she'd been doing on her twentieth birthday. Roxy had taken her out, they'd drunk too much, and they'd fallen asleep in the bus on the way home. The following day, her mother had called Roxy's mother and told her Roxy was a bad influence on her daughter.

'You were so young,' she told Samnang. 'How did you make that decision?'

'I went to a retreat taught by a Khmer Rouge survivor. He had been tortured during the war, and most of his family had been murdered, but he was such a gentle, forgiving soul that I felt humbled. If he could forgive the people who'd shattered his life, then I could do the same. So, on the third day, I decided two things: I wanted to be a monk and I wanted to live in Cambodia.

'For the next year, I studied and worked in the Buddhist centre. I cleaned the monks' rooms, took classes, and volunteered at a homeless shelter. On my twenty-first birthday, I made the commitment to take refuge in the Three Jewels—that means I pledged my life to Buddhism. And two weeks later I took my vows at a small monastery on the outskirts of London. Ghandivita conducted the ceremony and my mum stood in the back. My dad, of course, was too busy to come. To the most important event of my life.'

Charlotte looked down at her hands. She'd come to the pagoda to pour out her troubles to Samnang and never imagined he'd have challenges of his own. 'How did you know you were doing the right thing?' she asked.

'I never had a moment of doubt.'

A leaf fluttered from a branch above them and fell onto Charlotte's lap. It reminded her of the day she'd met Samnang, when she'd tossed a flower into a bowl of pomegranate seeds. 'Was it hard?' she asked.

He nodded. 'It was a constant struggle. But anything important is worth fighting for.' He shifted his posture on the bench. 'One of the most painful parts was leaving.'

'But you wanted to go.'

'More than anything. But I didn't realise what it meant until I started packing. I was so overwhelmed that I stuffed lots of useless things into my duffel bag, like a pair of jeans, and a sweatshirt.' He let out a short laugh. 'When would I ever need a sweatshirt in this heat?

'The worst moment was saying goodbye to Mum.' He paused. 'She was in her bedroom and I was afraid to tell her I was going. I considered leaving without saying anything but I didn't, of course. Before I left, I took a photo from the mantelpiece—a family picture of all of us. I thought it might keep me company when times got hard.'

She leaned forward, wishing she could grasp his hand. He'd done what she should have: followed his heart. 'Farewells are tough,' she said.

He nodded. 'We were both in tears. She clung to me for the longest time, then pushed me away and said, "Be happy". When I looked back from the doorway, she was staring into space. It broke my heart, but it was too late to turn back. And once I got into the car and waved goodbye, she blew me a kiss and called, "I'll tell your father you love him"'.

36

Charlotte wiped her eyes as Samnang finished his story. In the few weeks since they'd met, she'd been inspired by him in more ways than she could count. This latest revelation made her feel even closer and she felt privileged he'd shared so much with her.

After a moment of silence, he turned to her. 'What was it you wanted to tell me?'

She shook her head. 'It's not important now,' she said. 'I'm so sorry to hear about your father.'

He lowered his eyes and fingered his wooden beads. 'Death is part of life,' he said, then pointed to an enormous tamarind tree in the middle of the pagoda grounds. 'We're like trees, Charlotte. Leaves fall from the branches, then go back to the soil to nourish the roots. The following year, there are new leaves again. It was my father's time...I just wish—I wish I could...' He stopped, eyes brimming with unshed tears. 'I'll never know if he forgave me for disappointing him.'

Charlotte leaned forward. 'You once told me something I'll

always remember. You said if you harbour bad thoughts, the pain inside never ends, and that the only way through it is to accept it, let it go, and move on.'

'That is true. And I—ouch!' He gasped as Toyota scrambled from his lap, the cat's sharp claws scratching his arm. He wiped a streak of blood from his wrist, and Toyota ran across the courtyard and disappeared down a tree-lined path. Samnang shook his head. 'It's not a good idea for Toyota to go into those buildings. Some of the monks don't like having cats in their rooms.'

Charlotte leapt up. 'I'll get him,' she said, and followed the path to a clearing behind the pagoda. In front of her was a small stone building with the door slightly ajar, so she pushed it open and went inside. The room was dimly lit with coarse stone walls and a grey cement floor, giving the feeling of a cave. It smelled musty and damp, and she squinted into the darkness, waiting for her eyes to become accustomed to the light. Lined up along the back wall were four straw mats, and next to them four upended wooden crates, each holding a collection of personal items: combs, books, strings of beads, and plastic bowls. In one corner, orange robes were draped over washing lines like cinnamon-coloured flags, and four pairs of plastic sandals were lined up beneath a bench.

She froze, realising she'd entered the monks' private quarters. She turned to leave then heard a scratching sound from behind one of the crates. Toyota emerged, walked onto one of the mats, and started licking his paws, draping his tail over a book called *Learning Khmer*.

Charlotte crouched down and reached out her hand. 'Here, kitty. Come here, Toyota.' Toyota didn't budge. She took a step closer, eager to grab him and leave before anyone saw her. As she came toward him, Toyota ran from the mat, knocking over one of the crates with a loud clatter. The contents toppled onto the floor and Charlotte dashed to pick them up, hoping nobody would hear.

With a quick glance over her shoulder, she picked up a plastic cup and a toothbrush and put them back on top of the crate, then saw a picture frame lying face down in the shadows. She reached for it, turning it over as she placed it next to the other items, and glanced at the photo. A young boy stood between a man and woman and all three were smiling for the camera. The boy was wiry and suntanned, the woman petite and blonde. The man wore spectacles, his tall, lean frame dressed in a tailored black suit, one arm loosely draped around the woman's shoulders. Charlotte held the picture closer to inspect it. In the dim light, she could make out the man's expression and how his bushy eyebrows seemed to dominate his face. It was a face that was familiar to her. She gripped the frame tighter, heart pounding. It was Rashid.

37

Charlotte stared at the photo and held her breath. Not only did she recognise Rashid, but the little boy had the soft eyes and gentle expression of someone she'd grown to admire. Even as a child, he had a thoughtful expression as he clung tightly to his mother's hand and smiled for the camera.

Her finger grazed over an inscription on the frame and she noticed three letters: *L.I.F.* The same inscription as the one on the ring. She leaned back on a stone wall, her mind racing. Why hadn't she put two and two together before? The genocide museum, the dance performance, Monsoon restaurant, Kampot—all the places she'd seen Rashid. A chill swept through her. There'd been one common denominator in all of them: Samnang. The answer had been right in front of her all the time.

She walked slowly back to the garden. Samnang didn't move when she approached, so she stood next to him and cleared her throat. 'Bhante Samnang,' she murmured. 'I want to...I mean, I need to...there's something—'

Samnang looked up. 'What is it, Charlotte?'

'It's just that...' She cleared her throat. 'There's something I need to tell you...give you—I have a message for you, Bhante Samnang.' She paused and met his gaze. 'Or should I call you Chris?'

His eyes widened. 'How—?'

'I can't explain right now,' Charlotte said. 'Actually, I'm not sure I can ever explain. But I have something for you. Something you need to see.' She reached into her bag, took out the letter, and handed it to him. He opened the envelope and started to read, and she quietly slipped away.

❦

THE ROAD outside the pagoda was bustling with lunchtime traffic. Drivers jostled for parking spaces outside restaurants and trucks rumbled past, piled high with bulging bags of rice and enormous plastic jugs of water. A café owner came out of a Chinese restaurant, flapping a menu in Charlotte's face. She stepped aside, brushing past, and sat on a stone wall overlooking the river. Closing her eyes, she took a deep breath, picturing Samnang opening the letter from his father, finding the ring.

A gentle voice next to her made her jump. 'Sua s'day, lady.' It was the crippled beggar, looking up at her from the pavement. 'Look. I have new legs,' he said, pointing to the wheelchair next to him. 'Very lucky.'

Charlotte smiled. 'How wonderful,' she said, dropping a dollar into his bowl. She turned to walk away, but the man reached out his arm and beckoned. He twisted his torso, reached into a large cloth bag sitting on the pavement, and took out an enormous green coconut. Holding it in two hands he held it up to Charlotte.

'For me?' she asked, pointing to herself.

The man nodded again and held it higher. Charlotte bent down and took it from him then reached out and touched him on the shoulder. 'Thank you,' she said. '*Akun*.' She bowed and gave a sampeah and as she did so, noticed one of the man's eyes was cloudy and white. Her eyes welled up and she turned away to cross the street, once again touched by the kindness of a someone who had nothing, but still found a way to give. Deep in thought, she crossed the busy road, and as she reached the other side, her phone rang.

'Charlotte?' The person on the phone spoke with a French accent. 'It's Patrick.'

She ducked into the entrance of a small hotel to escape the street noise. 'Thank goodness you called,' she said. 'My phone can't make international calls.' A group of tourists walked by chattering loudly so she spoke louder, wanting to make sure he heard her next words. 'I'm in Cambodia.'

'Cambodia? What are you doing there?'

'I'll tell you when I see you. How long will you be in Bangkok?' She held her breath. *Please don't leave yet. I'm so close.*

'I'm not sure, *cherie*. We've been here three months so it could be a week, or it could be a year. It depends how your dad is doing.'

She let out a breath. 'I'm coming. Send me the address for the hospital and I'll let you know when I'm on my way.'

❀

Later that afternoon she walked back toward the pagoda, wondering if it would be too soon to return. It had only been an hour since she'd left, and she didn't want to intrude on Samnang's grief. But she also didn't want to leave without talking to him.

The courtyard was empty except for two gardeners whacking at tree branches with machetes, so she crossed the path, listening for sounds. Faint trails of smoke drifted from one of the rooms and the muffled sound of a gong echoed from inside. She stood on her toes so she could peer through a window and saw a large stone Buddha statue at the front of the room. In front of the statue, Samnang knelt on the floor, shrouded in a cloud of incense. His forehead was pressed to the ground, arms stretched out in front of him. A wisp of smoke drifted toward her and caught in her throat. She coughed and jumped back into a bush, hoping she hadn't been heard.

Minutes later, Samnang appeared at the doorway. 'Charlotte, I know you're there,' he said.

She pushed her way out of the bush, brushing leaves from her hair. 'I'm sorry,' she said. 'I didn't mean to disturb you. Just wanted to make sure you were okay and—' She paused when she saw him up close. The glow from the candles illuminated his slight frame and his pale eyes were softer than usual. He held his head straight, a peaceful expression on his face. He looked younger and more tranquil than when she'd left him.

He beckoned to her. 'I have something to share with you,' he said. 'When I was little, I thought my father was a superman. He healed people and worked long hours taking care of them. I used to tell my friends he was too busy saving lives to come to my school events. I thought if I said it enough, I'd believe it. But I knew the truth. He wasn't too busy. He just wasn't interested.'

'You don't have to tell me this.'

'I'd like to. It's important. When I was nine, he told me life wasn't about having fun, it was about being the best. But I was only average. And I had no interest in school. One day, when I was thirteen, he came home early and found me lying on the couch listening to music while my mate Harry was painting his toenails black for a Halloween party. I'll never forget the look on my father's face. He pulled Harry up by his collar and pushed him out the door. And do you know what he said? He said we don't entertain fairies in our house.' He twisted a ring on his middle finger.

Charlotte noticed the ring and a warmth spread through her chest when she recognised it. 'He sounds like a difficult father,' she said. 'I understand why you wanted to leave.'

He raised his eyes and met her gaze. 'That was the turning point. It hurt that he didn't just disapprove of me, but my friends as well. That's when I started drinking and doing drugs and created a world of my own. One where it was okay to be imperfect.'

A group of monks walked by and nodded a greeting. Samnang nodded back, then gently brushed a leaf from his robe. 'It's almost time for evening prayer, but I want to finish my story,' he said. 'I've learned a lot since coming here. I learned how to forgive him. I also recognised he might never accept me.' He looked down at his hands gripping the envelope. 'Then, this. He knew. Somehow, he understood. I can't tell you how much...' He stopped. 'How did you know?'

She shrugged. 'It's a mystery. If it hadn't been for Toyota, I might never have seen your photo or known who you were. But you told me your name was Robin.'

'It is. Christopher Robin.' He pulled a face. 'Awful, isn't it? You can imagine how much I was teased. So, I dropped

Christopher when I left school and told everyone my name was Robin. Only my parents knew me as Chris. And now you.'

'There's one more thing,' she said, fumbling inside her bag. She handed him the receipt she'd found inside the book and he read the scribbled words aloud: *One doesn't discover new lands without consenting to lose sight of the shore for a very long time.*

'It must be for you,' she said. 'Look what it says at the bottom: *You are my special messenger, Ch—* The last word got torn off. He must have been writing *Chris*'.

Samnang stared at the paper. He passed it back to her, and then did a deep *sampeah*. 'I think you're wrong this time,' he said. 'I'm not a messenger. You are. The word at the bottom...I don't think it's meant to be Chris. It's Charlotte.'

38

'What do you mean?' Charlotte's heart pounded. 'Why is it meant for me?'

'As you said earlier, it's all a mystery. I'll can't explain any of it, but there's a Bengali saying that says one cannot predict what a madman will say—'

'Or what a goat will eat,' Charlotte interrupted.

Samnang's eyebrows shot up. 'How do you know that?' he asked.

'Someone told me some things aren't predictable.' She swallowed a lump in her throat. 'You know who it was,' she said. 'Don't you?'

He nodded, a tear glistening in the corner of his eye. She wanted to reach out and take his hand, hold him close, and let him know she cared. But she could only look into his eyes and hope he understood what she was feeling. There was a special bond between them that started when she met his father on the flight and she knew it would remain long after they'd gone their separate ways. After a few moments, she broke the silence.

'There's one more thing I want to ask,' she said. 'What's the meaning of L.I.F?'

'The meaning of life?'

'No. The initials on your picture frame. They're also engraved inside your dad's ring.'

'It's a family signature. After my grandmother met grandpa, she started signing letters with it.'

'What does it mean?'

'Love Is Forever.'

The sound of a gong resonated into the courtyard. Two birds took flight from a nearby tree, their fluttering wings shaking the branches. Samnang looked toward the pagoda. 'I need to go,' he said. 'But I want to leave you with a story about a student who attended a lecture given by a Buddhist Master. After the lecture, the student said, "I've been listening to your lectures for years, but I still don't understand. Can you put it all in a nutshell?" The Master looked at the student and said two words: "Everything changes"'.

He turned and walked away.

CHARLOTTE SAT in the garden for a while, grateful for the silence. Her mind spun from everything she'd just learned, and the lump in her throat made it hard to swallow. She had found Chris. She walked through the gates onto the street and a voice rang out behind her. 'Jallod! Hello, Jallod!' SomOn's beaming face came into sight as he stopped the tuk-tuk next to her. 'You want ride? I pick up customer near your house.' He waved a shiny iPhone. 'See what I find near Russian Market. I not know who lose it.'

She took it from his outstretched arm. It was clearly an

expensive phone and somebody would be looking for it, so she flipped through the photo gallery to see if there was anyone in the pictures that she or Roxy might recognise. The first image showed an attractive Asian woman standing in front of the Phnom Penh airport wearing a floor-length skirt. In one hand, she held a small handbag and in the other she gripped a large red suitcase. Her immaculate style contrasted with her nervous expression as she stared into the camera, unsmiling. She looked like many of the middle-aged Cambodian women Charlotte had seen around the city, but her posture was stiffer, more anxious. In the next photo, the woman knelt on a concrete floor in what looked like a simple wooden hut. She was surrounded by a cluster of Cambodian children.

Charlotte showed it to SomOn. 'Have you seen this woman anywhere?' she asked.

He squinted at the phone and shook his head. 'Not see,' he said.

'I'll try to find the owner and give it back,' she said, dropping it into her pocket. 'Can you take me home, please?'

They drove to the flat, where she found Peter working at the dining room table. He looked up when she entered. 'Roxy's gone to make you a Boxy Wide Elephant T-shirt,' he said, grinning. 'The girl's on a mission. She'll sweep you along in a tidal wave of enthusiasm, whether you're ready or not.'

Charlotte held out the phone. 'Sorry to interrupt, but SomOn found this and I'd like to find the owner.' She pointed to the woman in the photos. 'Do you know how I can track her down?'

Peter took the phone, flipped open the cover and tapped the *phone* icon. A number popped up and he grinned. 'I'd like to say I'm a tech genius, but it's that easy. Just call the last number she dialled.'

Charlotte pushed the number and waited as it rang. After a few seconds, a woman answered. 'Chmoa Sandan,' she said. *I am Sandan.* The voice was weak and shaky as though it belonged to an old person.

'Sua s'day,' Charlotte said. 'Do you speak English?'

There was a rustling sound in the background, then a deep, masculine voice. 'Hello?'

'Hello. My name is Charlotte. I have a lost phone. The owner called your number, so I think you may know her.'

More rustling. Chatter in the background. Then another woman's voice, soft with a slight French accent. 'Hello,' she said. 'This is Malina. My nephew said you found my phone. I'm so grateful you called.' She paused. 'Can we meet?'

Charlotte gave her Jinjerbread's address then walked to the café and ordered a mango smoothie. Within minutes, a woman wearing a long silk skirt and an anxious expression came in and scanned the room. It was the woman from the photos. Charlotte waved and the woman nodded back then went to the counter, bought a cup of tea and a bottle of water, and joined her at the table. Deep wrinkles fanned from the corners of her eyes, and high cheekbones framed a delicate, heart-shaped face. She smoothed her skirt beneath her and sat on the edge of the wooden chair. 'You must be Charlotte,' she said, stretching out her hand. 'I'm Malina.'

Charlotte shook her hand then slid the phone across the table.

'It's kind of you to find me,' Malina said, looking down at long, tapered fingers resting in her lap. 'Gestures like this make me realise I'm back in a country where people look out for one another.' Her eyes softened. 'It's been so long, I almost forgot.'

She reached inside a silk handbag and handed Charlotte a small paper bag. Charlotte pulled out a pair of delicately crafted butterfly earrings. 'A token of my appreciation,' Malina said, unfolding a paper napkin and placing it on her lap. 'They were made by disabled women in the Philippines. My son owns a chain of boutiques in Paris selling items created by social enterprises and I often help him out.'

'They're beautiful,' Charlotte said. 'It's very kind of you, and quite unnecessary.'

'Good deeds should always be rewarded,' Malina said. 'And I appreciate you took the time to meet me.'

Charlotte pushed back her chair and started to get up. It was getting late and she wanted to get home. But Malina seemed to be enjoying her company or didn't have anywhere else to go as she kept talking. 'I'm looking for opportunities here,' she said. 'For my son's boutiques. He's interested in working with small business entrepreneurs and I've already made some contacts, but—'She shrugged. 'It takes time.'

Charlotte sat down again, suddenly interested. 'I might be able to help,' she said. 'My friend Roxy owns a shop that provides work for disadvantaged Cambodian women. I'd love to connect you.' She paused when Malina's eyes clouded over, sensing there was more she wanted to talk about. 'Are you here on holiday here?' she asked. 'I hope you don't mind, but I saw your photos with the Cambodian family.'

Malina turned her head away. 'That is my family, 'she said. Her smile faded as she peeled the paper wrapper from her straw, slid it into the bottle, and took a sip. 'Those who are left.'

'Excuse me?'

'It's been thirty-one years since I came back. I couldn't. Until now'.

Charlotte remained silent. 'I'm sorry if I touched a memory for you,' she said softly. 'Your family is beautiful.'

A shadow passed across Malina's eyes. 'Would you like to know about them?' she asked.

'I'd love to,' Charlotte said. 'If you want to tell me.'

Malina pushed back a strand of hair that had come loose from her bun. There was an expression in her eyes, a faraway look that made Charlotte think there was something deeper, something more intimate that haunted her. She shifted her chair and leaned across the table and said, 'I'm happy to stay. I have plenty of time and it's cool in here. Besides, it's a pleasure to meet someone like you.'

Malina smiled, and for the next half hour told Charlotte about her life. She was raised in a small Cambodian village where her mother had worked as a seamstress and her father repaired bicycles. As a teenager, she'd received a scholarship to study in France and had been the first in her family to receive an education, an enormous honour for a child from a poor family. In 1973, she'd left for Paris and a year after her departure, heard the devastating news that the Khmer Rouge had marched into Phnom Penh, evacuating thousands and beginning a purge that killed half the population.

'I watched it on television from my apartment in Paris,' Malina said. 'I couldn't reach my family. Didn't know what was happening to them. I had no money. No way to return.' She pressed her lips together. 'I stayed in France two more years, then went to Sudan for work. I tried to contact someone, anyone, in Cambodia who might know about my family. But nothing. Then, in 1980, a letter arrived from one of my sisters who'd managed to track me down. She told me most of my family had been killed.' She closed her eyes for an instant. 'I couldn't believe it. It was like I was living in a nightmare. A big void opened inside me that remains to this day.'

Charlotte didn't know what to say. A stranger had just

shared her personal pain in the same way Saran had done in Kampot. She reached across the table and touched Malina's hand. 'I'm so very sorry,' she said. 'I just can't imagine...' She paused. 'So, why now? Why did you come back?'

Malina stirred her tea. 'Do you believe in signs?'

Charlotte nodded. *If only you knew.*

'About three weeks ago, when I was at home, I dreamt I was in my childhood home in Cambodia and a butterfly flew through the window. It landed on my finger and I spoke to it: "At least you can fly away, little butterfly. My family never had the chance". When I awoke, the dream was still vivid. Then a strange thing happened. A butterfly flew into my room and settled on a photograph of my family. It was wintertime—not a time for butterflies. I felt it was a message, telling me it was time. Time to return to my country'. A muscle in her jaw twitched. 'I had much love for Cambodia, but hatred for the people who destroyed my home and family. I was terrified of coming back, and of what I might find. Then something happened as I was on my way.' Her lip quivered as she took a sip of tea. 'Please, excuse me a moment.' She walked toward the ladies' room.

Five minutes later she returned, eyes swollen. 'I'm sorry,' she said.

'Can I get you something?' Charlotte asked.

Malina shook her head. 'On the way here, I changed planes in Bangkok. I almost didn't continue as I was overcome with sadness about returning to Cambodia.'

Charlotte watched Malina's body language. Her hands remained clasped in her lap and her head bowed until she mentioned Cambodia. Then she raised her eyes and stared at Charlotte.

'I was afraid of what I'd find,' she said. 'I broke down in the airport and hid in a corner so nobody could see me. That's where the old man found me—a man with a kind expression who thought I might need someone to talk to. I was embarrassed, but he gave me courage and said I'd make it through the bumps in the road. He told me he'd left his own country when he was young and had never gone back. He understood.' She reached into her handbag and took out a bookmark. 'He also gave me this,' she said, holding it up to the light so she could read from it. '*One doesn't discover new lands without consenting to lose sight of the shore for a very long time.*' He said there was nothing in the world more important than family. I'm only here now because of him.'

Charlotte held her breath. 'Why doesn't he go back to his country now?' she asked.

'He said he was losing his eyesight, and this would be his last trip.'

Charlotte sat up straighter as a chill ran through her. 'Where was he from?' she asked.

Malina stirred her tea before replying. 'Bangladesh.' Her eyes softened and she reached across the table and touched Charlotte's hand.

'You saw him too, didn't you?' Charlotte asked, quietly. 'Did he come with you to Cambodia?'

Malina nodded. 'I saw him.' Her lips hardly moved as she spoke. 'But he stayed in Bangkok. He said he was waiting for someone.' She squeezed Charlotte's hand. 'I saw him one more time. Last night. In a dream. He said I was going to meet someone special today; a special messenger.' Her eyes shone with unshed tears. 'That is you, my lovely girl. He wanted me to tell you something. He wanted to say thank you.' She let go of Charlotte's hand and rested it on the table. For almost a minute nobody spoke. Then Malina glanced at her watch and pushed back her chair. ‘It’s late. I must go now.’

She stood and walked to the exit without looking back. Then she was gone, the door ajar behind her. All that remained was a smear of lipstick on her teacup and a whiff of floral perfume in the air.

39

Charlotte opened the door to the flat and tiptoed through the darkness into the kitchen. Her mind was still buzzing from the conversation with Malina and she wondered if she'd ever see her again.

Suddenly a shape appeared in front of her. She shrieked. Roxy emerged from behind the fridge door. 'Shh!' she hissed. 'You'll wake Peter.'

'What the hell!' Charlotte said. 'You scared the stuffing out of me.'

A sequinned panda design shimmered on Roxy's knee-length T-shirt as she moved closer, clutching a doughnut in her hand. 'I couldn't sleep,' she whispered, her body silhouetted against the glow of the fridge light. 'Come over here where we can talk without waking Peter.'

She steered Charlotte into the living room and spoke in a normal tone. 'I was lying in bed thinking.' she said. 'First, I started imagining all the things you could do at the shop. Then my mind flashed back to those wonderful cakes you used to make. Then I realised I had a couple of doughnuts in the freezer, and then...' She shrugged and pointed at the doughnut.

'You're eating a frozen doughnut! What kind of person puts doughnuts in the freezer?'

'Why not? It's a bit hard, but the icing's great. Here.' She thrust it toward Charlotte. 'Try some.'

Charlotte held up her hand. 'Read my face.' She pointed to herself. 'Does this look like someone who'd want a frozen piece of sugary dough? Besides, I've had a weird night. And I've got to look into flights to Bangkok.'

'Oh, shit, I totally forgot. What did your lovely monk say about your dad? Come, sit.' She plopped onto the couch and patted the seat beside her.

Charlotte sat and folded her feet beneath her. 'You ready for this?' she asked. 'That lovely monk. He's not Samnang. He's Chris.'

'He's what? Who—?' Roxy stopped chewing. 'Hang on a second, I need a drink for this.' She went to the cabinet, took out the nearly empty bottle of Ballantine, and poured some into two glasses.

Charlotte pushed the glass away. 'None for me.'

Roxy dipped the doughnut into the whisky, took a bite, and recoiled. Then she shrugged and popped the rest into her mouth. She chewed as she spoke. 'You've gotta tell me what on earth you're talking about.'

'I found Chris.' She took a deep breath. 'You're not going to believe this...' Half an hour later she paused. 'So that's all of it.' She rubbed her eyes. She was exhausted and needed to sleep but her mind was speeding.

'Jesus Christ!' Roxy stared at her. 'Let me get this straight. Rashid *was* on your flight? Or you imagined him. And Samnang is Chris, who is the son of Rashid, who's dead.'

Charlotte nodded.

'And your dad's in Bangkok with some Belgian dude named Patrick, who I believe was my art professor.' Roxy drained the glass of whisky. 'Bloody hell. If I didn't have the taste of whisky-infused doughnut in my mouth, I'd swear I was hallucinating.' She gave Charlotte a concerned look. 'You okay?'

'I guess so,' she said. 'I don't know what just happened. But I'm even more convinced Rashid's mantra is true.'

'What's that?'

'Things aren't always foreseeable.'

'The old fella's got that right. But you're starting to sound crazier than I am.' Roxy glanced at the clock. 'Babe, my mind's about to explode and I need to get some sleep. I bet you do, too. But there's something you've got to do first.' She pointed to the laptop. 'Book that flight. Or I'll force feed you doughnuts and make you start work at sunrise. Which is basically five hours from now.'

Charlotte opened a browser and typed, *Cheap flights from Phnom Penh to Bangkok*, then she paused and turned to Roxy. 'I don't know what I'll find. And I've never met this Patrick fellow.' She closed the laptop. 'D'you think I should go?'

'Are you mad? You've waited seven years to find your dad. Now he's an hour away'.

'What if—'

'I know, I know... What if he no longer remembers you or he's upset with you? But what if he's been waiting seven years to find you, too?'

Charlotte gripped Roxy's hand. 'Will you come with me?'

'Nope. This is something for you and only you. Like coming to Cambodia.'

'Not the same.'

'Sure it is. You told me you were scared to fly and gave some bullshit excuse about not being able to leave work. And look how it turned out.' She raised her eyebrows. 'So, who made that happen? Me? Your mum? Your boss? Nada. It was *you*, darling. You are entirely, completely, utterly capable of doing this.' She pointed to the screen. 'Just buy a frigging ticket, will you so I can go to bed.' She grabbed the laptop, scrolled through a selection of travel websites, and pointed to a list of flights. 'Look. There's a cheap ticket to Bangkok on Thursday at two o'clock. That gives you three days to find a place to stay.' She seized Charlotte's bag and rustled through it. 'Now where in this cavernous collection of nonsense is your credit card? I'm booking it for you.'

CHARLOTTE LAY on top of her bed watching the ceiling fan spin. The flight was booked and there was no turning back. She looked at the clock on the bedside table: 3:15 a.m. Her heart raced. She was going to see her father. An image of him sprang to mind: a tall, handsome man with a full head of golden-brown hair, strong shoulders, and dark blue eyes. There had been so many times she'd dreamed about finding him. So many scenarios she'd played out in her mind. He'd show up at their house, sweep her into his arms, and tell her how much he'd missed her. But the dream always ended there.

Rolling onto her side, she scrunched a sweat-soaked pillow beneath her head, her elbow brushing against *The Buddhist Way* on the bedside table. She switched on the lamp, picked up the book, and turned to the section where she'd last stopped reading:

Imagine you're walking to the top of a mountain: You can affect how you take the next step, but you can't affect the mountaintop.

Sometimes you don't realise your greatest strength until you come face to face with your greatest weakness. Nothing ever goes away until it has taught us what we need to know.

She re-read the last line. *Nothing ever goes away until it has taught us what we need to know.* That could mean her father, or Rashid, or Samnang. Possibly all three. She placed the book on the pillow and closed her eyes. She had a feeling she'd find out soon.

40

The next morning, Charlotte found Roxy hunched over a stack of binders at the kitchen table. She looked up when Charlotte walked in and tossed a packaged croissant at her. 'Come on, lazy bones! It's almost ten o'clock and we've got work to do. I've asked Rithy to pick us up a bag of coffee.'

'Rithy?'

'The landlord's son. I spilled our last pot of coffee down the sink when I tried to swat a gecko off the window.' She pointed toward the cupboard. 'There's some weird Chinese melon seed tea if you want it.'

Charlotte rubbed her eyes and sat down next to her. 'I'll wait for the coffee, thanks.' She yawned. 'So, what's the plan? Is there something I can do before I go to Bangkok?'

Roxy handed her a folder. 'Read this,' she said. 'It's my business plan.'

Charlotte opened it, then paused. 'I wanted to tell you about the woman I met last night,' she said. 'The one who lost her phone. Her son owns a couple of shops in France and she's helping him find arts and crafts to sell. I thought you might want to get involved.'

Roxy grinned. 'Trust you to meet someone. I always said you had the magic touch.' She picked up a pen and waved it in the air. 'Let's do something really cool. How about some...?' She stared at the ceiling and chewed on the pen. 'No, that wouldn't work. What about a picture of...? No, that's no good.' She bit the end off the pen and spat it on the floor. 'I know! Silk berets. The French love berets.'

Charlotte rolled her eyes. 'And how about silk lederhosen for the German market? Or silk kilts for the Scots?' She took a bite of the croissant. 'What on earth are you thinking? That's a ridiculous idea. Don't you think you're jumping the gun just a teeny bit?'

'*This* is why we make a good team.' Roxy leaned back and grinned. 'Your brains and my beauty. We'll soon have a chain of Boxy Wide Elephants all over Southeast Asia and then we—' A knock on the door interrupted her. 'Must be Rithy,' she said, scrambling to her feet. She opened the door and Charlotte heard muffled conversation from the hallway. A moment later, Roxy shouted, 'Charlo, it's for you,' and walked into her bedroom.

Charlotte went to the door where a young man stood in the hallway, facing away from her. The back of his cotton shirt was damp with perspiration and his baggy trousers were cinched tightly around a narrow waist. In one hand he clutched the handle of a large wicker basket.

'Can I help you?' she asked. He turned and her mouth fell open. 'Bhante Samnang! What are you doing here?'

'Actually, it's Chris. Chris Farouk.' He placed the basket on the floor and flashed a shy smile. 'Samnang's gone.' He peeked inside the flat. 'So's your roommate, it seems. I think I scared her away'.

Roxy peered around the bedroom door. 'I'm really busy right now, you guys. Need to polish the silver. Why don't you go out and get a coffee or something?' She shrugged. 'I'd offer you some, but there's none left.'

Chris lifted the lid of the basket. 'First, there's something I need to leave here. If you want it.' He nudged the basket and Toyota crawled out and strolled into the living room, where he curled up on a bean bag and started licking his paws. 'Looks pretty happy to me,' Chris said. 'I thought you might like him back since I can't keep him anymore.'

Charlotte looked beseechingly at Roxy who shrugged then disappeared back into her bedroom. Chris stood at the entryway, holding open the door. 'Come on,' he said. 'I'll fill you in on the details over coffee.'

❦

Once they were seated in Jinjerbread with two large cappuccinos, Chris leaned back in his seat and took a deep breath. 'Boy, that tastes good. I didn't realise how much I missed caffeine.' He took another sip then placed the mug on the table. 'So, there's not a lot to tell, but there are going to be plenty of changes in my life now. After you left, I meditated for a long time, I thought about my dad and read his letter over and over again. Then, I called my mum.' His eyes misted over. 'When I heard her voice, I felt as though something burst inside me. I realised how much I'd been holding in, and how much I missed her, how much I want to be with her. Specially now.' His voice caught in his throat. 'I've learned so much since I left home. Not just about myself but about my family and my role in it. Now I just want to help my mum.' He wrapped his hands around his mug.

'You're leaving?' Charlotte asked. 'What about Lokru? And the other monks? Can you leave all this behind?'

'I've already told Lokru. I spent two hours with him after Morning Prayer.' He sighed, a peaceful expression on his face. 'He was wonderful and said there'd always be a place for me if I wanted to come back. So, I'm leaving Samnang in Phnom Penh and Chris is going to London. I'm not sure for how long—could be a month, could be a year, could be longer. My heart will tell me.'

Charlotte stared from across the table. He's only twenty-four, she thought. The same age as I am. She wanted to reassure him everything would work out, then caught herself. He was the one who'd taught *her* about acceptance. He'd changed his life around for his beliefs and was about to do the same again, this time for his family. A warm sensation washed over her. Samnang had been the only calm presence in her life when it had felt as though everything was falling apart. His departure would leave a huge gap in her life.

As though he'd heard her thoughts, Chris reached across the table and took her hand. 'I owe you so much, my lovely friend,' he said. 'You brought a special meaning to my world, and I've enjoyed watching you grow. You're strong, Charlotte. I think you know that now.' Then he grinned, revealing an impish side Charlotte hadn't seen before. 'And I'll always think of you when I see pomegranate seeds.'

He drained his cup and stood. 'I'd better go and pack my bag. Then I need to find a guesthouse for a couple of nights.' He pointed to himself. 'My khakis and T-shirt don't blend in too well with the monks at the pagoda.'

Charlotte jumped up. 'Wait. You didn't say when you're leaving.'

'Thursday. I'm on a two o'clock flight connecting through Bangkok. I'll drop by to say goodbye before I go.' He pushed open the door and vanished into the throng of people on the street before Charlotte was able to tell him she was on the same flight.

41

Roxy thrust a foil-wrapped package into Charlotte's hand. 'I packed you something for the trip,' she said. 'It's not much but there's a box of durian biscuits, a bag of spicy nuts, and a few pieces of fudge. You can also take the leftover chicken if you—'

Charlotte rolled her eyes. 'For goodness sake, Roxy, it's a one-hour flight. And I can get food at the airport or on the plane. You're more nervous than I am.' She slipped her feet into a pair of sandals and stuffed a jacket into her overnight bag.

'I know!' Roxy wailed. 'Maybe I should come with you after all. I'm gonna be so stressed worrying. I'll see if I can borrow the landlord's car and drive you to the airport.'

Charlotte hoisted her bag onto her shoulder and wrapped her arms around her friend. 'Relax, darling. I'll call you when I arrive. And I'll be with Chris, remember.'

A honk sounded from the street below, so Charlotte descended the stairs to the pavement where SomOn greeted her with a smile, tossed her bag onto the seat of the tuk-tuk, and revved the engine. 'Now we get Bhante Samnang,' he said, and drove away from the kerb. Charlotte didn't try to explain that Bhante Samnang was now Chris. It would be too complicated for the tuk-tuk driver who, like all Cambodians, looked up to monks as revered members of society. Chris could break the news if he chose to.

As the tuk-tuk turned the corner, Charlotte glanced over her shoulder to see Roxy waving a sequinned scarf from the upstairs window. It felt as though their roles had reversed—now Roxy was the nervous one and she was the one heading out on a new adventure. She sighed. It had been less than two months since she'd arrived, and it felt as though her world had changed. She was now comfortable in unusual places, and the chaotic maze of Phnom Penh felt more like home than her neatly manicured neighbourhood back in England. The trip to Bangkok would be overwhelming, but it made her happy to know she'd be coming back—to Roxy and Peter and a new job, and an entirely new life.

As they pulled onto Monivong Boulevard, the tuk-tuk skidded on a patch of sand and tilted to one side. SomOn steadied the vehicle and turned to look at Charlotte with a nervous laugh. She grabbed her bag before it slid onto the road and laughed with him, no longer afraid of toppling off or crashing into a car. She remembered how scared she'd felt on her first ride from the airport and how different things were now. Then, the traffic had felt threatening and scary and she'd been suspicious of the strange man driving the tuk-tuk. Now, the bumps and swerves were part of a regular day, and SomOn had become a trusted companion. She caught a glimpse of herself in the overhead mirror. Her face glowed and her eyes sparkled. Her lips curved into a slight smile and there was a sprinkle of freckles across her suntanned nose. She took a deep breath and inhaled aromas from the street which now aroused her taste buds instead of repelling her. The world hadn't changed; she had.

SomOn drove through a spiderweb of side streets, skirting the busy riverside boulevard to avoid the traffic, and pulled up in front of a tiny blue building. The sign outside read *Kleenex Hotel* and Charlotte laughed out loud. I hope nobody ever changes these crazy signs, she thought. It's one of my favourite things about this country.

Chris stood in front of the worn, wooden doors, clasping a large duffel bag against his chest. He was dressed in jeans and a blue linen jacket and wore an apprehensive look. In the courtyard next to him, a group of children ran around a small fountain, splashing one another and squealing with laughter. Chris watched them with a slight smile, paying no attention to the waiting tuk-tuk. Charlotte observed him for a few minutes, her heart warming at his awkward stance. It had to be hard for him, walking away from this life he loved. After a few minutes, she called out and he walked slowly toward the tuk-tuk. SomOn climbed from his seat and reached out for the duffel bag, then hesitated and looked at Charlotte then back at Chris. 'Bhante Samnang?' he asked, a confused look on his face.

Chris touched him on the arm as he got into the tuk-tuk. 'Bhante Samnang is taking a holiday,' he said.

'Okay,' said SomOn. 'We go now.' He got back on the tuk-tuk, started it up, and pulled into traffic.

Chris looked at Charlotte and they both burst out laughing. 'No need to explain, eh?' Charlotte said. 'Just your typical Cambodian response of accepting and moving on.'

'I'm going to miss this so much,' he said. 'Cambodia's worked its way into my heart and London's going to feel quite boring by comparison.' He pushed his bag beneath the seat.

'But I know I'll be back. Perhaps I'll even bring Mum. I've got someone special to visit here, don't I?' He grasped her hand, tears welling up in his eyes.

They drove in silence as the tuk-tuk headed out of the city. On the edge of town, they passed a twelve-storey, half-built office building and Charlotte shook her head in amusement. It looked as though nothing had progressed since she'd arrived. The same construction workers were sitting under the same trees, probably having the same conversations, and doing the same miniscule amount of work. She waved to one who looked back, his mouth breaking into a wide grin, white teeth flashing in a handsome brown face. All along the airport road, enormous billboards loomed above their heads advertising companies with such names as *Tomato Bank, American Idol International School,* and *Laughing Internet Services*. Filthy, white dogs that looked the same as every other dog in the country scavenged for food on the edge of the road, and street vendors loaded vegetables into large plastic bowls, chattering with their customers as they went about their daily business. As they passed a small pagoda, the sound of chanting drifted toward them and they both turned their heads to look. Chris' gaze lingered longer, and Charlotte imagined what he must be thinking. He'd come to Cambodia to further his Buddhist studies and create a new life for himself. Now he was leaving it all behind. A lump caught in her throat as she wondered if he'd be going if she hadn't come into his life.

For the first twenty minutes, traffic moved smoothly. Then, as lunch hour approached, the three-lane road started to back up and the tuk-tuk came to a halt. SomOn twisted in his seat. 'We stop at light. Many cars.' He pointed to a red traffic light in the distance.

Ten minutes later they hadn't budged. Motorbikes

zigzagged between stalled vehicles and ear-splitting honks resounded from cars around them. Drivers wound down their windows to stare along the road into the muddle of traffic and Charlotte pulled her arm inside the tuk-tuk, trying to shield it from the sun. Her pulse raced as she worried about the clogged road. Perhaps they should have left earlier. After the third light change, they edged forward. A taxi forced its way in front of them. Then the next traffic light turned red just as they pulled up to it. They stopped again. She nudged SomOn. 'We need to be at the airport in thirty minutes. Will we be okay?'

SomOn stared straight ahead. 'You fine. I go now.' Throttling the bike, he veered sideways, bounced onto the pavement, and cut in front of a tour bus. Charlotte gasped as they narrowly missed a dog, then groaned out loud when they were forced to stop at another traffic light. Cars, buses, and bikes streamed across the road in front of them, jamming the passageway. The light turned green. Nothing moved.

She leaned forward again. 'SomOn, how much farther to the airport?' Her palms were sweaty. This wasn't looking good.

'Not long. You fine.'

Aware of the Cambodian tendency for understatement, she looked at her watch, then at Chris. 'I don't think we're fine at all,' she said. She scanned the street for any sign of traffic movement and saw none. They were stuck.

Chris unzipped his duffel bag, took out two bottles of water, and handed one to her. 'This is why I never wear a watch,' he said. 'Some things you can control, some you can't. If we miss the flight, we're not meant to be on it.'

'But we've got to.'

'There's no point getting stressed,' he said. 'That won't help anything. Don't worry, it will work out.' He took a sip of water and waved to a child in a car who stared at them through the window. 'If it doesn't, we'll make other plans.'

She stared at him, quizzically. Then the light changed again and SomOn gassed the engine. The tuk-tuk propelled forward and SomOn forced his way between two cars. Nineteen minutes later, they pulled up at the airport. Charlotte jumped from the tuk-tuk, hauled her suitcase from the vehicle, and thrust money into Chris's hand to give SomOn. 'Quick. We need to move fast,' she said, then turned and sprinted toward the entrance.

As the doors parted, she turned and saw SomOn giving Chris a deep sampeah and handing him a plastic bag filled with something that looked like rice. She bounced from foot to foot, agitated. This wasn't the time to dawdle. Chris handed a wad of notes to SomOn and walked toward the airport terminal. 'Hurry!' Charlotte called, running toward the check-in desk, passport in one hand, her bag in the other. She stopped at the counter and looked around. There were two people in front of her, but Chris was nowhere to be seen. As she reached the front of the queue, he appeared, grinning.

'What took you so long?' she asked.

'Just getting a newspaper.' He raised an eyebrow. 'Did I miss something?'

'No,' she snapped, 'but I...' He was right. They were fine. She linked her arm through his. 'Sorry,' she said with a shrug. 'Just nerves.'

They walked to the airport lounge and sat near the window, sharing Roxy's spicy nuts and SomOn's sticky rice. Then they exchanged email addresses and phone numbers, vowing to keep in touch. A voice boomed through the loudspeaker: *Flight 811 to Bangkok is about to board at Gate Three.* Charlotte hoisted her bag onto her shoulder. 'See you in Thailand,' she said, and handed her boarding pass to the flight attendant.

Once inside the plane, she took her seat on the aisle seven rows behind Chris. She buckled her seatbelt and took a deep breath. This time there'd be nobody to meet her when she landed, and no affable travel mate sitting next to her. But she was about to open a door that had been closed for a long time. She was going to see her father. She peered down the aisle and saw Chris reading the newspaper, one arm dangling into the aisle. What would Rashid think if he could see her now? A warmth spread across her chest. She was with his son.

She glanced at the young woman sitting next to her. Her eyes were squeezed shut and she was gripping her handbag tightly. As the plane left the ground, the woman gasped, and her lips moved, mumbling inaudible words.

Charlotte gently touched her arm. 'I like to think of turbulence as bumps on a road,' she said. 'A couple of bumps here and there won't make any difference to a safe journey. Besides, there's less traffic up here.'

42

Charlotte disembarked the plane and entered the arrivals hall at the Bangkok airport, where Chris was already studying the flight information board. He pointed to the overhead signs. 'I guess we go our separate ways here,' he said. 'For now.' He wrapped his arms around her. 'Today will be a special day for you,' he said, softly. 'You've waited a long time for this, and I know things will be as they're meant to be. I'll be thinking of you, dear friend, and I know the universe will bring us together again one day.'

How appropriate, Charlotte thought. No platitudes about how everything would be great, or how they'd keep in touch, just a simple acknowledgment of the facts. 'I'll miss you so much,' she said.

He held her away from him and looked into her eyes. 'Always remember,' he said. 'The past cannot be changed, but the present and future are in your hands. Live for the moment, Charlotte, and keep moving forward.' He pressed a small bundle into her hands. 'It's time for me to go.' He bowed, gave her a deep sampeah, and walked away.

She uncurled her fingers and choked back tears when she saw what he'd given her. His string of wooden prayer beads.

*

LESS THAN AN HOUR LATER, she was in a taxi on her way to the city. Traffic in Bangkok was ten times worse than in Phnom Penh. There were more cars, more people, more lanes on the highways, and more impatient drivers. She slouched down in her seat, hoping it wouldn't be a long drive. In the distance, rows of skyscrapers pierced the skyline and as the buildings grew closer, the meter ticked over: *One hundred Baht. One hundred and twenty-five Baht.*

A trickle of sweat ran down the back of her neck despite the icy blast from the air conditioner. Questions tumbled through her mind like a washing machine on full spin. Would Roxy remember to feed Toyota? Did the driver know the way to the hospital? Would they let her see her father when she arrived? Her hand curled around Roxy's fudge in her pocket so she unwrapped it and took a bite. The meter ticked onto three hundred and twenty Baht. Ten dollars.

The taxi pulled up in front of the hospital. She didn't budge. Adrenalin coursed through her veins and she wiped her clammy palms on her skirt. After a moment, the driver turned and stared, an irritated expression on his face. 'Madam, you need to get out now,' he said, leaning across and unlatching the door. She handed him four hundred Baht, aware it was too much, hauled her suitcase from the car, and stood on the kerb. The sliding glass doors were in front of her, but she was unable to take the first step.

As she lingered on the pavement, a porter, immaculately attired in a grey silk suit and mauve tie, walked toward her. 'Welcome to Arinathai International Hospital' he said. 'Are you visiting someone?'

Charlotte nodded.

'You may leave your suitcase with me. Please take the glass elevator and register at reception on the third floor.' He pushed the button and ushered Charlotte inside before she was able to protest.

Stepping out on the third floor, she entered a large, brightly lit area outfitted with white leather couches, low teak tables, and shiny white desks. An elegant woman dressed in a form-fitting mauve silk skirt and jacket approached her. 'Good afternoon, madam,' she said. 'How may I help?'

'I'm looking for...I mean, I want to find...I need...' She sank onto a chair and her bag fell with a loud thud, spilling its contents onto the tiled floor. Heads swivelled in her direction.

'Madam, you are all right?' A pair of brown eyes looked compassionately into hers.

Charlotte looked down to the pile on the floor. The prayer beads poked out from beneath a small bottle of hand sanitiser. She remembered Samnang's message: *The present and future are in your hands,* and took a deep breath. 'I'm fine, thank you,' she said, then bent down and picked up her things. She put them in her bag and stood up. 'I'm here to see my...to see Olivier Fontaine.'

The receptionist nodded. 'Of course, madam. You are a friend? A relative?'

Charlotte squared her shoulders and looked the receptionist in the eye. 'I'm his daughter.'

43

The nurse pointed down the hallway. 'Mr. Olivier Fontaine is in room twenty-six. Third room on the left.'

The corridor loomed ahead: thirty or so steps that felt like miles. Thirty steps to bridge a gap of seven years. To a door that, once opened, would never again be shut. Fingering the prayer beads, she took a step then stopped, frozen in place. The icy draft from the air-conditioning prickled her flesh. She rubbed her arms then slowly walked along the corridor until she stood in front of her father's room. Classical music drifted from unseen speakers and murals of exotic scenes adorned the walls. An orderly pushed an elderly woman in a wheelchair along the hallway. Charlotte stared at the number on the door: *Room 26*.

As she reached toward the handle, the door opened and she found herself looking up into a pair of hazel eyes. A male voice spoke her name and strong arms wrapped around her, enveloping her in a swirl of Valentino cologne. 'You must be Charlotte,' he said. 'Every bit as beautiful as the photos.' His soft French accent made her name sound exotic. 'I'm Patrick. I was on my way to the café for an espresso. Your journey, it was good?'

She pulled back and studied him. Tall and slender, with a closely cropped silver beard and matching full head of hair, Patrick looked like the kind of man who would sleep on Egyptian cotton sheets and own season tickets to the opera. There was an air of class about him and she could imagine him mingling in the circles her father had been part of when she was a child.

Her voice, like a whisper, replied. 'Yes.'

He closed the door behind him. His eyes were gentle and reminded her of Chris. 'I know this can't be easy,' he said, gesturing toward a leather couch in the corridor. 'I'd like to talk for a few minutes before you see him. Permit me?'

She sat, crossing one leg over the other and wrapping it around her ankle.

Patrick took her hand. 'As I told you on the phone, he's not the same,' he said. 'He's been through a lot.' He summarised the preceding years, telling her about the brain specialist her father had seen in Belgium after his surgery in England and the many follow-up appointments. 'There were several operations and a great deal of therapy,' he said. 'He can speak a little better now, but he still has very few memories from the past.'

As he talked, Charlotte was unable to look him in the eye. It took all her self-discipline not to pull her hand away. This was the man who'd broken up their family. He seemed pleasant, but she knew nothing about him and was reluctant to share her feelings with a stranger. She just wanted to see her father.

'He was lucky,' Patrick said, smoothing his beard. 'Doctor Farouk was the best surgeon in the country. We spent so much time with him we considered him a friend. He wasn't very approachable at first; I don't think he approved of our lifestyle. But he warmed up once he got to know us.'

Charlotte laughed nervously. She was having a conversation with a man who knew her father better than she did. Someone who'd shared his heart and his home. Possibly even saved his life. And he was referring to Rashid, the man who'd opened a door to this moment. 'I think I know him,' she murmured.

'Doctor Farouk was very well-known,' Patrick said. 'And he had a special connection with your father.' He smiled. 'He wanted to know about you, too, as he thought it might jog his memory to talk about his family. One day, Doctor Farouk brought his son to visit when he was up in London for the day. What a nice young man. The doctor wanted him to follow in his footsteps.' He shook his head. 'But the poor lad appeared to be intimidated by his father.'

Charlotte opened her mouth to comment, then stopped herself. Not the time or place. 'How did you get here?' she asked. 'Why Thailand?'

'Doctor Farouk told us about this hospital when he retired, and we trusted his advice. I expected to hear something more from him but...' His eyes clouded over. 'Perhaps he felt his job was done.' His gaze drifted toward the floor and in that moment Charlotte knew she'd made the right decision to come to Bangkok. Patrick shared her pain. He probably felt it even more.

'Your father's health is all that matters now,' he said. 'And I keep reminding myself how fortunate he was. Fifteen percent of people with aneurysmal subarachnoid haemorrhage die before they reach the hospital.'

'Aneurysmal—?'

'Bleeding in the brain. Actually, in the area between the brain and the tissues around it. Once an aneurysm bleeds, the chance of death is thirty to forty percent. The likelihood of brain damage is twenty to thirty-five percent.' He cast his eyes downward. 'If he hadn't been in London when it happened...'

Charlotte pulled her jacket closer around her shoulders and faked a strength she didn't feel. 'What should I expect?' she asked.

Patrick let out a deep breath. 'His vision's almost back to normal. But it's his memory that's the main concern. His doctor here works with dementia and Alzheimer's patients, and he's hopeful your dad will make a full recovery. He told me there are triggers—triggers that make him remember things from his past. He's had a couple, then slips back again. Nobody seems to know long it will take.'

A nurse walked past, and Patrick nodded at her then glanced at the clock on the wall. 'I don't want to hold you up any longer,' he said to Charlotte. 'I know you're anxious to see him. I told him you're coming but...' He smiled, compassionately. 'I will leave you alone, *cherie*.' He walked down the corridor, leaving Charlotte standing outside the room.

She stared up at the number on the door. Room twenty-six. Twenty-six letters in the alphabet, twenty-six bones in the human foot, twenty-six miles in a marathon. This door was all that separated her from her father. The feel of the wooden prayer beads in her hand pulled her back to the present, like an undertow in a stormy sea. She hesitated, hoping someone would come down the corridor so she wouldn't feel so alone. *The only way out of the pain is through it*. Then, taking a deep breath, she opened the door.

On the other side of the room, a man in a maroon silk robe sat upright in an armchair. He looked through the window, his profile silhouetted against the late afternoon sun. Thick, chestnut-coloured hair streaked with grey lay flat on his head, and he reached for his water glass with neatly manicured fingers. Her hand flew to her mouth. She dropped her bag, ran across the room, and knelt on the floor beside him. Reaching up, she took his hand in hers, squeezing his fingers as she murmured, 'Daddy.'

Her father turned his head and a pair of vacant eyes looked down into hers. He stared for a moment, then leaned forward and ran a hand through his hair. 'Oh my,' he said. 'What a surprise to see you.'

Joy almost made her laugh out loud. She started to stand up, but he leaned back and sighed. Then, he spoke again, and the laughter died in her throat. 'I must apologise, but I'm not quite ready for my haircut.' He smoothed his hair with a shaky hand. 'You're not the same girl who came last week, are you? Would you mind coming back a little later?'

The lump in Charlotte's throat silenced her voice and she gripped her father's hand. 'Daddy. It's me. Charlotte.' A tear slipped out. 'Don't you remember me? I'm your daughter.'

He unfolded a pair of spectacles and put them on as Charlotte held her breath waiting for an answer. 'Daughter? Oh, that would be delightful. I'd be very happy to have a daughter like you. I'll talk to Patrick about it. By the way, where *is* Patrick?' He swivelled his head. 'He *did* come today, didn't he? I'm sure he was reading to me this morning.' He picked up a novel and flipped through it. 'I have an excellent book if you like reading. What's your name again?'

'Charlotte.' Her voice was a whisper. She resisted the urge to run from the room and fumbled through her bag for a couple of photos. 'I have something to show you,' she said. She held out a picture of her and her father in their home in England, hoping it would spark a memory.

He studied the photo then looked at her with a polite smile. 'How very clever of you to find this,' he said. 'That man looks just like me. I just wish I had his physique. I'm rather out of shape these days.' He dropped his hand and the picture fell to the floor. 'I have to excuse myself. I believe dinner's on the way. Funny how I never forget that, isn't it? Even though it's not particularly memorable.' He shook her hand. 'Perhaps we can chat again another day.'

She ran from the room and bumped into Patrick who was walking along the corridor carrying a cup of coffee. Some of the coffee spilled onto the floor and Charlotte spun around, desperate to hide her tears from him. 'I'm so sorry,' she gasped. 'I can't...it's not...' She clasped her hand over her mouth. 'I don't know...' Tears spilled down her face. Patrick touched her on the shoulder, and she crumpled into his arms.

'I knew it would be hard, *cherie,'* he said softly, handing her a handkerchief. 'Give it time. It's important to be a consistent presence.'

'But there's nothing I...'

He put a finger to his lips. 'Be calm. We just have to be patient and wait.'

With trembling hands, she fiddled with the clasp of her bag, embarrassed Patrick had seen her break down. Then he gently raised her chin to look into her eyes and she realised she was not alone. In a voice that was barely audible, she said, 'I don't know what to do.'

A nurse walked along the corridor toward them, and Patrick held up a finger, signalling for her to wait. 'Just be here, *cherie,'* he replied. 'But right now, take a moment for yourself. Go downstairs to the café. Get a coffee, something to eat, a glass of wine. Take as long as you need. I'll stay with Olivier.' He walked over to the nurse.

Charlotte flinched at the use of her father's name. To Patrick, her father was a partner, a companion, a lover. It would take a while to get used to. She studied him as he talked to the nurse. There was a strength about him that was reassuring; a calmness that helped reduce her anxiety. It was clear he was in control, and Charlotte was grateful to know there was someone like him looking out for her father.

He came over and took her arm in his. 'Would you like to stay overnight?' he asked. 'There's a couch in his room I often make up into a bed. It's no *Astrabed*, but it's comfy enough for a night and I'll stay in a hotel. The nurse is bringing your suitcase now.' He took out his wallet and handed her a wad of bills. 'Please buy yourself dinner. My treat. Hopefully the first of many. I've waited a long time for this moment.'

44

Charlotte had just ordered a chicken sandwich and a cup of mint tea when her phone buzzed. It was a text message from Roxy; the eleventh she'd received since leaving Cambodia less than six hours earlier. Her messages had become more and more urgent as the hours had gone by, and this one read, *What's going on??? Call me!!* Charlotte realised Roxy's excessive use of punctuation marks meant she wanted an immediate response, so she moved to a quiet corner of the café and called Roxy on *WhatsApp.*

Roxy answered instantly. 'You've been gone six hours and you didn't call me,' she wailed. 'I'm dying. What's happening?'

'Calm down,' Charlotte said. 'I'm in a hospital, remember.' She took a deep breath and told her about her father. She described the conversations with Patrick and how he'd warned her not to expect much, and about the moment when her father hadn't recognised her. 'So, I'm not sure what to do now,' she said. 'What do I say? How do I…?'

Silence.

'Rox? You there?' Charlotte asked.

'I am, darling. How can I help?'

Charlotte took a deep breath. 'You can't,' she replied. 'It's just good to hear your voice. There's nobody else in the world who would understand.'

'But I want to do something,' Roxy said. 'Did Patrick say there's anything that might jog his memory?'

'It's unpredictable,' Charlotte replied. 'There seem to be moments when he remembers things, but...' She shrugged, fighting back tears.

'Then let's give him one of those moments,' Roxy said.

'What are—?'

'Wait. I'm thinking.' She went silent for a few seconds, then said, 'How about telling him a story? Like the day he caught us hitchhiking to Hastings. Or the time when we accidentally burned the tickets to *La Boheme*.'

'I don't think—'

'Give him some of my homemade fudge. I bet he'll recognise the taste.'

Charlotte smiled as she listened to Roxy. She knew her friend didn't like to feel helpless and was doing her best to comfort her. She also realised Roxy had stepped out of her weekly art class to take the call since she'd heard a male voice in the background followed by Roxy's sharp, 'Piss off!'

'I should be with you,' Roxy said. 'I'll book a flight.'

'No need,' Charlotte interrupted. 'I have to do this myself.' She glanced at her watch and realised she had been in the café almost an hour. 'I've got to go now. I'll be in touch later.' She closed the phone and walked back toward her father's room.

The night nurse was taking away the remnants of dinner when Charlotte entered the room, so she sat on the couch and waited for her to leave. A flimsy blue curtain separated her father's bed from the couch where she was going to sleep, and it fluttered in the draft from the air conditioner like a butterfly. After the nurse left the room, Charlotte surveyed her surroundings. The couch was pushed up against the window and there was a small Buddha statue on the table next to it. Her suitcase had been placed next to the chair and a white orchid blossom lay on a small pillow on the corner of the couch.

Patrick was no longer around, so she pushed her suitcase under the bedside table, slipped into her pyjamas, and fluffed the pillow. A garlicky aftertaste from the pesto chicken sandwich lingered in her mouth so she reached for a bottle of water, peeking around the curtain. Her father was asleep, one arm tucked beneath the pillow, the other dangling from the bed. His spectacles sat on the bedside table next to a hardback copy of *A Tale of Two Cities*. She gazed at him, remembering how she used to find him asleep on the couch at their home, one arm dangling onto the floor. His hair was greyer now and his face a little thinner, but if she tried hard she could pretend he was the same man who'd wake up and catch her staring, then suggest they make popcorn and watch a movie on the telly.

She lay back and looked up at the ceiling. It was so white and smooth. Not like Roxy's place where the paint was cracked and peeling. A sound came from outside. She opened the blind and peeked through the window. It was raining. Fat, round droplets pounded against the windowpane, tapping a rhythm onto the glass, and in the distance, a blinking light flickered in the sky. Could it be Chris's plane? His flight was due to take off around now. She wondered when she'd next hear from him. She thought about Roxy and pictured her at home with Peter and Toyota. She'd probably be eating frozen doughnuts and burning through late-night worksheets. Her gaze fell on a pair of brown suede shoes peeking from below the couch. They must belong to Patrick. She wondered if he was alone in a hotel room in Bangkok, and realised she knew nothing about him. Waves of cool air swept across the bed as she closed her eyes. The plastic water bottle slipped out of her hand to the floor, landing with a soft *thunk.*

Then, suddenly she was on a horse, sitting in front of her father on the saddle. The wind was raging, and waves crashed higher and higher all around. 'It's okay, Dad. We can do it!' she shouted. The horse whinnied in fear as currents dragged them farther from the beach.

A voice bellowed, 'Grab it. Quickly!' and a rope flew through the air. Charlotte seized it and looped it through the bridle as the horse was pulled to the shore.

'We're safe! It's going to be all right,' her dad yelled, jumping onto the sand beside her. 'Who saved us?' he asked. 'There's no one here.'

Charlotte scanned the beach. There was nobody in sight. Then, in the distance, she spotted a slender figure at the top of the hill, his silver-topped walking stick glinting in the sunlight.

'Who's that?' her father asked.

The man continued walking up the hill and Charlotte sprinted after him. 'Wait!' she cried, scrambling up the slope, her feet sinking into the soft sand. She tripped on a piece of driftwood and fell onto her knees, then quickly got to her feet and looked around. He was gone. She took a step and her foot bumped against an object in the sand. A mobile phone. She picked it up, flipping to the list of contacts, to see if there was a name so she could return the phone. Then, she gasped and gripped it tighter, her heart racing. There was only one name on the phone: it was hers.

45

Charlotte awakened to the faint sound of music. It was almost midnight. She rubbed her eyes and swung her feet onto the floor then tiptoed across the room and peeked around the curtain. Her father was sitting in a large leather armchair, his gaze glued to the television screen.

She studied the contours of his face and the way the corners of his mouth curled at the corners when he smiled. She'd forgotten his habit of tapping the fingers of his left hand in time to music and how he always kept his fingernails buffed. She noticed he no longer wore his wedding band and wondered why she hadn't noticed earlier. There was so much she'd missed about him—it would take some time to get used to having him back in her life. She tiptoed back to her bed to get her phone and quietly took a couple of photos so she could capture the moment.

His hand tapped faster on the bedside table and she crept closer, still gripping the phone. He was watching *The Sound of Music*, their favourite film. Charlotte remembered the first time they'd seen it together. She'd been nine. It had been raining for days and she'd been stuck in the house doing homework. Her mother had been out shopping, and her father had slipped a note under Charlotte's bedroom door: 'If you finish your homework before dinnertime, you can watch my favourite movie with me.'

She'd rushed through it and finished it before lunch, excited to have time alone with her dad. He'd made popcorn and sprinkled it with paprika and Parmesan cheese for movie time. It was the most exotic thing she'd ever tasted. Since then, they'd seen *The Sound of Music* at least seven more times, and the hours spent with her father became etched into her memory as *their* time. Her dad always made popcorn—sometimes with paprika and Parmesan cheese, sometimes with butter and salt. And, when she got older, with truffle oil.

As she stood watching her father, the door slowly opened and she caught a whiff of Valentino cologne. Patrick stood in the doorway clutching two mugs of steaming liquid. He winked and backed out, easing the door shut behind him.

Her father continued to stare at the television, a faint hum coming from his throat. On the screen, Julie Andrews sat on her bed surrounded by the Von Trapp children. '*Raindrops ...and whiskers...*' He turned up the volume. Fingers tapped faster. '*... kettles... and mittens...*' A smile crept across his face. His lips moved as he mouthed the words to the song.

Charlotte pressed her hand against her mouth and held her breath. Please don't let Patrick come back now. Her father's voice came in clearer. 'Raisins on tables...Chocolate on mountains...'

She took a step toward him and put her hand on his shoulder, and he kept on singing. Then she leaned down so that her face was close to his and murmured, 'Monkeys that fly through the air like a jet. These are some things that I'd like to forget.'

His head swivelled and he looked into her eyes. 'How do you...? Where did you...?' His brow furrowed.

She knelt beside him and took his hand. 'Remember, Dad?' she whispered. 'Do you remember?'

'Did we...Did we sing that song?' An anxious expression flashed across his face. 'Did we make it up?' He gripped her hand. 'Was it a long time ago?'

She nodded, unable to speak. Her father reached for the remote and switched off the television. The room was silent, except for the ticking of the clock. She held her breath. Her chest ached. She was on edge, hopeful, afraid.

Her father pulled her toward him. 'Are you—? Did you—? Charlie horse?'

Tears spilled down her cheeks. She clutched his hand and nodded. He drew her into his arms, and she fell against him, his closely shaven cheek pressed against her face, wet with tears. She closed her eyes, and in her mind she was seventeen again. The Jonas brothers were playing on the radio, the snow falling outside the window, the aroma of freshly baked cheesecake wafting through the house. Daddy was there. He'd come home.

She breathed in his familiar scent and savoured the strength of his arms around her. Then a short, sharp buzz from the phone in her hand:

It's March 3. Welcome to your new life.

ACKNOWLEDGMENTS

There are always other people who contribute to the creation of a book and I am blessed to have many who provided me with their expertise.

Most significantly, this book would never have been created if it had not been for my husband, Skip. He encouraged me to come up with the concept then became my editor, critic, supporter, reader, and cheerleader. A huge thank you to him and to my mum, Colette Said, who told me she felt as though she knew Charlotte and Roxy personally by the end of the story.

Thank you to my beta readers, Pete Lawson, Francie King, Sheila Consaul, Tim Lundergan, and Wendy Anderson, and to Michelle Baillat-Jones for her thoughtful edits. Each one of them gave me hours of their valuable time as well as excellent feedback that helped shape my story. To Vandong Thorn, Founder and Executive Director of BSDA (Buddhism for Social Development Action) thanks for providing me with insights on

Buddhism, and to the wonderful Sue Timpson for creating the beautiful cover art.

Finally, this primary inspiration for this book came from my experiences while living in Cambodia and from the wonderful people I met there. Many are featured in these pages and all will live in my heart and soul forever.

Made in the USA
Coppell, TX
09 November 2020

41043688R00215